# Night Diver

## ALSO BY ELIZABETH LOWELL

Dangerous Refuge

Beautiful Sacrifice

Death Echo

Blue Smoke and Murder

Innocent as Sin

The Wrong Hostage

Whirlpool

Always Time to Die

The Secret Sister

The Color of Death

Death Is Forever

Die in Plain Sight

Running Scared

Moving Target

Midnight in Ruby Bayou

Pearl Cove

Jade Island

Amber Beach

# Night Diver

## Elizabeth Lowell

HARPER LUXE

*An Imprint of* HarperCollins*Publishers*

To my fellow authors
You keep me sane!

NIGHT DIVER. Copyright © 2014 by Two of a Kind, Inc. All rights reserved. Printed in the United States of America. No part of this book may be used or reproduced in any manner whatsoever without written permission except in the case of brief quotations embodied in critical articles and reviews. For information address HarperCollins Publishers, 10 East 53rd Street, New York, NY 10022.

HarperCollins books may be purchased for educational, business, or sales promotional use. For information, please e-mail the Special Markets Department at SPsales@harpercollins.com.

FIRST HARPERLUXE EDITION

HarperLuxe™ is a trademark of HarperCollins Publishers

Library of Congress Cataloging-in-Publication Data is available upon request.

ISBN: 978-0-06-232633-1

14  ID/RRD  10 9 8 7 6 5 4 3 2 1

# Prologue

The moment Kate Donnelly heard her brother's too-cheerful greeting on the phone, she wished she had let the call go to voice mail. She loved Larry, yet right now she had nothing but bad news for him.

And fear.

"I hope you're calling to tell me that everything is fine," she said.

"If you were down here, everything would be fine."

"No," she said, more curtly than she had meant. "I just finished a job with a very nervous gallery owner."

"Then what you need is a little vacation on white sand beaches, blue sky, warm sea, and—"

"No." Cold chills rippled from Kate's nape to her fingertips. The ravishing tropical paradise of St. Vincent was the heart of her nightmares.

"C'mon, Kate," he said impatiently. "Get over it. It happened almost fifteen years ago."

"You weren't there. I was. No."

"You won't have to get near the water. Cross my heart."

*And hope to die.*

She forced herself to take a slow deep breath, then another, as she listened to her brother's pleas. Finally the urgency beneath his coaxing penetrated the deeper, older nightmare of the death of her parents. She began listening instead of staring out the window of her condominium at the haze of humidity and car exhaust.

Larry's voice was both hoarse and sharp over the crackling satellite connection. "We're at the point where you can't do things from there anymore. We need you here."

"Anymore? I've barely started. I only got those files two days ago and I've hardly begun to put them in order after I work on my own business all day. And calling them files is charitable. Rotting cartons of receipts and shopping lists are not files."

"I know. I'm sorry. It took more time than I thought to get stuff together. You know that I never was good with papers and numbers."

"You're in charge of the salvage business," she said. "You have to keep books or hire someone to do it for you."

"Look, I've kept it afloat since you ran out. Grandpa hates records, much less balance sheets. Everything I know I learned from you before you bailed. I'm a diver, not a businessman."

Kate closed eyes that were an echo of St. Vincent's clear turquoise water. "I've known about your lack of interest in bookkeeping since I was ten and started keeping the ledgers for Moon Rose Limited." Their family salvage business had never been wealthy, but it had kept them in food and living quarters.

"No doubt about it. You got all the number smarts in the family. That's why we need you. Please, sis? If you don't help us, we're going under, and you know that will kill Grandpa."

She felt the door to the trap closing softly, relentlessly, like sinking into warm salt water. She couldn't live with herself if the family business went bankrupt because she was too frightened to revisit the scene of her nightmare.

*I'm barely living with myself now. Running hasn't ended the nightmare. Maybe facing it will.*

*Certainly there's nothing in North Carolina to hold me right now. Not even a houseplant. And I've been promising myself a vacation.*

She shuddered lightly. St. Vincent wouldn't be a vacation. It would mean facing things she had been running from her entire adult life. Part of her, the part that was no longer a teenager, knew she had to get over the past. The rest of her wailed in remembered terror.

*Do flies trapped in amber scream?*

Sunset flowed through the floor-to-ceiling windows of her Charlotte condo, making the room hotter than it should have been, but it was cold in the shadows of her mind.

"You've at least had a chance to read the contract, haven't you?" Larry asked.

"Enough to know that you shouldn't have signed it," she said, sensing she had lost the fight but not wanting to give up.

"Beggars can't be choosers. It was sign up with the Brits to salvage that maybe-Spanish wreck or sell the boat. That would have—"

"Destroyed Grandpa, I know," she finished tiredly. "Larry, I advise small businesses, not pass miracles. You should have called me before you signed that contract."

"We tried, but you were in the Yukon working with those native carvers. You got them going in a business, so we should be a piece of cake after that. Kate, please, you're our last hope."

She closed her eyes and fought against what she was afraid was going to happen anyway. "Hope? I don't know how you're putting diesel in the tank right now. Was your advance on expenses approved?"

"Not yet. The Brits are sending C. Holden, some kind of fancy accountant, out to evaluate whether the dive is worth the advance. We're heading into the stormy season."

Icy fingers tapped down her spine. "I know about the storms in St. Vincent," she said tightly.

"So we're really under the gun. You'll find a way to convince this Holden dude that we're okay. You talk numbers better than anyone."

"Larry . . ."

"I'm serious," he said quickly. "You're brilliant. You're the only one who has a chance of getting this guy to agree to a stay of execution."

Kate sighed and knew the trap was shut. "When does he arrive?"

"Tomorrow. I've timed your flight so that when you get here, you'll be able to bring him to the little house we rented at the beginning of the dive. I'll meet you there and take him to the *Golden Bough.* You don't even have to go on the water if you're still scared."

*Scared,* she thought. *What an easy word for cold-sweat terrified.*

"All right," she said in a rush, before she lost her courage. "I'll do it. But I'm not sleeping on the boat."

"Thank you, thank you, thank you! You can stay at the rented house. There's no room aboard anyway, what with the extra divers we hired. I'll even have someone leave a meal or two in the fridge so that . . ."

No longer really listening, she let out a cautious breath, relieved that she wasn't expected to stay aboard anything that floated.

Or sank, in the case of the family business. Nothing she had seen in the few hours she had sorted through the invoices gave her any confidence that she could keep the company alive. Wages and air supplies, food and fuel, maintenance and debt service, and a thousand other expenses drained the accounts. The Donnellys had poured three generations of work into a seventy-foot hole in the water called the *Golden Bough*.

And it had been her home until that terrible night.

*Don't think about it,* she told herself fiercely. *I already promised to go. Larry sounds like the weight of the world has been lifted off his shoulders.*

" . . . and you'll keep the Brits off our back," her brother all but sang. "Nobody can baffle with numbers like you can."

She started to protest, but her brother was still talking fast, relief in every syllable. She listened with half her attention while he made silly comments about her skill with numbers. It was good to hear something other than fear and defeat in his voice.

Idly she wondered what the rental was like. Grandpa Donnelly didn't waste money on anything having to do with land.

"I'm not diving," Kate said when Larry paused for breath.

"You don't have to even come aboard unless you want to. Hell, sis, if you get in the water, then things will really have gone in the toilet."

"Things are already there. If you knew numbers, you'd understand that."

"Yeah, whatever, I promise you won't have to dive."

"Fine. I'll stay as long as I can, but no more than two weeks. Three at the outside."

"You're the most incredible sister ever," Larry said. "I've booked space on a flight that leaves tomorrow morning at nine. I'll park the old pickup in the airport lot, with directions to the house. It has a dock so it's easy to come and go from the ship."

Kate looked at the phone. The fact that her brother had bothered to see to the details of her trip told her more than words how worried he had been.

"See you soon, sis. I love you."

He hung up before she could say anything.

Or change her mind.

He and Grandpa Donnelly were so much the same that often it was scary, like looking in a mirror caught in time. Grandpa had been pulling treasure out of the water too long to have been just lucky or smart or canny. He had a generous helping of all three. Larry had the luck in spades.

*Too bad our parents didn't share that luck,* Kate thought sadly.

Then she closed the door on the haunted past. There was no time to dwell on it. First she had to call and make sure that Larry had followed through with the ticket. Her brother meant well, but the details of daily life quickly dissolved in the lure of diving.

A call to the airport assured her that a ticket was waiting.

The lock on the trap clicked shut.

*Don't think about it. Breathe slowly. One . . . two . . . three.*

When her skin no longer felt cold, Kate went about preparing for travel with the efficiency of someone who always kept a suitcase of basics packed. Her life revolved around the inevitable, urgent calls from small businesses who trusted her to keep them out of the quicksand of red ink that always awaited people who were entrepreneurs, not accountants.

*People like Grandpa and Larry.*

Ruthlessly she shut off the thought. With tight motions she pulled business clothes out of her to-go suitcase and substituted shorts, sleeveless tops, sandals, and bathing suits. Remembering the penetrating tropical sun, she threw in some lightweight long pants and blouses, plus a hat and major sunblock. Unlike most residents of St. Vincent, she didn't have the lush, dark skin that would allow her to ignore the sun.

When she was finished, she eyed the two cartons of "business" papers that had arrived on her doorstep two days ago. On the subject of bookkeeping, Larry had raised malicious compliance to an art. Whoever wanted to check expenditures would have to spend days sorting out things in order to begin the real work of setting up spreadsheets to track expenses.

*It doesn't matter. The contract they signed is a guaranteed loser for Moon Rose Ltd. Even if they discovered the richest galleon ever, the Brits would get it all and the Donnellys would get expenses plus three percent of the net profits.*

*And the net is determined by the Brits. Articles given to museums aren't part of the net, because they are donated, not sold.*

She couldn't believe Larry had signed such a punitive contract.

While she cleaned her condo—she hated coming back to a mess after a long trip—she mulled over the ways she might be able to help her family. By the time she had finished, showered, and set her alarm, she was fighting to stay awake. She was asleep before her head touched the pillow.

And she dreamed.

*The sun was brilliant over the turquoise water and white sand. Lazy waves surged and rolled, making the boat lift and fall with the languid grace of a dancer. Laughter from below, her parents teasing one another as they checked dive gear . . . teasing sliding into screaming and the water closing around, sun overcome by night, wind and water bleeding into darkness and screams.*

*Her screaming while her parents kept sinking, sliding from her grasp, she was spinning, screaming, reaching, the night sea devouring them, her, screaming no no NO NO . . .*

Kate awoke in a cold sweat, throat tight from remembered screams, heart racing, breathing almost impossible, her radio alarm shrill in her ears.

*Just a dream,* she told herself.

*Just another nightmare.*

She should be used to them by now. She'd had them since the night her parents died. Since she hadn't been able to save them from the ravenous sea.

Night diving was dangerous.

And now she was headed back to her greatest failure, her greatest fear.

# Chapter 1

Holden Cameron surveyed the interior of St. Vincent's modest airport with the eyes of a world traveler who had lived and worked in war zones. Instinctively he searched for danger in the body language of the people around him. He didn't expect any, but had learned that the unexpected was a killer.

*You're medically retired now,* he reminded himself. *You're a bloody consultant.*

*And you're walking into a family of thieves.*

A smart man would be wary. Holden hadn't survived this long by being dumb. And if he needed any reminder, the stabbing ache in his left thigh obliged. The scar from the shrapnel wound had faded somewhat, but pressure changes caused by flying or especially diving played merry hell with him.

Idly he rubbed his thigh and wondered which one of the Vincentians who eddied through the arrival lounge would be his native guide. Most of the people were dressed in loose, colorful clothes that allowed them to be comfortable in St. Vincent's unvarying heat. The only exception was the silver-haired, transparently pale Englishman who had boarded the plane with him at Heathrow.

*Poor bastard will get heatstroke. Canary Wharf suits don't work well with St. Vincent's climate, but appearances have to be kept up whilst living among the natives and all that utter rot.*

With faint amusement, Holden's glance moved past the man, searching the faces of the people who were searching the faces of the people getting off the plane. Nobody seemed interested in him. He stepped aside from the main flow of traffic. Back to a wall, he watched and waited for someone to care, never taking his attention from the people milling about.

Almost everyone in St. Vincent's airport had hair as black as his, but considerably more curly. With it came the many shades of skin that resulted from hundreds of years of intermarriage between Europeans and the Africans who had once been slaves. What genetics began, the tropical sun burnished. The music in the voices was soothing, like the lapping of the sea on a moonlit shore.

The glow of deep auburn hair caught his attention. The woman was casually dressed and subtly anxious. Her hair was sleek, pulled back into a ponytail, and looked natural rather than dyed. Wisps of hair curled gently in the humidity, clinging to her face and neck. Her curves would have done credit to an exotic dancer. Her skin was pale, with just enough freckles to tempt him into touching and tasting.

Though Holden liked women of all shapes, colors, and sizes, he'd always had a weakness for redheads. Eyes that were the luminous turquoise of tropical shallows glanced at him, hesitated, then moved on, still searching.

*Pity,* he thought, looking at the redhead from behind his mirrored sunglasses. *I'd love to spend a few weeks lazing on the island with her, discovering and licking each freckle. But I'm here to oversee a scurvy lot of divers who appear to be keeping more than they should.*

*Human greed, as reliable as gravity.*

Shifting to ease the weight off his bad leg, he waited, watching. If nobody showed up, it would be one among many demerits in the file of Moon Rose Ltd.

The crowd swirled, shifted, and eddied like richly colored water.

Kate kept searching for a pale-skinned Brit, but saw no likely candidates.

*Did he miss the plane?* she thought, then instantly rejected the idea.

Accountants were precise. It came with the job. More likely, Larry had fouled up the arrival hour, or even day. Divers had their own way of keeping time. She and her brother had been born and raised aboard the *Golden Bough,* but she was able to shift gears to match whichever culture she found herself in. Larry . . . well, Larry liked the idea that time was divided into later, much later, and never.

Again she searched among the Europeans who had arrived. The man leaning against the wall, watching the crowd through mirrored sunglasses, was too fit and had too much physical presence to make a convincing accountant. The man in the tropical suit and big belly was speaking what sounded like Russian, not London English. Another man had a flashy playmate hanging from his arm, English speaker by way of the Bronx. The pale, thin man in the heavy suit was diffident, searching for someone, and looked old enough to be her grandfather.

Her attention kept wandering back to the man leaning against the wall. He had drawn a lot of female glances, but he greeted no one. His dark blue shirt was short-sleeved and square at the bottom, meant to be worn outside his khakis pants. Two waterproof duffels lay at his feet. Without moving, he dominated the place. His features were an unusual mixture of strength and refinement, his face oddly Celtic, his skin a silky dark honey.

*Wonder what color his eyes are,* she thought.

Then she mentally shook herself. She had only been on the island long enough to get her baggage and stow it in the old VW pickup Larry had left in the parking lot. Yet she already had succumbed to the lazy sensuality of St. Vincent, where the language was music, the temperature was made for bare skin, and the surface of the sea was always warm.

*The sea.*

Kate rubbed the cold bumps that rippled over her skin. Abruptly she made her choice. The pale man might be older than she had expected, but the rest of the package looked right. He was standing about ten feet from the intriguing man with the two duffel bags.

The gray-haired, gaunt man was beginning to look worried. His eyes were a vague blue. The weight of his suit appeared on the edge of taking him down.

"Welcome to St. Vincent, Mr. Holden," she said, extending a hand. "I'm Kate Donnelly, from Moon Rose Limited. I was told to meet you here."

The gentleman pressed her hand lightly and smiled. "Very kind of you, but there seems to be a mistake.

I am meeting my daughter-in-law here." He scanned the crowd briefly. "Ah, there she is."

Bemused, Kate watched as an ebony-skinned woman embraced the smiling Englishman. He returned the hug and began asking eagerly after his grandchildren.

*Okay. Wrong guy,* Kate thought.

"Pardon me," said a deep voice from behind her. "I couldn't help but overhear." The accent was upper-class British with something else just beneath. "I am waiting for someone from Moon Rose Limited."

She turned around and reminded herself to breathe. It was the man who didn't look at all like an accountant. "I'm Kate Donnelly. Moon Rose is owned by my family."

"At your service."

*If only,* she thought. But what she said was, "You're the accountant from the British government. Are you here to replace the other Brit aboard?"

"Not quite. My understanding is that Farnsworth is to remain on hand to catalog the results of each dive. I am a consultant on dive projects. My job is to see that everything is in good order."

"My mistake. Good to meet you, Mr. Holden," she said, taking his offered hand with a firm American shake and quick release. She had learned that it was expected in business.

And this was business all the way.

Then he took off his sunglasses and she forgot about proper office manners. He had the most striking eyes she had ever seen, like shards of blue and green and gold crystal had been turned in a kaleidoscope and then frozen in place.

"The name is Holden Cameron."

It took her a moment to understand. "Sorry. I was just given the name C. Holden. It's a pleasure to meet you, Mr. Cameron."

He shrugged slightly and put on his sunglasses again. "Pity that pleasure and business don't mix. But they don't, and there it is."

*All righty,* she thought. *Business and only business. You could use that voice to refrigerate the entire island.*

"Any luggage beyond the duffels?" she asked.

"No. I'll be here only long enough to see whether I should recommend shutting this project down."

"You might be surprised at how well the dive is going," she said, lying coolly, covering the fear that she had arrived too late to do any good.

All he said was, "Shall we begin?"

It was an order, not a request.

Kate set her teeth. The first man she had seen in ages who might tempt her out of sexual hibernation had blood the temperature of the ocean one hundred feet down.

"Sooner begun, sooner ended," she said under her breath. Then, "Follow me."

As she headed for the door to the sunbaked parking lot, she wondered how the British ice cube with the startling eyes would stand up to conditions on a dive ship.

*That's Larry's problem.*

*And I can't wait to hand it to him.*

Without looking back to see if the "accountant" was coming after her, she cut through the diminishing clumps of people and headed toward the parking lot.

Holden found it easy to follow the woman with flame in her hair and beautiful, wary eyes. She had a motion to her walk that brought every one of his male senses to predatory alert. He wondered if she might be a red herring meant to distract him from getting to the bottom of whatever lay beneath Moon Rose's sketchy accounting and pitiable salvage recovery. The idea appealed— sex was a useful weapon.

But the more he thought about it, the less likely it seemed. She had been friendly in a casual American way, yet when he had gone into his right-British-bastard routine, she had retreated with a finality that put paid to any flirtation.

*Pity my job requires that I be a stiff prick,* Holden thought ruefully, *but divers are a hard-shouldered lot. They don't respect any man who isn't like them.*

Holden should know. He was one of them.

Or had been.

He followed Kate's gently swaying hips outside where the air was hot, humid, and heavily scented with a mix of tropical plants and petroleum fumes from idling taxis. Violently green shrubs overflowed with pink and purple flowers. Stands of palm trees framed the colorfully painted airport building, filtering sunlight through crisply cut, fanlike leaves.

The partial shade was short-lived. Holden was sweating before he reached the bleached gray asphalt of the parking lot. While the temperature wasn't nearly as hot as the deserts of northern Africa, the humidity was an unwelcome blanket. He knew he would stop noticing the humidity after a few hours or days, so he ignored it now. Sweat was a fact of life, like the ache in his thigh or his uncommon eyes.

"Throw your duffels in the back," Kate said.

He eyed the unimpressive transportation. He wasn't surprised that the doors were unlocked and the windows rolled down. No self-respecting thief would steal the ancient truck. The hood was a different color from the truck bed, the tires were bald, the tailgate was missing, the doors were mismatched, and the whole lot was as faded as the asphalt.

Kate's smile was all teeth. "Grandpa only puts money into things that float or dive."

Holden lifted both black eyebrows, lowered his bags into the back of the truck near a smallish, rusty toolbox that had been welded to the truck bed. He searched for cargo straps, but the best he could find was a rope that had once seen hard duty at sea. With a few deft knots, he secured the duffels.

She saw what he was doing, thought about telling him that she wouldn't be going fast enough to shake anything out, then simply got into the steaming cab and started the engine. After four tries, the engine backfired a cloud of diesel smoke and settled into a reliably uneven rhythm.

After a few hard bangs with her fist, the glove box opened. The map to the rented house was primitive, but combined with what she had looked up online this morning, she wouldn't get lost.

Finally her cheerless guest abandoned his baggage and got into the passenger seat. The truck settled deep into its worn suspension. Surprisingly deep.

*He must be all bone and muscle,* she thought. *I think his kind of consultant is called a troubleshooter. Real bullets optional.*

"Do you dive?" she asked.

"Why do you ask?"

"Because you're really solid. Divers don't have much body fat. They burn it off."

"Interesting," he said.

The call of voices and piercing cry of birds filled what otherwise would have been the silence following his neutral comment.

*What a fascinating conversationalist,* she thought. *Boy, is this going to be a fun drive. Let's see, maybe fifteen minutes to the side of town, and another mile to the rental.*

She shifted gears, let out the clutch, and drove slowly onto the airport road.

"Is it long to the ship?" Holden asked.

"Depends on Larry's dive schedule."

"Why?"

"He's picking you up at the cottage the company rented for your friend. The rental itself is about a ten-minute walk from the fuel dock, chandlery, and commercial marina Larry uses. This isn't a big island."

The fact that Holden followed her elliptical conversation told Kate he was a lot smarter than the average diver.

"Malcolm Farnsworth is a contract employee, as I am," Holden said. "I don't know the man personally, much less call him a friend."

"How unsurprising."

Something close to a smile disturbed Holden's features, but all he said was, "I thought Farnsworth was staying aboard the *Golden Bough*."

She shrugged. "Larry would know. I just got here."

"That explains it."

She told herself she wasn't going to ask, but she did. "Explains what?"

"Pale skin. Hard to maintain in the tropics, unless you only go about at night."

"Sorry to disappoint. No vampire blood in the Donnelly family."

He looked sideways at her. "How terribly ordinary."

"Certainly makes our lives easier. I don't think I've ever heard of a diving vampire."

Something that could have been a smile changed the line of Holden's lips. "Do you know how long it is to the rental?"

"No. But again, it's a small island."

Five minutes and a lot of greenery went by, broken by occasional brilliant views of the ocean.

"Is it always this warm here?" he asked.

"You'd have to ask a tourism minister. I haven't been here for years."

"But you're one of the diving Donnellys, correct?"

"I don't dive anymore." Her tone of voice didn't encourage questions.

Holden thought about pursuing it. Until he had met her in the airport, there had been no mention of anyone called Kate Donnelly being on the payroll or on board the dive ship *Golden Bough*. He would have to ask the Antiquities Office for more information.

"Couldn't take the calloused hands and bad hearing?" he asked. "Or was it the nerve damage that put you off diving?"

"I was a careful diver. No damage."

"You must have quit young."

"Young enough."

"So you won't be suffering dysbaric osteonecrosis either," Holden said. "A wise choice."

"I understood about half of that," she said. "Osteo. Bone. You mean arthritis? A lot of divers end up with it. Grandpa has his share. Are you a doctor?" She glanced at him, then back to the road.

"Diving can lead to arthritis," Holden said. "Sometimes it just leads to a joint replacement due to bone death, hence the name 'osteonecrosis.' And no, I'm not a doctor, but I know my way around underwater operations. Otherwise I would be rather useless for this job."

That this was his first and only civilian job since he'd been injured was a fact that he kept to himself. The people in Antiquities had conferred with the military doctor and deemed him competent to consult on salvage diving, especially as it had been made clear he was to find reasons to shut down the dive. No diving would be expected of him.

Holden wasn't unhappy with that. He had been diving enough since the mishap to assure himself that the injury was manageable underwater. Hurt like a bitch, but he could dive.

Kate slowed to match speeds with a tourist bus. It was painted bright green and looked like a giant beetle crawling around the road. Sticking out of open windows, a scattering of hands waved in the breeze like flowers reaching toward the Caribbean sun.

As the silence stretched, she decided that being nice hadn't worked, so she'd move on to direct.

"My brother wasn't very clear about what your job is, so I don't know what kind of information you need."

"Call me a dive consultant."

"Grandpa and Larry could be called dive consultants," she said, keeping her voice neutral. "What is your specific purpose?"

"To evaluate the operation. Surely your brother mentioned that they have precious little to show for all their diving. AO—the Antiquities Office—sent me to plug the money holes, as it were. Our weather people are predicting at least one good gale within the week.

There is no point to keeping a losing project on standby while the weather sorts itself out."

"According to the receipts I've seen," she said carefully, "there are no 'money holes' except the normal expenses of any dive."

Holden considered pointing out the obvious—he had been sent out because incompetence or theft or both were suspected—but decided to save that little gem for another time. From the files he had been given, Moon Rose Ltd. was one buggered operation.

*Too bad, how sad, and failure is more common than success,* he thought. *The nondiving member of the Donnelly clan could be the most beautiful woman ever born and it wouldn't change the outcome. Every dive the department underwrites must produce profit or prestige, and profit is preferred.*

"If there are no money holes, there is no problem for me to find," he said.

The rest of the drive was completed in silence but for the wind rushing through open windows and the occasional cry of birds.

The rental was on land the jungle had pretty much reclaimed from whatever agricultural use had been its previous life. As required in a tropical paradise, the beach sand was a blinding white in the sun, the palms were elegantly graceful, and the sea clear and gentle.

St. Vincent had quite a few black sand beaches, compliments of its resident volcano, but this rental wasn't on one of them.

Kate stopped the rattling truck at the end of dirt ruts that served as a driveway. She made it a point not to look at the water. Smelling it, hearing the seabirds—that was enough.

Too much.

She gripped the wheel with clammy hands and concentrated on her breathing. Without driving to distract her, the reality of where she was kept pulling at her like a cold undertow.

Holden gave the scenery a sweeping glance that missed nothing, lingering over the canted floating dock and the aluminum workboat loosely moored to it. There was a faint path from the house—barely a cottage, really—to the dock. Off to the back of the property there was nothing but tangles of vines, shrubs, and trees.

The dwelling itself was rustic to the point of dilapidation. If the exterior wood had ever been painted, it had worn away. The foundation looked like a kind of cement mixed locally by unskilled labor. The roof had been shingled once; now it was a patchwork of corrugated tin pieces nailed on whenever and wherever a leak became a problem.

Without a word Kate got out, took the cartons of bookkeeping from the bed of the truck, and walked up the rocky, overgrown path to the front. The door was unlocked. She stashed the boxes inside the house. A quick look around told her that the furnishings were as shabby as the house. At least the electricity worked, if the loud hum of the refrigerator was any indication.

She shrugged. Knowing her grandfather and the financial problems of his salvage company, she hadn't been expecting the Ritz. With a little more exploration she found two tiny bedrooms, one bathroom, and a kitchenette. The back door led to the jungle.

When she returned to the truck for her luggage, Holden was still studying the house and its surroundings from behind his mirrored sunglasses.

"It's not much," she said, "but it will get the job done. The bedroom at the back has two bunk beds. You and your fellow employee can share."

"I've stayed in worse," was all he said.

"Such confidence. You haven't even seen the inside."

"Irrelevant. I'll be bunking on the *Golden Bough*."

Kate hesitated, remembering her brother's comment about how crowded the ship was. Then she decided that where Holden slept was Larry's problem. All she cared about was that she was staying on land. Period. With a little effort and a lot of concentration on cleaning up

Larry's laughable bookkeeping, she would hardly know she was within breathing distance of her nightmare.

And if she told herself that often enough, she might really believe it.

Holden met her at the front door, holding her luggage. "Which room?" he asked.

"The one with a single bed, thank you."

Kate watched his easy stride as he walked down the narrow hall and thought again that it was too bad such a nice package was wrapped around a block of ice. Then her eye caught the piece of paper held to the tiny refrigerator with a garish fish magnet.

> *Hi, sis,*
>
> *Welcome back. Diving rotation got changed. Bring him to the ship, okay?*
>
> L

She read the note three times before the roaring in her ears eased and she remembered to breathe.

*He can't do this to me!*

But he had.

# Chapter 2

Kate's first impulse was to grab her luggage and head back to the airport—and to hell with the family business. But she had fled once, years ago. She was still running. No matter how tempting at the moment, in the long run giving in to fear wasn't going to get her anywhere she wanted to be.

She blew out a hard breath, breathed in deeply, and repeated until her head no longer felt like it would explode.

*It's calm and sunny. Even the trade winds have taken a vacation, just like they always do in August and September. I was operating workboats when I was eight. I can do it now. That's one of the reasons I came back, right? To get over what happened. To stop waking up screaming in the middle of the night.*

She kept breathing, waiting for it to become automatic again.

Holden walked into the kitchenette and saw Kate standing stiff and motionless, her fist clenched around what looked like a piece of paper.

"Is everything all right?" he asked.

"Just peaches and cream," she said through clenched teeth. *I'm so going to kill my brother.*

Holden raised both black eyebrows and said nothing.

"Looks like you won't have to wait for Larry to pick you up after all," she said, throwing the note into a small trash can. "I'll take you to the *Golden Bough* now. Right now." *Before I go from fury to fear.*

"Excellent," he said.

And he wondered why she looked angry and fierce and afraid, like a cornered animal.

While he went to the truck for his duffels, she grabbed a wind shell and a sun hat from her luggage. He fell in behind her as she marched down to the dock. Although her shoulders were rigid, her ease on the uneven, wobbly dock told him that she was hardly new to the movement of water under her feet. It was the same for her graceful step from dock to the gunwale, and then down to the open cabin of the boat.

Holden glanced at the aluminum workboat. It was between five and six meters long, powered by two muscular outboard engines, and driven from a forward cabin that was little more that two bench seats with backrests and a windscreen. A fuel compartment filled the area under the stern bench. Various permanent clamps and anchors for ties studded the cargo area. Most were in use, holding down everything from compressed air tanks to fuel and food, waiting to be ferried to the *Golden Bough.*

The boat had the patina of metal that had been hard used, beaten and bitten with thousands of tiny scars and scratches. Pieces of tread from old tires had been fixed on the outer side of the gunwales. The resulting rub rail wasn't fancy but would get the job done. TT *Golden Bough 2* was painted in faded letters across the stern.

*One of the main ship's two tenders,* Holden noted, mentally checking it against the list of equipment that had appeared on the contract. *Wonder where the other one is, plus the pricey speedboat Farnsworth uses.*

A few moments after Kate stepped into the open cabin, the boat engine fired up with less stink and rattle than the truck had. Holden looked at what he could see of the aluminum bottom of the boat. There was some sign of water along the center seam, but nothing unexpected. Less than a cup of tea, really.

*Right,* Holden thought. *At least the Donnellys keep diving and support gear in decent order.*

Kate came back from the cab and looked at him, silently asking why he was still on the dock.

"Would you like me to cast off for you?" he asked.

"No need. Our tenders are rigged for single handling."

Holden took that as an invitation and stepped from gunwale to the centerline of the tender, making almost no disturbance to the motion of the boat. His thigh protested, but he was used to it. He stowed his bags under a seat in the open cabin, watching while Kate stepped up onto the dock and cast off with a minimum of fuss.

She pushed the boat away from the dock with her foot, landed lightly aboard, and moved quickly but not carelessly to the controls. Soon she had the speed up to the maximum that the hull was designed for. While she drove, she checked her heading against the simple navigation screen. A multitude of dotted lines pointed out to sea, converging on a spot in the distance.

Despite the strain on her face, he could see that she knew her way around boats—perhaps even as well as he did. Her body flexed to the changing movement of the water, she handled the controls with unconscious expertise, and yet she had the air about her of someone being forced to do something quite frightening.

"You don't like being on the water, do you?" Holden asked, pitching his voice to be heard above the hearty roar of the engines.

For a moment she acted like she hadn't heard him.

"I don't like collard greens, but I eat them," she said finally. "Life is rarely about what you like."

As she spoke, she felt something loosen just a bit inside her. She could do this. She really could. It was just a matter of keeping her mind from being sucked back down into the nightmares.

*The ocean around St. Vincent is quite beautiful,* she reminded herself. *All those clear, luminous shades of blue.*

Resolutely she kept her eyes to the surface of the water, where things were warm and lazy and full of light.

"The dive site is about five kilometers out from one of those islets, yeah?" Holden asked, pointing toward the dark dots that were growing from the sea.

Her tentative peace evaporated at the word *dive.* Her parents had died off those islets, searching for Bloody Green's legendary treasure ship.

"I don't know," she said. "I'm just following a route someone else entered in the nav computer."

Yet even as she spoke, a combination of memory and instinct and nightmare assured Kate that the

*Golden Bough* was anchored uncomfortably close to the site where her mother had vanished and she had pulled her father's convulsing body from the stormy sea.

Kate shoved the thought down into the part of her mind where darkness waited. She concentrated on watching the *Golden Bough* take shape in the distance. Its black hull and dark red superstructure stood out from the blue expanse of sky and sea like a checkmark. The closer she got, the more she could see that the ship had been on the water for a very long time. A thorough bottom cleaning and paint scraping was in order.

*I don't see how Grandpa will make enough money for basic maintenance on this lousy job.*

To deflect the panic gnawing at the edges of her self-control, Kate concentrated on separating the real *Golden Bough* from the pitching, careening black blob of her nightmares.

Festooned with antennas and radar domes, the ship's conning tower rose up off the elevated forward deck. It was a patchwork affair, having been added to and built up over decades. A huge metallic arm dominated the stern deck. Grease and hydraulic fluid leaked out in rusty brown streaks from every joint, announcing that the *Golden Bough* was a hardworking, seagoing pack mule. Like her captain, she was salty and pragmatic, and she refused to be consigned to history.

*Nothing to be afraid of,* Kate assured herself. *Nothing at all.*

"She hardly looks a day over sixty," Holden said, his voice dry.

"The *Golden Bough* was purchased in 1966, built in 1959 in Providence by Cooper Shipping Works," she said absently. "When its most recent owner went bankrupt, Grandpa bought the ship."

Holden made an appreciative noises. The builder had a reputation on both sides of the Atlantic for making exceptionally sound, affordable ships.

"It's difficult to get that kind of quality anymore," he said.

"So Grandpa always says."

She eased back on the throttles as they approached the starboard side, where part of the gunwale on the lowest deck was hinged to open inward. Deckhands or divers off rotation popped their heads over the rails, looking down curiously. She waved to them as she brought the tender around to the side opening.

Holden assessed the dive boat in his mind. Despite its lack of flash and polish, the ship could take about anything the sea felt like dishing up—so long as the engines had been cared for regularly and competently. Sometimes the appearance of clean and shipshape was just a pretty wrapping on a rotten package.

"There's Larry," Kate said, cutting the throttles to idle as the tender bumped gently against the larger boat. "He'll be down in a moment. Throw your duffels aboard. I'll keep you close enough to step up on the gunwale and then onto the lower deck of the ship."

"Shall I take a line?"

"I'm leaving," she said. She heard her own clipped voice edged with fear and winced. *Way to win friends. Think of his sexy exterior and not the robot inside.* "My work is ashore, thank you. I'll wait here until the crew unloads the supplies."

No sooner had she finished speaking than her brother was calling to her.

"Hurry up, sis, and get a line up here. I haven't seen you since Christmas before last!"

She looked up at all the faces peering down, shades of skin from ebony to brown to the sun-reddened, freckled face of her brother. Wisps of orange-red hair stuck out from the hat he wore.

For an instant she was five again, looking up into the face of her father. Tears stung.

*Damn you, Larry. You know I don't want to come aboard again. And you know I should.*

*So do I, now.*

*But I won't dive. There isn't enough treasure in all the Caribbean to make me go underwater again.*

Holden threw the line to Larry, who tied it off quickly, giving Holden time to watch his beautiful pilot go pale, flush, go pale again, and then turn off the engines. Her mouth was a grim line of determination, a difficult feat with her full lips. They usually made a man think of kissing and nibbling. Everywhere. All inappropriate, of course. This was an assignment, not a holiday with a side of sex.

Too bad his mind and body kept pointing that way.

"After you," he said politely.

Holden watched while Kate went from the tender to the ship with the speed and temper of a scalded cat. The man who was apparently her brother swept her up into a big hug. For a moment or two, she was stiff. Then she hugged him in turn.

Holden envied the brother even as he wondered about the family dynamics. The murmuring of the crew reminded him to pull his mind away from the woman and concentrate on his job.

According to the briefing he had received, Larry was captain of the ship and head of the dive operation but always deferred to the elder Donnelly. Patrick Donnelly was at best a rapscallion, and at worst a thief. He was also a legendary treasure hunter who had lost his son and daughter-in-law during a dive to find a pirate's hoard. Like all treasure hunters, no booty that

Patrick Donnelly ever found had the allure of what was still out there, waiting in the depths for him to discover. The death of his son hadn't even made him pause.

*It's an illness,* Holden thought. *Or a madness. By all measures, he has infected his grandson with it.*

*But not his very curvy, tempting granddaughter.*

Again, he pulled himself away from thinking about Kate and focused on the crewmen who had come to greet the newcomers. From the look of their dark skin, most were native to some part of the Caribbean. They had the lean, sinewy bodies of divers. So did the fourth man, though with his ragged, straight dark hair and brown skin, he looked like he was Spanish or South American. All were clean-shaven. Divers only grew facial hair on their time off. Beards, mustaches, and any combination thereof got in the way of the seal between dive mask and face, which got in the way of survival.

A shaggy blond-haired man appeared, his unruly mane tied at his neck with a leather thong. His beard and the dough-covered wooden spoon in his hand pegged him as the cook.

To a man, they watched Holden with open suspicion.

*Very well,* he thought with wry satisfaction. *I'm not here to adopt the lot of them or be the new bloke at the pub buying pints. It is time to polish the right-bastard act.*

He threw his duffels up onto the deck and followed them aboard.

Kate sensed him behind her, hesitated, then said softly to Larry, "If you try to trick me into a dive suit, I'll take the pressure regulator and shove it up so far you'll be spitting metal."

Her brother went still, then let out a shout of laughter. "There's the old Kitty Kat. Welcome home!"

She tugged on his hair to let him know she meant every word, then turned toward Holden. Before she could say anything, Larry stepped around her, his hand extended.

"Mister Holden?" he asked.

Holden shook his head as he pressed Larry's hand with a patented dead-fish shake. "It is Mister Cameron. Check your paperwork. You may give me a tour of the operation after you show me where I'll be bunking."

Kate gave Holden a sidelong look. He seemed bent on sharing the least appealing side of his personality.

"You'll be sleeping ashore," Larry said tightly. "We don't have any room." He swept his hand around. "This isn't a damned tour boat."

"Excellent. I'm not a tourist. Do keep up, mate." Holden waited, watching behind his impenetrable sunglasses while Larry flushed stoplight red. "My quarters, if you please."

Behind Larry, the crew shifted restively, their distrust giving way to curiosity about who would come ahead in this shouldering contest.

Though Holden appeared not to notice the crew, he was aware of every shifting expression. Their responses would tell him if Larry was leader only in name, or if the divers actually would back him in a brawl.

At the moment, the crew was simply waiting and watching.

So was Kate. Her rather skeptical expression told him that she wasn't quite buying his entire act. Holden tried to regret not being a complete bastard in her eyes, but couldn't. She was just too appealing to him, and her intelligence was a growing part of her allure.

Fortunately, her brother was a much easier sell. He was ready to toss Holden overboard.

"Who died and left you king of the universe?" Larry muttered.

Holden heard. "Must I repeat? Check your paperwork. The contract specifies that you will provide food and housing for whichever representative or representatives of the Antiquities Office request—"

"We'll feed and house you," Larry cut in. "Just not on the dive ship. You'll stay ashore with Kate and Malcolm, unless he's still aboard catching up with his logs."

"Not bloody likely," Holden said with a disdainful curve of his mouth. "What little of worth that you have found shouldn't tax his abilities to that degree."

Kate wrapped one hand around her brother's wrist. He had an uncertain temper at best. When he was under pressure, he exploded regularly.

"Actually," she said to Holden, "it takes just as much time to find and enter a potsherd properly as it does a gold doubloon." Her tone of voice said he should know that.

"Pity that potsherds don't pay the overhead," Holden said.

"Last time I checked," Larry shot back, "you were the ones who needed a job done and weren't able to do it yourselves. How we got it done wasn't supposed to be your problem."

"The job has yet to be done," Holden said. "That is your problem."

Kate's grip on her brother's wrist tightened, holding his fist to his side.

"You're lucky we've found what we have," Larry said. "The storm last year that uncovered the wreck scattered as much as it revealed."

"And another storm can cover it all up again," Holden said. "Given current conditions, British Weather Service has projected that this area is in a likely storm track due to become active within six to eight days."

"But last year's storm," Larry began, then changed tack. "The chances of two big blows in a year on the same track are—"

"The weather, Mr. Donnelly, does not give a tinker's damn about your opinion. If you flip a coin and get heads ten times in a row, what are the odds of getting heads on the eleventh?"

Holden watched Larry do some math in his head. He had to work at it. Perhaps that was due to the bruises of fatigue under his eyes or the smell of stale beer on his breath. More likely, he simply lacked mathematical competence, unlike his very bright, much younger sister.

"The odds are—" Kate began.

"The question is to your brother," Holden said over her.

"Less than two percent," Larry said.

She sighed.

"Wrong," Holden said. "The odds are fifty-fifty. Apparently you are lacking in more than the ability to read and understand simple paperwork. At this time the AO believes that wreck H-37 holds far more than we have yet seen cataloged. With the storm brewing out there, we have little time to find treasure and secure it. That, Mr. Donnelly, is a problem for both of us. Shall we get on with it?"

Kate's clenched fingers kept Larry from speaking the first words on his tongue. The crew watched Holden now, not supporting him, but recognizing that he was ahead on points at the moment.

"There's no guarantee of treasure," she said distinctly. "The contract only states that the Bureau of Historic Reclamation, a branch of the Antiquities Office, gets to keep what Moon Rose Limited hauls up. Without a manifest for and a positive identification of the hulk in question, nobody knows what's down there, thus there is no assurance of worth."

Unlike Larry, her attitude wasn't defensive. She had learned as a younger sister the truth about offense being the best defense.

"So the AO should be content with the cannonballs and trinkets that you've pulled up so far?" Holden asked. "This operation has cost—"

"Precisely what the signing and commencement fees of the contract have stipulated," she cut in. "Which, by the way, is far less than it would have cost you to get a British naval salvage crew out here, assuming you had one to spare, and also assuming you could get in place before the doldrums ended."

"Yeah," Larry said, putting his arm around Kate and silently saying, *See? This is why we need you.* "It's our necks on the line down there, not yours. So don't walk in here and start pissing all over everything that we've done."

"In any case," Kate said, "we've brought up nearly a hundred silver ingots and a scattering of silver jewelry. All of which you can happily melt down and put into the Crown's coffers. You're hardly empty-handed at this point."

"Even if it is determined that the silver is of no historical significance and melted down," Holden pointed out, "at the price of silver in today's market, my employer is uncomfortably distant from recovering its investment."

"That's why it's called a treasure *hunt*," she said. "There is no guarantee of success."

"Point to the lovely lady," Holden said, smiling in spite of himself. He turned and looked directly at the crew. "That should take care of the formalities. At the moment, time is of the essence. Go back to work. If need be, I'll talk to you individually about your dive jobs."

The crew stirred uncertainly, but turned away, accepting Holden's authority.

*Which was the entire purpose of that little farce,* he thought. *Good old Larry no longer has to figure the odds of lightning striking twice. He is still feeling the voltage.*

Kate didn't move. The smile Holden had given her had changed him from robot to something that made her pulse scramble. She suspected that his personality had more facets than the average diamond.

And when he cut, it was to the bone.

# Chapter 3

Following the direction of Holden's glance, Kate saw that he was watching her grandfather on the upper deck, and probably had been from the beginning. Cultural glitches aside, very little escaped Holden's striking eyes.

Something in the silent exchange between Holden and her grandfather kept Kate from running up to the wheelhouse to give his wiry body a hug. Lit by sun that was almost directly overhead, Grandpa appeared stark and dramatic. His head—bald but for a longish sliver fringe spreading from ear to ear—had been burned a dark teak from long hours in the sun, as had all of his body save the parts covered by faded shorts. His stance was casual, but somehow distant. His teeth were clamped on the stem of an unlit pipe, his elbows were resting on the rail, and his pale eyes gleamed with intelligence as he watched the newcomer.

"Patrick Donnelly, I presume," Holden said.

"On the *Golden Bough* they call me Captain."

Holden's black eyebrows rose. On paper, it was grandson Larry who had that title. Reality, however, was often different from paper. It was that difference which gave Holden a job.

"I trust you will have time for a chat with me after I've checked out the dive center," Holden said, again as much a command as a request.

"I'm here."

"Yes, I rather imagine that is preferable to being in court fighting to hold on to various treasures," Holden said blandly.

"Bloodsucking governments are worse than insurance companies. You don't see any of them risking their pampered arses on a dive, do you? I research, I dive, I risk, and sometimes I pull up treasure. Me, not your god-rotting bureaucrats. By the law of the sea, what I find is mine."

"At one time, yes," Holden agreed. "Unfortunately for you, that time is past."

"God-rotting, gut-eating vultures."

Holden didn't take it personally. He had read files where Patrick Donnelly had been quoted at length in court records and the less formal pages of newspapers. At one time Donnelly had been seen as a kind of folk hero for spitting in the eye of various governments and lawyers. But since the turn of the twenty-first century, that respectability had ebbed.

*Not that Patrick Donnelly had changed because of it,* Holden thought. *Nothing will change that crusty old bastard except death.*

Silently Kate watched as Grandpa Donnelly looked away from Holden to the eastern horizon. With a faint grimace he headed inside the wheelhouse once more.

She let out the breath she had been holding without realizing it. From where she stood, it was obvious that Larry had been relegated to bit player in the drama of the *Golden Bough.* Grandpa and Holden were shouldering each other for the lead.

*Poor Larry. Grandpa's contempt for any point of view but his own can be really hard to live with.*

But somehow her brother managed. He always had.

"I'll see the dive center first," Holden said, looking at Larry.

The other man didn't move. If his mottled skin color was any indication, he was struggling to keep his temper leashed.

"Have you changed the location of the dive center since Dad was in charge?" Kate asked her brother.

He shook his head. "Everything is pretty much the same, but more crowded. We've stashed supplies and replacement parts everywhere aboard to minimize trips ashore. Fuel is expensive. Which reminds me . . ." He called out to the first crewman he saw, "Unload the tender."

"Apparently I'm the designated tour guide," Kate said as she turned to Holden, trying to keep her voice level.

It was bad enough being on the *Golden Bough* again. Going belowdecks was much, much worse, memories clawing at her. With a deep breath she opened the salt-rimed door and stepped into the relative darkness beyond.

She had manned the dive center often, but what raked her guts with fingernails of ice was the memory of the last time she'd stood in this doorway.

*The green glow of the dive cameras recorded that the divers were coming up from the bottom far too fast, not even pausing at the decompression stations that were clearly marked on the weighted line hanging from the dive buoy.*

*"What's wrong? What's wrong! Answer me, Dad!" she yelled into the mic.*

*At first he didn't answer.*

*Then he didn't have to.*

*Obviously something had gone wrong with her mother's dive gear. Her mother's figure was slack as her father finned his way at reckless speed to the surface.*

"*Oh, God. No. Dad, the bends!*"

*If he heard her, he ignored her, his whole being intent on getting his wife up to the air.*

Holden was the only one who noticed Kate's unnatural stillness. He eased off his sunglasses as he moved through the door and shielded her from her brother's view. With a gentle touch to her cool cheek, Holden pulled her out of her trance.

She shivered convulsively as he touched her. His unusual, shattered-crystal eyes yanked her out of memories of terror.

"Ready to go to the dive center?" he asked in a low voice.

"Your eyes . . ." she whispered. "So beautiful. Dragon eyes."

Then she came fully into the present with a start. A flush crawled up her pale cheeks.

"Ready," she said, lying without a pause. She had to be ready. Everything depended on it. "You, too, Larry," she said in a carrying voice. "I'm sure our guest will have more questions than I have answers."

"In a minute," Larry called from the deck. "I want to make sure the crew gets those supplies stowed properly."

Once her eyes adjusted and she got a better grip on her nerves, she stepped farther into the belowdecks opening. Just inside and to the right, a steep stairway—more a ladder with wide rungs—led up to the main deck. The sight of it sent memories breaking over her in cold waves.

*Scrambling up the pitching ladder, more desperation than judgment.*

*Screaming . . .*

*Launching the tender in an awkward rush. Sweeping the stormy sea and darkness with a heavy light.*

*Screaming . . .*

*Trying and trying and trying to haul them into the tender despite the wild ocean and lightning scoring the sky, thunder like body blows.*

*Screaming . . .*

*Her mother sliding out of sight beneath the water. Her father convulsing in the final stages of the bends as she hauled him aboard and searched the dark storm waters for her mother.*

*Screaming. . .*

*"I'm sorry, Mother. I'm sorry, sorry, sorrysorrysorry!"*

"Kate," Holden said softly, touching her clammy skin. "Easy, Kate. Come back. You're safe."

Without realizing it, she leaned closer to the comfort she had so badly needed when she was seventeen and hadn't been able to save either of her parents. There had been too many hours alone in the storm searching for her mother's body while her father grew cold in the bottom of the tender.

Her mother had never been found, just one more body taken by the ravening sea and the cursed wreck called *Moon Rose.*

Strong arms came around Kate, rocking gently, a deep voice murmuring reassurances into her ear. She wrapped herself even more tightly to his warmth, holding on, just holding on, until the sound of her brother shouting something at the crew cut through the moment.

Hastily she straightened and stepped back from Holden.

"Just getting my bearings," she said without looking at him. "I haven't been aboard this ship since I turned eighteen."

"Of course," he said, his voice gentle, his tone saying that he knew she was telling only a part of the truth—the most unimportant part.

And he would have all of the truth.

Holden could have told himself that it was only business that drove his curiosity, but he knew better. With a final touch on her cheek, he released her and stepped back just moments before Larry appeared at the door, still yelling orders over his shoulder.

Looking straight ahead, Kate walked toward the dive center, ignoring the brightly painted doors on either side of the narrow hall that led to crew quarters. One door was ajar, showing unmade bunks. The odor of stale alcohol competed with the usual smells of engine and sea.

Holden paused, looking into the small room. He couldn't be certain, but what appeared to be an empty bottle of rum had been tossed into a corner with some dirty clothes. Obviously alcohol was either uncontrolled or ignored aboard the ship.

She knocked at the last door and was told to "Open the damn door yourself, I'm busy."

The voice was flat, nasal, and impatient. The accent was more Dutch or German than English.

Kate shoved the metal door wide and gestured for Holden to follow her inside. He saw her glance lingering on his eyes and mentally sighed. It always took people time to get accustomed to his colorful eyes.

Deliberately he looked past her at the dive center.

No one made any introductions. The crew member manning the dive center didn't even look over his shoulder to see who had come in. Holden decided not to take it personally. When a diver was working on the bottom, he deserved full attention from the liaison up top.

Because the dive center was in the bow of the ship, the space was shaped like a funnel with the wide end toward the entrance. At the narrow end, a curving bank of pale, flickering screens dominated the small room. On the screen just to the operator's right side, the seabed was mapped out in a series of green topographical grids, waiting for a diver to appear or simply focused on a part of the dive area that wasn't under active exploration at the moment.

Holden sized up the piles of electronic equipment—some with leads exposed and running together to tangle like a nest of snakes—that lined the walls. From what he could see, the nerve center of the dive ship had been cobbled together using everything from the streamlined black cases of modern Japanese consumer styling to snarls of coiled wires and green motherboards that would have been at home in a tech museum.

The mismatched equipment obviously did a satisfactory job. Video feed from a diver filled the main screen. The wreck was deep enough to be in the twilight zone, where everything was a watery gray blue except in the swaths cut by dive lights. There, corals showed their true colors in rainbow array.

Most of the heavy work of removing the overburden of sand and silt from the wreck had already been done by directing the wash from the ship's propellers through tubes, literally hosing off loose material on the bottom. Because the process took a lot of expensive diesel to run the main engines, only the areas deemed most likely to reveal treasure had been uncovered. The rest waited, still laden with the accumulation of centuries of debris.

The delicate work of going through cracks, crevasses, and other areas where heavy metal had slowly sunk through the loose sea bottom to the hardpan beneath—sometimes many, many feet beneath—was left to divers. One of the divers was presently sifting through sand left in the lee of a clump of coral. With each motion of his hand, sand floated up like a slow, silent echo.

Holden was familiar with the strange disconnect divers encountered their first few times down. For humans, the water beneath the surface was a slow-motion world, rather like the old videos of men on the moon. Everything seemed to take place with a time delay.

He remembered that unearthly feeling of diving, an alien ballet that took place when gravity was largely subtracted from the equation. Largely, but not entirely. Heavy objects could still fall and pin unlucky divers, and nobody moved as fast underwater as they could on land.

*Not nearly as fast as the shrapnel from an exploding underwater mine,* Holden thought, rubbing his thigh absently. His blood had been a muddy green until he was hauled out of the water and put in a decompression chamber with a doctor in attendance. In the air his blood had been scarlet drying to black.

From the corner of his eye, Holden watched Kate's reaction to being in the crowded space belowdecks. She had a faint sheen of sweat on her face, but that could have been due to the minimal ventilation in the room. Her face was calm, her hands still. She looked good. Beautiful, in fact.

*I'm going to have to check very carefully into her background. I wouldn't be the first investigator caught in the net of a sexy thief.*

The pragmatic part of him hoped she was indeed part of the family scam; it would be so much simpler. But the part of him that sensed she was as honest as she was compelling knew that his life had taken a complex, unexpected turn.

The diver's wrist-mounted dive computer's face flashed as it reflected the spill from the dive lights. The compact lightning drew Holden's attention. Gray-green sea fronds danced lazily in the twilight, undulating to a rhythm all their own while neoprene-gloved fingers whisked like a clumsy broom over the bottom. The motion made sand lift in lazy curls that bent toward a nozzle off to the right side of the screen. An invisible, man-made current siphoned off the sand as it slowly settled into a low, eerie cloud around the diver's black-clad hand.

A big tiger shark swept into view with the ease of a supreme predator. Holden tightened instinctively. So did Kate. Larry scratched his cheek with a total lack of interest.

The diver ignored the shark.

As for the dive center operator, he was too busy reaching into a bag of fried pork rinds to react to anything, including the people behind him. From the look of his fleshy neck and cheeks, he spent a lot more time eating than exercising.

*Not a diver, that one,* Holden thought. *Far too much body fat. I've seen bored divers go through thousands of calories, but they burn it off as soon as they get back to work.*

Crunching sounds filled the room as the operator shoved in some more crispy bits.

"Goddam, Volkert," came a voice over a loud-speaker. "Sounds like you be eatin' right in my ear."

"It's bloody boring up here," Volkert said indifferently.

"You think it be better here? You say you put me in the right place this time," the diver said in a long-suffering tone, "but I not be findin' a shaggin' thing and the tank be runnin' on fumes."

The diver's accent was Spanish, but with the lilt of the Caribbean dancing through the words. Then the man added a few more phrases in blistering Spanish.

Holden looked at Kate.

Sensing his attention, she gave him a wry smile and said softly, "I was raised around divers. I could swear in three languages and five dialects before I was four. As long as the cursing isn't directed at me, I don't really notice it."

Holden had worked alongside women in the military who had the same attitude. They were every bit as competent as the men and could be as blunt in their language.

"Hullo," came a new voice over a different speaker. "Hullo, *Golden Bough*."

The London accent was unmistakable to Holden.

"This is Malcolm on board," the voice said. "Someone pick up, please."

Volkert pushed his mouthpiece aside and reached for an intercom handset. "Got you, Malcolm. Go ahead."

"Oh, good," Farnsworth replied, as if having things working was something unexpected and delightful. "I've got the latest lot entered and cataloged, ready for our overlords in Britain. Should I expect anything new from down below or am I sitting on my hands for the rest of today?"

The only British overlord within hearing raised winged black eyebrows.

"And when is it that the bloody busybody arrives?" Farnsworth continued. "Tomorrow morning?"

Larry laughed.

Volkert turned, reacted to his first look at Holden's startling eyes, and drew the obvious conclusion.

Holden held out his hand for the unit.

After a glance at Larry, who was yawning wide enough to swallow a fist, Volkert handed over the com set.

"Farnsworth, is it?" Holden asked, clipping each word like the well-educated Brit he was. Although he spoke several languages, plus various English dialects—including American English—he found that this particular accent worked best with most English speakers. It radiated upper crust and intimidation. "It seems that your overlords have stolen a march on you. The 'bloody busybody' is already present."

Air noise filled the connection. Then Farnsworth cleared his throat. "Nothing personal, mate. It was just a bit of a lark. Dives can be boring."

"You don't say. Are there any further notable acquisitions beyond the report that you filed on twenty-three August?" Holden asked.

"The next report isn't due until—"

"That wasn't my question," Holden cut in.

"Yes, of course. I, ah . . ." There was a quick clacking of keys on a computer and some rustling papers. "Just a moment. Hold on. It's right here." More rustling.

Holden imagined the man rummaging about a messy cabin, trying to find the daily dive reports. Apparently Larry wasn't the only one on the operation who disliked proper filing.

"Ah, here we are," Farnsworth said. "Yes. Oh, excellent. Very nice. Silver ingots, marked M23 to M56. That's 7.65 kilograms, give or take. We won't know until all the corrosion is cleared."

Holden did a quick conversion in his head. "Roughly forty-eight hundred pounds sterling. At today's silver prices, that is hardly a fortune to dance and shout about, especially considering all the costs on the debit side of this operation's ledger."

"There might be some additional value from the metallurgic or historical perspectives," Farnsworth pointed out.

Holden recalled the very succinct orders he had been given. "Do remember that this is the Crown's silver, and the Crown wants it back in circulation, not lining a museum vault."

Kate looked at him sharply. He might have been talking about scrap metal for all the passion or avarice in his voice.

*He isn't like my parents, captive to the lethal lure of treasure. Or like Larry, in love with the sea itself and treasure just an excuse for doing what he would do anyway.*

*Or like Grandpa, driven by the need to prove that his only child's death wasn't in vain.*

"Indeed, Mr. Cameron," Farnsworth said. "Quite correct. Would you care for an accounting of the pottery and porcelain finds?"

"Intact artifacts?" Holden asked.

"Ah, no. I would have filed a special report on such a find. Just as I shall for the silver ingots," he added hastily.

"By tonight," Holden said. "Copy to my e-mail, of course."

"Of course, sir." A subdued Farnsworth signed off.

"So your real job," Kate said, "is to rummage between couch cushions for loose change."

"That is your brother's job," Holden said. "Mine is to ensure that all the change makes it to the piggy bank."

"Larry wouldn't—" she began.

"What the hell?" her brother said over her. "Just because we haven't found a lot doesn't mean we're stealing!"

"I didn't even imply that," Holden replied. "However, since you've opened the subject, in the past some people working on contract have found more than has been reported. That will not be happening on my watch."

# Chapter 4

The quiet in the dive center was so profound that Kate could hear her heartbeat. Even Volkert had stopped crunching. Then came a sound over the dive loudspeaker.

"Holy," whispered the diver, almost inaudible over his respirator. "Holy holy holy holy holy. *Golden Bough,* you be seein' what I be seein'? Or maybe I be down here too long?"

Kate looked at the screen and gasped, which drew Holden's attention from Larry. Volkert dropped a chip from his thick fingers and began muttering words in his native South Afrikaans.

The diver's glove gleamed red as he put his hand closer to the camera and light, driving out the normal blue filter of deep water. Something glimmered in his hand, a glow that only came from high-quality gold. The links were about as big around as a pencil.

"The sixteenth-century version of a portable ATM," Kate said, recognizing it from the books that had filled her childhood. "The gold links are pure, soft enough to be parted and re-formed without tools. Need a blanket, food, a horse? Just break off the right weight in links and pay on the spot."

"Indeed." *And how very lovely to find for my arrival.* Holden took his smartphone out of a pants pocket and snapped a picture of the screen. "Lucky timing, eh? This might not be a total cock-up after all." With a quick motion he leaned over and took Volkert's headset. "How long is the chain?"

Holden's brisk question jarred the diver into a more formal kind of English.

"The length of my arm, twice. Maybe two meters. There might be more, but I'm running low on air."

"Right. Good work." He handed the headset back to Volkert and looked at Larry. "Tell your divers to concentrate on that part of the grid. I will see you in the main salon after I check in with Antiquities. Do be sure that your grandfather attends our little meeting."

Nodding, Larry got out of the way.

Kate didn't.

Holden looked at her, wishing he had more time to enjoy the effect of her smoldering in the light bath from the monitors.

"Are you going to tell me what is going on?" she asked in a level voice.

"That is what I'll be discussing with the chap who is actually running the show—Patrick Donnelly. Do join us."

Though the words were polite, it was another command.

Holden was gone before she could tell him what a nice man he wasn't.

After a moment to check her temper, Kate tilted her head toward the door and raised her left eyebrow at her brother.

"What?" Larry asked, yawning. Then, "Oh. Damn, Kitty, I should be taking a nap."

He followed her out the door and waited while she closed it firmly.

"You should be hiring a permanent business manager," she said, "not napping."

"Easy for you to say. I've been pulling extra dive shifts. Damn divers these days like drinking better than working."

"At the wages you're paying, you shouldn't be surprised."

He shrugged. "If we get above a certain amount in expenses, there are penalties. That's why we asked for an advance and got bloody Holden Cameron instead."

"You never should have signed that contract," she said.

"You'll get us sorted out."

"And we've had this conversation before." She hesitated, lowered her voice, and went to the point that had been worrying her. "How well do you know the diving crew?"

"They're cheap and competent enough. Same for Volkert, except the amount he eats, he should be paying us."

"That's not what I asked. How *well* do you know them? Are they trustworthy?"

Larry's pale blue eyes narrowed. "Even though you hate everything about diving, that's no reason to think divers are rotten."

"Do you think any of them are thieves?" she insisted.

"I don't hire thieves," he shot back at her. "Just because we aren't making a big haul doesn't mean there are crooks aboard. Besides, we just found some gold. We should be celebrating, not arguing."

"You don't have to yell, I hear you just fine."

"You're not acting like it."

Kate rubbed at the headache that was waiting behind her forehead. "I'm sorry. You know I love you." Then she heard herself and made a choked sound. "Time machines are real."

Her brother gave her a shocked look. "Are you okay?"

"Fine. Just time lagged."

He began to look worried.

She smiled crookedly. "Remember when you'd yank my ponytail and I'd yell at you?"

"Yeah?"

"And then you'd somehow work the conversation around to me apologizing for having gotten the ponytail in your way?" she asked.

"Sure. It was fun, then," he said rather wistfully.

"Maybe for you. I got tired of always being in the wrong."

"I love you, Kitty. That hasn't changed."

She let her forehead bang lightly against his shoulder. "I know. It's the only reason I haven't killed you. Come on. Let's watch Grandpa and the handsome Brit go at it."

"Handsome? That arrogant son of a bitch?"

"Part of that is the situation," she said, not knowing why she bothered to defend Holden. "Part is cultural. You're used to a relaxed island atmosphere and he is used to a right-and-tight city."

"Culture, huh." Larry yawned and said, "I thought he was just a prick."

"That, too. I suspect it's the lead item in his résumé."

She could hear her brother's laughter following her as she climbed the steep stairway up to the main deck. The sound helped her ignore the terror gnawing at her soul, memories of the night she had bolted up the stairs like her heels were on fire.

But there was no fire, only storm and the ravenous sea.

*Don't think about it,* she told herself. *It won't do any good. It will just get in the way of helping the family.*

*I really wish they had waited for me before they signed that awful contract. Oh well, spilled milk and all that.*

She climbed the ladder up to the wheelhouse, reading the words that her grandpa had painted between the steps long ago and repainted every year since.

ANYONE CAN HOLD THE HELM WHEN

THE SEA IS CALM

—Publius

She half smiled. The saying was so like Grandpa. Whatever the sea threw at him, he overcame. Whatever it gave up to him, he spent. Whatever it took from him, he mourned. But not for long.

It was an outlook Kate was still trying to master.

She hesitated before knocking on the steel door of the wheelhouse. The porthole, which as usual was opened for air circulation, reflected sunlight in blinding flashes that kept time with the lazy swells rocking the ship.

*So calm. So beautiful.*

*So deceptive.*

Larry's voice drifted up behind her, telling divers about the new area of concentration.

Kate knocked briskly on the gray door. "Grandpa, it's me."

"Come in, Kitty darling. I'll be yours in a moment."

Though he was a second-generation American, the lilt of County Cork curled around the words like a hug, telling her that he was in a good mood.

*Finding gold will do that for you,* she thought, and pushed the door open.

The wheelhouse was still a time-dulled stainless steel and lacquered teak, old and new materials mixed together with an eye to function rather than fashion. A sonar screen burned with brilliant blue, red, and yellow, mapping the bottom, which changed as the *Golden Bough* shifted lazily on anchor. The coiled line of a communications handset hung near the wheel like a corkscrew snake. Another screen lay beneath a light blue cotton shirt.

"I see you're still keeping all your displays clear," Kate said as she pulled the shirt away and hung it on the chromed hook behind the door. When she turned back, she realized that she had revealed a screen displaying a satellite relay of current weather overlaid on a graphic of the area. "I don't see the storm that Holden is worried about."

"It's coming," her grandpa said calmly. "Don't need fancy machines to tell me. I can feel it in the motion of the sea. If not in the next few days, then within the week." He wrote in the captain's log before he said, "Holden, is it? Do you fancy our new Brit?"

"He has gorgeous eyes," she said, then laughed when Grandpa turned swiftly toward her. "Gotcha."

"That you did, Kitty darling. Give an old man a hug."

"You're not an old man. You're my grandpa."

She went into his arms and was engulfed in the scents of the past—sea and tobacco and last night's rum. His fringe of hair tickled her cheek. She was nearly as tall as he was, which surprised her. Age had compacted him, making his work-scarred hands and thick knuckles look too large for his wiry frame. When she was young, she used to believe he could hold up the sky with those hands.

Everything aboard the *Golden Bough* was so familiar. She could almost hear her parents laughing on the dive deck.

Part of Kate tensed, waiting for the nightmare to break free.

Nothing came but the clank and creak of a working boat, with the steady undertone of the generator making electricity.

"Did you hear what a diver pulled up?" she asked.

"Mingo," her grandfather said.

"What?"

"Kid's name is Mingo."

"Oh. He pulled up almost two yards of gold chain," she said.

"About time that whelp earned his keep."

"Once you would have been shouting to the sky about the chain."

"Then the treasure was mine. I don't waste energy on another man's gold. So what do you think about the Brit? You always were a shrewd little one."

"Don't be misled by his proper accent. He's not just a stuffed shirt."

Grandpa grunted. "Larry calls him Cookie Monster."

Kate took a moment to absorb that her brother had already briefed her grandfather.

*Just like the old days. Nothing personal. I'm a little girl, not a big manly man. Fun to tease, a decent cook, a good diver, and a great bookkeeper.*

*And if Larry thinks Holden is as amiable as Cookie Monster, he's in for an unhappy surprise.*

"Well," Grandpa said philosophically, "maybe the new Brit will be more use than Malcolm the Geek. If it's not in a dive log, Malcolm doesn't see it. On the other hand, he doesn't get in the way. Hope this Cameron fellow doesn't, either."

"Sharks don't get in the way," she said. "They just follow their teeth."

"Shark, huh? Maybe I'll arrange a meeting between him and Benchley, show him what real teeth look like."

"Who's Benchley?"

"The fourteen-foot tiger shark that began cruising around the *Golden Bough* not long after we set up shop out here."

Kate remembered the muscular black shadow cutting across the dive screen, a shark overwhelming a rectangular goldfish bowl. "You dive with a tiger?"

"You've been away too long," Grandpa Donnelly said. "Sharks are a fact of life for divers here. To the crew, Benchley's good luck, so long as he isn't hungry.

This Cameron fellow gets in the way, we'll feed him to Benchley."

"It wouldn't help. The Brits would just send someone else." *But he probably wouldn't look like Holden, all surefooted and dragon-eyed.*

Kate cut off the thought. She'd clearly been knocked loopy by being aboard again.

"Maybe the Brits would lose interest," Grandpa said.

"That's not going to happen. Especially now that we've found some more signs that this is an old Spanish wreck."

The old man smiled bitterly. "What Mingo has in his hands is a trifle. I've pulled out money chains that could girdle the wheelhouse three times and have enough left over to put diesel in the boat for a month of cruising."

"Grandpa, you were lucky to find even this wreck. There's only so many left out there in easy reach."

"What makes you think I found this? I'm just an errand boy diving on a grid someone gave me. But sure as hell, I'd have found her by now. We were so close . . ." He shrugged. "Not close enough. Like chasing the devil's own rainbow. God-rotting bureaucrats. The sea was meant to be free to anyone with the wit and guts to survive her."

"So was the New World once. Now it's all claimed several times over."

"Vultures feeding on the carcass of men's dreams."

"At least you don't have a court fight ahead of you," Kate said. "Silver lining, Grandpa."

He said something under his breath, raised his pipe, and clamped his teeth around the stem.

"And you're only having to go about eighty feet down, ninety if it's on the slope to the drop-off. Much easier on the divers," she added. "Faster salvage, too."

"No point breaking your balls on those deep wrecks. Most of the time it takes more millions in equipment to recover anything and then a battalion of lawyers to keep governments at bay. Recovery costs far more than any treasure is worth. Besides, having robots do the work of men is for nancy boys and bureaucrats. I'm neither."

Kate braced for the rant to come. Even when she'd been a child, Grandpa had hated modern technology almost as much as he hated modern laws and the governments that thought them up.

*He's afraid,* she realized suddenly. *The past is gone and he doesn't fit in the present.*

"I'm sorry," she said softly.

"For what? Last time I looked you were family, not bloody government."

*For being young,* she thought. *For fitting into the present better than you do.*

"Please don't take it out on the messenger," she said softly.

"You?"

"Holden Cameron."

"That miserable bastard. Who is he to be talking about thieves?"

Kate stepped into her usual family job. Peacemaker. "For what it's worth, if the Brits wanted to shut down the operation and revoke the contract, Holden would have done it the second he set foot on the boat. Or sooner. A radio call would have taken care of it."

"So he's here to spy," Grandpa snarled.

She sighed. "More like a guard to make sure that the *Golden Bough* doesn't disappear into the sunset with a hold full of treasure that the British government claims."

He gave her a narrow-eyed glare. "If I'd intended to do that, I never would've taken this contract."

"You didn't. Larry did. It's his signature on the bottom line."

"Larry's a good boy, but he couldn't tie a proper flat knot without being reminded how to. You only needed to be shown once," he said, looking directly at her. His faded green eyes held the regret of a dream that hadn't come true. "You should be running this show. We'd not be in a pickle if—"

"Don't start," she cut in. "I didn't come here so that you could rail at me in person for letting the family down."

"You have your father's intelligence and your mother's fire." A faint smile softened the weathered lines of his face. "All right, Kitty darling. No more on that subject. So tell me, have you found a way to drain the red ink filling the bilge?"

She shook her head. "For someone who's as old-fashioned as you insist you are, this operation has spent a saint's ransom on electronics and expensive air mixtures for the divers."

"That's all Larry's doing. The boy thinks he's going to find the next hundred-million-dollar wreck. I put my foot down when it came to rebreathing gear. He can play all he wants with his own toy, but old-fashioned scuba gear is good enough for me. Cheaper, too."

Neither mentioned that her parents had died using rebreathing gear.

"Even if Larry found a lifetime wreck," she said, "and you could reach it, some government would claim it. Spain, Portugal, Britain, France—even Mexico and South American countries are trying to claim sovereignty over old shipwrecks. People are very possessive about history."

"Only when it's worth money," he said cynically. "So far this job is red ink and frustration. Can you keep us afloat?"

"I can see about restructuring various old and new debts." *Which never should have been taken on.* "With less going out to service debts, you'll have a chance." She hesitated, then said, "Don't sign another contract until you run it by me. Moon Rose can't survive it."

"I'm not the captain."

"That's not what you told Holden."

Grandpa resettled the pipe stem in his teeth. "Larry can't handle that stuffed shirt. I can."

She let that go by. "What about the crew? Can Larry handle them?"

"He hired them."

"That's not an answer."

Grandpa bit down on the pipe stem.

"You've worked with divers all your life," she said. "Are these men honest?"

"As honest as anyone is." Then he added impatiently, "Larry has been *Golden Bough*'s official captain for five years."

"Larry is the best first mate you could ask for and an even better diver," she said. "But after two minutes aboard, I knew he wasn't the captain in anything but name."

"I'm an old man, Kitty darling. It was never supposed to be this way. But your father died, you left, and Larry stayed."

*Cold to the soul, tugging at her father's slack body, screaming "Where's Mom? When did I lose her? Where's Mom!"*

*Nothing answered but the spray of salt water over the workboat's gunwale.*

*Nothing ever had answered.*

Kate forced memories aside. She couldn't change the past. She just had to live with it.

"I'll do what I can," she said, "but I can't help if you know more than I do. I think that Holden Cameron is the kind of man who is sent out when his bosses don't trust the salvage crew."

"So what? If I had the treasure, I'd have taken it and sold it in Venezuela or any other place that wants to spit in the eye of the West. But I'm here, so I don't have the treasure."

"Don't be so contrary," she said. "I know you and Larry, but I don't know the crew. This is serious. Holden was taking pictures of the gold that we just found, as if he suspected it wouldn't make it up to be cataloged."

"God-rotting bureaucrats."

"I'm not happy about being on the god-rotting sea, but here I am." Then she remembered his house in

Florida, his collections, and an explanation she really didn't want to hear. "Grandpa, you aren't keeping this dive afloat out of your own pocket, are you?"

He bit down on the pipe stem. Hard.

And ignored her.

"That's your retirement," she said, "and Larry's legacy from our parents. Without it, there is nothing for either of you!"

He looked at the distant horizon where a coy storm was flirting with the future.

She wanted to scream at him, to shake him, to make him listen. But she couldn't rage at the man whose eyes were so like her dead father's. She could only do the best she could with what she had right now.

"Come with me," she said. "It's time to meet with our very own bureaucrat."

"I belong up here."

"We're at anchor and you have an alarm set," she said, pointing to the small inset on the nav screen. "If we drag anchor, the whole boat will know it. Stop stalling."

With that, she turned and opened the wheelhouse door, only to find herself looking into Holden's startling eyes. He was standing on the narrow walkway just to the side of the door.

"There you are," he said. "Larry is waiting for us. I told him I would fetch you and your grandfather."

*How long has he been standing here?* she wondered. *Could he hear us?* Then she remembered the open porthole. *Of course he could.*

"A boat is too small a place to keep secrets," Grandpa said behind her.

Holden smiled.

It was nothing like the sexy smile that had startled Kate earlier.

# Chapter 5

Larry hadn't moved from where Holden had left him, head propped on his crossed arms on the long wooden table, eyes closed, body slack in one of the swivel chairs that were bolted to the deck around the table. Holden had seen enough soldiers in combat to know that Larry wasn't done yet, but he was closing in on exhaustion. He was forty-four and diving was a young man's game.

The old-alcohol smell on Larry's breath wasn't helping, but it wasn't nearly as bad as that of an end-phase alcoholic. If a company deep-sixed every diver who drank, there would be very few divers left.

Grandpa Donnelly sat beside Larry, jostling him awake. Holden sat across from them. When Kate hesitated, he smiled a very different smile and patted the chair next to him.

"I won't bite," he said. *Although a bit of nibbling . . . yes, I'd quite like that.*

Warily she sat down. The chairs were so closely spaced that she could feel his body heat like a ghostly caress with every breath he took. She tried not to notice it. The others certainly didn't seem to be aware of the muscular dragon coiled beneath the proper accent, but she could think of little else when he was near.

"Now that I've had a chance to do a brief recce, it appears that this dive isn't as badly off as my superiors feared," Holden said. *I suspect it's worse, but until I can prove it, I'm just another British prig. Or as the old man says, a god-rotting bureaucrat.*

"Not a total 'cock-up' after all?" Larry asked in a gritty voice.

The elder Donnelly snorted.

"Are you here to shut the project down?" Kate asked bluntly.

"Not after we just struck the lode," Grandpa said. "Right, Mr. Cameron?"

"Not at the moment, no," Holden agreed. "My employer's interest, which is very keen, is based on a single coin that was minted in the mid-seventeenth century. The coin was found on a rocky beach not far from here after—"

"A gale ripped through some coral reefs and generally rearranged some sea bottom last year," Larry interrupted, yawning. "We're clear on all that."

"The sea is a fickle bitch," Holden said. "That coin could have come from anywhere. It could be the first of a hoard or a one-off kicking around on the storm currents. We believed that it would lead to more. The handful of coins and raw metal you have found so far is welcome, but it's not the weighty kind of proof my superiors expected."

"And they're all worried that either they were wrong about diving on this wreck and will be shown up for it," Larry said, "or that someone on *Golden Bough* is a thief. We're clear on that, too."

Kate shifted, wondering if she could kick her brother under the table.

Holden pinned Larry with his unusual eyes. "Antiquities was divided on that very subject. However, after the money chain was discovered, they are quite excited that you are on the right track."

"How clever of them. Ouch!" Larry gave his sister a look.

She lifted one eyebrow at him.

Holden hoped his own amusement didn't show. Under other circumstances he probably would have enjoyed Larry, who was a very well-regarded diver and drinking companion. However, the circumstances were what they were and Larry might well be a thief or simply an incompetent captain who drank when the pressure got too intense. In either case the result was the same.

The advance on expenses wouldn't be made and the dive would be shut down.

"Antiquities is hoping that the treasure isn't scattered over the entirety of the seafloor between St. Vincent and Grenada," Holden said. "Again, opinion is divided. I'm told there is quite a lively discussion at the moment. Anything you find will be weighed carefully in the decision whether or not to advance the monies you have requested or invoke the weather stipulation and terminate the dive."

"Look, this isn't anything new," Larry said impatiently. "You come on board and throw your weight around, but you don't know any more than we do about what's below. You're hoping for a big payout but you're reaching for shadows."

"Is that what you believe?" Holden asked, switching his attention to Larry's grandfather.

The old man shrugged. "Nothing's sure but death."

"What have you heard about the coin that started this whole scramble?"

"It was gold," Larry said sarcastically.

Holden kept looking at the real captain, who finally spoke.

"It's a gold sovereign, no more than an inch across. It was minted in England, not just poured and stamped in Jamaica or made in a Spanish mold from the New World. It's marked with Charles II's head on one side." Grandpa Donnelly's voice was dry, leathery, whispering of a crossroads where Ireland and Jamaica met. "The other side has the cross and the shields of the four kingdoms. The portrait side had Charles's long nose pointed to the left. Not many of that particular coin was minted."

"Which makes them all the more valuable today," Holden said.

"But you and your god-rotting bureaucrats already knew that, didn't you? It's the only reason you offered the salvage contract."

"Grandpa," Kate said. "Please remember the difference between honey and vinegar."

Holden had to work not to show his amusement at her efforts to civilize the old salt.

"They're English coins and England is trying to recover them," she said to Holden. "This is hardly a surprise."

Yet even as she spoke, ghostly fingertips slithered down her spine. There was only one treasure she knew of that was reputed to contain coins minted in England with the portrait reversed. Her parents had died looking for it.

*No,* she thought as her heartbeat speeded in dread. *It can't be.*

"They're far from ordinary coins," Holden said. "Legend has it that these coins were a shadow currency, used to pay off acts of official treachery and other covert ventures. The story had it that Bloody Green himself was worth a hundred such coins, fully a tenth of the rumored thousand that were supposed to exist. It was the Crown's bounty on the head of a renegade English privateer, Declan Horatio Smyth-Fothergill, better known as Bloody Green."

Kate's nails dug into her palms. When she sensed Holden's attention, she slowly unclenched her fists. But she could do nothing about the tension that had seized her body and iced her blood . . . the vision of a dead man who was also her father sprawled in the bottom of a dinghy.

*Breathe. Just breathe.*

*One way or another, you'll get through this.*

From the corner of his eyes, Holden watched color slowly return to Kate's cheeks. He wanted to gather her close again, inhale her unique scent of sunlight and flowers and the underlying woman heat that drew him like a compass needle pointing true north.

"I assume you know the story?" he asked the men across the table.

Larry yawned.

"Which one?" asked the old man, taking the cold pipe from his teeth. "Hero or villain, lover or rapist, privateer or pirate?"

"Agreed," Holden said. "It rather depends on the point of view of the person experiencing Bloody Green. In the version the Antiquities Office cherishes, the man was no better than he had to be and of great use to the Crown. While pillaging—or helping—a foundered English merchant ship, he risked his own life to rescue a beautiful young aristocrat. Apparently it was love at first sight, as the story goes."

"My parents," Kate said hoarsely, then cleared her throat. "They said it was like that for them."

"That it was, Kitty darling," her grandpa said gruffly. "It was a blessing they died together."

*Not for me.* But she kept the bitter words to herself.

"In any case," Holden said, drawing attention away from the shine of tears and terror in Kate's eyes, "her family was quite furious. Seems they had sent the girl to wed a rich old man who had essentially purchased her. They had enough influence in court to get the Crown to issue the bounty."

"Hardly the first time titled blood was sold to untitled riches," Larry said around a yawn. "The part of the tale that my parents loved was that in order to keep the girl and get back into the good graces of the Crown, Bloody Green sacked and pillaged until he had her weight in jewelry and gems. And the bounty coins. Bet he laughed his ass off when he took them. Then he offered everything to the girl's father for his daughter. The father accepted, the Crown took its cut, and Bloody Green was a citizen in good standing again."

Holden listened carefully. Larry's tone was that of someone retelling a story he had heard so often it had become part of him.

"The happy lovers and the treasure set sail for London on the pirate ship called *Moon Rose*," said the elder Donnelly. "It vanished, as did the *Cross of Madrid,* a merchant ship Green was sailing with. Have we covered the high points?"

"Admirably. My superiors assumed from the name of your company that you were familiar with the legend."

The old man shrugged. "Around here, everyone knows it."

"But everyone doesn't name their company after a pirate ship."

"Mom and Dad did," Larry said. "They left a whole trunk of maps and speculation on the location of those ships when they went down. It used to be a family game to trace possible storm tracks and old records and currents."

"My daughter-in-law was very fond of Bloody Green's story."

Holden looked at the old man whose eyes had seen more of the sea and sorrow than most.

And treasure.

"My parents died looking for the wreck of *Moon Rose*," Kate said flatly. "It's not my favorite story. Are you telling me that we're parked over that hulk now?"

Silence followed her words.

Grandpa Donnelly shifted his pipe and looked unhappy.

"It is a possibility," Holden said carefully. "Experts in London have decided that the ribs of the ship down there aren't big enough to belong to a merchant ship such as the *Cross of Madrid*."

The thought that she might be anchored on her mother's unmarked grave had Kate on her feet and out the salon door, fighting for breath every step of the way. She grabbed the deck rail and hung on, forcing herself to breathe through the panic attack.

*I can't be here anymore. The sea took too much from me that day.*

*The only reason it didn't take Larry and Grandpa was they were ashore while Grandpa had a bad appendix taken out. If they had been there, the sea would have eaten them too.*

*Don't they understand that?*

*Don't they know that the sea is still hungry?*

The door opened and closed behind her as someone came out.

"Hey," Larry said. "Are you still having panic attacks? It was years ago, Kitty."

*Not for me. It's as fresh as my next nightmare.* And she would be having one tonight, no doubt.

It didn't make her look forward to sleeping.

"Hey," he said softly. "You should be glad it might be a rich wreck. Even with that lousy contract, we'd come out ahead."

"Assuming we're in the right place and not just finding occasional scattered pieces," she said stiffly.

"We're not," Larry said. "I have a feeling about this one. This is the big one we've looked for all our lives."

"Every treasure diver gets that feeling and then they follow it too far down," she said. "It's a sickness."

"I know you're thinking about Mom and Dad," Larry said. "But you can't blame them for following their dream."

"I can. Especially when their dream turned into my nightmare."

Even as Kate spoke, she knew she was wrong. Yet that was how she felt. That hadn't changed since she was almost eighteen and found out that everything could be taken away without warning. The sea she had once loved was unpredictable and treacherous.

"They were my parents, too," Larry said. "Do you ever think of that?"

She let out a careful breath. "I know I'm not being fair. But damn it, you were a man when they died. I was seventeen, had basically lived on board all my life. Just a child in some ways. Important ways." *And at night, I still am. Panic and terror and screaming.* "I've done enough for today," she said abruptly. "Too much. Being out here is making me crazy."

"You're making yourself crazy."

"Because I realize that when I'm out here, I'm at the mercy of a sea that has none?"

"Okay, okay, go back to the rental. Just don't run off. We need you. Most of the time you're all brains and common sense. You know that between Grandpa and me, we don't have enough of either to fill a coffee cup."

A ghostly smile flickered over her lips. "That's the truth."

"There's my Kitty Kat," he said. The pinched lines around his eyes and mouth relaxed. "You ready to go back in there before Grandpa does something stupid, like throw a punch at the Brit?"

The child in Kate wanted to pitch a screaming fit. The adult in her knew she had to find a better way to live with the past, took a deep breath, and headed back inside. It quickly became obvious that she was indeed needed. Grandpa was standing up, pointing his pipe stem at Holden.

Which meant that Grandpa was about to lose his temper.

"I didn't ask for the captain's cabin," Holden said in a reasonable tone of voice. "I simply want a place to sleep aboard. It's difficult to oversee a dive from shore."

"We don't dive at night," Larry said. "On the wages your AO demands, we're lucky to find enough men to dive during the day. Kate can taxi you back and forth from the rental along with supplies."

"I don't have time to be shopping for—" began Kate.

"There's no room aboard," Larry cut in with the irritation of the sleep deprived. "You saw the crew quarters on the way to the dive center. Men are doubled up as it is. We're doing all we can and more just to keep the Brits off our backs."

Holden supposed the mess he had seen through open doors could be the result of crowding, but he was much more interested in the fact that no one wanted him aboard. "The contract—" he began.

"Says we house and feed our overseers," Grandpa cut in. "Doesn't say where. We rented the house for the geek out of our lousy expense allowance, and that's where you're staying. If you don't like it, whine to your bosses."

"Bugger," Holden snarled. Then he looked quickly at Kate. "Apologies."

She shrugged. "Why? It's rather refreshing."

Larry snickered. "You can double up with the geek. Mingo's brother is onto a cache of broken pottery found near the gold chain. Malcolm will be doing pictures and measurements and log entries aboard until sunrise."

"Where does he sleep?" Holden asked blandly.

"In a cubbyhole the size of a coffin, with his feet propped on his desk and his chair tipped back against the door. You'd rather be ashore and so would he."

Leaving the argument behind her, Kate walked out to the workboat and got in. The craft rolled in the gentle afternoon swell. She fired up the engines on the second try and then let them roar, signaling just how out of patience she was.

"This water taxi leaves in one minute," she yelled above the noise.

Holden made a command decision and scrambled down into the workboat.

The ride back to the rental was swift and silent but for the engines. Behind his sunglasses, Holden thought about how eager the Donnellys had been to see him off.

*Could be hiding something.*

*Could be responding to my persistent lack of charm.*

At the moment, the possibilities were about even, but his orders hadn't changed. If anything, the Antiquities Office was more eager than ever to pursue the salvage. The cynical side of Holden kept coming back to the oh-so-terribly convenient find just after he came aboard. The rest of him kept pointing out that coincidences happened. That was why the English language had a word for it.

Any pursuit of answers would have to wait until tomorrow. Which meant other pursuits were available tonight.

He concentrated on Kate's profile. She was an intriguing woman, seemingly unaware of her beauty, making no attempt to ingratiate herself with the man who held her family's fate in his fist. Yet he had caught her more than once looking at him the way a woman looks at a man who interests her. During the brief time he had known her, she had ricocheted between fear and anger and aloofness more than many women he had known over years of acquaintance.

Yet he didn't think being volatile was a natural state for her. She didn't have the pinched, nervous look of someone perpetually balanced on the edge of panic. Her hand on the steering was as competent as her posture was confident. She looked more and more relaxed with every minute.

*Maybe it's just her family that makes her nervy.*

It would be a long time before he forgot her terror at the sight of the narrow staircase leading to the main deck. It would be even longer before he forgot the feel of her in his arms. The embrace had been meant to be soothing, but he was a man, after all. He had felt the woman heat as fear receded.

He wanted to feel it again.

Soon.

*You're rushing your fences,* he advised his body.

His body didn't listen.

*I'm a man, not a randy boy.*

His body didn't listen to that bit of reason, either.

Holden was relieved when the rental's dock came into view. The sun was close to the horizon, setting sky and water afire, making the dock leap out like a welcoming hand. The engines dropped to a conversational hum as Kate slowed for docking.

Though the tides weren't as pronounced in the tropics as they were in the North Sea, they did exist. But tidal swings weren't the reason many seashore buildings sat on stilts. It was the storms that shifted huge masses of water, making and remaking the sea bottom in a few hours, rearranging beaches and shorelines in their paths.

"Amazing that the rental hasn't washed away," Holden said.

"It's on the leeward side of the island, protected from the worst of the storm surges," Kate said, coasting into the dock. "If the storm you're so worried about materializes, we might get wet but we won't be swimming."

While she tied off, he grabbed his duffels and stepped lightly onto the dock. As always since the mishap, his thigh protested. As always, he ignored it. Some of his team would have been happy to be as lightly injured as he had been.

"I'm not worried about the storm," he said as she joined him. "My boss is."

"Has anyone ever thought that the whole supposed treasure was dreamed up by a long-ago bookkeeper to cover up losses or even theft?" she asked.

"I have. It was not a well-received observation." As he spoke, he reminded himself of the considerable intelligence behind her wide turquoise eyes. He could have ignored the curvy body, but he had always been drawn to smart women.

Kate didn't notice his assessing stare. With every step she took away from the water, she felt her nerves uncurling.

"The idea of bean counters getting treasure fever would be funny if it wasn't for my family's business," she said.

"Oh, we bean counters have our romantic moments."

This time she laughed.

"You don't believe me?" he asked, pretending to be wounded.

"Holden, you aren't a bean counter and we both know it."

The undecided breezes of the doldrums riffled over him like a lover's fingers. "You seem quite certain."

"Am I wrong?" she said, turning to face him as they approached the house's sagging porch.

"What gave me away?"

"Your eyes were the first clue. Your fitness was another."

"I limp when I'm tired," he said before he could think better of it.

"Your point? I've seen men in wheelchairs who were incredibly fit."

"Another point to the lovely lady," he said. "As for the rest, the eyes came to me at birth, no work required. They're quite common in some areas of the world, crossroads of civilizations as it were. My eyes are a case of Pashtuns meeting soldiers of the British Empire in what we now call India, Pakistan, and Afghanistan. More recently, I have an Irish grandmother and an ex-pat American mother. The men in my family have a real weakness for redheads."

"And a lot of redheads have a weakness for tall, dark, and different." She put her shoulder into opening the front door. Humidity and wood made for sticky doors. "Your English is excellent."

"London boarding schools will do that to a man," he said, sliding his sunglasses up on his head. He had never understood the trendy affectation of wearing unneeded sunglasses on the back of the neck, where they invariably got sweaty.

"You must have a good ear for accents," she said. "Sometimes there is a difference to your inflections and word choices that is almost American."

"Caught again," Holden said. "I was raised in a very mixed household, linguistically speaking. As I said, my mother is American; my father's childhood was divided between his father's clan and his own preference for life in Wales. Unless I guard myself carefully—and really, why would I—I have quite a few accents and word choices."

"I hope one of your languages is cooking."

He gave her a sideways look. "It won't be fancy."

"I'll settle for edible."

"You don't cook?"

"All the time. And then I clean up, all the time. I'll take half of the chores, thanks. A love of housework does not come down in the female genes."

He laughed. "Fair enough."

She stared. His laughter was beautiful, rich and full and warm, and his dragon eyes gleamed in the twilight inside the house.

"You've got to stop doing that," she said.

"What?"

"Being human. It makes your robot turns all the more unsettling."

She flipped on a light, pushing away the dangerous feeling of intimacy that the hushed twilight gave.

# Chapter 6

Holden looked around at the accommodations. Nothing had changed. Spartan was the first word that came to mind, followed by shabby. But it was as clean as anything ever was in the tropics, where the greenery and insects fought humans for every bit of space.

"Cozy," he said.

"That's a word I hadn't thought of," Kate said. "My reactions were more along the lines of wonder that the whole thing is still standing."

"The fake wood paneling is particularly tasteful, don't you think? The contrast with the broken louvered windows is quite witty."

His deadpan delivery sent amusement fizzing through her. Added to her relief at being on land again, the result was almost dizzying.

*Or maybe it's that I haven't eaten much today.*

"I hope you're a believer in early dinners," she said.

"Supper. Or tea."

"Ah, the robot returns, and we are again divided by a common language."

"As a child in school I was twitted mercilessly for my 'odd' speech," Holden said. "So I learned, only to be cut by an American for my odd speech."

The thought of him as vulnerable child with exotic eyes caught Kate off balance. It was so much easier to write him off as an upper-class British robot.

Safer, too.

Then a nonrobotic choice of words or inflections would remind her that he was a man, and a handsome one at that. Add in humor and intelligence and a kind of heat that made her itchy, and she was in trouble.

"I'm hungry," she said abruptly. "Are you?"

"Quite."

The speculative fire in his eyes made her wonder about the mating habits of dragons.

She looked away.

Holden was trying to decide whether to snack on her and forget supper when he grabbed his wandering mind and put it to use. He did a quick recon of the kitchenette, which consisted of single electric coils plugged into an exposed junction box, a bar refrigerator, a sink that sat on four metal legs fashioned out of galvanized pipe, and a dubious-looking burner sitting crookedly on a small propane bottle. He lifted the bottle. If it wasn't empty, it was close to it.

"Do you have spare propane bottles?" he asked.

"I don't know. I didn't see any by the back door."

"Right. Electricity it is."

He opened the cube-shaped refrigerator that was balanced precariously on a counter made of two-by-fours nailed to some packing crates. "So for protein we have reef fish." He sniffed it. "Fresh. Lovely." He kept searching. "Garlic. A pitcher of fresh tea. And an onion that has gone to the dark side. No wine or beer."

"No problem. I rarely drink. Don't like the taste."

While Holden was looking in the refrigerator, Kate began rummaging in the cupboards. "Rice, coffee, tea, sugar, salt, canned milk—yuck—spices, and a bowl of fresh fruit, including coconuts," she said. "Oh, and a really good olive oil. Do you suppose Farnsworth is a closet foodie?"

"Doubtful. How fresh is the fruit?"

She sorted through it. "Very. The oranges look yummy."

"That takes care of the scurvy issue."

"Thought that was limes."

"Any citrus will do," he said, closing the refrigerator door. "Limes travel well."

"We have some of them, too."

Kate watched him cook out of the corner of her eye. He was efficient and quick to improvise. After he washed his hands, he opened a coconut with a kitchen knife that looked like a machete—and had probably been used as such on the resident greenery. He poured the coconut milk into a small pot and turned to the rice.

"Instant rice," he said, looking at the box. "Puts paid to the closet foodie theory."

"A foodie in a hurry?" she offered.

"Contradiction in terms."

She smiled and relaxed even more.

He poured rice into the pot, added water, and put the pot on one of the electrical coils. To his surprise, it heated very quickly. He stirred in spices and put one of the three unmatched dinner plates on top as a lid.

In surprisingly little time, the whole rental smelled of spice and coconut, sliced fresh fruit, and fish fillets being seared in olive oil. He singed his palm on the handle of the cast-iron frying pan, swore about "not a bloody potholder in the place," and wrapped a piece of his shirt around the handle before he speedily transferred the half-cooked fish to the plate that rested on top on the rice pot. The steam from below would take care of finishing the fillets.

"You're lucky that the electricity hasn't yet gone out," Kate said, trying not to drool over the food and the man. "All it takes is a tree frog or a sizable cockroach in a junction box and *zzzzzt!* you're back in the Dark Ages."

"Raw fish in coconut milk is quite good," he said. "But I agreed to cook, and marinating doesn't quite make the cut."

Quietly she noted that he was a man of his word, even in such a minor detail. Too many men didn't carry business ethics into personal life, assuming the men had any ethics to begin with. She had met a lot who would lie to get in a woman's bed. She'd met her share of lying women, too.

He squeezed lime juice into the still-sizzling fish pan and left it to simmer while he put slices of fruit on two mismatched plates. He dished rice onto the plates, put a fillet on top of each mound, and dribbled the pan sauce over.

Kate wondered if she'd ever had a savory meal cooked by a man who was tall, dark, and different. Then she wondered if it would be shallow of her to be seduced by a handsome man who could cook.

*Good thing he isn't wearing an apron. I'd lose all dignity.*

Silent laughter bubbled through her.

"Glasses?" he asked.

"I'll see." She opened the cupboards until she found two cracked teacups.

He filled each from the pitcher of cold tea and placed everything on the tiny, chipped Formica bar that had two stools crowded along it.

"I hesitate to inquire after forks," he said. "Or chopsticks."

"Forks are in the basket on the counter," she said, washing her hands.

She sat down at the bar while he served the food. When he sat next to her, she barely had room to breathe. Part of it was the tiny eating surface. Most of it was Holden. Somehow he took up an unreasonable amount of room.

Both of them fell on the food with barely civilized greed.

"Wonderful," she said after her first bites. "I nominate you chef."

"I decline. Who knows what we'll find in the refrigerator tomorrow."

"You'd make something tasty of it."

"Ever had snake in coconut milk?"

"Right," she said. "I'll cook tomorrow."

He saluted her with his cup of tea.

In a comfortable silence she demolished her food, shook her head when he went to dish himself seconds, and sipped at her tea. A dreamy kind of mood settled over her, a mixture of time and food and fatigue. Idly she wondered how many hits she would get on Holden Cameron, UK, if she did a computer search.

"Some, I would imagine," he said.

She started. "Do you read minds?"

A smile flickered over his mouth. "Only when people speak clearly."

"Oh." She felt heat moving over her face and knew she was blushing like a stoplight. "Want to save me some trouble?"

"You don't even have a network connection here," he said, neatly scraping up the last morsel of his second helping.

"Everything's cellular on the island. St. Vincent is wired to the max. When it comes to the tropics, towers are cheaper to maintain than cables. Talk about yourself and save me a trip to the bedroom to get my computer elf."

"What is it you're so keen to know?" he asked.

"What did you do before you worked for the Antiquities Office?"

"I was a sailor."

"Breaking hearts in every port," she said, looking at his forearms. Golden brown, muscular, with a sheen of dark hair. Very different from the First Nations people who had been her clients in Canada. "How many years did you serve?"

"I believe I've answered your one question for the evening. Perhaps you can try again tomorrow."

"Google never sleeps."

"If you're that curious, I suggest you take it up with him."

"I will," she said. "So you were a sailor . . ."

Holden shot her a look. "Royal Navy, ABCD."

"What happened to the rest of the alphabet?"

He shook his head and held up the tea pitcher in silent question. She held out her cup. He filled it, then his.

"ABCD was my rank," he said. "Able Seaman Clearance Diver."

The lazy curiosity vanished. "You're a diver." She knew she shouldn't be surprised, much less disappointed, but she was.

"Clearance diving is hardly glamorous work to a family of treasure divers," he said.

"What exactly does a clearance diver do, rake debris out of shipping lanes?"

"I spent most of my time deactivating mines."

"Mines?" she asked. Suddenly treasure diving seemed like a positively safe way to make a living.

"Yes. Dreadful business."

"I didn't know British harbors had that many mines left over from World War Two."

"That would explain why I spent most of my time in other places." When she opened her mouth to ask another question, he shook his head. "My turn. Where were you raised?"

"Why do you ask?"

"You eat like you're in a mess hall, surrounded by larger upperclassmen."

Kate half laughed. "Well, that's a pretty apt description of my childhood, the smallest person at the table."

"You were raised institutionally?"

"No, but perhaps I should have been institutionalized after it."

He gave her a look that said he would wait for a real answer.

"That ship we were just on was where I spent my childhood," she said. Her tone of voice said she didn't want to talk about it.

"You lived aboard the *Golden Bough*?"

"With my grandfather, parents, and brother, plus assorted divers."

"Close quarters," Holden said.

She got up and began clearing the plates. "You have no idea. I had to share a cabin with Larry until that became impossible. He went to bunk with our grandfather."

She rinsed, soaped, and rinsed the dishes again. There were no dish towels and no rack to drain wet cutlery. With a mental shrug, she put the plates back into the cupboard.

"I can understand how you might have wanted to get away from that," Holden said into the silence. "How did the rest of your family take your departure?"

"Grandpa was angry. Larry was relieved because if I'd stayed, I would be captain. Grandpa made that very clear." Her voice was ruthlessly neutral.

"Be careful what you wish for," Holden said. "Your brother is looking thoroughly shagged. I gather that you were called in to pretty up the books?"

"Pretty up. Is that the Brit way of saying cooking the books?"

Warily Holden eyed the fork in her hand. "No."

"Good answer," she said, turning back to the sink. "I was brought in to translate Larry's eccentric way of bookkeeping into something anyone can read."

"I'll be glad to help."

"A diver and a bookkeeper, too. Fabulous." Her tone of voice said the opposite. "Too bad you haven't been aboard all along."

Silverware hit the basket with a ringing sound.

"Is that a yes or a no?" he asked.

"Sorry, what was the question?"

"May I help you with the books?"

"If I hit a wall, I'll run up a flag," she said. "Excuse me, I've got a pan to scrub on the beach. It should give you plenty of time to go through my stuff. Just put everything back where you found it and we'll both pretend nothing happened."

Kate felt him watching her every step of the way. She crouched where water met dry beach, grabbed a fistful of sand, and scrubbed the pan. It took several tries, but finally there was only the smell of the ocean on the metal.

When she got back to the rental, Holden was nowhere in sight. The murmur of a deep voice coming from the back of the house told her that he was in his room, either talking to himself or to someone at Antiquities.

The cartons of papers she had left out looked exactly the same as they had when she went to clean the pan. A mess.

With a sigh, she put the pan away, pulled her computer from her luggage, booted up the spreadsheet she had been working on, and settled in for a few hours of sorting and entering.

From the back room, Holden listened to the small sounds Kate made while she sorted papers, dropped something, cursed softly, and began clicking away on the computer keys.

*Probably entering receipts in columns, for all the good it will do. Whatever she digs out of that snarl of papers in the cartons won't be enough to save the dive, so why did her family bother to fly her in?*

No answer occurred except the obvious—a bit of sexual distraction. The oldest game in the world. Because it worked.

Holden couldn't deny he was attracted. But distracted?

*Bloody hell. Yes, I'm distracted, sitting here mooning about her, envying every bit of food that touched her lips. Sexy lips, those. Full, made for—*

With a phrase in Pashto, he stopped his wandering thoughts, pulled out his cell phone, and hit Farnsworth's number. While he waited for an answer, he shut the door to the tiny bedroom and booted up his own computer.

"Malcolm here."

"About bloody time," Holden said.

"The main generator's packed it again. We're down to flashlights because the captain is too stingy to eat fuel running one of the main engines. Have you ever tried describing, entering, and photographing under these conditions? Took a bit to even find my phone."

"Try doing everything underwater," Holden said, "and then complain to me. What's wrong with the generator?"

"It's older than dirt. Old man Donnelly is down below cursing rather frightfully while he works on it. The crew took the big tender to shore for the night. Bloody hot belowdecks."

"Why didn't you go?"

"I already had everything set up in the room," Farnsworth said. "It's not my first time in the tropics. Actually, I prefer the heat."

"Going native?"

"Not until I'm a pensioner."

"Where is the gold chain the diver brought up?" Holden asked.

"With me. I take all important finds ashore, personally. I'm the only one with the key to the warehouse where I pack important salvage for the trip home to London. Natives pack the rest."

"Are they honest?"

"It doesn't matter," Farnsworth said. "The strongbox with the valuable goods is bolted to the floor of the warehouse. Locked, of course. Again, I have the only key."

*Are you awake every moment of every day?* Holden thought, but he knew what the answer was.

He considered telling Farnsworth how thin the security was, but didn't. When Holden had brought the subject up in London, he had been told that security wasn't his area of expertise, and to let the professionals do their work.

"I'll have a look at the warehouse, of course," Holden said.

"Any time, but not right away, I hope. I'm up to my arse entering bits and pieces. As the warehouse key never leaves my custody, I will be the one to show you around."

Holden wondered how many duplicates of the key were in circulation—a man had to sleep, after all. But all he said was "Anything valuable among the china bits found today?"

"Trifles. A gold ring that might have held a stone. A clump of metal that might have come from a money bag or the galley. A pewter cup that had been banged about. Another bit of gold that could have been part of a brooch or earrings. A rather nice carnelian, or it might be if it survives the baths. Also what appears from above to be a cannon. I'll send photos to AO to see if they think another cannon is worth concentrating on in what time we have before the storm comes."

Holden switched over to the dive software on his computer. It opened on a picture of the seabed in light blue and black. There was a suggestion of a rib cage—crescent forms laid out in a repeating pattern, though it was crumbling and uneven. He clicked a few more keys and a grid appeared over the wreck.

"Which section had the recent find?" Holden asked.

As the other man answered, Holden entered notes on the computer program and said, "These finds don't seem to follow any pattern."

"The bottom has been stirred a time or two," Farnsworth said dryly.

"The ribs and keel appear in decent shape under the coral camouflage."

"I wouldn't know. My work is cataloging, not diving. Is Antiquities really going to shut down this operation?"

Holden switched over and looked at the weather program, which was always running in the background on his computer. Any significant variation in the prediction would set off an alarm.

"As far as I know," he said, "the home office is in a holding pattern. The storm has stalled. Nothing predicted for a day or three, but the five-day forecast looks dodgy, to say the least. The fiddly bits you just described certainly won't put anyone back home in a hopeful frame of mind."

Farnsworth sighed. "Any more news on the black market?"

"It is doing considerably better finding treasure from *Moon Rose* than we are."

"Bollocks. They should have locked up that bastard."

"Which one?" Holden asked.

"The idiot who thought he could wriggle away from the cops by giving information on antiquarian black market trinkets fenced in St. Vincent. That's how the head of our department heard about the coins."

"Ah, that one." Holden shrugged. "As thieves go, he was rather deft."

"Stanley Chatham—our *boss*—is a thief?"

"I was referring to the weasel who decided to tell the Crown all about some shady doings that began in St. Vincent and ended with secret auctions. Because his information was good, he was allowed to slide back into the pond to continue his business, instead of being gutted and grilled as he deserved."

While he talked, Holden switched screens again. The image that came up was breathtaking.

"I would very much like to talk to the weasel about the Marquez Crest," Holden continued, looking at the screen.

"What is that?"

"A quite valuable ring. The gold was said to come from a melted pagan statue. Inca, I believe. The man who commissioned the ring apparently took great satisfaction in knowing he had helped subdue the heathens and become monstrously wealthy in the process."

"Why couldn't I have been born into that family?" muttered Farnsworth.

"Ugly mother?"

"Sod off," the other man said without heat.

"The ring was topped with thirteen square-cut emeralds, shaped into a Templar Cross. It was a statement of rank and wealth, and a subtle twist of the nose of the Church, hinting that Captain Gabriel Mignola Brandon Marquez remembered the order that the pope himself wanted forgot."

"You've seen the ring?"

"Two photos, one from an unnamed source and the other a closeup of an old painting of the proud captain displaying his wealth. The captain's ship was called *Cross of Madrid,* last seen in company with *Moon Rose,* which is rather like pairing a fat tuna with a shark. In all likelihood, Bloody Green was wearing the Marquez Crest when *Moon Rose* met its fate."

Farnsworth's breath sucked in. "Larry told me about the legend of *Moon Rose.* A fortune in gold and gems. No wonder Antiquities has their knickers in a twist."

"I received my marching orders to St. Vincent shortly after Chatham discovered that the ring had been auctioned on the black market," Holden said.

"So Chatham thinks the Donnellys aren't bringing up all they find and handing it over to me for cataloging?"

"That's one possibility. There are others. The divers themselves are a dodgy lot. They could easily be concealing small finds such as rings or coins and selling them ashore. The dive cameras can't be everywhere at once, and in any case they are only meant as a safety measure and historical record rather than as security."

"Volkert is a bit of a swine, too."

"I don't know the man," Holden said.

"Has a piece ashore, if you can imagine that."

"I can imagine she is rather well paid by island standards, but that is neither here nor there. If having women ashore was illegal, a great many seafaring men would be locked up."

Farnsworth laughed.

"Now, which grid did the pottery and jewelry come from?" Holden asked.

While Farnsworth answered in numbers and compass settings, Holden typed. Very soon the cramped position holding the phone in place between his tilted head and shoulder became uncomfortable. And without the door open, there was precious little air movement. The room was getting hot enough to make a rock sweat.

"Stand by," Holden said.

Before Farnsworth could answer, Holden was on his feet.

# Chapter 7

Deliberately Holden made a lot of noise opening the bedroom door and walking down the short hall to the living area. The first thing he saw was Kate asleep over her paperwork, her computer on screen saver.

*I'd love to have the right to tuck her in bed,* he thought. *Next to me.*

*Naked.*

But he didn't, so he went back to his room, left his door open for the cross-ventilation, stripped down to minimal underwear, and picked up his cell phone.

"I'm putting you on speaker," he said. "Bloody hard to type otherwise."

"Where were we?" Farnsworth asked, smothering a yawn.

"The site map, all twenty-five sectors of it. Overview."

"Right." There was a pause. "Don't know how much AO gave you."

"Just tell me what you have," Holden said. "I'll worry about correlation with the AO information."

"Personally, I'll go with Larry's gut belief that the wreck is too small to be the *Cross of Madrid.* He says it's the right size to be a two-deck sloop, stripped down for speed and boarding larger, slower boats."

"Merchant ships," Holden said.

"Right. They weren't protected like a treasure galleon with its escort of armed vessels."

"That's in line with Chatham's theory of the wreck being the *Moon Rose.*"

"Wouldn't that be lovely?" Farnsworth said. "AO mentioned a plump bonus if the salvage went beyond a certain amount."

"There was nothing about that in the dive contract I saw."

"Oh, the crew wouldn't get much. I was speaking personally. Although it is about as likely as a blind man finding a needle in a haystack. *Moon Rose* was perhaps twenty-five meters at the waterline, according to the documentation AO gave me, and presently is spread out like an egg smashed onto concrete from a third-story window."

"That's the problem with wooden ships," Holden said. "The sea bottom constantly changes, coral grows, and things come apart in storms. Radar scans were reasonably clear, though. The wreck is indeed down there. Has anyone recently run metal detectors over the site?"

"Volkert would know about that. Or Larry, if you can catch him awake and above water. Poor devil is doing the work of three men. The most recent detailed metal scan that I have a file of was"—papers rustled, computer keys clacked, and Farnsworth continued—"sector C2, just off center of the main hulk. That's where the ingots and a handful of the gold coins came out. Two were unique. Lovely coins, so much history in the reversed face. AO was quite excited and told me not to say a word."

Holden hadn't been told about finding more of the special coins, but it explained why some people at AO were so determined to continue with the dive. Hoping his superior was correct, Holden studied the images of the wreck that he had. "In theory, every grid square should be producing something, if only pottery."

"The gold chain was rather nice."

"My inbox is full of specific requests that one grid or another be hoovered up and spilled out onto the dredge platform," Holden said.

"Did they give you specific depths to search in each grid?" Farnsworth asked eagerly.

"No. I pointed out that lack to Chatham. He said they were doing the best they could with the information at hand, and if I needed more, I should get it without interfering with the salvage process itself."

"I think that would be rather difficult and probably a waste of your time. On the subject of wasted time, AO hasn't demanded a visual review of the dive records, have they?"

Holden thought of the hours and hours and hours of dives recorded and archived as .mpg files. Going through them would be less interesting than watching grass grow.

"Some poor drone spends her days in London doing just that," Holden said. "If Ms. Pinkham had found anything dodgy, the local constables would already have boarded the *Golden Bough* and locked up everything in sight."

"Isn't that your job?"

"Not at all. I'm here to assess the efficiency of the dive itself," Holden said. It wasn't the whole truth, but the rest was nothing Farnsworth needed to know. "You've spent a lot of time on board. Have you noticed anything unusual in the crew or the salvage operations?"

"Sorry. Usually I work on land. This is only my second time on a marine salvage site. I wouldn't know what is common, much less out of place."

Holden tried another angle. "What's your impression of the elder Donnelly?"

"I've had almost nothing to do with him. His grandson seems a hard worker."

"What of the granddaughter?"

"Larry mentioned once or twice that he had a sister. Sorry, mate. I'm not being much help, am I?"

"Why don't you ask me?" said a cold voice from the doorway.

Kate's voice.

Abruptly Holden ended the connection with Farnsworth and turned to her. When he saw her eyes widen, he remembered that all he wore was briefs.

"If it bothers you," he said, "I'll dress."

"No," she said, then cleared her throat, trying to remove the husky catch in her voice. "I was raised on a dive boat. I knew all about the difference between male and female before I was old enough to put it in words."

It was half true. The other half was that Holden Cameron had the kind of body that the ancient Greeks had immortalized in marble. Except he was much warmer than white marble. His skin was a bronze-gold over muscles shifting as fluidly as the sea, shadows curving across his body like a lover's fingers.

*Don't stare. Don't stare. Don't stare*, she told herself firmly. *God, would it be wrong to stroke him?*

*Yes, it would be wrong.*

She dragged her attention from his body and said the first thing that came to mind. "I'll bet that scar has a story."

Holden glanced at his left thigh, where a piece of an exploding mine had played merry hell with it. The scar was inches long. "Job hazard. Mines do have a tendency to blow."

She went still. "How far down were you?"

"Not far enough to die."

"I'll bet it was . . ." *Horrible. Terrifying.* "Painful," she managed finally.

"Most of the time it looks worse than it feels." Automatically he kneaded the torn flesh. "It healed improperly, leaving a cyst. Pressure changes make it flare up until things equalize out, so I'm rather good at predicting weather changes."

Her eyes kept straying to his lap. She closed them for an instant, then focused on his face. "Flying must be hard on you." *Hard. Could I have chosen a less loaded word? And speaking of loaded . . .*

Kate prayed that her straying thoughts weren't revealed on her face.

"Smaller aircraft can be a problem in terms of pressure changes," he said, wishing she was as stripped down as he was. Though her blouse was loose, it clung in intriguing places. He hoped he was doing a better job of keeping his glance from wandering than she was. "Larger planes are pressurized enough that it only hurts for half an hour or so at a time."

"I remember the weird feeling I got in my joints and lungs when I rushed too much coming up from a dive. Even when I did it right, the sensation was uncomfortable for my first few times." She hesitated. If the lower pressures aboard an airplane hurt him, then the higher pressures of diving would be a lot worse. "You don't dive anymore, do you?"

"The doctors tell me they can cut out the cyst any time I get tired of it. The idea of months more physio doesn't intrigue me, however."

"Physio?"

"Therapy of the physical variety."

"Do you miss diving?" she asked.

"Do you?"

Echoes of terror, denial, rage; a tidal wave of emotions from the teenager she had been. She drew a careful breath. "No. I don't miss diving."

"Odd."

"Why?"

"Diving for treasure with your family as a child is the stuff of dreams for land-bound children," Holden said.

She forced herself to look away from his tempting golden brown skin. "It was all I knew."

"Normal, in a word."

She nodded and looked into his changeable eyes, almost gold in the low light. "When I went to college, I found it exotic and strange because everyone had an address that wasn't just a mail drop, and classrooms didn't float around, and I could walk all day and not end up where I started."

"Still, getting your allowance in doubloons must have been nice," he said.

She accepted his teasing with an ease that should have worried her, as if she had known him for years instead of hours. "Allowance? Why would I need something like that? I was fed, had a roof over my head most of the time, and only had to do the minimum amount of schoolwork to keep the State of Florida off our backs. What ten-year-old wouldn't love that?"

"But not an eighteen-year-old?"

"You grow up," she said with a shrug. "You realize that the thing you've built your life on isn't going to last. Particularly when your competition has the resources of say, the United Kingdom."

"We're not competition. We're a client."

"Not the way Grandpa sees it. Remember, it used to be that those wrecks down there were his. He just hadn't gotten around to pulling up the gold yet."

"Or hadn't found it," Holden pointed out.

"Academic," she said with a wave of her hand. "For him, finding was just a matter of time, work, and luck, and he has the luck of the Irish." A shadow darkened her eyes, a reminder that luck sometimes ran out. "After he found gold, he worked hard, in case the sea changed her mind about letting him have access to the treasure."

With a few smooth motions, Holden pulled his shirt on. He needed something to hide the erection that kept growing despite his attempts to reason with it.

Kate both regretted and approved his action. Seeing just how much the man she wanted also wanted her was eroding what little control she had over her wandering eyes. The feeling was unsettling, rather like her first deep dives—excitement, nerves, fascination, exhilaration, every bit of her *alive.*

Just how alive was something she shouldn't be thinking about right now. Her nipples were tight and tingly, hungry for touch.

Rather desperately, she looked for a distraction and spotted his computer. Though the screen was dark now, she remembered what she had seen when she first looked into the room.

"Why do you have Cartomancy on your computer?" she asked.

Holden let out a careful breath, trying to lower the sexual tension in his body—and in the bedroom.

"Not many people would recognize the program," he said. His voice was too deep, too husky, almost a growl, but he ignored it as he was trying to ignore the swelling tightness of his body.

"Not many people had my childhood," she pointed out, her eyes fixed on the screen because it was the safest thing in the room to look at. "Cartomancy was the standard for reading and interpreting ESRI maps back when Grandpa first had computers on the boat because Dad badgered him into it." Her eyes softened with amused memory. "Then Dad had custom software modules written up to directly map live radar and sonar results into the software in real time, so that any readings taken on the *Golden Bough* could be marked up and added to permanent records seamlessly. Of course, Grandpa thought it was foolish, expensive bunk."

Holden grabbed the conversation like the lifeline it was, pulling himself out of the dangerous sexual currents rushing between Kate and himself. "Cartomancy was a few versions ago. Some wags dubbed the new version Cartocracy. The older version is still the standard for marking underwater data sets."

"So you have no problem reading and understanding *Golden Bough*'s digital logs."

"If they were filed logically, no, I'd have no problem. Apparently there was a change in dive center operators a week or so ago. Volkert hasn't begun to clean up the mess left by his predecessor. Or predecessors. The file on wages only lists positions, not individual names."

"At the rates Larry is paying," she said, "you have to expect a high turnover."

"Inefficient."

"But cheap. You get what you pay for. If the mess Volkert is facing is anything like the snarl I'm working on, my sympathies to one and all. Divers are terrible businessmen."

"That's why the smart ones hire someone to take care of all the fiddly details," Holden said.

"Don't look at me," she said, shaking her head. "Hiring implies payment for work. I'm here on vacation."

He watched her with changeable eyes, reminding her that dragons were reputed to be as intelligent as they were lethal.

*Lord, what extraordinary eyes. Hypnotic.*

*Sexy.*

*Too bad that I'm not really here on vacation. He would be one wild fling, a lifetime of hot memories to curl up with on cold nights.*

"Vacation?" His voice was deep—and deeply skeptical. "Why would a woman who doesn't care for the ocean come to an island for a holiday?"

"Family."

"A family you've rarely seen in the flesh since you turned eighteen."

"You sound quite certain. Checking up on me?"

He watched her out of his disconcerting eyes. "I find it strange that you come onto this project some six months after bidding and three months after the boat has set anchor at the site. What makes the whole situation really curious is that you haven't had a thing to do with Moon Rose Limited in an official capacity since shortly after your father died and your mother was presumed lost at sea."

Kate froze.

"You were seventeen and alone on board this ship the night the accident occurred," he said. "You pulled your father out, searched the storm for your mother, and found only salt water and loss."

Silently, fiercely, Kate fought her memories in silence, shoving them down and down until her throat loosened enough to speak rather than scream.

"I see I'm not the only one who uses Google as a research assistant," she said tightly.

He looked at her transparently pale skin, each freckle a tiny bit of gold, her eyes huge and haunted. He wanted nothing more than to hold her, warm her until her skin was flushed with heat and life. Then he would share it with her, the heat and the life.

*Would that be before or after you destroyed her family business, boyo?*

The sardonic question echoed in his head, reminding him that he was here on Crown business, not monkey business.

"What baffles me," he said, "is why. Why did you come back now? There is no way you can add, subtract, multiply, or divide numbers that will keep the family business afloat."

He waited for her to say something.

She simply watched him with shadowed turquoise eyes.

"You're a highly intelligent woman," he said finally. "I suspect you knew the family business was sinking within hours of getting what your brother laughably calls business files, and you certainly knew it after you read the contract Larry signed. AO gave him a right rodgering on that one."

"Is that Brit for screwed over?"

"Close enough." Then he waited for his answer.

And waited.

*Patience,* she thought. *Dragons are noted for that, too.*

"You're a highly intelligent man," she said finally. "Yet you dismantled mines. Why?"

"I could plead orders from above."

She gave him a skeptical look.

"Right." He sighed. "Bloody idiot that I was, I thought I could do some good."

"You'll be happy to know you aren't the only bloody idiot in this room."

He shook his head and said gently, "Poppet, there's nothing you can do for Moon Rose Limited. Your brother signed the contract in front of witnesses. No coercion was involved."

" 'Poppet.' Is that Brit for fool?"

"Dear. Love. Darling. Honey."

She blinked.

"Poppet is an endearment," he said. "I apologize if I have offended you."

"Oh." She felt a flush climb her cheeks. "Er, no, I'm not offended. You didn't use the word in a demeaning way. In fact, I like it." She closed her eyes as she felt her flush heighten. "And as soon as I get my foot out of my mouth, I'll go walk back to my numbers. They're more my speed than dragons."

"Dragons?" His steeply arched eyebrows climbed upward. "How did they get into this discussion?"

"It's hard not to notice when there's one in the room," she shot back, eyes still closed.

*Okay. Now I will get my tongue under control,* she told herself rather desperately. *And my foot out of my mouth.*

She opened her eyes just in time to see Holden smile like a dragon. She put her hands on her hot cheeks.

"Being a redhead sucks," she muttered.

He would like to suck on a particular redhead, but managed not to say it. She would dislike him enough when he told AO what a cock-up this dive was. If he seduced her along the way, she would hate him.

"Don't put yourself through the wringer," he said neutrally. "There is nothing you can do to save your brother's business."

"I can find proof that he isn't stealing."

"No one has said he is."

"No one has to," she shot back. "Stealing is the second-easiest explanation for why so little has been salvaged, and the only explanation that will get the overlords off the hook for funding a dry well. 'Dry well' is American for—"

"Paying good money for bad results," he said coolly, reminding her of his mother's origin. "Even if everything you have said is true, there is nothing you can do but hold your brother's hand while he goes broke."

"Going broke is one thing. Grandpa and Larry have built up from nothing more than once. Having your reputation destroyed is catastrophic. You can't rebuild from that. No one will loan you money to try."

Holden wanted to argue, but couldn't. She was all too correct.

"If there are thieves aboard *Golden Bough*," she continued, "then there is also proof that Donnellys aren't involved. It's up to me to find it."

"Why you?"

"I've always been the sensible one in the family. I don't go crazy at the thought of treasure. The history of a wreck is exciting. The artifacts are a fascinating time capsule. But the money value," she said with a shrug, "is just numbers."

Holden forced himself to look away from her nipples pushing against soft cotton.

"Sleuthing, even sensible sleuthing," he said, "would involve your being aboard the ship in the first place. We both know that you're frightened of the sea in general and the *Golden Bough* in particular."

For a long moment, the memory of her terror at confronting the stairway rippled between them, as did the simple warmth of his comforting hug.

"Love, don't look at me like that," he said in a deep voice. "I'm only a man, and you're a woman fighting for your family. If I took what I see in your eyes, it would end in guilt and tears. You don't deserve that—and neither do I."

Kate wanted to argue that it was her choice, he should let her make it.

But it was his choice too, and he had made it.

"I'll let you get back to important work," she said.

Holden watched the door close behind the woman he wanted until he felt like his skin would split with need.

Honor and decency were cold bedmates.

# Chapter 8

B y the fourth day in St. Vincent, Kate had settled into a kind of rhythm. She and Holden made coffee and scrounged breakfast from the previous night's leftovers plus whatever she had managed to sneak when the cook aboard *Golden Bough* had his back turned. Then she drove Holden and his ever-present duffel to the dive ship. He divided his time between divers and dive center, plus reviewing random snippets of the video log. She prowled the ship under cover of making an inventory and went to the dive center at the least sign of excitement she heard.

So far she hadn't found any stash of illicit treasure aboard. She hadn't overheard any incriminating—or even interesting—conversations, and the dive center excitement was over potsherds, pewter, and the like.

If a woman's weight in gems and jewelry had been aboard the wreck, no one had found it.

Other than discovering that Volkert and Farnsworth each had a woman ashore to fill their downtime—when they weren't in the local dive bars—Kate had little to show for her aboard-ship hours. Her nights were spent talking with Holden over dinner, trying not to touch him, and then staring at spreadsheets until her eyes blurred and she fell into bed.

And each second, each minute, each hour, she had become more at ease with the sea. Not at peace, just not constantly terrified.

The relief that came with her realization was like breathing a straight shot of oxygen.

"Now that's a lovely smile to wake up to," Holden said as he walked into the kitchenette.

"No nightmares last night," she said without thinking, watching the coffee gather in the stained glass pot. Three seconds and she could drink some.

"Excellent," he said. He stood close to her while he poured two cups of the coffee she had made. She smelled like sleepy woman. Kissable woman. "It's impossible for a sane person to sustain a high level of fear when nothing occurs to reinforce it."

She took the cup of coffee he handed her, touching his fingers in the process. She told herself it was an accident. It would have been, too, if they hadn't both lingered to increase the almost caress.

"Sounds like you learned that the hard way," she said.

"Is there another method? After the mishap," he said, absently kneading his thigh, "my mind and my emotions fought a pitched battle on the subject of diving. Many battles, actually."

"What made you dive again? Orders from on high?"

"Six months behind a desk. Thought I would go mental. Plus, I'm a man. I wanted to look in my shaving mirror and not see a coward."

Kate flinched. "Glad I don't have to shave."

"You're not a coward."

"I don't dive."

"Childhood trauma is the hardest kind to overcome."

She let out a slow breath. "It sure has been for me. Perhaps I shouldn't have run, but I did."

He tipped up her chin so that he could see her eyes. "What matters is that you came back."

She looked into his eyes and saw nothing but acceptance and a beauty that still surprised her several times a day.

"How did you force yourself into the water again?" she asked, wanting to stroke against the fingers touching her chin.

"It was better than the alternative." He dropped his hand and began rummaging in the kitchenette.

For long minutes there was no other sound but the fitful wind, the cry of birds fighting over food, and the soft, relentless sigh of sea against sand.

"I can't think of anything worse than diving," Kate finally said.

"You will."

She shivered despite the sultry air. "You're not comforting."

"You're not the first to notice."

An alarm cheeped from the back of the cottage.

"What's that?" she asked, seeing Holden come to alert.

"My computer," he said. "It's tracking the storm that can't seem to decide whether to grow up or die."

"Welcome to St. Vincent toward the end of the doldrums." Sipping her coffee, she followed him down the tiny hall.

He opened his computer, tapped a few keys, and frowned. "Looks like she decided to grow up."

"Who decreed that storms were female?"

"Sailors."

"ABCD?" she asked blandly.

He gave her an amused look. "I doubt that the ancient Chinese used our alphabet."

"Chinese?"

"Probably the first sailors. Or the Egyptians." He tapped more keys and lifted his eyebrows.

"What?" she asked.

"Despite the turn in the weather, you'll be relieved to know that the overlords have released enough funds for another week."

"Overlords, huh?"

He didn't even pause. "When in Rome, use the local dialect."

She laughed. "Come on. We can eat our fruit and biscuits on the way to the ship."

Holden smiled as she hurried out of the room. Of all that had happened in the past few days, watching her emerge from terror had been by far the best. Next to that, a gold money chain was simply a historical trinket.

He didn't have the right to hug her in celebration of her progress, but he was going to claim that right soon. It was the least he could do to appease the hunger prowling through his blood.

The very least.

He settled back and tried to find signs of the weather tempest that was brewing over the horizon. All he saw was the luminous water and the increasing light of day.

By the time Kate and Holden reached the ship, the divers were suiting up. While Larry tied off the tender, waved, and disappeared, Holden climbed aboard with the duffel that went to and from the *Golden Bough* with him each day.

Kate came on board the ship quickly, easily, childhood reflexes taking over more completely with every moment she was on the sea. There was no terror clutching at her stomach right now, making her clench against fear.

She hoped it stayed that way.

The ship rolled a bit at anchor, caught between the strengthening breeze from one direction and the usual swell from another. The sky was still silvery with the last of the morning clouds. Beneath the sullen weight of the sun, the breeze was a soft whisper of life. Ripples slapped at the hull and fell away gently.

Holden was feeling a lot less gentle. After days and nights of being gnawed on by his superiors, plus the persistent ache in his thigh from the undecided weather and the near-constant beat of need for Kate, he was ready to take off heads. The fact that an unknown diver had been added to the rotation—again—didn't help. New people had to be taught the routine, which meant more time wasted.

Right on schedule some early bird from Antiquities called Holden on his phone. When he saw it was

Chatham, he knew it wouldn't be good. He answered and listened to what had become the standard rant—too much money spent and not enough valuable salvage to show for it.

"Respectfully, sir," Holden said when Chatham ran down, "the miserable wages necessitated by the . . ."—*unconscionable and ultimately self-defeating*—"contract the government offered require that Moon Rose Limited scrape divers from bar floors and drag them to the *Golden Bough*, where they have to be slapped sober and instructed as to their duties. Rather like England's merry old days of rum, sodomy, and the lash."

"I am not amused," Chatham shot back.

"Neither are the divers, I assure you. The point remains that miserable wages equal miserable hires."

"So you are telling me that Larry Donnelly is running an inefficient operation and should be cashiered."

Holden took a better grip on the phone and his temper while he moved to a part of the deck that was empty of people.

"I'm telling you that if you pay for sour beer, you shouldn't be surprised when you are served just that," he said.

Chatham had quite a bit to say on the subject of sour beer.

Holden pretended to listen while keeping an eye on his surroundings.

" . . . all we have to show for it is pails of junk that won't pay for the cost of shipping them to England!" Chatham yelled.

"I do believe that is why this is called treasure *hunting*," Holden said, smiling as he echoed Kate's words. "The outcome isn't guaranteed."

"You are there to make sure we come up with more than pails of junk."

Holden sensed someone approaching behind him. He turned just enough to catch the red flash of Kate's hair.

"I'm here to judge the efficiency of the dive," Holden said crisply. "Considering the monetary handicap Moon Rose Limited is working under, the operation is reasonably efficient."

"What about theft?" Chatham asked.

"Has Ms. Pinkham found anything dodgy in the dives she has reviewed?"

"Not yet."

"Has anything else appeared on the black market?"

"No," Chatham said reluctantly.

*So you called me to vent your spleen. Lovely,* Holden thought. *AO must be crawling up your arse.*

"Farnsworth has been working overtime to catalog what the divers have found," Holden said.

"I get the reports," Chatham said sharply. "I don't see gold or precious gems, and bloody little silver from the wreck of the *Moon Rose*. Why don't they use the device they call the 'mail box' again?"

"It's expensive to run, mucks up the clarity of the water, and stands a good chance of destroying any fragile artifacts on or close beneath the surface debris, which really upsets the scholars who—"

"Sod the scholars. We need to pay for this dive. Tell the divers to quit farting about and get to work."

Holden thought about inviting his superior to fly down, suit up, and grub around in the crevices of the sea's vast twilight zone for bits and bobs of gems smaller than his fingernails, but he held his tongue. People who didn't dive simply couldn't grasp the difficulties involved.

"Diving is a tedious, dangerous, costly undertaking," Holden said calmly. "You would get better odds of return on your money in Monaco."

"The Crown does not gamble." There was frost on every syllable. "Are they using the siphon yet?"

"Not that I've seen. In some situations a siphon is inefficient. In all cases it costs petrol to run. As you well know, the captain is extremely limited as to expense money."

"Not my problem. Adding to the Crown's coffers is. See that those lazy bastards get on with it."

"Would you rather I suit up and dive than oversee operations ashore and aboard?" Holden asked.

"Bugger," Chatham muttered. "Carry on. I have a report to prepare for my superiors. They will not like it."

Holden shut down the phone and put it in one of the pockets of his cargo shorts. When he turned, Kate was there, watching him.

"Thank you," she said.

"For what?"

"Defending us against your boss."

Holden wondered how much of his defense had been due to his growing interest in her, but all he said was, "Chatham isn't a diver, much less a salvage diver. He has no way of actually understanding the difficulties involved. Also . . ." Holden realized what he was about to say and closed his mouth.

"What?"

The turquoise eyes watching him with something very close to trust made a knife turn in Holden's conscience.

*Sod it. Of all the people involved, she deserves the truth.*

"The contract my superiors gave Moon Rose Limited was a glass of salt water handed to a man dying of thirst," he said roughly. "Chatham has no pretense to serving any higher purpose than greed."

"Kind of like Bloody Green," she said. "Until he met a woman who was worth more than gold and gems."

Holden's fingertips traced the softness of Kate's cheek and the strength of the bone along her jaw. "Men have done many things, both stupid and sublime, for a special woman."

Her heart stuttered. Then she did what she had been wanting to do for days—she ran one fingertip around the line of his sensual lips. "The same could be said about women."

"We're both mental, you know that," he said softly. Then he touched her fingertip with his tongue.

Watching his eyes, she put that same fingertip against her own tongue. "Yes."

Two crew members called to each other in a liquid creole that was a meld of English, French, and Spanish, all of which had held the islands of the Caribbean at one time or another.

The wheelhouse door opened.

Kate jumped back like a kid with her hand caught in a cookie jar. "I'd better get to work."

Holden glanced up at the wheelhouse, saw no one watching, and went to see which divers were going down this morning. When they came back up, he would be the one to go through their diving gear, checking for any concealed packets of gems or coins or chain. He hadn't found any yet, and he liked the job about as much as he would going through other people's soiled underwear, but he did it every day.

And every day Grandpa Donnelly watched him like a bald bird of prey.

*Ah, trust,* Holden thought sardonically. *Such a satisfying way to work.*

There were times when he really missed the camaraderie of dismantling mines.

Holden reached the stern dive area while Larry was double-checking Mingo, the lead diver. He was cocky as always, closing his red-and-black dive suit while talking about the women waiting ashore for his special kind of sexing, and making side bets with his brother Luis, the second diver going down.

"The gold, she is already mine," Mingo said.

"The gems are waiting for me," Luis said. His grin flashed. "Just like your women are."

"Ha!" Mingo fastened a dive computer on his left wrist and clipped a second computer to a leash on his suit. This was the ship's computer that every diver wore and handed over at the end of a dive to Volkert for downloading. "The women, they know who can ride them all night."

Luis adjusted the position of his own computer on his wrist. Like most of the divers, he also wore a watch in case the computer failed and the backup ship's computer on his leash didn't agree with the flagged stages of decompression. Properly timing each stage of decompression was the difference between health and death.

Mingo gave the computer screen a final loving wipe with a soft cloth that Larry handed to him.

"Oh, beauty, you be worth more than the ship, yes?" Mingo crooned.

Larry didn't rise to the familiar bait.

Holden assessed Kate's brother, knowing that he was under a lot of pressure. Larry's color was bad, and his hands were slow and sometimes unsteady. His breathing was a bit too rapid.

Holden wondered if the other man had been drinking himself to sleep. Nothing in Larry's files indicated a real problem with alcohol, but that didn't mean much. Hard drinking was only noted when it got in the way of the job.

"You sure your mix is good?" Larry asked Mingo. "You haven't even checked it, and you're diving a lot of hours."

"I be getting the bonus for first gems," Mingo said, his smile brilliant against skin darkened by sun and genetics. "You see."

"You won't be getting anything but sick if your air mix is bad," Holden said.

Luis snickered.

Mingo gave Holden a look out of dramatic dark eyes that had lured many a local girl astray. "I be good." He tugged the cuff of the neoprene mask around his face, pushing his black curls behind. When he spoke again, his Caribbean accent was barely a whisper. "This is my own special blend. Minimized compression and decompression is my specialty. Higher time efficiency. More salvage."

"He's right," Larry said. With a grunt he heaved a silvery tank onto Mingo's back so that the diver could secure it. Sunlight glinted against the tank's countless nicks and scuffs and scratches.

"Don't mind the looks," Larry said to Holden. "Only new tanks are shiny. As long as the old tanks are clean inside, no grease and corrosion, they're solid. If you're worried about these tanks exploding, you've been watching too many movies. It takes a hell of a lot of force to make one of these babies blow."

"I am reassured," Holden said gravely.

"It's the special blends inside that cost," Larry said.

"That was noted on the bills you submitted when asking for an advance on expenses."

"So tell me, boss man," Mingo asked Holden mockingly, "should I be using a normoxic blend? We're not going all that far down."

Holden looked at him. "Just as long as it's not a moronic blend, which would suit you."

Larry shifted and busied himself checking straps and buckles on Luis, who was watching Holden and Mingo warily.

"What did you just call me?" Mingo asked Holden.

"A moron, because you suggested using a normoxic blend at the surface." Holden's voice was neutral, almost bored. Mingo had been pushing him at every opportunity. It was time to push back.

"I no say nothin' 'bout surface. But I be fast enough goin' down to suck on a normoxic can straight off the deck."

Holden's phone vibrated, telling him a new message had come in. He pulled it out.

"Check his mix," he said to Larry without looking up. "That sort of manly idiocy kills divers."

"I do it before. Me!" Mingo said, pointing at his chest.

"You underline my estimation of your intelligence," Holden said, working over his phone. "Frankly, I doubt you should decant your own mixes."

"Back off, Cameron," Larry said, double-tapping Luis's tank in a signal that he was ready to go. "You can read up real fast on mixes on that fancy phone of yours or you could get out of the way and let us work."

"Mixes?" Holden's black eyebrows lifted.

He turned the phone so Larry and Mingo could see a photo of a blue-eyed, blond little girl with straight hair smiling devilishly through the gap in her missing front teeth. Her skin was pearl dusted with freckles. Next to her was a boy with curly black hair, brown skin, and teeth missing from his smile. The boy had Holden's striking eyes.

"My niece and nephew, fraternal twins," Holden said. "Quite a handful for my brother and his wife."

The other men looked astonished that Holden was related to anything human. Then they smiled.

"Oh, she be heartbreaker," Mingo said.

Larry smiled in spite of himself. "The look in her eyes reminds me of Kate before . . ." His voice trailed off.

Holden knew Larry was thinking about the death of his parents. If Mingo knew, it didn't show in his expression. Holden pocketed his phone.

"Chitchat aside," he said to the diver, "we all know that your dive computer is going to talk to the little compressors on your back and shunt around the proper amounts of helium so that you don't get nitrogen narcosis, unless you deliberately bugger it."

Mingo looked at him, but there was humor instead of malice in his eyes. "I could do it without the little box."

"The little box is what allows you to enjoy a longer life expectancy than you have any right to, which will no doubt please a lot of ladies in St. Vincent."

Mingo laughed.

Larry gave a final check to the diver's equipment and double-tapped on the tank.

Mingo fixed his mask in place. His fingers went to the hand-sized silvery box on his wrist, made a few adjustments so that it would start counting the instant he hit the water, and went in flippers first, dropping like a rock thanks to his weight belt.

"He's a better diver than the wages I give him," Larry said. "So is his brother."

*That's not saying a great deal,* Holden thought. "From the looks of it, you're thinking of employing the siphon today."

"Weather isn't giving me much choice."

Both men looked to the horizon. The difference was subtle, like someone was slowly, slowly dimming a light. Nothing would happen today, perhaps not even tomorrow. But the storm was strengthening, sending ripples through the ocean, changing the way *Golden Bough* rode at anchor.

Sensing another presence, Holden glanced up. Grandpa Donnelly was looking at the same horizon, his fingers clenched on the rail until his knuckles stood out like white stones. Then he turned away and went back into the wheelhouse.

"Grandpa will oversee the siphon," Larry said. "If you want to watch a lot of sand and muck pumped into the barrel, feel free. If you want to help fish out anything worth keeping, you can pay for your room and board."

Since Holden hadn't smelled alcohol on the other man's breath today, he assumed that fatigue was dragging on Larry.

Or the realization that this dive was a dead loss.

# Chapter 9

An engine Holden hadn't heard before ripped into noisy life at the stern of the ship. Diesel smoke poured out an exhaust, then largely disappeared as the engine warmed up. A few minutes later, a stream of sand, salt water, silt, and debris began gushing into the large barrel on the stern.

Grandpa Donnelly brushed past Holden and went to stand near the dredge receiving bay, which was a huge tub six feet across with walls about a foot high, formed out of stainless steel. One side was open like a dump truck's back. The whole bin could be levered up and spilled overboard once the muck had been checked for artifacts.

Coiled by the barrel was about one hundred feet of six-inch-diameter black rubber hosing that could be used as needed, depending on the depth of the dive. One end of the hose was manned by Luis on the bottom. On top, the siphon was run by its own diesel engine to create the suction required for the process. Sand that was sucked up from the sea below the siphon's mouth went up through the hose and poured out onto the stainless steel grate. Grandpa Donnelly grabbed a short rake and began separating out chunks that looked promising.

"Going to the whip, are you?" Holden asked the elder Donnelly, pitching his voice to be heard over the racket.

"Not much time left in this race. The weather is going sour."

Holden looked at the horizon where the storm would appear. It had changed very little from previous days, but his thigh was still aching. Nothing definitive, simply an early warning of changing pressures. The more steep the changes, the more likely a weather shift.

And the pressure had been shooting up and down like a yo-yo in the past few days.

"The scholars at AO are going to curse," Holden said looking at the sludge.

"We're recording the sector Luis is siphoning on camera," Grandpa Donnelly said impatiently. "It'll have to do. There's no time for titty fingers anymore. Your bosses can have treasure or they can have some bullshit papers published in places no one reads."

"Actually, AO will be pleased. Going through the siphon's output is a lot faster than having divers fan sand with their fingers until their air runs low."

"Scholars," Donnelly hissed. He pulled a cold pipe out of his pocket and clamped the stem between his teeth. "They act like the sea bottom never changes unless humans muck it up. Any fool knows that the bottom is alive, and living things move and change all the time."

Farnsworth popped up from his belowdecks workshop. "Heard the siphon. Anything?"

"Noise. Burning fuel. Salt water," Donnelly said curtly.

Something pale flashed among the muck. His hand shot out with surprising speed. "Pottery." He tossed it into one of the buckets standing by the barrel.

Farnsworth started to record it on his small computer tablet, then shrugged. No point in being meticulous with a siphon at work.

A few minutes later the rake turned over a several links of gold chain.

"Retrieving it," Farnsworth said.

He picked up the bit of jewelry, held it up to the camera that was recording the dredging area, and popped the gold into a clear plastic bag that was already marked with the date, hour, and sector being siphoned.

For a time, watching the siphon was fascinating—the gush and swirl of water, the clink of coral debris, the occasional fragments of pottery or ancient wood that began to decompose the instant it struck air.

"Any sense of what the wood was used for?" Holden asked Farnsworth.

"Feels like wet cardboard and is about as anonymous in small pieces. Could have come from a trencher, a bucket, a spar, or a crumbled chest that once held gems and gold. And wouldn't that be lovely?"

"It would go a long way toward making AO smile," Holden said.

Donnelly said something about "god-rotting vultures."

After the first hour the constant noise and swirl of water became almost numbing. The occasional spurt of pottery, or the even more rare gleam of metal, did little to shake the dreamlike trance of the men watching. Yet nothing escaped the old man's experienced eye.

Green flashed and tumbled in the barrel. A large-knuckled hand shot out and closed around the stone, pulling it free. Slowly his hand opened. A thumb-sized crystal spear of gemstone glowed in unearthly beauty.

"Emerald," Farnsworth said. "Uncut."

Donnelly nodded. "Spaniards killed a lot of Indians in the mines. Royalty loved emeralds. On the treasure galleons, the officers smuggled their own gems aboard. It was a perk, like wine at meals."

"Some historians," Farnsworth said absently, his mind captive to the intense green crystal, "speculate that ships sank due to the excess tonnage of silver and gold smuggled by the crew."

"Greed is always deadly," Holden said. "And so very human."

Word of the emerald went through the ship like a shock wave. Everybody but Volkert appeared to gawk at the valuable bit of crystal and speculate on its worth. Donnelly allowed it for a few minutes, never taking his own eyes off the barrel where the siphon disgorged a continuous stream of sand, silt, and water.

"Go back to work," Donnelly said without looking up. His hand closed around the emerald, concealing it.

The crew filtered back to wherever they had come from.

Holden barely noticed. He had been watching Kate from the corner of his eye since she had appeared to check out rumors of gems spreading through the ship's grapevine. She was watching Farnsworth as he closed the raw emerald in a bag and set it in the pail with the other bits that had been collected from the barrel.

"Gold, jewelry, gems, and other valuable items should be entered into a written and photo log immediately," Kate said. "Then they should go to the ship's safe and only be removed by someone who signs a receipt for the items."

Grandpa Donnelly didn't even bother to answer, but Farnsworth said, "If Holden agrees, I'll take care of the extra work."

Holden nodded. "Now that we've found a real gem, AO will be reassured by the extra steps."

"Larry isn't going to like being awakened to open the safe for every bit of gleam we pick up," Grandpa Donnelly said. "And I'm not going to leave the barrel until the siphon is off and the bed is empty."

Kate thought about it, then nodded, rubbing absently at her cheek. Her fingers left a smudge on her skin. "Put everything valuable in one pail and make certain the pail is in the camera's view at all times. That way we'll have a record and Larry will get to sleep."

Farnsworth took an empty pail, put it in the camera's field, and transferred the plastic packages with valuable goods inside to the pail one at a time, ensuring that each was recorded.

"Thank you," she said. "I'll work with Larry on some protocol to sign things into the warehouse ashore. I don't want anyone to doubt that what comes up from the dive goes directly to our British *partners*."

Holden heard the emphasis on the last word and hid a smile.

He left Farnsworth and Donnelly to their work and followed Kate down to a storage area where tanks of various compressed gases waited to be used. From the looks of the deck and storage racks, it had a been a long time since the place had had a good scrubbing.

"I'm surprised your face is only a bit smudged," Holden said.

Like everything else below the deck, the quarters were close and tight, smelling of brine, grease, and sweat in equal parts. Even on tourist vessels, keeping places like this spotless was hardly a high priority. On a working vessel, such areas got wiped down when there was literally nothing left to do.

Holden looked at the grimy lightbulb that barely illuminated the area.

"A good cleaning sounds great," she said. "You volunteering?"

"I'm not an ensign."

"And here I thought you were perfect." She turned away before she grabbed him with dirty hands and pulled him close enough to bite.

Holden surveyed the row of five tall canisters of pressurized gas—oxygen, helium, and nitrogen—waiting to be mixed and locked in scuba rigs. Then he looked at her. He wanted nothing more than to pull her against him and breathe in her scent, feel her soft heat against his body. The hunger burned up the back of his neck and spread across his body.

"How is the inventory going?" he asked, his voice too deep.

She stared back with a hunger that equaled his. "This isn't inventory. This is damage control. Tanks are low, particularly the nitrogen and oxygen, but really all of them."

"Leaky valves?"

"Lazy bookkeeping. People haven't bothered to log out each time they use the tanks. And that helium is expensive."

"Maybe Volkert's sneaking up here for a giggle."

Her lips curved at the thought of Volkert squeezing into the storage room to get high on gas mixtures. "The idea has comic possibilities."

He smiled slowly. "I don't envy you sleuthing after missing helium—colorless, odorless, and near weightless. Even Sherlock Holmes would be baffled."

She watched the line of his lips and remembered how he had looked in the tropical sun by the siphon, with the light from the water rippling off his bronze skin. He was beautiful down to his bones, and his eyes were more compelling than any gem. She wanted to sink into them, into him.

"Kate?" he asked softly, wondering where she had gone in that intelligent mind of hers.

She realized she was holding her breath. She let it out in a soft rush.

"I can't get the dive hours to jibe with the remaining gas in the storage cylinders," she said.

"A fair amount of heavy salvage has been floated to the top with cables and balloons," he said. "Cannons aren't light. Neither are ingots of metal."

"If the divers are using expensive air mixes to float iron, I'm going to tear strips off their hides. We have a compressor aboard with a long hose we use to blow up floats for the big stuff. Or we use the balloon lifts that are self-inflating. At least we used to."

Frowning, she tapped out a quick note on her computer to check with Larry. She hated to bother him, but someone had to keep an eye on supplies, especially the expensive ones. Since no one else was doing it, she would.

A random larger swell caught the ship, changing its motion.

Holden watched Kate closely. Beyond the automatic adjustment of her body to keep the computer stable, she didn't seem to notice the ship's motion. No sudden pallor, no tightening of her mouth or shoulders, nothing but a supple shift to accommodate the changed motion.

He smiled.

"What?" she asked, looking up.

"The first day or two aboard, you flinched at every unexpected shift the *Golden Bough* made."

She looked confused.

"You're getting past your fear," he said, touching the smudge on her cheek.

Before she could answer, the light in the storeroom went out and the familiar grumble of the generator went silent.

"Bugger," he said, dropping his hand. "There goes the power again."

"Grandpa will fix it." Even as she spoke, the siphon shut down. "See? He's on his way."

"Is he a proper ship's engineer?"

"For the *Golden Bough*, yes. He could probably take it apart and reassemble it in his sleep." *Which is very close to what I'd like to do to the lickable man with the dragon eyes.*

Her cheek still tingled where he had touched it. Her nipples wanted his touch, too. Not to mention his mouth. She wondered if his nipples were sensitive. Not every man's were. In fact, most men just went for the finish line like there was a prize for the fastest orgasm.

Male, of course. If the female couldn't keep up, well, that was her problem.

*And I'd better stop thinking about sex.*

" . . . work by flashlight?" Holden asked.

She blinked, had an image of them in the dark, naked, laughing and grappling for possession of the flashlight's revealing beam. She fought a blush and tried to drag her thoughts away from how Holden's every movement made her want to find out if his follow-through in bed was half as good as his looks.

Or even a third.

"Flashlight," she said, her thoughts racing furiously. "Um, I didn't think to bring one. Did you?"

He shook his head.

She stretched stiffly. "Grandpa will probably fire up the starboard engine to top the batteries off and keep the operation going. Expensive as hell, but at least the lights will work."

"Take a break and come to the dive center with me," he said.

"Why?"

"Why not?"

She blinked. "Point to the gentleman. Assuming you are one."

"In the right circumstances I can be very gentle. Thorough, too."

Heat shot through Kate. "Not touching that."

"Pity. We'll talk more about it at supper—dinner."

A big engine fired up, adding a pulsing rumble to the air.

"You're prescient," he said.

"Experienced on this ship," she corrected.

"Come to the dive center with me. Your back must be cursing you."

"What do you want at the dive center?"

"Volkert's cooperation. With you along, I'm less likely to have to resort to kicking his lazy arse."

"I doubt it. He made an offer and I declined."

"A hard offer?" Holden asked sharply.

"There's not a hard inch on that man."

Holden smothered a smile. "Don't be too sure."

"Gak. Mind bleach." She shuddered. "I'm sure some women lust for his type, but I really don't want to think about it. He goes through junk food faster than divers go through oxygen. His snacks are all imported because he hates the cook's food. And if the dive logs have been updated in the last week, I haven't found them."

Holden's black eyebrows lifted. She sounded ready to tear a strip off Volkert.

*Maybe she'll let me help. Or at least watch.*

"Okay," she said, stretching again, "let's go see what Volkert has on the screens."

"While we're watching, I have a few questions about previous scans done by metal detectors," Holden said.

"I've been curious about them too, but there are things a lot higher on my to-do list."

Holden really hoped he was one of them. He gestured for her to precede him out of the storeroom.

She tried not to take any extra time brushing by him, but it felt so good she wanted to linger. Every step of the way to the dive center, she could feel him watching her rear.

So she put an extra little swing into her stride.

The narrow hallway was alive with the thrum of power, sending vibrations through every surface. The bulkheads and walls were so close that the sensation of life rushed through them, like resting a palm on the heart of a sleeping dragon, raw power coursing.

*Like Holden,* she thought, then tried very hard to think about something else.

Kate opened the door to the communication room, bathing them both in the flickering glow of the dive screens. The insistent thump of electronic music poured out the open door.

The smell of stale food and sweat clung to the room like a bad reputation. An iPod plugged into a small speaker was the source of an incessant electronic beat with a sweet-sinister girl-voice winding through it like a snake.

"Dial it down," Kate said loudly. "You may be deaf but I'm not."

Volkert either didn't hear her or ignored her.

"What in hell is that noise?" Holden asked roughly.

The electronics phased into a hammering digital drumbeat, all bass. Then more singing over it, the words in Dutch or German.

"Die Antwoord," Volkert said without looking up. "You should get out more."

"Why? The English invented that electro-pop you're deafening yourself with."

"Pity that you English don't sing in Afrikaans. What do you want?" Volkert crunched on some more chips.

"I'm having trouble syncing up my computer map with the ship's daily dive record," Holden said loudly.

*"Geen woord gevind nie."*

"Excuse me?"

"Afrikaans for 'I'm so terribly sorry.' A bad habit. I used to work tech support for a company based in Johannesburg."

"Can you get me connected?" Holden asked impatiently. "I'm already on the network, but I keep getting shunted off."

"Yah, sorry, we got some new procedures that I'm catching up with. And doing my normal job. And trying to fix the mess I found when I came aboard."

Kate wanted to put her fingers in her ears. Volkert's whine cut right through Techno-pop and put her teeth on edge. That and the fact that he was ignoring her like grease on the deck.

"The new procedures," she said clearly, "are the accepted standard for entering and cross-referencing digital files. Remember? It was in your job description."

Volkert ignored her.

She leaned over him and shut off the iPod. "Maybe that will help you concentrate."

He gave her a cold-eyed glare. "What do you want?"

She looked at Holden and said, "You first."

"I have a few questions about the metallurgic scans you've been working from," Holden said. "It appears to me that the data you're using is rubbish."

Volkert sighed and pushed a meaty arm across the keyboard. The main screen went from a view of Mingo's camera to the five-by-five grid of the whole wreck area. Overlaid was a false color map, showing small concentrations of red and yellow here and there, but mostly a faint scattering of blue. "This data?"

"Precisely. Is it current?"

Volkert shrugged. "Current as I've got. You should know. It's the map that the Brit survey team provided us."

"I recognize it, and its limitations. Why aren't you running your own surveys?"

Volkert stared at Holden as if he had a flower growing out of his nose. "You Brits are running the show. If you couldn't be arsed to get a better survey to us, then you're going to get what's coming to you."

Holden stiffened, shirt tightening across his shoulders. He had had enough of the insufferable Afrikaner.

Kate decided that her peacekeeping act was in order now. After all, they had deprived Volkert of his noise cocoon. "What Holden meant to ask is if the divers had done informal surveys based on this original scan. In other words, is there better information in the digital file?"

Holden flexed his lean fingers, but kept quiet.

Volkert stared at both of them with eyes that were almost lost in the curves of his face. "One of the advantages of being a fungus is that I sit in the dark and am fed bullshit. I see what the divers are doing when the cameras are running. That's it. If you want, I can get you an overlay of everywhere the divers have gone and you can put it over whatever other information you can pull out of the files. But it will take a time." He turned back to the screen. "I should be watching the divers and taking notes. *Someone* has suggested that we tighten up."

"Someone who is your boss," Kate reminded him tightly.

"You didn't hire me."

"You can bet your next bag of cookies on that. But I can fire you."

He ignored her.

Holden started forward.

Kate beat him to it. She leaned over and got right in Volkert's face. "Listen, you miserable pile of grief, you will look at me when I'm talking to you and *do your job.*"

He glanced at her blazing turquoise eyes and shrank back against his seat. "I've been here less than two weeks. It's not my fault the people before me were incompetent."

"Check the records for the most recent metal scan," she said flatly.

"All I have is what I was given. The guy before me told me to do it the same way he had—no instructions. I've barely learned the system."

"Not good enough. If anyone has been waving a metal detector around on that grid, the findings are recorded somewhere. Ferret them out."

"Well, yah. I guess. If they wrote them down or entered them into their dive boxes."

"Go through all the reports that you've gotten and search for anything about metal deposits. Send the result to me." Kate stood up, having had enough of the smell of his sweat. "Got that?"

Volkert nodded rather sullenly. "When do you need those records?"

"Before you open your next sack of chips."

"It will be at least an hour, probably two. Mingo's been streaming up data faster than I can chew it down."

"Pretend the data are cookies and get me that report."

Holden watched as she pushed away from Volkert and walked closer to the bank of monitors. For a moment she was a stark female silhouette against a shifting glow. Her shorts and shirt were stuck to curvy parts of her by the heat and humidity.

"Anything else you need?" she asked Holden.

*Oh, love, I want you to ask me that question again in the dark.*

Volkert glared into the monitors and hammered his fingertips over the keyboard. Noisily.

"Some of the files are ready now," he said, looking at Holden. "Do you want them in your inbox?"

"Just leave them in a public folder. Mark them clearly."

More clicks. "Done and done. But I can't promise the information isn't shite. This isn't what I would call a tight ship."

"Then do what you can to tighten it up," Kate suggested.

Holden watched the screens where the divers were working their way through the decompression stages.

"Looks like they have full bags," he said, referring to the mesh bags divers used to carry small finds.

Silence, then openmouthed crunching as Volkert chewed.

"What did they find?" she asked.

Volkert chewed and looked at her, giving a great view of a mouth full of mush. His expression said he knew how little she liked it.

Holden waited, understanding that Kate had to live in a man's world on board the ship. If he stepped in, it would be worse for her the next time she gave orders to a crew member. *Now, if I could just stop imagining how delightful it would be to mash that fat toad's mouth all over his face . . .*

"Gold jewelry," Volkert said, the words almost buried in half-chewed chips.

"Intact?" she asked.

He swallowed. "A few small pearls left. They're junk."

She wasn't surprised. Once a pearl left the oyster's protection, it began degrading. Salt water acted like a slow acid on the natural gems.

"A collector or a museum will overlook that," she said, "if the piece is unusual enough. Anything else?"

"Such as?" he mocked.

"Emeralds," she said, "diamonds, sapphires, rubies, money chains, coins, ingots of gold or silver. The usual stuff of a treasure diver's dreams. But then, you wouldn't know, would you? You aren't a diver. Tell me about significant finds or I will fire your ass right now and run the dive center myself."

Volkert looked at Holden.

"I hear she's quite good at your job," Holden said, his voice indifferent.

Volkert turned to Kate. "Some coral that grew around a purse of coins, silver. Five earrings, no stones." He looked down at the notes he had made in Afrikaans. "In fact, it looks like Bloody Green pulled out almost every gem and stored it separately. If he was true to type, he had some chest or chests locked in his own quarters."

"Translate your notes and put them in my inbox," she said. "Farnsworth will debrief the divers."

She and Holden headed out, followed by the blare of the Techno beat as Volkert crawled back into his cocoon.

# Chapter 10

Under Kate's watchful eyes, the small, valuable goods from the dive had been touched, photographed, packed, taped, and signed across the tape by her so that any opening would breach her signature. The temporary high from seeing the artifacts faded when she sat at the galley table, her computer running on battery power because she felt guilty about every bit of energy she took from the engine's expensive heartbeat.

Grandpa had gotten the generator going twice, and twice it had died, so everyone was working on batteries or sleeping. Or sitting, like her, staring at a screen, hoping somehow to change the figures, but they were what they were.

Bad.

Soon Larry would have to buy more of the expensive compressed gas, especially helium, or chance running out in a few days. Assuming the generator worked and the divers were in the water and the weather didn't go to hell.

*I can't control the weather,* she told herself. *So concentrate on what I can control.*

Dutifully she focused on the screen, staring at the list of what the divers and siphon had brought up:

325 grams gold in linked chain

2 cannonballs, now soaking in a chemical bath to strip away the rust and the corrosion that had built up over the centuries

1 uncut emerald, thumb-sized

1 gold facial pick that was both ear, nose, and tooth cleaner, badly bent

17 silver discs, presumably coinage, total weight of 520 g, also bathing

assorted pewter drinking and table vessels, damaged and essentially worthless beyond historical value

6 silver rings, settings empty, now soaking in a bath

7 silver earrings, settings empty, now soaking in a bath

1 gold necklace, settings empty but for a few corroded pearls

1 gold brooch, central setting empty, surrounded by small diamonds

metal hasp, probably bronze, probably from a small chest, soaking in a bath

13 gold coins, portrait oriented right, in a mass of coral and silver coins, now soaking in a bath

It was moments like this that she understood the appeal of gold on an almost physical level. Submerged in water for centuries, yet it still gleamed, tears of the sun, always bright, always valuable, heavy with the weight of time and human adoration.

"There you are." Larry's voice, too hoarse.

He sat heavily next to her.

Kate turned. "You look terrible."

"Thanks," he said around a yawn. "Way to make me feel good."

"I'm serious. Go get some sleep and shake off whatever bug has you so hollow-eyed."

"Sinuses are clear. So are lungs. I'm good to dive. And quit trying to change the subject."

"What subject?" she asked.

"Cameron."

"Were we talking about him?"

"Yeah."

"What were we saying?" she asked.

"Volkert's a pig, but that's no reason to take Cameron's side against a crew member. Morale is bad enough without that."

At first she thought her brother was joking. Then she realized that he was serious.

And seriously wrong.

"Volkert's attitude toward me needed adjusting," Kate said distinctly, "and I adjusted it."

"In front of Cameron."

"Volkert was being a dick because I turned down his charming offer of sex the second day I was aboard. Holden and I needed information directly related to Volkert's work and he wasn't cooperating. He got exactly what he deserved."

"Holden and you, huh? How chummy." Then, before she could say anything, he was talking again. "The Brits have been asking for ridiculous levels of documentation. Check it yourself. Volkert didn't need you jumping in his shit on Cameron's behalf. And if they think I'm stealing, they should just come out and say it. They've got me looking over my shoulder so much my neck aches. I'm diving my ass off and all I get is grief. Grandpa says the treasure is down there and then he starts yelling about how these idiot Brits have us looking in the wrong place. I'm tired of being on the hook for their opium dreams."

Kate leaned over and gave her brother a hug. After a moment he returned it.

*His bones are too close to the surface,* she thought. *He's pushing himself too hard. He knows it as well as I do.*

*And we both know he'll keep pushing because it's all he can do.*

She tightened her arms around him, wishing she had something besides red ink and gloom to give him.

"From what I've seen of the dive records," she said, "they match up to the early metallurgical surveys, and they are consistent when looked at in the aggregate. The divers have gone over areas that showed hits, and sometimes those hits paid off."

"And sometimes they didn't," he said hoarsely. "Those are the times I hear about."

"Maybe I can get Holden to push for someone to come in and run a close survey over the wreck."

"We've been doing that on the fly when we had an extra diver who happened to be sober. Problem is, just because you get a hit doesn't mean the goods are at the surface or that we have the equipment to dig down to the metal. The Brits knew it was a crapshoot from the start. That's what they paid us—crap—and that's what they give me." He gave a broken laugh. "The idiots think that holes in the sand we suction out of the wreck don't fall back in on themselves the moment we look away."

She rocked slightly, holding him, trying to comfort him. "I remember watching Dad. As soon as he'd manage to suction out a hole, the sides would dissolve and he'd have to start all over again."

"Yeah. When I sleep, sometimes I wake up in a cold sweat, thinking of what will happen if the salvage is a bust."

Kate knew what that kind of waking was like. "Hush. You've brought up plenty of stuff."

"But no treasure chest of jewels. None of the staggering weight of gold Bloody Green's ship carried."

"We don't know what was aboard when *Moon Rose* sank. History is as much lies and brags and wishes as truth. Anyone who's in the salvage business knows that."

"Our bosses are bureaucrats," Larry said with tired savagery. "They're button pushers and box checkers looking to blame me for their own stupid orders and inflated promises of wealth."

She held him, trying to tell him silently that she loved him and supported him.

"I've had about all I can take," he said roughly. Then he released her and stood up, using the chair as a prop. "I need to know for certain that you're on my side, okay? You can't be sticking up for Cameron if he goes pissing off the crew. We have enough trouble keeping crew as it is. Word ashore is that we're cursed."

"I'm on your side."

He nodded. "Okay."

"Now you promise me one thing."

"What?" he asked.

"Be careful down there."

He gave her a crooked smile and a pull on her ponytail. "Every time, Kitty Kat."

With worried eyes she watched her brother shamble out the door and heard him call to one of the divers.

*He needs a week of sleep. Or a really big find.*

And she couldn't give him either one.

Grimly she went back to the computer, hoping she would discover something that would help her family out.

In the end, the best she could do was sign off on today's manifest for the divers. She hit the forward key.

*One more time,* she told herself, and switched to the accounting software.

"You need a break," Holden said from the doorway.

She looked up and smiled wearily. "Who doesn't?"

"I've signed off on the manifest. My computer pinged at me, so I know you have, too. Farnsworth will meet us at the warehouse after he refuels. He can sign off on today's haul and lock it down. Shouldn't take us more than an hour, total."

"Us?"

"As in you and me," he said with satisfaction. "I'm required to have a representative of Moon Rose Limited accompany me and the goods, due to your new protocols."

"Oh. I assumed you'd take Larry."

"Why would I do that? He hasn't signed off on anything. Even if he had, he's so knackered I wouldn't trust him with custody of a flea. Tag, you're it, but I'll buy you lunch afterward."

"I don't think the dive expenses cover lunch out."

"I won't expense it," Holden said.

With a smile she gave in to what both of them wanted. "Okay."

**Wearing khaki** pants, a loose, ratty Manchester United T-shirt, and his habitual frown, Farnsworth met Holden and Kate at the warehouse. The clothes emphasized his compact, wiry build. Except for frown lines, he looked about eighteen.

"There you are," he said to them. "Good to see you in person, as it were. Seems like we spend all our time in tiny boxes looking at life through little screens and speaking though small microphones. Seeing people in the flesh is always a bit of a surprise."

Kate smiled. "You have a particularly small box to work out of."

He gave her a smile that was almost shy. "I'll give you a quick recce of the warehouse after we lock up today's valuables. It went well, didn't it? The emerald is particularly nice. AO was quite excited. The brooch is lovely, too. At least on the screen."

Kate thought of the piece of jewelry, its silky weight and winking diamonds. "The brooch is fine in person, too. The emerald is wrapped in a separate, cushioned box. The color is incredible, like the heart of summer condensed into a single crystal."

"Should fetch some pounds on the market," he said, nodding.

"Certainly more than that disreputable T-shirt you're wearing," Holden said, shaking his head.

"A vestige of my heavier days," Farnsworth admitted. "I can't quite bear to give it up, though. Reminds me of home."

"Sounds like you've been away for a time," Holden said. "It softens the edge of the accent."

Farnsworth ran a hand through close-cropped hair that was in need of another going-over.

"Actually, I went to school in the United States, Boston to be precise. Worked abroad far more than at home. Feel like a tourist when I go back. It's all high-tech and no factories. Though the apartments are still there. Bloody horrible things, all slabs and no personality. You?"

"London, London, and London. They let me out of my cage occasionally, but not often. Turns out that I can yell at people almost as well via teleconference as I can in person."

"Ah, yes. Unfortunate, that. It just makes our little boxes even smaller. At least this box," he said, opening the warehouse door, "has breathing room."

After the tropical sun, the industrial lighting looked dim and unnatural, a not-quite-twilight that never changed.

"You haven't shipped the silver ingots yet?" Holden asked.

Farnsworth followed the other man's glance to the stack of ingots sheathed in gleaming, semitransparent plastic. The heavy columns were wrapped in metal bands, sitting on a pallet and waiting to be forklifted aboard a truck for transfer to a cargo ship. There were other boxes and crates laid out around the warehouse, each sealed and stamped and ready for transport.

"AO is waiting for one of our ships to take the heavy goods, except if we find gold ingots. Then we make special arrangements with a licensed, bonded courier service," Farnsworth said. "London doesn't trust the natives with gold."

Holden said, "Antiquities doesn't trust anyone with gold."

"Looking at the sheer volume of boxes," Kate said, "how can your AO complain about the efficiency of the dive operation?"

Holden and Farnsworth glanced at one another. And laughed.

"Right," Kate said. "They are human and they complain." She looked at the packet she was carrying and gave it to Farnsworth. "They'll probably complain about this, too."

Farnsworth took it, checked that the packet's seal hadn't been disturbed, and compared the manifest tag to his pocket computer's entry. He approved everything as in good order before he tucked the packet under his arm.

"Lovely. The second length of money chain," Farnsworth said almost caressingly. "What was it—three hundred grams?"

"Three thirty," Holden corrected. "Thirty grams is thirty grams."

"Right you are." Farnsworth walked to the steel desk in a nearby corner, placed the packet in a drawer, and locked it.

Holden's eyebrows shot up.

Kate said, "Is that it? A locked desk in a shabby warehouse near the docks? How can your bosses be sniffing around my family as thieves? This place is a sieve!"

"Oh, it's safe enough," Farnsworth said with a small smile. "Though you can't see them, there are cameras in every corner, motion triggered and wired into the alarm box over by the roll-away door. The cameras work in darkness and in light as well."

"Unless things have changed radically since I was last here," she said, "the local police will sleep through anything but a woman's invitation."

"The lock and hinges on the warehouse door couldn't be shot out," Farnsworth said, "though they could be drilled if you had a diamond tip and three hours. But the instant you touched the exterior openings to the warehouse, an alert goes to the ship. If you're here, you would be bloody well deafened by the alarms." He ducked his head. "I spend quite a few nights with my lady friend, whose house is about a hundred meters away. I'm hardly James Bond, but I do know which end of a pistol to hold."

"Thus the reason you insisted on that expensive speedboat so you could race around at all hours," Kate said.

"It costs less than a night guard would. Your brother approved it."

Holden spoke up when Kate still looked unhappy. "Looks like you're almost as secure here as the local bank."

"More, actually. The light goods go out by a bonded carrier tomorrow. I'll take them to the airplane personally. The heavy goods are just that. Too heavy for local thieves to bother with, and too distinctive to fence even if you could manage to steal them. AO has a whacking great reward posted for information resulting in the trial and punishment of any locals trafficking in England's sunken treasure." He turned to Holden. "Speaking of heavy goods, did you bring any?"

"Some bits and bobs," Holden said, pointing at the Volkswagen, which had been parked close to the rollaway door. "Cannonballs, anchor chain, shot, that sort of thing."

Farnsworth looked out at the truck in the steaming early-afternoon sun. "Now then, who can I enlist in assisting me in the unloading and conveyance of submarine treasures?"

Kate glanced sideways at Holden and smiled. "Tag, you're it. I've already signed the material over to you, and you've accepted. The designated weighty marine treasures are the property of the Crown, which means they're all yours."

Holden sighed at the thought of heavy lifting in the tropical sun. "All right then," he said to Farnsworth. "And while we work, you can explain to me how Man U is going to keep the Cup out of Arsenal's hands this year."

"It's quite clear that the superior ball-handling . . ." Farnsworth's voice faded as he and Holden disappeared outside, leaving Kate alone with the boxes of salvage from *Moon Rose*.

*Awful lot of boxes for stuff that is coming out of a so-so salvage dive,* she thought. *But what do I know? Grandpa was never much for preserving scraps of wood and broken crockery.*

*If this setup is any indication, it costs a lot to preserve history.*

She thought it was worth every penny, but she wasn't the one paying the bills.

" . . . and that's why they'll win," Farnsworth said, returning to put a cannonball and a box of lead shot on a processing table.

Despite his wiry frame, he must have had decent muscle, because he wasn't huffing or dumping the weight with relief.

Holden eased a big armload of metal chain onto the table, saying something that was buried in the clatter.

Two Vincentians came in a side door and walked to the long packing table. As they went to work, they talked in an island creole that was as soft on the ears as a sea breeze, except for the occasional, startling upper-crust British phrase. From what Kate could catch, their lunch had been almost as delectable as the woman who served it.

Kate's stomach growled.

"You may oversee the packing if you like," Farnsworth said, looking at his watch. "I have to stay anyway to enter their hours and lock up when they finish."

"Not necessary for me," she said, looking at Holden.

"Time for lunch," he agreed, turning away. Then, as they reached the rolling door, Holden called over his shoulder, "Call me instantly if any alarms go off."

Without looking up, Farnsworth nodded and waved.

"I heard the divers talking about the food at a local café," Holden said as they closed the doors to the battered truck. "It's only a kilometer from here, called the Dive In. Or would you like something fancier?"

"Go for dive food," she said instantly. "It's cheap, filling, and the portions are big enough that I won't have to cook dinner. We'll just eat the leftovers."

"What if the food is awful?"

"Then dinner will be, too."

He laughed as she put the truck in gear and followed his directions.

When they broke out of the forest, the sky was silver blue with heat, the breeze almost nonexistent. Flat-bottomed clouds drifted lazily, sending deep blue shadows over the water. The darker blue looked as cool as ice cream.

Though the area she drove to could most charitably be described as semi-industrial waterfront on the cheap, children shrieked with laughter as they played tag in the sand and debris or slipped like little seals into and through the warm water. Hearing them, she felt something in her relax. She remembered being that young, laughing and playing on the beach and jumping off the dive step of the *Golden Bough* in the shimmering heat of the doldrums. She had loved it, and no matter how her mother had hovered over her with sunscreen and broad hats, Kate still had some freckles to show for it.

Vincentians, mostly older men, but some young ones, sat in the shade of palms and other trees. Many were drinking from shared cans of beer or slicing bits of mango off with pocket knives. The end of the workday was close, though the lion's share of men had been off work for several days by the look of them. Or longer.

Employment didn't seem to be the most important goal of island life.

The Dive In was an outdoor affair, with a small, weathered cottage where the cook and the serious drinkers could keep their red eyes out of the sun. Even in the shade of the trees, it was sultry, especially when the indifferent breeze vanished. Banners of purple and yellow and orange threw colored shadows over the mismatched tables and chairs. There wasn't a female in sight, not uncommon for a dive bar during the day.

When the waitress appeared, she wasn't holding a pad and pencil, much less a portable electronic device. She recommended the spicy seafood chowder, told them what else the cook was serving today—mixed-meat stew and fish every which way but swimming—and took their drink orders. Kate asked for cold tea. So did Holden. The waitress walked away with a languid grace that Kate envied.

"Does it come with being born on a tropical island?" she asked after the waitress disappeared.

"What?" he asked.

"That walk."

He looked puzzled.

"The waitress," Kate explained. "Her walk is so graceful."

"Ah." He smiled. "The difference between sand and concrete, bare feet and tired feet. Island time, a lovely slow motion. You have it, you know. The longer you spend here, the more it shows."

"No way I walk like a panther."

Holden slipped his mirrored glasses up on his hair. "But you do. Makes me want to growl and pounce."

The multicolored crystal blaze of his eyes against his sun-darkened skin was like a caress.

She flushed and changed the subject. "Did you know that the red chowder you ordered comes with a wicked hot-pepper kick?"

His lips quirked. "I'm looking forward to it. To me, spice is like red hair, something that gives life a special fire."

"You're doing it on purpose."

"What?"

"Making me blush," she muttered.

"I find it charming."

"You wouldn't if you did it."

He laughed, picked up her hand, and kissed it—with a sneaky little lick thrown in.

"You're not acting at all the proper Brit," she said, pulling her fingers back. Slowly.

"If Brits were as proper as you seem to think, how would we ever reproduce?"

"Lie back and think of the Queen," Kate retorted.

Holden's rich, deep laughter drew smiles from the scattered diners. "I've never tried it that way. Would you care to demonstrate the technique?"

She gave up and gave in to the teasing, sensual side of Holden Cameron, letting her worries and fears and hopes dissolve as quickly as ice cubes on a tropical beach. She'd never met a man like him, one who intrigued and exasperated and charmed without giving up a whit of his intelligence and sheer animal presence.

The speed of service and size of the servings lived up to the diver's recommendations. Kate looked at the steaming heap of seasoned rice and black beans, fruit chutney, and a pile of reef fish that was as fresh as any she'd ever caught and cooked herself. She inhaled the steam rising from seasonings shy and bold, a whiff of cinnamon and bite of peppers, a cuisine that was both simple and a complex melding of flavors from many cultures and countries.

Her plate held enough for two, four if they weren't divers. Holden's platter was enough for a family of six and included a vat of seafood chowder. The waitress also left a bowl of fruit that must have weighed four pounds, a loaf of French bread, a pitcher of cold tea, and a smile as bright as the sun.

Holden waited until Kate took a bite before he all but dove into the chowder. He ate steadily, ignoring the sweat that began to leave a sheen on his forehead and upper lip. If his skin had been pale, it would have been flushed now.

"Spicy?" she asked innocently.

"Try some," he said, nudging the huge bowl into the middle of the table.

She took a spoonful, sniffed, and licked it clean. "Hoo doggies, that's hot."

"Are you certain?" he asked gravely as a drop of sweat ran down one cheek.

She dipped in again, lifted a heaping bite of crab and octopus, and chewed happily. She ate some rice and beans to soak up the heat, then went back to the soup even though she hadn't ordered it.

"The rest of the food will keep better than the soup," she explained, "and it's way too good to let go bad."

Holden looked amused as she ate steadily, ignoring the heat rising on her cheeks as her body reacted to the intensely spicy chowder. He scooted his chair closer to hers so that they could both easily reach the chowder and dug in. The level of the red broth and chunky seafood retreated down the bowl until they were both reduced to soaking up the last of the soup with the bread.

She sat back and flapped her loose blouse so air could circulate beneath. She knew her face was red and didn't care.

He wiped his forehead on a paper napkin, drained his glass of tea, and moved on to what the waitress had called a "mixed-meat" stew. He hadn't asked what kinds of meat and the waitress hadn't offered.

"How is it?" Kate asked between sips of tea to cool her mouth.

"Excellent. The goat, particularly. Beef is lean to the point of leather, but full of flavor. Some meat that could be snake or eel, hard to tell after hours of cooking."

"Snake? You're kidding."

He shrugged. "As I said, hard to tell."

"And you don't care."

"Protein is protein."

He glanced sideways and laughed at her look of horror. "Should I warn you that I have younger sisters and cousins, as well as an older brother?"

"And you're used to teasing them. I'm relieved." She started to ask if he really ate snake, then decided she didn't want to know. The stomach didn't care, but the mind flinched.

She forked up a bite of eel from the sauce on top of her fish and chewed happily, then looked at Holden as he laughed.

"What?" she asked.

"Do explain to me the difference between eel and snake."

"One I eat, one I don't."

Shaking his head, Holden ate the rest of the mixed-meat stew. Then he cleansed his palate with several tiny bananas with lime squeezed over them, drank another glass of tea, and went to work on rice, beans, and fish.

She watched from the corner of her eyes as she ate, wondering if there would be any leftovers. His manners were excellent, yet he went through food with a speed she associated with mess halls and stopwatches. After a few more minutes he leaned back in his chair, sipped at his third glass of cold tea, and smiled rather blissfully.

The waitress came by with another pitcher of tea and dark eyes that approved of Holden's appetite.

"Please tell the cook that the chowder is among the best I've ever had," Holden said.

"My grandmother will smile. The recipe is hers. My mother, she buys from only the best fishermen and divers."

Holden looked around the open air café. "Do a lot of divers eat here?"

The waitress smiled. "Yes. My father and brothers, they dive."

"Do you know of anyone looking for dive work?" Kate asked.

"They come, they go." The waitress shrugged. "Are you looking for a quick dive trip?"

"No," Kate said. "The *Golden Bough* is doing salvage work. We can always use more hands."

The instant the waitress heard the words *Golden Bough* she began shaking her head. "Divers talk. They don't like that boat. They say she is cursed."

# Chapter 11

The honking of a scooter shooing chickens from the road filled the silence that followed the woman's words.

*Cursed.*

"Utter rubbish," Holden said cheerfully. "There is nothing wrong with the ship but the pay scale."

"Of course," the waitress said with a polite smile. "The divers, they gossip like old women. Would you like more chowder?"

Holden looked at Kate.

"No, thank you," she said to the waitress. "But we would like the ticket and some boxes for leftovers."

The waitress nodded, retreated to the shabby kitchen, and returned with a handwritten bill and a plastic bag lumpy with boxes waiting to be filled with food. Holden paid the bill—adding a good tip—and helped Kate empty the contents of the plates into boxes. Carrying the plastic sack full of food in his left hand and snagging her hand with his right, he led her back to the side street where they had parked.

"I wonder which diver started that nasty rumor," Kate asked as she slid into the steamy cab of the pickup.

"If your brother kept a personnel roster, I'd have a go at the local dive bars and ask questions," Holden said. "Not that it would make any difference. Rumors are harder to pin down than smoke."

She frowned, not liking her brother's lack of interest in bookkeeping any better than the output of the local divers' rumor mill.

Holden touched her cheek. "Let it go. We're on holiday, remember?"

"We are?"

"Yes, we are. Even wage slaves get a day off now and then."

She blew out a breath and started the truck. Twice. The fact that it kicked over after only two tries made her feel better. She glanced over at Holden, who was touching his forehead experimentally.

"Headache?" she asked.

"No. I think it's numb from the chowder."

"Thank God. I thought I was the only one."

They drove in a peaceful silence to the rental where the metal workboat was tied to the sagging dock. The thought of going back to the dive ship didn't appeal.

The gleaming, pale shades of the protected water did.

"You know what I'm going to do?" she asked.

Holden watched her through half-open eyes, thinking of a lazy, horizontal kind of dancing.

"Swim," she said. Then she saw the expression on his face. "You don't like to swim?"

"It's my second favorite thing to do."

She noted the wicked gleam in his eyes and didn't take the bait. "I saw an extra sheet that would make a decent beach towel."

Indecent would have better suited his mood, but he didn't object. He just changed into faded black swim trunks, folded his khaki pants for a makeshift pillow, and met Kate at the front door.

She almost dropped the tube of sunscreen when she saw him. She had spent a lot of time trying not to remember how he had looked wearing only lamplight and tight briefs. He had been aroused then.

He was aroused now.

Heat shot through her. Her nipples tightened as her lower body loosened in ancient female preparation to take her mate. She knew he noticed the change. A flush burned along his cheekbones that had nothing to do with spicy lunch or the tropical sun.

"Are you sure you want to swim?" he asked in a gritty voice.

"I've always dreamed of playing in the water with a dragon." Her voice was low, husky, invitation and plea at once.

"Ah, the dragon again. I'm going to get jealous."

"Of yourself? Holden, you must know how sexy you are."

His lips curved in a gentle smile. "You're the only one who thinks so. But you never seem to notice when men look at you, tongues hanging out."

She laughed. "That's because it never happens. Even if it did, the only tongue I want hanging out for me is yours." She looked startled, put one hand over her eyes. "That came out wrong, didn't it?"

He was still grinning when she peeked him from between her fingers. He walked close and tugged at the tube of sunscreen she had clenched in one hand.

"We'll talk about it while I put sunscreen on the places you can't reach," he said.

"I'll have you know I'm quite limber."

He gave her a smoldering look. "You're tempting me."

"Just saying."

"Limber. Yes." He licked his lips. "Let me help you anyway. I promise I won't peel you out of that screaming green bikini."

*Yet.*

She turned around. "Have at it."

He all but groaned. The promise of her walk was fulfilled by her beautifully shaped rear. Perfect for his hands, his teeth, his tongue.

*Is she freckled beneath that hip-spanning strip of green? God, I hope so. Ginger and cream and then pink, so pink and simmering with sexual heat.*

She looked over his shoulder and saw him studying her butt. "Yes, I know it's too big, but that's the way it came."

Slowly, slowly, he met her eyes. "Too big? Love, it's perfect." He filled his hands and squeezed slowly, savoring the flex and lush heat of her flesh. "Bloody damn perfect."

He moved so close she couldn't help but feel the hard, thick ridge of his erection nestling in the seam of her rear. Her eyes widened. He moved once, slowly, and then released her.

In a silence that hummed with things unsaid, undone, anticipated, Holden put some mango-scented cream into one palm and rubbed his hands together. When he raised them, his khaki pants dropped softly to the floor.

"Lift your arms," he said.

"The sheet . . ."

"Let it go."

With a whispering sigh, the sheet slipped to the floor.

The flush on Holden's cheekbones darkened as he surveyed the graceful lines of her body. He raised his hands and began massaging sunscreen into her neck and shoulders, sliding his fingers down until they caressed the top of her bikini.

"I—" Her voice caught as he traced the swell of her breasts. "I can reach there."

"So can I."

She shuddered when his fingers pinched her nipples with sensuous care beneath the thin bikini material. When his hands moved away, she sighed.

"Too much?" he asked.

"And not enough."

He laughed softly and squeezed more sunscreen onto his palm.

She felt the warm rush of his breath and shivered. Her skin felt tight, hypersensitive, fully alive to the lightest touch. And that was what he did.

Touch her.

Lightly.

"You're going to drive me crazy," she whispered.

"Fair enough. You've already made me mental. Your freckles look tasty."

"The sunscreen isn't."

"That's all that is keeping me in check," he admitted.

He spread his big hands across her back, working in the cream, sliding beneath the bikini bottom and flexing, savoring her lush curves as he groaned almost soundlessly deep in his throat. Reluctantly he slid his fingers free, pressed out more sunscreen, and went on his knees to knead the cream into her thighs, her calves, her feet.

Eyes closed, she felt each touch as a smooth whip of warmth, a promise of the pure fire to come.

Dragons were very good with fire.

By the time he finished with her legs, they were trembling. He ran his palms from her ankles to her hips, flexed his long fingers, and then stood in a coordinated rush. Bunched sheet in one hand, sunscreen and pants in the other, he ran the knuckles of his right hand up the long, shallow crease of her spine.

"Ready for the sun," he said, his voice a sensuous rasp.

Kate was ready for a lot more than that, but she had just enough sense not to say it. "This will be my first time in the ocean since . . ."

"Your parents died?"

"Yes." Her voice was so faint that it was barely a whisper.

"I'll keep you safe."

She gave him a look from shadowed turquoise eyes. "I should have done this years ago. In some ways, I gave up as much as the sea took."

He shifted everything to his left hand and laced the fingers of his right hand through hers. "Let's take it back."

She led him out the door and down to a patch of dazzling white sand that was shaded by palm fronds shimmering in the uncertain wind. He shook out the sheet, put his pants and the sunscreen in one corner, and waited. She took a deep breath, let it out very slowly, and concentrated on how good he made her feel now rather than on the old fears of the past. Kicking off her sandals, she headed toward the water.

The sand was hot enough to make Kate hurry to the edge of the sea. The water itself was so warm she barely felt its first touch.

"I expect to hear my feet sizzle," Holden said from just behind her.

"The water will be cold farther out, where it turns to cobalt and drops steeply away from the volcano."

"Born of fire, yet surrounded by the sea," he said. "I've always been caught by the collision of opposites and by the delicate balance they achieve. Such an intricate, slow-motion dance."

"I never thought of it that way . . . but yes, it's a balance, a dance, and it changes every moment."

"Rather like us," he said, tucking a strand of red hair behind her ear. "Ocean and land simply live on a vastly different time scale than the two-legged mayflies known as humans."

Smiling, Kate curled her toes, enjoying the fine texture of the sand with every step. The shallow water was so clean it was virtually invisible and the air was the temperature of her skin. She felt suspended between sky and sea.

And the water was above her waist.

She waited to feel fear. She was still waiting when a swirl of tiny fish flashed around her ankles, like colorful confetti tossed in a wind. The tiny brush and nibble of their mouths tickled her toes and she laughed.

Motionless, Holden watched her, seeing what she must have been like before tragedy shadowed her turquoise eyes. He wanted nothing more than to lean into her and drink her laughter like golden wine.

As though she sensed his thoughts, she turned and held out her hand.

"You'll keep me from floating away when it gets deep," she said, closing her fingers around his.

"Whatever you want, Kate."

She saw that he meant every word and felt more fear dissolve away, fear she hadn't even known she had.

"I've always blamed the sea," she said after a few minutes. "Hated it."

"It's easier than blaming your parents for diving when they bloody well should have stayed on board," he said calmly.

Her fingers clenched. "How did you know?"

"It was rather well documented that they were diving at night with a tropical storm barreling down on them."

After a long time Kate's fingers unclenched. "Yes, hating the sea was easier than hating them for being so foolish, so *selfish,* choosing the gleam of gold over their own daughter." And then she made a broken sound. "And I'm selfish for wanting to be more important to them than anything else, including the wreck they had been looking for longer than I'd been alive."

"The *Moon Rose,*" Holden said.

"Yes."

She walked deeper, bringing him with her. Clumps of coral grew like shadows from the bottom, reaching toward the light. But not too far. Just enough to let the organisms living in some corals transform sunlight to food. Other corals combed the water with fragile, restless fingers, millions upon millions of tiny hands begging for crumbs of life.

"I wish I had my mask and fins and snorkel," she said softly.

He was close enough to hear. "Are they aboard the dive ship?"

"Yes, for all the good it would do. I haven't touched them in years. They're probably rotted by now."

"You'd be surprised."

"What do you mean?" she asked.

"First chance I had, I checked the dive locker. It's a quick way to size up a dive operation. If the gear isn't cared for, it's a bad operation. Period."

"Larry might suck at bookwork, but he's always had a magic touch with diving gear."

"He's thorough, too. I found a locker with 'Kitty' on it. The gear inside was as well kept as anything on the ship."

She stumbled, but Holden and the water held her upright.

"Grandpa," she said, tears standing in her eyes. "He always hoped I would come back."

Holden half smiled. "Your grandfather is a man of great stubbornness."

She made a sound that could have been a laugh or a sob. "And very thrifty, yet when my parents died, he took my father's rebreather and threw it overboard."

"That explains why I didn't find but one in the dive lockers. I thought it was because this site is relatively shallow."

"No. Grandpa won't have them aboard. Blames them for my parents' deaths."

"Why? All dive equipment has its own hazards." *And the biggest of them is the diver.*

"That's what Larry told Grandpa," she said. "It's the only time I remember them having an in-your-face shouting match. In the end, Larry kept his rebreather. Says he loves the silence and maneuverability."

Holden thought of the many times he'd used a rebreather at night in places where a trail of bubbles was an invitation to get strafed by enemies on the surface. The fact that a rebreather allowed extended dives with much less time in decompression was a bonus.

A fish shot by, pursuing other fish. Unlike the rounded, colorful reef grazers, the bigger fish was streamlined, ghostly silver blue, and wicked fast.

As Kate turned to watch the racing ghost, she realized that she was up to her breasts in water. It was cooler now that she was out of the extreme shallows where sunlight heated water to the temperature of blood. If she took a few more steps, she would be swimming.

So she did.

She didn't know what she had expected, but it wasn't the sudden exhilaration that shot through her as the water accepted her with forgotten ease. A sleek, delicious feeling of freedom swept over her. She turned onto her back and laughed like a child rocked in loving arms.

"I've missed this," she said, seeing Holden's wide smile. "I didn't even know. How could I not know?"

"The sea is what you make of it. Like life. The child in you made the sea evil. The adult always knew better."

He could have kept wading. Instead, he turned onto his side, kicking alongside her with a lazy strength that radiated his ease in the water.

"I can't believe you had trouble getting back into the water after you were injured," she said, watching him.

Wanting him.

"Believe it," he said. "I came close to vomiting."

"Were you in scuba gear?"

"That's what kept me swallowing hard," he said wryly.

Her laughter rose above the lagoon like another kind of sunlight.

Holden paused in midkick, realizing he had never known the kind of peace he felt watching her languid glide through the water.

*She was born for this,* he thought, *not for business suits and spreadsheets and fear.*

Watching her, he could almost forgive her brother for making such a cock-up of the dive that he'd been forced to call his baby sister to save the family business, which was sinking like a ship with open seacocks. Not that Holden's people had helped; the contract was shameful on the face of it.

*That's why I'd make a lousy businessman,* he thought, keeping pace with Kate. *Taking advantage of desperate people so that I can advance and enrich myself . . . I'd rather deal with live mines.*

And he had.

Kicking easily, he shifted to a breaststroke, then to a backstroke.

"Does this hurt your thigh?" Kate asked.

"Not at all. It's far more congenial than the heavily chlorinated pool I used for my physio."

She made a face. She hated pools and chlorine, but that kind of swimming was better than nothing.

"I know I asked you before," she said, "but do you miss diving?"

"I dive, love. It's part of my work. What about you?"

For a time there was only the cry of birds and the rush of the sea foaming over a reef of rocks and coral farther out.

"I miss it," she said finally, "but I'm not ready to dive. Not yet. Maybe not ever. I don't know. There's nothing down there I can't live without."

Holden didn't try to coax or wheedle or shame her into diving. He just followed her through the protected water, occasionally diving down when something on the bottom caught his interest, mostly staying close enough to touch her. Sometimes he swam beneath her, stroking her with his body, teasing both of them, sharing his sensual pleasure in being with her in the water.

Kate's breath shortened the third time he caressed her chest to chest, body to body. He was aroused again and so was she. She went beneath the surface and returned the gliding caress, lingering against him until she ran out of breath.

"Can you stand on the bottom?" she asked, breathless from more than swimming underwater.

"If you're tired, I can just tow you in."

"Not that. I wanted to kiss you without worrying about drowning."

His eyes changed, focusing on her lips with crystal intensity. "Come closer. I'll keep you above water."

Even as she reached for him, he drew her in. His skin was smooth except for the hair that slicked over his chest. As he stood, his muscles flexed and bunched beneath bronze skin. Drops of water clung like a net of diamonds that shifted with every breath he took.

Then his arms closed around her and all she knew was the heat and textures of his kiss. He was spice and fire, salt and sweet, rough and slick and alive, so alive. She wanted to consume him, to crawl inside his skin and know him, flesh and blood and heat.

The soft whimpers she made were whips of fire on his hungry body. He took what she offered and demanded more, then more again, until there was nothing between them but need and more need, primal fire consuming them.

Vaguely Kate sensed motion, water sliding away.

"Put those beautiful legs around me," Holden said roughly against her mouth.

Large, strong hands wrapped around her buttocks, lifting her. A single, heart-stopping rub over the length of his cock told them both just how good it would be. She locked her ankles around his waist and her arms around his neck, kissing his shoulder and neck as though afraid that something would tear them apart.

He dipped his head, ran his teeth over the curve of her neck, and bit her with exquisite care. She cried out, a husky female sound of approval, and he sucked hard, making her buck against him, clawing to be closer than skin.

Lifting his head, he saw the flushed circle that still held red dents from his teeth. "Your skin marks so easily, I'll have to take more care."

Her answer was a bite over his heart that was just short of fierce, then the gentle scrape of teeth over his nipple. She licked him slowly, circling, before she caught the dark nubbin of his nipple and sucked hard. His muscles locked and he shuddered.

"Enough, love," he said almost roughly. "I have to get us to shore."

"Why?"

"Condom."

"Oh."

Her eyes opened slowly, a smoldering kind of turquoise. She sighed and lifted her lips, snuggled against his biceps.

"I want to taste you," she said, licking his taut skin. "Everywhere. I've never wanted that before. Never needed."

Holden was sure his heart stopped. Then it kicked and began pumping like he was racing a wildfire. Except he wasn't running away. He was running toward the flaming center so he could burn within it.

Within her.

The sea clung to them as though reluctant to release them to the shore.

Kate licked drops of salt water from every bit of Holden's skin she could reach. She loved the heat, the taste, the supple feel of his skin on his neck and the rougher skin of his jaw shadowed by the beard lying just beneath.

Everything spun and she felt the sheet touch her back from nape to hips and then her legs as she unlocked her ankles. Moments later her bikini was a pile of emerald by his khaki pants. His swim shorts appeared next to them.

Naked, he knelt between her legs and looked, simply looked at her stretched out beneath him. Her skin was luminous pearl dusted with tiny flecks of gold.

And she was a redhead everywhere.

"Your eyes," she whispered. "So beautiful. Dragon."

She reached for the proud male flesh jutting toward her, only to have him catch her hands and put them next to her head. He stilled her murmur of complaint with a soft kiss.

"My turn," he said. "I've been wanting to do this since the first time I saw you."

Before she could ask what he meant, she felt the tip of his tongue touch the freckles across her nose, cheekbones, the top of her shoulders, the slope of her breasts.

"Freckles," she said breathlessly.

"My weakness," he said. "They appear in such tasty places."

His mouth roved up one arm, nibbled on tender flecks of color, then down the other.

"Tickles," she said.

"Suffer. I have."

She laughed, then gasped when his lips roved over the curves of one breast, then the other, never touching either sensitive tip. Her nipples pouted.

"You're missing some," she said, her voice husky.

"Really? Show me."

He saw the flush that rose from her breasts to her forehead. Slowly she lowered one hand and touched her left nipple. "Here." Her fingers moved to the right. "And . . . here."

Holden lowered his head until his breath rushed over one stiffened nipple, making it harder still. He sucked it into his mouth with slow deliberation, tasting and enjoying each ridge and seam, sucking, pulling until her hips began writhing against him. He pinned her in place with his lower body, sweating with the force of his own need.

"Not finished yet," he managed finally.

"Save some for dessert."

He laughed and felt the tension within him both ease and increase. The urgency was still there, still clawing deep, yet he was held in check by the velvet ropes of her humor. He had had his share of sex, but he'd never wanted to play with a woman, to share laughter as well as passion.

"You're going to be trouble," he said, turning to her neglected nipple.

Whatever she had intended to say escaped as a needy cry when his mouth closed on her again, tongue rubbing, teeth just edgy enough to provide a balance to the rushing pleasure. By the time he released her, she didn't have enough breath to argue.

Then he began kissing the freckles below her breasts, lingering, licking, nipping. His shadow beard was just rough enough to give contrast to his lips as he drifted lower and lower until suddenly she came off the sheet with a gasp.

"No freckles—there!"

"You sure?" he asked.

Then he sucked her clitoris between his teeth, rubbed it with his tongue, and felt her come apart. He gentled his touch, bringing her down even as his own need twisted into burning wires of hunger. Slowly, slowly, he licked her, nuzzled her, told her without words that she was beautiful to him.

"Dessert was exquisite," he said, reaching for a condom in his pants pocket. "Now I'm ready for the main course."

Through half-closed eyes she watched him put on the condom. "Next time I get to do that."

"What?" he asked.

"Everything. I want . . ." Her voice unraveled when she felt him rocking into her, stretching her, filling her until all she could do was give and give and give until she had taken all of him.

She moved her hips in slow counterpart to his sexual dance, feeling both ravished and ravishing, until her breath was short and she felt his whole body tighten, rocking, pulsing deep within until she could take no more and came undone in her own shimmering rings of ecstasy. His body suddenly went slack over her, yet he held back enough of his weight that she could breathe.

"Don't move," Kate said, holding him.

"Not planning to," he managed.

They held each other until their breath became the slow rhythm of an ocean's measured caresses along the shore. And then they still held on, because peace was a bond as deep and as ancient as fire.

# Chapter 12

Kate toweled her hair dry and looked into the cloudy mirror nailed just above the wash basin. Her eyes looked back at her, turbulence and peace and wonder.

*Does he feel this way?*

She almost laughed at her own naive question. Holden was a man. All man. He enjoyed sex and made sure his partner did, too. A generous lover.

*Savor it,* she told herself, *for as long as it lasts.*

And that would be until her newly acquired lover destroyed an old family business.

*One more thing I can't control.*

"You're frowning," Holden said from the doorway to the tiny bathroom, deciding she looked edible in her sleeveless tank top and shorts. He hoped to get her quite naked. Soon. "'Let the lover be disgraceful, crazy, absentminded,'" he said in his deep voice. "'Someone sober will worry about things going badly. Let the lover be.'"

The words shimmered in the red of the dying sun.

"Beautiful," she said. *Like you.*

"Rumi has kept me company on many a long night's watch."

"Rumi?"

"A Sufi mystic and poet." Holden took the towel from her and began to gently rub water from her hair. "Rumi was also Pashtun, from what we'd call Afghanistan now."

She met Holden's eyes in the mirror and felt her heart take a slow, lazy spin. He wore only dark shorts. The rest was a breath-shortening expanse of golden brown skin tight over shifting muscles. She knew she should pull back, keep more of herself aloof, not chance the kind of pain she had felt at seventeen when the world had shattered and re-formed in nightmare.

*I'm not seventeen anymore. I'm not terrified of darkness and storm and being alone. I'm not running away from something that is always in front of me no matter where I turn.*

"'Let the lover be,'" she repeated softly. "Do you think the world will?"

He smiled almost sadly. "Doubtful. That's why you take what you can get for as long as you can keep it."

"It won't be long, will it?"

"That depends on the lovers." He set aside the towel. "It was very, very good with you. I want more. Do you?"

Memories shivered over her. "Yes."

The faint growl of his stomach in the silence made her smile.

"Then let's fuel the machine," he said, nipping lightly at her neck, "so it can run at full throttle again."

While she made tea, he warmed up beans and rice. As he arranged fruit on a chipped plate, he asked, "Do you want the fish warmed?"

"Just put it on top of my rice and beans," she said. "That should take the chill off it without giving it that cooked-too-much taste. Sweet tea or plain?"

"I'll take sweet. I seem to be in need of calories, as if I've been diving."

"Skin diving," she said without thinking. Then she flushed as her words echoed in her mind.

He laughed softly and touched her hot cheek. "That I have. Some of the best work I've ever done, by the way, thanks to my thoughtful, thorough dive partner."

She stirred sugar into the tea until her cheeks no longer felt hot.

They ate quietly, finishing off the leftovers and lingering over the fruit. Both of them accepted silence with the ease of people who didn't need to talk in order to feel alive.

Finally she stood, stretched, and said, "I have to put in some time on the computer. Did Farnsworth leave anything on your phone?"

"Such as?"

"Whether the generator is running yet."

Holden pulled his phone out of his cargo pants and pushed buttons. "Nothing about the generator. The light valuable goods shipped out a few hours ago. The new diver quit. He decided one day's pay was enough to stay drunk for two or three. Your grandfather took the *Golden Bough* in to refuel, offload the unwilling diver, buy more cylinders for the dive mix, and secure a part for the generator. He'll be anchored back on the dive site by now."

"I bet Larry is headed for the dive bars or is already there," Kate said, "trying to talk someone into working rather than drinking."

"It won't be easy, especially if word is out that the dive is cursed. Divers are a superstitious lot."

She just shook her head. "Larry can't seem to catch a break. At least Mingo and Luis are reliable."

"How long have they been diving for Moon Rose Limited?"

"Let me check." She got her computer and cleared a place for it at the little bar. Eyes narrowed, she scanned what work logs she had been able to put together. "They came on after the wreck was cleared of most of the overburden, so they've been here longer than any other diver but Larry."

"Which makes them prime suspects in any theft." *After Larry.*

Her head snapped up. "Why?"

"They've been working the wreck from the moment the heavy lifting was done. They've kept at it despite rumors of a cursed dive. They could even be the ones who started the rumors just to keep away the competition."

"I know Volkert's a pig and can't be counted on for much more than his next meal, but the digital files don't show anything suspicious about any of the divers."

"Files can be doctored," Holden said calmly. "Sand and silt can be 'accidentally' kicked up, obscuring the view while the divers stash some small goods for retrieval after the dive is shut down. Really small goods can be smuggled ashore."

"How?"

"I check the dive gear, but not body cavities." He laughed. "The look on your face . . . Be grateful you're not worrying about diamond miners in South Africa. Man is an extremely clever monkey."

She started to say something, then simply shook her head. "Even if the divers are stuffing things up and down their wazoos, we have no way of proving it. In fact, unless you catch someone with the goods, there's no proof at all."

"Yes."

"Then even if no one is stealing, you can't prove that, either. But you can ruin Moon Rose Limited by simply saying that someone must be stealing, because not much has been recovered from what is historically believed to be a rich wreck."

"Yes," Holden said. *And Chatham is just the sort of prick who would do that. Far better to tar the Donnelly family than to get tarred himself for paying out good money to dive a dry wreck.*

"We were screwed from the day Larry signed the contract," she said.

*We,* Holden thought. *After all these years away from it, she still identifies with the family business. Will I have a chance to convince her there could be an us before this whole bloody mess blows up?*

"Now who's frowning?" she asked.

"Was I?" He stood up and began methodically cleaning the dishes. "Must be all the spicy food. As for the rest, yes, it's difficult to see any way for Larry to come out on the winning side of this game. I'm sorry, Kate."

"It's not your fault."

The curve of his mouth was too unhappy to be called a smile. "That's very adult of you. In truth, I'm both messenger and executioner. That would be hard for even an adult to accept."

"You can't know that for sure. There's still time to dive, to find enough to please a reasonable man, enough to save Larry's reputation."

Holden didn't want to be the one to quench the hope in her eyes by pointing out that possible and probable rarely had a bridge between them. "I hope you're right."

"You mean that, don't you?"

"Yes."

Relief made her a bit light-headed. She hadn't known until that moment how much it meant to her that he was pulling for the dive's success.

"Such a beautiful smile," he said, coming over to her. "Thank you for believing me. I doubt that your brother would. Your grandfather certainly doesn't."

"They're . . . frightened."

"They have reason to be."

She closed her eyes for an instant. "That's why I trust you. You don't avoid the hard truths or try to pretty them up."

Holden gave her a long look. "Most people would dislike me for those very things."

"I've spent too much of my life hiding from the truth of death. My parents died. I tried to save them. I failed. And then I ran."

"Love," he said softly, tracing the line of one cheekbone, "you were a child. Even if you had been an adult, you couldn't have changed anything. Very likely something went wrong with your mother's rebreather. She blacked out, lost the mouthpiece, and breathed water. Your father couldn't get her to the surface in time to save her, but gave himself a fatal case of the bends trying. It's a miracle you got him into the workboat at all. I've seen men convulse hard enough to pull muscle from bone."

Tears stood in her eyes but she said nothing.

"Even if you had had a bariatric chamber aboard the *Golden Bough*," Holden said, each word gentle, relentless, "you couldn't have got him aboard in stormy seas alone and it would have been too late in any case. Air bubbles in the heart are quite fatal."

A tear slid down her cheek and caught at the corner of her mouth. He bent, sipped at her lips, and rested his forehead against hers.

"You did as much as any trained man of twice your weight and four times your strength could have done," he said. "It rips at me knowing you think you failed when you never had the least chance of succeeding. It tears at me listening to you pace the room when your dreams won't give you peace."

"How did you know?" she whispered.

"Post-traumatic stress is a fact of life in war zones. It exists in civilian life, too, for all that we ignore it. You went through bloody hell the night your parents died. You're still going through it. At least let me sleep by your side so you'll know you aren't alone when you awake in a panic."

"You make me sound like a child seeking comfort for nightmares."

"In nightmares, we're all children."

She looked into the shifting colors of his eyes, more gold than green or blue in the lamplight, except for the stark indigo ring separating white from changeable crystal. And within those magnificent dragon eyes, the certainty of nightmare lurked.

Hers were not the only haunted dreams.

She couldn't change the past, couldn't lift the burden of failure from her brother's shoulders, couldn't save her grandfather from change or age; but she could have a few more hours of being fully alive in this incredible man's arms. She could pull something from the wreckage of hopes, salvage something of value from the depths of nightmare and black water.

"Yes," she breathed against his lips. "Sleep next to me."

She took his hand and led him toward her room. The bed was narrow, sheets pulled up, a light blanket folded at the foot. The tropical night was unrelieved by moonlight and the encroaching greenery closed out all but a few stars.

"It doesn't have to be more than tonight," Kate whispered, as much to herself as to Holden. "But I have to have tonight."

He came down onto the bed with her, lying on his side facing her, bringing with him the scent of salt and life and man.

She leaned into him and inhaled deeply. "This is what I've missed and never knew it," she said, pressing her lips against his neck. "How could I? I'd never met you. Fill me so I won't miss you when you're gone."

He whispered her name, almost afraid to breathe, to shift the moment from the now when she was his to the uncertain future. His calloused fingertips traced her eyebrows, her cheekbones, her lips.

She tasted his fingertips and murmured her pleasure, touching him in turn. His body was taut, hot, almost violent with life, and she wanted him all the way to her soul.

They didn't know when they began kissing. There was no past, no future, only now and a need that was greater for having been fully satisfied. Now they knew what awaited. Now they wanted even more. Tongues and lips blended, breaths quickened, pulses beat in ancient rhythms of passion, and fire consumed.

His hands were sweet and heavy on her shoulders and the curve of her back, fingers sliding down to catch the hem of her shirt.

As much as she wanted his hands on her bare skin, she stopped him. "You first."

She pressed her body against his as she moved her hands down, savoring the flex and shift of muscles tight beneath his skin. He waited for her to open his shorts and find out how much he wanted her. She tugged at the waist of his khaki shorts, but her fingers weren't responding to her mind, only to her need to soak in the heat of his skin and the texture of the tight line of hair sinking beneath his shorts.

"You sure you want me to go first?" he asked roughly as she stroked him.

"I like the feel of you. And I want . . . I need to see you, too." She reached across him for the light on her bedside table, but all her fingers could reach was the flashlight she always kept in case the electricity failed.

"May I help?" he asked when it remained dark, and his hands were sliding up her waist and beneath her scrap of T-shirt.

When his fingertips pinched her nipples, she gasped and arched against him. The beam of the flashlight made jagged patterns on the ceiling.

"You're cheating," she said breathlessly.

"Am I? Show me."

A cone of light slid down the wall and centered on her breasts as he caressed them. Her nipples were poking up between his fingers. He felt the heat of her blush flare beneath his hands and she started to move the flashlight.

"Keep it there," he said, his voice thick with the beating of his blood.

Slowly he eased her pale T-shirt up until one breast was revealed. Even the harsh light couldn't pale the rose of her nipple or the life of the creamy flesh that quivered, waiting for his touch.

"Holden . . ."

His tongue touched the pouting pink invitation of her nipple. The sight of the caress spotlighted made her hand shake, and with it the flashlight. His eyes burned in the reflected light, watching her heartbeat quiver through her breast. Then he lowered his head and took the stiffened nipple into his mouth and sucked. Heat snaked through her at the sight of his beard-shadowed cheeks hollowed out with the force of his caress.

Part of Kate felt that she should be embarrassed by the stark sexuality of seeing him suckle, of watching his fingers slide beneath her twisted shirt and stalk her other nipple, fingertips pressing and plucking until her whole breast stood up and begged for him.

"Beautiful," he said, nipping, playing, his fingers dark against her skin.

His other hand guided the flashlight clenched in her palm, stroking her with light and shadow.

"Take off your shorts," she said.

"Let me hold the flashlight."

"Not a chance." Her voice was husky, determined. "It's my turn to give orders."

His teeth gleamed in the reflected light as he stood and stripped. He kicked his clothes aside and stood next to the bed, hands on hips to keep from reaching for her, waiting to see what his sexy, unpredictable lover would do next.

She made a humming sound of pleasure as the cone of light traced his shoulders, his chest, the midnight hair leading to and surrounding his naked, proud flesh and the tightly drawn globes beneath.

"I know men aren't supposed to be beautiful," she said in a whispery voice, "but you are."

She watched the jerk of his erection and the gleaming pearl that appeared at its broad head. Slowly she leaned forward, holding the flashlight steady until she tasted him, salt and musk and man, the taste of life on her tongue. The flashlight slipped from her fingers. She had found something much more satisfying to hold.

Holden saw the light jerk and caught it before it left her hand. He would have set the flashlight aside, but the sight of her tasting him, licking his violently sensitive flesh, then taking it into her hot mouth was too beautiful to give up. He hissed through his teeth and fought not to come.

She tasted what escaped his control and hummed again, enjoying him.

Sweat broke over him from forehead to feet. He could feel the orgasm gathering at the base of his spine. Slowly, slowly, he freed himself from the sweet suction, ignoring her murmured complaint.

"But I like your taste," she said.

"I can tell. You're killing me, love."

She kissed the glistening head. "I'll be gentle, I promise."

"I won't be."

As he bent and twisted toward his shorts, the light clicked off. There was a soft thud as the flashlight rolled away.

"Hey, that's mine," she said.

"Don't worry, you'll get everything you have coming," he said, rolling on the condom by touch.

"But—" she began, then words turned into a squeak when she felt her shorts and underwear whipping down her legs.

She moaned and rolled her hips as two long fingers tested her readiness.

"Ah, you liked playing," he said, both hunger and satisfaction resonant in his deep voice. She was hot and slick around him, squeezing his fingers in deep reflex, needing more. "Next time, I won't throw away the flashlight. You'll glisten and weep so sweetly. All that beautiful pink flesh so wet for me. I'd like to bury my tongue in you, but you have me so primed I'll be lucky to last past the first stroke."

She opened her knees wider. "Now, Holden. *Now.*"

"Or what?" he teased.

"I'll—" Her voice became a soft keening as her body convulsed around his fingers.

He spread her wide and pushed through her orgasm, stroking her even higher. She writhed and cried and clenched around him, taking him deep, milking him with her body until his muscles corded and he slammed home, shuddering and groaning her name, giving himself to her until he had nothing left, not even breath.

It was a long time before either of them could move. Or wanted to.

Finally he lifted his head. "Want to shower again?"

She gave a mumble that he took as no. Then she definitely complained when he pulled out of her.

He slipped through her hands, kissing her fingers as he withdrew.

"Hush, love. I'll be back before you're asleep."

She made a grumpy sound and settled deeper into the rumpled sheets. When he returned moments later, he pulled the sheet over them, settled her against his body, and both of them fell headlong into sleep.

# Chapter 13

Kate came awake to the persistent ringing of her cell phone. The sounds traveling through the thin walls told her that Holden was showering. It was still dark out, though the birds were yammering in the trees, announcing that the sun would soon be along. She turned on the table light before she fumbled among the clothing tossed carelessly around the room. She smiled, remembering how it had been last night.

"Hello," she said, finding and answering the phone in the same motion.

"I know it's early," Larry said. "Wanted to catch you before you came to the dive site."

She yawned. "I'm caught. What's up?"

"I need you to go to the fuel dock and check to see if the other tender is there. If it isn't in the marina, rent another one for a few days."

"Why do—" She stopped, realizing that she was holding a dead phone.

Larry had hung up.

"Something wrong?" Holden asked from the doorway.

He was fully dressed and he still looked good enough to eat. Memories of yesterday blazed through her in a rush of blood.

"I don't know," she said. "Larry wants me to check the marina for the *Golden Bough*'s other tender. If it's not there, I'm supposed to rent another."

"What happened to the first tender?"

She shook her head. "Another thing I don't know. Larry just gave me marching orders and hung up."

"Odd."

"Very," she said, shrugging. "But he never took pressure well, except when he was underwater. Lately he has been so tired and scattered I don't think he should even be diving." *Or drinking.* But that was something she didn't want to talk about.

Holden asked softly, "Does he have a real choice?"

She bit her lip. "No, not if the business is going to survive. While I take a fast shower, will you raid enough fruit and bread for us to eat breakfast on the way to town?"

"For a kiss."

"If I kiss you, Larry will be waiting until noon. You're addictive."

Smiling, Holden went to scrounge breakfast. When Kate hurried out of the shower, he was waiting by the front door with his customary duffel and a bag of food. Very quickly they were in the workboat and rounding the head to the harbor where dive bars, cafés, and fuel docks waited like old friends. Very old. From the water it looked like all the buildings were leaning against each other.

After half an hour spent cruising various places where the tender could have been left, Kate decided that renting another boat was a better use of their time. The only one available was a workboat just slightly smaller than the one that had mysteriously disappeared. Holden helped her rig a bridle to tow the rental before they headed at reduced speed for the dive site.

As the *Golden Bough* solidified on the horizon, Kate could no longer ignore the cold knot strangling her throat. She didn't know what was wrong, but she knew something was. Even if Grandpa had an extra nightcap or two and Larry was cross-eyed tired, the Donnellys just didn't misplace large equipment.

No one appeared when she brought the two boats alongside the larger ship. Holden took his duffel and a line and went aboard.

"Larry?" Kate called. "Grandpa?"

One of the Spanish brothers shambled over from the galley side as Holden tied off the workboats. Luis looked like a man who had taken an unexpected blow and was still trying to understand why. He noted the rental behind one of the *Golden Bough*'s tenders and looked even more confused.

"Wasn't Mingo ashore? Did you see him?" Luis asked.

"We don't know where Mingo is," Holden said. He called to Kate. "Bring both keys with you."

She hesitated, then went against family practice and took the key from the ignition. The key to the rental was already in her pocket.

Muffled yells came from the front of the ship, hammering through the glass and steel of the galley.

"Where is everyone? Where's your brother?" Kate asked, coming quickly aboard.

He shook his head sadly. "Mingo, he left."

"Left? Why?"

Luis shrugged. "Dive is cursed. He took his gear and the first tender. He went to town. Wish he take me."

"When did this happen?" Holden asked, stepping close enough to test the other man's scent for alcohol. Nothing fresh. Luis might have passed out in his bunk last night, but he was sober enough now.

"I was sleeping," Luis said.

"It sounds like Mingo was planning on a solo," Holden said. *Or drunk.* "Why else take a dive rig and a boat unless you're going diving alone?"

Luis shook his head. "Maybe Larry knows, but he was sleeping. So was the old man."

"Does Mingo make a habit of diving alone or taking off in the middle of a dive?" Holden asked Luis.

"Mingo, he does what he want. Guess he want to play with the ladies. Maybe I take the extra boat ashore and go have fun."

"No one is going anywhere until we get to the bottom of this," Holden said. "The keys aren't in the ignition on either of the tenders, so unless you want to swim some kilometers, you're staying."

The other man looked stubborn. "You go ashore, I go."

"We'll talk about it when we know more," Holden said.

Kate left Luis to Holden. The sounds from the bow of the boat were getting louder. Too loud. She turned and hurried toward the shouting. She sensed Holden behind her, but didn't slow down. Larry almost never argued with his grandfather, but it sounded like that was exactly what was happening.

The door to the main cabin was open. Inside, two Donnellys glared at one another.

"I told you Mingo was trouble!" Grandpa Donnelly yelled, putting a rasp on every syllable.

Larry was slumped at the table, elbows on knees, head propped up on his palms. His customary Atlanta Braves cap was off, dangling from one hand like a dirty flag at half-mast.

"He'll be back," Larry said wearily. "He always comes back. I've told you that every time he goes AWOL."

"You don't hire shirkers!" Grandpa shouted. "Even if they're the best divers when they show up, they end up making more work for everyone else."

"I'm not worried about him so much as I am the others, especially Raul," Larry said, his voice hoarse from yelling.

"Not worried? About your lead diver?" Grandpa said. "Sonny, we can have an army up here and without at least two divers down there, you can kiss your personal playpen good-bye." He swept his hands about, indicating the whole of the ship. "That's all this has ever been to you—play!"

Holden watched as Kate stepped between her grandfather and brother.

"Grandpa," she said calmly, "what happened? Luis told me a little, but it didn't make any sense."

"That son of a bitch Mingo snuck off in the middle of the night. Nobody knew it until we saw the tender was missing. If he's put one scratch on it, I'll shove my boot so far up his ass he'll be chewing leather."

"From what I saw of the roster yesterday," she said carefully, "we still have three divers aboard, plus Larry."

Grandpa said something that she chose not to hear. He glared at her for a long moment, then looked out the window toward that storm that would neither break nor go away.

"We have Luis and me," Larry said into the silence. "Malcolm took the others ashore in his speedboat when they refused to get in the water this morning. They said the whole dive was—"

"Cursed," Holden cut in. "We heard it in town. Rubbish, but people love to talk rubbish. Did Mingo own the diving gear he took?"

"Most of it." Larry rubbed his eyes. "Half of the wrist dive computer was ours. He was working it off for part of his pay. The cylinder was ours, but so what? He'll be back when he runs out of cash. It's not like this is unusual," he added, giving a sideways glance at his grandfather. "He dives for thirteen, fourteen days and then he gets itchy for a woman and some nonstop drinking."

"Then why did you hire the lazy bastard?" Grandpa demanded.

"Because he would work for us," Larry said through clenched teeth. "Shit wages and bonuses paid out of pocket change aren't much of a lure."

"Did the other divers quit or are they just hitting the bars in town?" Kate asked Larry.

Her brother shrugged. "Three divers quit outright. The fourth one, Raul, insisted on going and finding Mingo. What was I supposed to do, knock them out and tie them up?"

Through the open galley door, wind gusted off the water, thick with moisture and surprisingly cool. That, and the gnawing ache in Holden's thigh, told him the pressure was taking a downward turn. It wasn't a guarantee the storm system had finally gained enough energy to be a problem, but the increased ache wasn't good news, either.

"The point is that you have only two divers aboard and deteriorating weather," Holden said. "Is there anyone on rotation ashore you can call?"

Larry shook his head.

"Right," Holden said. "We need divers."

Kate wondered if she was the only one who noticed that Holden had said *we*.

"Have you checked the weather recently?" Larry asked. "Sometimes the Venezuela forecasts are more accurate for us than the British version."

Grandpa muttered something about looking through a window and making up his own goddamn mind.

Holden said, "I checked both before we came aboard."

"And?"

"The weather is still there. We're still here."

Larry smiled tiredly. "Okay. I'll get Luis and go suit up."

"Luis is riding a hangover," Holden said.

"So what else is new? The only perk I have to offer is that I allow alcohol on board. All I care is that the divers show up in shape to dive. If they've got a headache and bad stomach, it's their damn problem."

Holden's black eyebrows arched up. He had figured out that alcohol was aboard the first day. At first he had assumed it was limited to the Donnelly men—captain's privilege and all that—but the crew quarters stank of alcohol and soiled laundry. There was a watermaker aboard ship, but no laundry facilities.

"When will Farnsworth be back?" Holden asked.

"Who gives a damn? He's not a diver," Grandpa said without turning around.

Kate ignored him and talked to Holden. "I know the routine. I can rake the barrel and bag and tag anything we bring up with the siphon."

A stream of curses in Spanish and English and creole poured through the galley door. Kate reached the opening first and looked out. Luis was bent over the gunwale, cradling his left hand.

"What happened?" she called to him.

She made out enough of his answer to wonder if the dive was truly cursed, or if Luis had just found a quick way to go ashore to see a medic.

Larry had heard enough, too. He shook his head. "Clumsy bastard."

Grandpa snorted and poked his head out the door and started for the dive deck, his voice fading as he moved. "Get some antiseptic from the cook, wrap it up, and quit whining. It's just a cut."

Luis cussed and demanded a medic for stitches.

Grandpa cussed him back and offered to stitch it himself. With a gaff.

Kate watched while the men argued in low voices as the cut was examined. Blood dripped onto the deck. Then Grandpa hollered for the cook and came back upstairs.

Larry waited like a man who already knew lousy news was coming.

"How bad?" Kate asked.

"To the bone," Grandpa said angrily. "Sheathing his own damn diving knife and he cut himself. He won't let me stitch it."

"Are you a surgeon?" Holden asked.

"It's meat, not major blood vessels," Grandpa said. "I've stitched worse on myself."

"Hell," Larry said, and blew out a long breath. "It doesn't matter. Kate can take him to a medic. I can handle the siphon alone down below and Grandpa can rake up on board."

"No," she said instantly. "Diving solo is too dangerous. Our insurance specifically forbids it."

"Are you offering to make it safer and dive with him?" Grandpa asked quickly, something close to satisfaction in his voice.

"No." She looked over at her grandfather. "I won't dive. You know that." Her voice was cold rather than panicked.

"But—" he began.

"*No.*"

"It's like riding a bicycle," Grandpa said.

"What, it only hurts when you fall off? I already fell off that bike." *Sometimes I'm still falling.* "I am not going to get in the water. Not even for you."

There was a sheen of tears in her eyes, but no weakness. She was on fire at that moment, as fierce and determined as she had been the night when she'd pulled her father out of the water.

"Then do it for David," Grandpa said. "And for Mary Katherine."

The names of her parents were rarely spoken aboard the *Golden Bough*. They seemed to echo in the room, louder than wind or seabirds or the grumble of the repaired generator.

Past and present flip-flopped and she was yanking at her father's body, trying to get him into the work-boat as he convulsed and blood frothed at his mouth and a terrible knowledge chilled her.

*Dying. Her father was dying.*

Then she took a breath and looked at the echo of her father in her brother, in her grandfather.

"How could you?" she asked through pale lips.

"Did you ever stop to think that I lost my only child that day, Kitty?"

*Don't let him do it,* Holden thought urgently. *You aren't Kitty, a child unformed and needing guidance. You're a woman grown. It's your choice to make.*

Holden realized that Larry was watching him as if he'd just discovered that there was a large predator in the room. Holden didn't care. Kate was talking again.

"I drove this ship back to shore with my father dead not ten feet from where you're standing." Her rage was focused, a rapier of fire. "I docked it in a storm with no help. I was seventeen." A single tear slid down her cheek. She ignored it. "I almost died more than once looking for my mother. If I had, the ship you love so much would now be at the bottom of the ocean you love even more. I couldn't save my parents, but I saved the *Golden Bough.* Don't you dare insinuate that I've failed in my family obligations unless I dive now. Without me, you wouldn't be captain of anything more than your memories."

Grandpa Donnelly looked as if he had been hit by a rogue wave that had come without warning, pouring water over the gunwales and sending the ship staggering.

With outward calm, Kate walked past her grandfather and out of the main cabin. "I'll take Luis ashore. If I see the first tender or hear anything about Mingo, I'll let you know."

*Bravo, Kate Donnelly,* Holden thought.

He wanted to grab her and kiss her until the flush on her face came from something hotter than anger, but this was her family, her moment. He would wait until they were alone to tell her how magnificent she was.

Larry and Grandpa exchanged a long look.

"I'll suit up," Larry said to his grandfather. "You can check me out."

"Diving alone?" Holden asked. "Bad form. Especially when there is another diver aboard."

"Grandpa's doctor told him if he did anything more than snorkeling, he would be at risk of dying," Larry said. "That leaves me."

"I'm a highly qualified diver," Holden said.

"Oh, so you're all about helping now," Larry shot back bitterly.

"No. I'm about facilitating. Helping implies some sort of altruistic attachment. Altruism isn't any part of what I'm feeling for you two at the moment. If it weren't for Kate, I'd let you sink like waterlogged rubbish."

He pulled out his smartphone and went to work.

"Are you really a salvage diver?" Larry asked after a few minutes.

"I spent too many years dismantling and placing explosives underwater. I'm used to working deeper than the bloody wreck you're picking over." *The thigh will hurt like hell burning, but I've taken worse and survived.*

His phone vibrated. He read quickly. "Excellent. Farnsworth is only a few minutes out. He can handle the cataloging. Someone go shake the charming Volkert from his carb coma so that he can man the dive center."

Larry looked at Grandpa, who hissed a word between his teeth and went to kick Volkert out of bed.

Nobody mentioned that Holden was now in charge, but no one pushed back. He was their last hope of pulling the dive out of the toilet.

"Shall we suit up?" Holden said.

"Why do you care about Kate?" Larry asked.

"She's too good a woman to be dragged down by a manipulative old man. In any case, I doubt that my diving will make a difference."

"Then why do it?"

Holden looked at Larry and said patiently, "So that Kate knows the fact of her *not* diving didn't matter, either."

Larry absorbed that, put his hat in place with a tug, and followed Holden down to the dive locker. Kate's boat was already little more than a white wake pointing toward the shadow that was St. Vincent.

As Holden unzipped the duffel, Larry watched with open interest.

"You expected to dive," he said finally.

"A camera only tells you what passes within the field of the lens. In case more is needed, I always carry the minimum of dive equipment with me."

"Makes sense," Larry said. "As long as you're not a pro basketball player or a sumo wrestler, dive suits with a reasonable fit aren't that hard to come by, and water pressure can smooth out a lot of bumps. But a personally fitted mask like yours takes time—and a hell of a lot of money—to replace. Nothing like being able to breathe and talk to the surface at the same time. Righteous dive computer, by the way. I'm hoping to buy that model."

"It's a nice piece of kit," Holden agreed.

He headed for the dive storage room, Larry on his heels. Holden had already decided which suit he would wear if he had to dive. He opened a locker and pulled out a Pinnacle full-body suit that was just about his size. Like nearly everything else on the *Golden Bough,* the suit had survived a good bit of wear in its time. Still sound, though, which was all that mattered.

"I was going to recommend that one," Larry said. "Thick enough to keep you warm but not so thick you're too buoyant. You really do know your business."

Left unsaid was that anyone with money could buy expensive dive accessories and still not know enough to be a decent dive partner.

They took the gear and the cylinders out to the stern to dress. Dive gear was wonderful in the water, and clownishly clumsy out of it. When Holden was fully suited, Larry checked him out. Holden returned the courtesy, right down to two taps on the dive cylinder. They began breathing canned air as they did the awkward shuffle required by fins on a solid surface. Going feetfirst into the water was a relief.

While Larry talked with his grandfather over the com about the siphon's placement, Holden finned slowly, keeping just beneath the surface. This part of the water column was bright. The sensation of freedom from gravity was as heady as the beauty of the surface bending light into flowing patterns across his arms.

Years of dive training took over, regulating Holden's breathing. In the first instants below water, the reptilian brain said *hold your breath hold your breath hold your breath.* But that only led to patterns of oxygen conservation followed by hyperventilation, followed by increasing anxiety, followed by conservation—a brutal feedback loop all divers learned to short-circuit. If they didn't learn, they didn't dive again.

When Larry finned slowly past him, headed down for the wreck, Holden bent at the waist, put his fins where his head had been, and followed. Getting down to the bottom was the easy part, the compression stops short. Going up, decompression, was another animal entirely, with boredom enforced by stabbing pain for the impatient. Or in Holden's case, pain no matter how patient he was.

Silvery light gave way to a twilight world as the water filtered out all but the color blue. Everything became a thousand nameless variations on the theme of blue. It added to the feeling of growing chill as the water went from warm to cool to cold. The dark line of the siphon hose swayed all the way back to the blinding silver of the surface, a long, thick line showing the way back to the ship. Between that and the weighted dive line that went from a buoy to the bottom, with fixed markers for decompression stops, a diver would have to be drunk to miss the home ship.

Quite different from a lot of dives Holden had made, where stealth was the first safety rule.

Like the water itself, Holden went down in easy stages, stopping at prescribed depths to compress. The sea was clear, a welcome change from the dives that had taken him through algae soup to search blindly for active mines. Today he could see far enough down to recognize some of the topography from the map. The white plastic pipe of the grid that divided sections of the wreck was the color of bones. The spreading ribs of the ship were darker shadows.

With the ease of long practice, his brain blended the static, one-dimensional maps rendered by photography and cartography into the living, tridimensional landscape of the undersea world. When the blending was complete in his mind he would be ready to find his way around the wreck without needing to come up for an overview.

Even after Holden was certain he was oriented, he stayed for a few minutes more, suspended in the water, studying the wreck and enjoying the luxury of clear water. As he finned toward his designated work area, he ignored the piercing ache in his thigh and wondered if anyone had spotted Benchley lately.

Not that it mattered. If a large tiger shark decided you were food, it would try very hard to eat you. Bad luck happened, but a diver was in more danger from his own mistakes than from any shadow lurking where blue shelved off steeply into water so deep it looked black.

He found his designated grid and went to work. For all the hours a diver spent in the water, only a few included actually working the wreck. The dive computer was a relentless machine, recording elapsed minutes and water pressure and computing how much time the diver would require to decompress.

*The ascent will be a right bitch,* Holden thought, looking up to the quicksilver shimmer of the surface. *So few feet. Such a long time.*

And his thigh would make him pay for every centimeter.

He accepted it as he had accepted the other factors limiting his dive capability. His body had closed off the last bits of the thigh injury with a cyst, but the interior of that cyst was still subject to the same laws of physics as the rest of him, just more slowly. Until the exterior and interior pressures equalized inside the cyst there was pain. Period.

A silver swirl of fish flashed in the sunlight far above, gathering around the thick siphon hose.

Then Holden focused on the blue world around him instead of on his thigh. The bumpy, always-changing coral growths gave way to the geometric grid. He settled in to work very carefully, slowly, creating currents by hand that lifted the sand away and reaching with equal deliberation for anything of interest beneath the sand.

Whether intended or not, every motion he made created a temporary swirl of current. So instead of touching interesting bits he spotted, he touched the water around them. Every motion had to be deliberately planned and executed with careful restraint. The simple act of closing a hand around a piece of debris became a carefully synchronized ballet. A good diver didn't rush anything.

Hours of the careful dance yielded what appeared to be a handful of grapeshot, a hunk of iron so rusted he couldn't guess at its original function, random bits of waterlogged wood, half of a teacup, and a mangled circle that could have been a gold ring. From what he could hear over his radio, the siphon wasn't coming up with much of value, either.

*If this is a good part of the wreck,* Holden thought, *I'd hate to work a bad part.*

Yet that could change in the next second, the next thin layer of sand lifting to reveal a cache of gold or gems or coins. Treasure salvage was like gambling, and like gambling it could be addictive.

Holden's dive computer told him it was time to head up. Depending on how closely Larry shaved safety margins, he should be heading up too.

*I'm staying within my margins,* Holden thought. It was stupid not to.

He signaled Larry, received a curt "Five minutes," and began to fin slowly up the dive line. At the first decompression stop marked on the line, he checked with his own dive computer and waited with a diver's patience for the signal to continue. By the time he reached the second stop, his past experience with his injured thigh was confirmed.

Decompression was a right bitch.

When he finally surfaced and got unsuited, the first thing he discovered was that Kate was still ashore.

Trolling dive bars.

Alone.

# Chapter 14

As hours went by and Kate visited dive hangout after dive bar after dive café, including a strip club, she began to admit that she was wasting her time. The later the afternoon, the more divers filtered in from various jobs, and the more they drank. The last bar had been peppered with drunks who were way too proud of and anxious to demonstrate body parts she had zero interest in hearing about, much less seeing. Bartenders and bouncers had become her new best friends.

No one had seen Mingo recently.

No one wanted to dive for Moon Rose Limited.

Everyone had heard bad things about the *Golden Bough*.

Kate looked at the circles she had drawn on the map. Most had been crossed out. She glanced around an area that probably looked a lot better at night and decided she would try one more place before she went to the cottage and washed the smell of smoke out of her hair and clothes; the enduring mystery of divers was how many of them smoked.

She looked around carefully, choosing where to go. There were always more bars to check, but once the sun went down, a woman alone in some of those bars would be assumed to be looking for more than alcohol. In the end, she selected a bar that was on the wrong side of the line between seedy and disreputable. But it was the closest bar on the map and daylight was wasting.

The sign above the place said MCNAMARA'S TAVERN and was decorated with a weathered painting of a red-haired, bushy-bearded, and thoroughly dissolute mariner, head tilted back in laughter. The wind had increased to the point that it rocked the sign on its chains, making it shimmy and swing, lending an air of drunken revelry to what was otherwise an outright shabby, no-tourists-wanted divers' dive.

*I'll bet Grandpa used to drink in places like this. Probably still does when he's ashore. Larry, too.*

Not that either had helped her to compile her list of dive hangouts. She had done that the hard way, one bartender or waitress at a time, asking after Mingo and divers looking for work, and settling for the names of other dive hangouts.

A man who looked like he had posed for the McNamara's sign in his youth—and had been a friend of henna ever since—stood at the till, waiting for something to happen.

*Must be the infamous McNamara,* she decided.

Since he looked about as friendly as razor wire, she glanced toward the bar. Another man, younger and much fitter, was tending bar. His mixed heritage resulted in cinnamon skin and wildly curly, red-streaked brown hair. He smiled and chatted up patrons, poured refills, and nixed a request from a man who was wobbling on the bar stool.

"Slow down, Javier," he said easily, pouring tonic with lime for the man, no gin. "If your lover come back to you tonight, you have nothing left." A wink and a sympathetic smile. "Man want to be ready for his lover, yes?"

Javier drank the tonic down in a few gulps, frowned, but didn't object when more tonic came as a refill, also without gin.

Kate gave the people in the bar a discreet once-over. As she had expected, the men defied racial and political boundaries, mixing with the camaraderie of alcohol and shared experiences underwater. Gradually she realized that this bar had a different vibe. Not bad, just different. It smelled like gin and pulsed with Lady Gaga.

And more than one man looked surprised to see Kate.

*It's a gay hangout,* she realized. *Thank God. I don't need to worry about drunks hitting on me.*

She made her way over to the long bar, hoping the smiling young man with the mop of hair wouldn't mind answering a question or three, especially if she put some currency on the bar while she talked.

The bartender did a double take and gave Kate a slow smile that had her rethinking her conclusion about the patrons of the tavern. Or at least this man.

"Are you lost, pretty lady?" he asked.

He watched her with appreciation and a silent promise of restraint that made her feel like an exotic butterfly that had landed on a tiger's paw.

"Not yet," she said. "I'm looking for a diver called Mingo. Has he been in here recently?"

The bartender shook his head. "We been expecting him, but . . ." A shrug said Mingo hadn't come yet.

"How about the men in here now? Are they divers?"

His grin widened. "Nothing but. McNamara's is best dive bar on the whole damn island. Most tourists take one look and leave."

"I'm not a tourist," she said, returning his easy smile. "Anybody looking for salvage work?"

The bartender hollered out, "Any of you looking for salvage work?"

"Which ship?" called a man from the back table.

"The *Golden Bough*," Kate called back.

A murmur went through the room and the patrons went back to their drinks and gossip. The refusal was as clear as it was final.

"Sorry, miss," the bartender said.

"So am I. I can't even find where those rumors came from."

The fact that the bartender didn't ask which rumors told Kate it was as bad as she'd feared.

"The sea, she whispers to her men," the bartender said. "Smart ones listen."

"Thanks, anyway," she said, pushing some money toward him.

"Drink?"

She realized she was thirsty. "Have any iced tea?"

He reached below the bar, came up with a pitcher beaded with cold drops of water, and poured her a glass.

"Thank you," she said, pulling more money from her shorts pocket.

He shook his head in gentle refusal of the cash and went down the bar where a patron had knocked his knuckles on the wood, signaling he wanted another round.

Kate sipped her tea and enjoyed being out of the hazy heat and humidity of the day.

Behind her the entrance door opened and closed. The fact that nobody hollered a greeting told her that whoever had come in wasn't a regular. She took a final long drink of tea, stood, turned around—and almost stepped on Holden Cameron.

"Hi," she said. "I was just going to go back to the cottage after I picked up dinner."

He hesitated, seeming to choose his words carefully. "What in bloody hell are you doing trolling dives in the wrong section of town?"

She blinked. "It isn't dark yet. I was looking for information about Mingo and any divers who wanted to work."

"Not dark yet," he repeated, looking like a man trying something's taste and finding it unpleasant. "Did you know that men don't need darkness to want to shag a pretty woman, and bugger whether she's willing or not?"

Kate realized that underneath his calm exterior, Holden was furious. "Let's talk outside," she said.

"Bloody good idea."

She waved good-bye to the bartender. "Thanks again."

The bartender smiled at both of them. "You ever looking for a third, I'm your man. Ask anyone. They tell you I'm amazing."

"Er, thanks," she said. The open sexuality of the islands was something she hadn't quite gotten used to, much less all the variations on the theme of sex.

Ruthlessly Holden herded her to the exit. She ducked her head, knowing her cheeks were on fire.

"Any more sewers on your to-do list?" Holden asked.

"I thought it was a gay bar. Safe enough."

"Some men shag both ways."

"I'm shocked," she said. "Tell me you're not one of them."

He gave her a sideways look. "Cocky, aren't you?"

"I leave all things cocky to you."

He laughed in spite of his earlier fear for her, fear that had flared into anger the instant he saw her in what was obviously a locals-only dive. "Cheeky, then."

"So I'm told." Then, more seriously, she said, "If it helps, I was prepared to run. If that didn't work, the men in my family taught me some dirty tricks when I began growing breasts."

"Eyes, nose, throat, and balls?"

"Among others."

"Ever used them?" Holden asked.

"A few dates thought that dinner included a blow job and insisted on collecting what I 'owed' before taking me home."

He winced. "How old were you?"

"Eighteen. I learned fast how to be a better judge of whether a man wanted a date with the hope of sex or just expected sex for the price of a hamburger and fries."

"You'll have to show me what you know."

"Why? Are you into pain?"

Holden laughed again and realized that he had done more laughing with Kate than he had with anyone except the munchkins who crawled all over him when he visited family. She was far from a child, but she relaxed him just the same. Made him hard, too. An excellent side benefit.

By silent consent, they walked toward a nearby open-air market. They didn't talk about the problems plaguing the dive, or Mingo, or anything about business, including Kate's latest attempts to find divers willing to work for her family. Instead, they simply strolled through the market stalls that were still open and argued amiably over whether to buy a whole chicken or some wicked-looking blackened chicken pieces, or to settle for fresh eggs and whichever vegetables went best with spicy rice.

While he bargained over the price of chicken and if the shrimp really had come off the boat this afternoon, she selected fruit and piled it on the merchant's table. When she spotted the only remaining loaf of bread from a local French bakery, she pounced on it and carried off her prize to the counter.

By the time the sun was sliding into the ocean, they had walked to the marina, where the truck waited like an oven left to preheat. In minutes they were bumping down the ruts to the cottage. Kate was disappointed when she saw Farnsworth's racy little speedboat tied off on the dock. He was stowing something aboard and didn't notice them at first.

"Well, it was nice while it lasted," she said.

"Perhaps he'll already have eaten supper."

She smiled, glad that she wasn't the only one who had been looking forward to another meal alone with Holden.

"Maybe he has news," she said.

Holden simply carried the food inside.

When Farnsworth emerged from the cockpit of his boat, he was as surprised to see them as they had been to discover the speedboat.

"I didn't think anyone was here," he said to Kate. "Where's the workboat?"

"Tied up at the marina."

He looked puzzled.

"Long story short," Holden said as he reappeared, "Kate took some crew ashore, Larry dropped me later at the fuel dock, and I helped Kate look for Mingo."

"We didn't find him," she added.

Glancing at his watch, Farnsworth frowned. "Did you try the Buddy Bar? I heard Luis and Mingo talking about it a few times when I was listening in the dive center during their decompression stages."

Holden looked at Kate. She pulled the rumpled map from her shorts pocket and smoothed the paper flat against her thigh.

"It was on my list, but I didn't get there," she said, carefully not looking at Holden.

"Just as well," Farnsworth said. "It's not the kind of place I'd want my sister popping into for a pint." He grabbed a few pieces of fresh fruit. "I'm heading back to the warehouse after I leave my laundry off with my friend. Unless you need something from me here?"

"No," Holden and Kate said simultaneously.

Then she added, "I'm going to check out the Buddy Bar before it gets into the wild hours. Can I drop you somewhere in town?"

"Are you going with her?" Farnsworth asked Holden.

"Count on it."

"Would you like any help?"

"Thank you, but no," Holden said. "Kind of you to offer." Especially when the other man hardly looked the type to seek out a brawl.

Farnsworth nodded. "Then I'll be off. Unless something comes up at the warehouse, I'll see you just after dawn on the *Golden Bough*."

Kate hurried to the bedroom to change into long pants and a bright, long-sleeved shirt. The steadily increasing breeze was almost cool. When she found Holden, he was finishing off what looked like a blackened chicken sandwich.

"Just a bit to hold me until supper—dinner," he said. "Ready?"

She grabbed a few of the tiny, sweet bananas that had been part of their purchases earlier. "Ready."

Holden fed her bites of banana while she drove the familiar road to town. When the trees gave way to buildings and lights, she thought again how different everything looked after dark. The tourist centers at the beach had colorful crowds out to enjoy the carefully sanitized nightlife that catered to outsiders with money. Beyond that shoreline strip, the small shops and markets were shuttered. The dark patches came more often, and when there were lights, they tended to be neon liquor signs flickering in bar windows.

Though Buddy Bar was only four streets up off the industrial area of the beach, and a block over from McNamara's, the bar looked like a down-and-dirty dive where men went to brawl as often as to drink. Kate would have hesitated to go during daylight. Even with company, she wasn't exactly eager.

"Okay. Glad you're here," she said.

"Why don't you wait in the truck?"

"If Mingo is in there, he'll talk to me quicker than he will talk to you."

"Right. Good job you covered up those sexy legs," Holden said. "Stay behind me. If the place is too rank, neither one of us is going two steps from the front door."

She didn't argue.

Smoke and music from speakers poured out as Holden opened the door. He scanned the place hard and fast and decided that the atmosphere was rough but not vicious. As an ABCD, he'd seen some really savage bars. This wasn't one of them.

"Stay close to me," he said quietly to Kate.

"The corner on the left," she said, tiptoeing to reach his ear. "Isn't that Luis?"

"Yes. And Raul."

The two men were playing dominoes at a table as gloomy as their faces. When Holden saw what they were drinking, he signaled the bartender for another round. Experience had taught him that a paying customer was much more welcome than a stranger who kept his money in his pocket.

Holden carried the two beers over and set one in front of each man while Kate slid into one of the two empty seats.

"Thanks," Luis said.

He didn't smile, but no one took it personally. He and Raul looked like they were at a wake rather than a party. As Luis shifted to study his dominoes, the wrapped hilt of his dive knife knocked against the chair.

Kate was surprised by the knife.

Holden wasn't.

Luis matched a five with a five on a free domino and waited for Raul to make a move.

A tear slid down Raul's cheek.

Both men ignored it.

When Kate would have said something to Raul, Holden's hand clamped around her thigh in silent warning.

"What did the clinic tell you about your cut?" Holden asked Luis, looking at the already grimy wrapping around the diver's left palm.

He shrugged. "It heal. No dive for maybe few days. By then, the weather be good and the bottom clear."

*By then, there will be no dive,* Kate thought grimly.

Raul stared at his dominoes like they were quadratic equations. He was drunk, yes, but it was more than that. He had the shocky look that Holden had seen during covert skirmishes when a fellow soldier had been killed and the survivors were trying to accept it.

"You can rake the siphon barrel if you want," Holden said. "You don't have to dive."

Luis just waited for Raul to play.

Holden removed his hand from Kate's thigh.

"Are you okay, Raul?" she asked. "Everyone on the boat was worried about you."

A man who had been drinking at a nearby table leaned back and winked at Kate. "Don' worry about that one. He be dumped by his boyfriend. You come to Evgeni," he added, pointing at himself.

"That's very kind, but I have the only man I want," she said, putting her hand on Holden's thigh. It was like petting steel cables. "Are you looking for dive work?"

Evgeni looked Holden over and apparently decided that the pretty redhead wasn't worth a brawl. He saluted Holden with what looked like a glass of black rum and went back to drinking alone.

"Raul," Kate said softly. "What's wrong?"

Tears welled up in the man's huge brown eyes and his lips curled down. "Mingo," he managed hoarsely.

"Gone." He pushed his dominoes faceup, ending the game in a black scatter of tiles. "Gone!"

"Have you been lovers long?" Holden asked calmly.

Raul started to cry.

"Years," Luis said. "Mingo like women, but he always come back to Raul. Eat the soup I bought for you."

As he spoke, Luis pushed a bowl of callaloo closer, sending the chunks of green leaves floating in the broth into erratic flutters. Raul lifted a battered spoon and poked at the soup without interest.

"Where do you think your brother is?" Holden asked.

"Maybe look for a boat of his own," Luis said. "He talk big. Want his own business. He say Raul be cook, because he is better in the galley than breathing trimix, and I be his first diver."

"Mingo must have been saving money for a long time," Kate said. *God knows he wasn't earning boat payments on the wages we paid him.*

Raul smiled sadly. "Mingo is lover, not banker. No good with money. But he tell me it change soon. Big money come. Then he buy a boat and . . ." Raul's voice died.

"Did Mingo talk to you about this?" Holden asked Luis.

"He always talk, but not about his big money. He just say he be rich before the next storm."

"Was he selling goods on the side?" Holden asked, his voice matter-of-fact.

Raul and Luis exchanged a look. Then Raul turned back to stirring the soup that was the temperature of his tears.

Kate's fists were balled in her lap, but her voice was soothing when she spoke. "I won't go running to the cops. I just want to know."

"I don't know," Luis said in a low voice. "But he talk big."

"He always talk big," Raul said.

"Beer-for-life big or something else?" Kate asked. "I mean, there are beer dreams and then there's truly rich."

"Big enough that he use it as an excuse to sneak away after we . . ." Raul shrugged. "He say he go dive."

She made a startled sound. "Alone?"

"Not with me," Raul said.

Holden looked at Luis, who shook his head. "Not me."

"So he was the only one diving at night?" she asked.

Luis gathered up the dominoes scattered across the sticky table. "I dive. I drink. I sleep. I wake up. I dive. No trouble. That is the way of the *Golden Bough*. Smart men do same like me. Mingo, sometimes he not so smart."

Slowly Raul nodded.

Kate's expression said she wasn't satisfied, but Holden's hand was squeezing her thigh again.

"If Mingo has been peddling the odd bit of gold," Holden said, "the local police could be the least of his problems. The kind of people he would be dealing with make bad enemies, especially with the bounty offered for information on anyone selling the Crown's salvage."

The tears on Raul's face fell faster.

Luis went pale.

"Who was his fence?" Holden asked.

Silence.

"Have you had any luck finding out where Mingo is?" Holden asked, his voice both edgy and sympathetic.

Raul's tears were the only answer.

Without a word, Luis began turning dominoes face-down and mixing them up, preparing for another game.

Holden knew the conversation was at a dead end.

"If you hear anything," he said, standing up, pulling Kate with him, "get word to the boat." He put his hand on Raul's shoulder, squeezed, and said quietly, "I'm sorry."

Kate waited until they were in the truck before she said the words that were eating her up. "You believe Larry is in on it, don't you?"

# Chapter 15

Outside, it was dark, scented with rubbish bins cooking in the tropical heat.

"I would be a fool if I didn't consider the possibility that Larry is involved," Holden said evenly. "Mingo might have got away with the odd night dive to pick up valuables he'd stashed beyond camera range during the day, but if he made a habit of it, it's highly unlikely that no one aboard noticed."

Her fingers whitened around the steering wheel. "Larry is a lousy businessman, but he's not a thief."

"Even if theft is the only way to keep the *Golden Bough* afloat?"

"My mind hears you, but my gut knowledge of my brother isn't buying it."

Holden didn't point out that a lot could have changed in the years since she had been a part of the diving Donnellys. She knew it as well as he did.

"Do you blame me?" she asked hoarsely. "What if it was your family being accused?"

"Love, I don't think you're wrong to want to protect your family. My first instinct would be to do the same. My Pashtun grandmother would say it's a clan trait. My mother would say it's simply human."

Holden stroked the back of his fingers down Kate's cheek until the skin over her knuckles no longer looked pale in the dashboard lights.

The computer in Holden's ever-present duffel pinged.

She looked at him.

He hated adding to the shadows in her eyes, but he spoke anyway, "Pressure is dropping again."

The sky in front of the windshield was taking on that thick, translucent silver gray that told of weather changing. The waves would probably be picking up and the surface would carry some wind chop. Not dangerous, just different. A bit bigger, a bit stronger, a bit less predictable, forerunner of the raw power to come.

*No time limit, of course,* Kate thought unhappily. *Just one more thing waiting to break all over me.*

*Us.*

She felt like crying or screaming, anything to ease the tension growing inside of her, pushing at her like air bubbles in the blood of a diver who had rushed decompression. But there were no marked time-out flags along her way, nothing to signal how close she was to the surface. Or to drowning.

When they approached the cottage this time, the headlights of the old truck flashed over a dock shifting uneasily in the quickened water. No boat was tied up. They would have to go back to the marina to pick up the workboat before heading out in the early morning.

Kate didn't feel like eating, but when Holden put chicken and fruit and bread in front of her, she made herself chew and swallow. When she couldn't force down another bite, she pushed back her plate.

"What a mess," she said. "Mingo was going over the side during the night and picking up the lightest, most valuable salvage."

Holden made a noncommittal sound.

"He could have done it alone," she said. "Crazy. Stupid. But possible."

Deliberately Holden sliced a particularly ripe mango and put the best pieces on her plate.

"That would explain the shortage of breathing gas I discovered," she continued. "But one man can't keep up that sort of double-shift diving forever."

She looked at Holden, hope in her shadowed turquoise eyes.

"Having essentially done the same thing on several occasions," he said carefully, "I agree that such diving is quite possible. It requires a very fit, experienced diver."

She waited for the *but* that hovered between them, unspoken, because to speak it would be to strip away the last of her hope.

"It's all over for the business, isn't it?" she asked finally.

Holden stretched as he stood from what passed for a dining table. His thigh jabbed at him, still unhappy from the dive.

"All we're certain of," he said finally, "is that Mingo is missing and could have been stealing artifacts by means of solo night dives. A few quite valuable small goods have surfaced on the black market. How they got there is unknown. When I dove with Larry today—"

"You dove?" she cut in, startled. "What about your leg?"

"I saw your brother doing the best he could with the materials at hand," Holden said, ignoring her interruption. "Most important, I know that even if this dive goes straight to hell in a handbasket, you will weather whatever happens to Moon Rose Limited.

You're a survivor, love. Never forget that. The treasure sickness that haunts your family has no part of you."

Tears stood in her eyes. "You went diving in spite of your leg. Why?"

"Larry would have gone down alone."

"And if something had gone wrong, I would have blamed myself," she whispered. "That's why you went, isn't it? Even though it hurt you."

"The thigh aches anyway. Might as well do something worth the pain."

"Was it?"

"We found some bits and bobs of gold, the dredge brought up some loose gems," Holden said, rubbing his leg absently. "Enough to keep Farnsworth busy for some hours, but not enough to make AO pop champagne corks."

"We're almost out of time, aren't we?"

"Unless we make a very large find in the next twenty-four to thirty-six hours, the dive will be shut down, if that's what you mean."

"Maybe waterfront gossip is right," she said bleakly. "Maybe the *Golden Bough* is cursed."

"I know nothing about that. I'm simply pleased to dive in clear water where I'm not looking for nasty devices that are rigged to explode."

She waited for him to say more, but he only shook his head.

"We can talk for hours about what-ifs and maybes," Holden said, "and not one bloody word we say will change what happens on the *Golden Bough* tomorrow. So come with me to my narrow, wretched bed. The problems of the dawn will arrive much too soon."

She looked at his fascinating eyes, golden green now, blue against the tropic sky, green against the jungle, always different, always beautiful.

*Let the lover be.*

A weight lifted as she took his hand and walked down the short hallway.

"So this is a decompression stop?" she asked almost whimsically.

He smiled and tugged her down on his neatly made bed. "A breather," he agreed.

"I'd rather take your breath away."

His eyes changed even as his heartbeat did. "You just did."

"Then lie down, lover," she said. "Ease your leg and let me do the work."

"The leg isn't hurt, but the rest sounds good."

He made room for her on the bed as she leaned in and traced the curve of his lips with her tongue.

The change in his breath and the sudden heat of his body made her smile.

Whatever he might have said was lost when she lowered her head and kissed him until every muscle in his body was tight. Before the kiss was over, his shirt was open and hers was strained across her breasts, revealing her nipples standing hard and proud.

The sheen of his chest hair in the lamplight drew her eyes, then her fingers. The hair was surprisingly silky, the muscles beneath hot and vibrant with life. The skin stretched over his abdomen was dark against her pale fingers, a kind of dusky bronze that she knew tasted as warm and sweet as it looked.

She pulled her hand down, brushing past one of his nipples and under the curve of his pectoral, down over his ribs and to the tight abdomen below. He was wonderfully alive, skin responding to every touch, his sigh low and pleading.

"You always make me feel so sexy," she said, tracing his smile.

"You are."

She laughed. "Funny, but you're the only man to see me that way."

He framed her face with his big hands. "You really believe that."

"Of course."

Before he could speak, her lips were pressed to his again and her agile tongue was testing every changing texture of his mouth. They breathed each other and went in deeper, wanting more. His fingers worked between them until she was naked from the waist up. His uninjured thigh pressed up between her legs and found her hot enough to make him groan.

"I'm supposed to do all the work," she reminded him.

"Work faster. My pants are strangling me."

She laughed against his chest as she shimmied out of her pants and underwear. Then she carefully peeled his clothes down his long, muscled legs until he was as wonderfully naked as she was. While he struggled to put a condom on, her tongue traced the angry ridges that surgery had left on his thigh.

"Are you sure you're up to this?" she asked against his skin.

He took one of her hands and wrapped it around the only part of him that hurt at the moment.

She felt his heartbeat, his thickness, his sheer heat. He was on fire.

"That wasn't what I meant," she said, meeting his eyes.

"If you want to make the pain go away, take me into that silky body. I guarantee the only thing I'll feel is the kind of pleasure that makes the world stop." As he spoke, his fingers slid between her legs, testing, hoping. Then he groaned. "So hot, so wet. Let me in, love."

His fingertips, wet with her own need, traced her nipples. She shuddered like his touch sent an electric current through her. When his hands closed around her breasts and kneaded, she forgot who was supposed to be doing the work.

"Yes, more," she said huskily.

And the hand wrapped around him more than returned his caresses.

Through narrowed eyes he watched fire slide through her hair with every sigh, every quiver, her pale skin flushed with desire, her eyes a smoldering turquoise he could have happily drowned in. He would have told her how beautiful she was, but she shifted, taking his breath away as her body took him with a slow, hungry glide.

She rode him gently, completely, working her inner muscles to bring them both the greatest pleasure with the least effort on his part. His hands touched everywhere, caressing and demanding at the same time. When she leaned down to lick the sweat from the rigid tendons of his neck, his teeth closed on her shoulder in a bite that made her gasp. So he did it again, and then again, until her body began to undulate like a dancer's.

He shuddered and put his hands on her hips, holding her still.

"Patience," he said hoarsely, feeling none himself.

"Another attribute of dragons." She looked into his untamed eyes and smiled as she locked him inside her, squeezing and stroking him in a way he could neither control nor deny. "But I'm not a dragon. I'm a dragon rider."

He surrendered to her with a laugh and a wrenching groan, giving himself without hesitation or restraint as she came apart around him, filling her as she consumed him.

And in the stillness that followed, they slept, the heat of their bodies comforting and enclosing them while dawn with its tears and dangers slid closer to them with each breath.

# Chapter 16

By the time Kate and Holden had refueled the workboat, picked up some spare parts at the chandlery, and headed back to the tender, both of them were sweaty. The air was motionless, then it would move like hot breath, then go still again. The humidity was so high there was little difference between air and water. The sky had glazed over completely with moisture, becoming a nearly opaque, silver-gray dome. The sun was little more than a white circle barely seen through the lid of heat and humidity.

There was a sullen anticipation in the air, a sense that the doldrums were fighting a losing battle against the earth's motion and the returning rivers of air that humans knew as the trade winds. But the doldrums wouldn't give in easily. Before the rivers returned, there would be the kind of storms where sky and sea went to war. Until that happened, there would only be an oppressive kind of waiting.

"How is your leg?" Kate asked when they reached the workboat.

"Slightly more surly than the day."

"Ouch."

"It has been a lot worse." *And will be again as soon as I dive.*

But there was no need to share that tidbit with her. She felt bad enough about watching her family's business circling the drain. She didn't need to feel guilty about his diving, too.

"I just have this hunted feeling that something is going wrong," she admitted as she stepped into the workboat.

*It is,* Holden thought.

He could sense the coming storm, feel it in his thigh, taste it in the back of his throat. It could come in an hour. It could come in a day.

But come it would. The coy tropical depression that had been dubbed "Davida" had decided to quit fooling around and get down to the serious business of pushing around countless tons of air and water.

Kate brought the workboat quickly up on plane. It was good to have the air moving fast enough to make her feel less like she was wrapped in a sticky cocoon. That, and the feeling of imminence, had her pushing up the throttle, racing something she could only sense, not describe. She chased the feeling inside her head, trying to put it into words.

About a kilometer out, the wind came up, chopping the oily-looking water into sharp little waves that rode on top of the underlying swell. The workboat had to push hard across the dull surface of the sea, aluminum hull smacking as it hit the chop kicked up by the sudden exhalation of wind.

"Would you mind backing that down just a bit?" Holden shouted to her. "I'd like to be able to dive when I get there."

She realized that she was pushing the boat at a speed better suited to calm water. It made for a rough ride, and no doubt his thigh was already aching from the dropping air pressure.

"Sorry," she said, slowing so they could talk without shouting. "I wasn't thinking. Well, I was, but not about speed."

"So what were you thinking about?"

"The fact that people with vertigo aren't afraid of heights as much as they are tempted to jump. To fly. I understand that. Being on the sea again. Us. Do you think there's a chance for us?"

He almost smiled, because he'd spent a great deal of time before dawn, listening to her breathe, holding her, thinking.

"What is it they say in America," he asked. "All in?"

"Yes."

"I'm all in, Kate. The rest is your choice."

Wind gusted, pushing hard at the hull. She responded with automatic movements on the controls, evening out the boat's motion.

"Do we have a shot at the real thing?" she asked without looking at him.

"I didn't know we'd been feeling a false sort of thing."

She gave him a smile that turned upside down. "That isn't what I meant. It's just . . . the rest of it."

"The complication called life."

"Yes."

"I'd love to promise you it will be easy, but then, easy isn't worth much, is it?"

Her smile righted itself. "No, it isn't."

"You were heartbreakingly brave at seventeen."

"I was scared to the bone."

"That's what bravery is, love. Doing the right thing no matter how much it frightens you."

Before she could say anything, her pocket cheeped. She steered one-handed and pulled out her phone.

Holden saw tension draw her face before she even answered.

"It's Grandpa. He hates phones. He never—"

Abruptly she slowed the boat so she could hear over the engine. As she listened, her tension redoubled at the strain in his voice as much as his words. Then she went pale to her lips. When Holden gently pushed her away from the controls, she barely noticed. He took her seat, checked the dials automatically, and looked toward her.

"We're on our way," she said to her phone. "Ten minutes. Maybe a bit more. The sea suddenly went choppy."

Her hand shook as she pocketed the phone. Only then did she truly realize that she and Holden had switched places.

"I can drive," she said. "It will be hard on your thigh, but—"

"I'll drive. I can brace myself more effectively when I know precisely what's coming. Shore or ship?"

"Ship. Larry's sick. Grandpa called for a helicopter evacuation."

"Dive related?"

"I don't know."

Holden nodded and pushed the throttle as high as the boat could safely go given the water conditions. The scarred hull came up on plane and raced toward the unseen ship, assuring Kate that he knew what he was doing with the controls and the limitations of the workboat.

Safe wasn't the same as comfortable. Bursts of spray peppered over the windscreen and swirled to get both her and Holden damper than the humidity already had. She was forced to brace herself so that she didn't fly out of her seat, but she didn't complain. She felt like they were crawling, wanted to tell him to speed up, yet didn't say a word. It wouldn't be safe to go any faster, which meant Holden wouldn't listen to her.

*That's why he took the pilot seat,* she realized. *How did he know?*

Then she realized that her hands were quivering despite their grip on the dash. He must have seen how shaken she was before she even knew herself.

*Larry,* she thought, wanting to scream like the engines. *What happened to you? Don't you dare be really hurt.*

And she was afraid down to her soul that he was.

*Damn the ravenous sea!*

Yet even as she silently raged, she knew it wasn't the sea. It was choices, human choices, the freedom to be stupid that took so many lives.

A black helicopter with black pontoons churned by overhead just as they saw *Golden Bough*'s outline condense out of the thickened atmosphere on the horizon. The aircraft would reach the ship within two minutes. The workboat would take longer and be much harder on the occupants.

Holden didn't need conversation to know what was going on behind Kate's haunted eyes, so he concentrated on getting to the ship as fast as he could. When they finally pulled alongside, the helicopter was waiting a short way out, sitting up on fat black pontoons. It was old, almost antique, with a bubble-shaped cockpit and a body that was more empty space and framework than aluminum paneling. With its rotors turning lazily, the helicopter looked barely airworthy.

A crewman who was probably a med tech finished fastening a gurney to one of the pontoons, then slid a plastic cover over Larry, protecting him from stray water. The rental skiff with Grandpa piloting it was tapping gently against the big pontoon, held in place by the wind and the old man's skill on the water.

The pilot was seated, shouting across the open cockpit with Patrick Donnelly. Her tank top fitted over her lean body and her multiple neat braids were tied at her nape, out of the way of the helmet she was getting ready to put back on.

Grandpa's voice carried across the waves. "Move! You gotta get him to shore fast!"

Holden brought the tender alongside the fiber-glass rental Kate's grandfather had used to ferry the patient over to the helicopter. Even through her worry, she noticed that Holden made the tricky maneuver look easy.

"Take the controls," he said.

The instant she did, he moved to the gunwale rising and falling against Grandpa's boat. Timing the swells, he crossed over into the other boat in a single flowing movement that didn't jar either small craft.

Kate watched, impressed. Switching between two watercraft must have been part of his ABCD training. He made it look easy. It wasn't.

" . . . fly barely above the waves," the pilot was saying in a clipped British accent. "Until we are certain about the cause of the patient's condition, we have to assume the bends. If you want to take responsibility for him, we can fly up high, but standard procedure says we stay real low for evacs of scuba accidents."

When Grandpa opened his mouth to answer, Holden cut him off. "She is correct," he said. "Kate will take the workboat and I'll take this skiff. You fly in with Larry. Your information about him will be more up-to-date than anyone else's, including Kate's."

Grandpa turned on Holden as though happy to find an outlet for the emotions strangling him. "Who the hell are you to—"

"I'm a former navy diver," Holden cut in, nudging the older man away from the boat's controls. "We're wasting time. Crewman," he snapped.

"Yes, sir," the man said automatically, responding to the authority in the stranger's tone.

"When your patient is secure, help Mr. Donnelly aboard," Holden said.

"But the *Golden Bough*—" Grandpa began.

Kate heard. "I've already piloted the ship solo in a storm worse than this one is making up to be."

For a few tense moments, Grandpa chewed over his choices and she held her breath. He'd left the ship in someone else's care only once before, when he'd been too out of his head with pain and fever to object. When he had awakened after emergency surgery, it was to the news that his son and daughter-in-law were dead. Larry had been with him then, had helped him to cope. Though neither of them ever spoke aloud about it, both remembered it. Despite their occasional arguments, Grandpa loved Larry as he loved nothing but the sea itself.

And now he had to choose.

Grandpa muttered a few ripe words while he timed the swells and chose his moment. Then he stepped from the gunwale up onto the pontoon with the speed of a man half his age.

"Hand up that valise," he ordered Holden.

Holden looked down, grabbed the battered leather valise from an open locker, and managed to get the small suitcase up to the old man without either of them going for a swim. Grandpa squeezed Larry's plastic-covered shoulder and climbed into the helicopter.

"Which hospital?" Holden asked the pilot.

"Saint Swithin's in Kingstown," she said. "They have a pressure ward. It's old, but like this bird, it does good work."

The pilot put her helmet on and waited while everyone strapped in.

Carefully Kate backed the workboat away, giving Holden room to do the same. As soon as they were out of range, the helicopter rotors speeded until they were nearly invisible. There was a moment of hesitation while the pontoons broke the embrace of salt water and then the aircraft shot aloft. Flying very low toward the island, the helicopter quickly became a noisy black dot heading back toward shore.

By the time Kate and Holden tied off and got aboard the *Golden Bough*, the aircraft had vanished.

"That pilot could show the helicopter crews I know a thing or two," Holden said. "Most of them got up so fast that everyone was pancaked on the deck. To be fair, we were under fire at the time."

She smiled wanly, took a deep breath, and turned to what was left of the crew. Luis was splotched with dirt, sand, and water from working the siphon. Raul was out of his wetsuit and half dressed. Both men were pale beneath their skin's natural darkness.

"I quit," Luis announced. "The dive, it really is cursed."

"Me too," Raul said.

"Again?" she said.

"Nobody is going ashore until we know what happened," Holden said, standing beside Kate.

In silent agreement, she handed him the key to the workboat.

"Talk or swim," she said.

Raul looked like he would rather swim, but a glance at Kate's stance and Holden's disconcerting eyes got the diver talking.

"I don't know much," Raul said so softly he barely could be heard. Then, louder, "Larry, he say something over the com about feeling no good. We be down there, I don't know, maybe an hour after descent, maybe less."

"So, no more than ninety minutes since you went in?" Holden asked, looking at his dive watch.

Raul shrugged. "Larry, he go down quick. Me? Slow and easy, man."

"Go on," Kate said through pale lips. "You were down there about an hour and then . . . ?"

"He work the siphon and I work near. Then it sound like the siphon suck up something too big. Don't know. I don't see that. But I hear or maybe feel a big *clack* and he cry out on com."

"Was Larry all right up to then?" Holden asked.

"He don't say nothing, so I don't ask. He be working fast. That storm, she be coming soon."

Kate made a sharp gesture for Raul to keep talking.

"So I hear the funny sound and then Larry, he give me the wave."

In demonstration Raul put his arm out and bent the elbow. His hand was flat with the thumb pointing down. Then he brought the hand to his chest and tapped himself a few times.

"Got it," Holden said. "Universal dive signal for not good. No com required, just good visibility. Did you see the siphon stick?"

"Just feel it like a demon banging," Raul said.

"Could it have come from Larry dropping the siphon onto something, rather than trying to suck up something too big?" Kate asked. "The suction could have made the metal mouth hit harder than you'd expect."

Raul shrugged. "I be busy steering him to coins and such, all pretty and shiny. I don't watch him."

"Which grids were you working?" Holden asked. He hadn't seen anything the least bit shiny and beckoning when he had been down.

Raul wiped moisture off his face with a neoprene-covered arm. "He just tell me follow the siphon down. I do."

"Where's your backup dive computer?" Kate asked.

"Volkert take, same as always."

She headed for the dive center with Holden right behind her.

"What about me?" Raul asked.

"Stand by for orders," she said over her shoulder.

Kate hurried down to the dive center, shut off Volkert's cocoon, and asked, "What grids were Larry and Raul diving?"

"Larry was doing the real work. Raul isn't much good underwater," Volkert added, shoving a cookie into a mouth that was still half full.

"Which grids?" Kate asked again, baring her teeth.

He pointed at the screen that held all the grids. Two of them were highlighted.

"Were they bringing up gold?" she asked.

"Larry found it right on top of the ground," Volkert said. "Then he started siphoning and Luis started whooping about coins. Then the siphon must have slipped or Larry dropped it. The old man shut it down and the divers started up. You want to see the .mpg files?"

"Copy and send to my e-mail," Holden said. "I'll go over it. When was your latest weather update?"

Volkert's thick fingers moved with surprising speed over the computer keyboard. An inset appeared. "Two hours ago. Not good. Not bad. Unsettled."

"Right," Holden said. "The captain may want us to dive again before the storm makes it impossible."

"Yah, okay. How many come back up this time?" Volkert asked sarcastically.

"Shut it and do your job."

Kate saw Holden head out of the dive center and caught up. "What are you going to do?"

"Get my duffel off the workboat and dive with Raul."

"Why bother? A handful of gold coins won't make a difference."

"You saw the grids where Larry was diving?" Holden asked.

"Yes."

"When I dove with him yesterday, we were at the other end of the wreck and we didn't see anything but junk. Today he was diving a part of the wreck that is about as far away from the old dive spots as he can get and still be on the grid. The place he chose for today looks like a pile of lava overgrown with coral, right on the edge of the drop-off, dodgy to dive. I want to know why he did it."

Kate had noticed the same thing and hadn't wanted to think about it. It raised questions that made her queasy and answers that made her want to throw up. Chewing on her lip, reminding herself to breathe, she watched Holden retrieve his duffel.

"Mingo has to be the thief," she said when Holden returned to the deck.

"Circumstantial evidence tends that way, but only if there was a treasure actually found and then concealed. We have no proof of that." *Yet,* Holden added silently.

That was what he would be looking for today, in a very rough patch of lava and coral and wreckage.

"If not Mingo, then who?" Kate asked sharply.

"Do you really need me to say it?"

"No! It can't be Larry."

Holden dropped his duffel and put his hands on her shoulders. "Since I arrived, I've watched hours of dive files featuring the divers who are still with us. Luis is an adequate diver, but doesn't have the physical stamina or skill to work double shifts for this long and not get in trouble. Raul doesn't have any feel for the water.

He needs a keeper down there, especially since Mingo disappeared."

The stubborn expression on Kate's face told Holden that he wasn't getting anywhere he wanted to be.

"Larry made all the dive assignments," Holden said quietly. "Divers worked all over the grid *except* the place where Larry struck gold today."

"That doesn't prove anything except Larry was diving the safer parts of the wreck first."

Holden wanted to gather her close and hold her against the coming storm. But he couldn't weather it for her. Nor could he make her accept his help. It was her choice to make, her life to live.

"What if Larry was diving double shifts—one for the files in dry parts of the grid and one for himself where the valuable salvage was?" Holden asked gently. "It would explain his extreme fatigue."

"So would drinking." Her voice was as flat as her eyes. Her tone said that she didn't really believe what she was saying but had to say it anyway.

"Perhaps. And perhaps oxygen toxicity took him down rather than the bends. The hospital will tell us."

"Oxygen poisoning?" she asked, startled.

"When I was in Iraq," Holden said, "sometimes a squad of five divers had to do the work of ten. I've seen men who drank too much and I've seen OTS. Larry didn't stink of alcohol on his skin. He drank, but he wasn't a drunk."

Reluctantly she nodded.

"If Larry was ill, nobody else caught whatever bug he had during all the weeks of working in close quarters," Holden said.

She took a deep breath and nodded again. She didn't like where he was taking her. She liked that Larry was in the hospital even less.

"I have seen men dive until oxygen poisoning brought them down," Holden said. "Larry looked like those men."

"I can't believe my brother is a thief," she said hoarsely. "Mingo, sure."

"Oxygen toxicity is like falling off a cliff," Holden said, his voice level, relentless. "You can push against it and push it and still push and sometimes you don't move the needle far enough. But one time you do, and then something bloody stupid happens down there."

"I won't believe it until I see some kind of evidence. And I'm not in a hurry to look for it."

His smile was gentle and impatient and sad. "In your place, I'd feel the same. Give me permission to go through crew quarters and don't watch while I search Mingo's cabin." *To begin with. I'll get to Larry's, too, but I don't have to force her to confront what is most probably true. I don't want to be the messenger who destroys her world.*

*For the second time.*

*She'll survive it as she survived the death of her parents, but she'll never be comfortable with me again.*

That was an outcome Holden wanted to avoid.

"Mingo's quarters? I'll help with that," she said, relieved to be off the topic of her brother's guilt or innocence.

Moving quickly, she led Holden toward the crew quarters.

"What are you going to tell your bosses?" she asked.

"For the moment, I'm stalling. The instant they know, they'll shut down the dive."

"You have the power to shut us down right now, don't you?" she said, stopping in front of Mingo's quarters. The door was painted a bright yellow.

"I choose not to."

She blew out a breath. "Thank you."

"No need. On a number of issues, I don't share AO's opinions. They take apart events, number the pieces, and file them according to tick sheets made by other bureaucrats. Life is too messy to fit onto anyone's tick sheet."

She opened the door to the cabin that Mingo and Luis shared.

"Whew," she said, waving a hand at the mess. "This could use an airing."

"Porthole is already open."

"I was thinking more like dynamite and bleach."

Holden's lips quirked.

A nearby speaker crackled and produced a tinny voice: "Would the person in charge please pick up? We're getting fresh weather reports."

The message was relayed with a backbeat of Volkert's electronic music, but the voice was Farnsworth's.

Holden looked at Kate.

"Battlefield promotion," he said. "Captain."

# Chapter 17

Kate reached for the green plastic handset on the wall near the door. The com system hadn't been updated in her lifetime, and looked it, but it worked.

"Kate Donnelly here," she said. "Until Larry returns, I'm the captain. What do you need? And shut down that noise."

"Ah, right. I'm turning this over to Volkert," Farnsworth said. "Looks like I have packing to do before we head to port."

The music faded.

"Yah, okay," Volkert said. "Our friends at BWS are advising us to move our wide ass. They project a seventy-five percent probability of Davida dumping crap right where we are."

"Do they have a good track or is this a general warning?" she asked.

"Best estimates have the bitch hitting Venezuela and skimming along to us."

"How strong?"

"That's the good news. Only a tropical depression, but if the Brits are right, it might blow right past tropical storm and into Category One. We'll get the wash."

Kate closed her eyes. "Joy. When is it due?"

"Twelve to twenty-four hours before the center passes," Volkert said crisply. "Speed has been irregular."

"Like everything else about this damn storm," she said.

"So are we going to port like Larry talked about before he went diving?"

"When it's time to leave, I'll make a general announcement." She disconnected.

"You can take heart in the fact that the BWS is only right most of the time," Holden said.

"Not. Helping," she said, but almost smiled anyway.

Hands on hips, she surveyed the mess. There were two bunks along the left side. Clothes and bedcovers dangled everywhere, making the already small room look like an explosion in a closet.

"Be grateful the crew's head is across the hall, open to everyone. No need to start there."

"I'm just grateful I'm no longer the designated head cleaner," she said, frowning at the mess. "Obviously Mingo missed the memo about keeping things ship-shape. The first thing you learn living on a boat is that there really isn't room to be a pig."

"In the navy, there would have been three men bunked into a space like this. I could hardly get dressed without barking my shins on the lowest bunk. Of course, the officer who searched our quarters didn't leave everything on the floor."

"Searched?" she asked quickly.

"For contraband."

"No. I meant do you think this place has been searched? That only makes sense if Mingo wasn't working alone."

"Exactly." And that was all Holden said.

"You think he was stashing stolen salvage in his bunk?"

"Somebody appears to have thought so. Divers might keep their land apartments like a pigsty, but I've never known one to be this slovenly aboard ship. Certainly not to the point of tripping over things on a calm day."

She put her head in her hands for a moment, then straightened. "You make looking for helium sound easy."

He did a double take. "I beg your pardon?"

"*If* Mingo is a thief and *if* he brought the loot back to his quarters and *if* he disappeared without the loot and *if* someone knew and *if* that someone searched the place, is there anything iffy left behind for us to find?"

Holden's eyebrows shot up. "When you put it like that, it sounds like a joke."

"I wish it was. But Larry's in the hospital and I'm . . ." Her voice trailed away.

"I'll take the laundry pile," Holden said. "You take the crew lockers."

"Wonder what chewed on them," she said absently.

"What?"

"The lockers."

Holden walked over and examined the handles of the two lockers. Where a personal padlock would have been placed to secure the door, there was nothing but a few deep gouges.

"Bolt cutters can leave marks like that, especially if they slip," he said. "Do you have any onboard?"

"Probably. Grandpa has everything else. You know how it is with men in hardware stores and chandleries."

Holden smiled slightly and pulled something that looked like a hairpin from his pocket. He used the metal to probe around the door of the first locker.

"What are you looking for?"

"Anything with wires."

Her eyes widened. "A bomb? That's impossible."

"Actually, it's improbable but quite possible. Good job that I've been trained to deal with the possible. But at the moment, it looks like we only have to deal with the probable here. Good news, that."

He gave her a quick, almost fierce hug. "No matter what happens, I have your back."

For a moment she clung to his strength. Then she took a deep breath as he slowly opened the first locker, keeping a sharp eye out for nasty surprises.

The narrow opening held three drawers, a small rod for hanging clothing, and space for shoes and a rolled-up duffel on top of the drawers. Nothing surprising, nasty or otherwise.

And not a wire in sight.

"Luis," she said. "I recognize the purple shirt."

"It would be hard to forget," Holden agreed as he patted down the hanging clothes and found nothing unexpected.

He examined the face of the drawers, didn't find anything, and let Kate nudge him aside to check the contents—shaving gear and briefs that gave new meaning to the word—while he made sure the second locker didn't contain any wires.

"I didn't know men wore thongs," she said, poking at the contents of the first drawer. "Didn't want to know, either."

"Could be a souvenir."

Hastily she snatched her fingers back from the silky red strip of cloth and rubbed them over her shorts. "I need to wash my hands."

"Wait until we work over the mattresses. Don't forget to feel all sides of the drawers," he said as he went to work probing around the edges of the second locker.

No wires. None on the drawers, either.

He returned to helping Kate with Luis's locker. She had the first drawer out without a problem, but the second was balking. Salt water and metal were a corrosive combination.

"Check out Mingo's locker," Holden said. "I'll work this free."

"Fine. I now know more than I ever wanted to about Luis," she said. "On to Mingo, whose underwear hopefully went ashore with him."

Holden made a sound that could have been agreement or argument or anything in between as he felt along the top and sides of the drawer before pulling it out and doing the same to the exterior sides.

"Sure you aren't a cop?" she asked, watching him work.

"In boarding schools there are a limited number of places to hide things," was all he said. "The same is true in crew quarters."

She looked around the cabin with new eyes, but there was little to see. No hanging pictures to hide things behind, no floorboards or rugs to pull up, no baseboards to pull out, and all the recessed lighting revealed was the grime that always built up when diesel engines were at work.

After eyeing the bunks and mattresses with a mental cringe, she started on the second locker, copying Holden's method of searching. Mingo had about the same amount of clothing as his brother had, including underwear that should have made him a soprano.

"Looks like most of his stuff is still here," she said. "Except for a shaving kit."

Holden's hands paused, then resumed searching.

"He must have more clothes in his apartment, or in Raul's," she said. "Less to haul back and forth that way."

She dutifully felt around for anything concealed on the inside of the drawer. When she moved on to the outside, all she got for her trouble was a small cut from the razor-sharp rails. She grimaced and went on to the next drawer, which held nothing of interest inside, outside, or on the bottom.

The third drawer was stuck. She nudged, tugged, yanked, silently cursed, but the drawer didn't budge.

"Need some help?" he asked. He had gone through all the drawers in the first locker and found the same thing in each—nothing useful.

She stepped back. "It's you or a crowbar."

"Or a foot," he said. "Looks like someone kicked it in frustration."

Holden tugged, jiggled, tugged again, and said, "It's either stuck or wedged in place. Fortunately, there's more than one way get into a drawer."

He pulled out the two drawers above, lifted them off their tracks, and set them aside. The contents of the third drawer were some rolled up T-shirts—and a wedge along the rails that kept the drawer from opening.

"Low-tech lock," he said, removing the wedge. "But effective."

Ignoring the T-shirts, Holden pulled out the drawer and flipped it over to make sure nothing was concealed on the bottom. One of the rolled-up T-shirts hit the floor with an odd sound.

Kate shook out the shirt and found a wad of money wrapped in a rubber band. With fingers accustomed to counting foreign money, she fanned the corners of the bills for a fast overview.

"Pounds. Fifties. Probably a thousand or more," she said. "Looks like Mingo doesn't believe in banks, and it definitely indicates he is coming back after his binge."

*If he can,* Holden thought.

But she didn't want to go there and he didn't want to force her to until there was no other choice.

"Mingo must have been converting his pay into pounds at the bank. Less bulk for the same amount of money."

Holden glanced at the roll and then turned the drawer to examine the outside of the back, where there was a small space between the locker and the end of the drawer. All the drawers were shorter than the locker was deep, in order to clear any bolts that might be used to secure the locker itself to the wall and deck.

"What do you have?" she asked, glancing up from the money.

"Looks like the back of a dive computer."

A bit of fiddling and pulling freed the wedge-shaped object from its tape prison.

"Nice piece of kit," he said. "Thin, light. Expensive. Wireless relay to a wrist display. Don't remember seeing Mingo wear this one."

"That's worth a lot more than a wad of cash," she said. "Now I'm really sure he's coming back."

The fact that she kept returning to the subject told Holden that she was as disturbed by Mingo's disappearance as he was.

"Too bad he bugged out when we needed him most," she added.

"Wonder where he went wearing this?" Holden said, looking at the computer. *And who else knew about it?*

"Why would he need a second dive computer setup?" she asked.

"Backup. Plus, I'll bet this one doesn't automatically relay information back to the ship's dive center."

She caught her lower lip between her teeth, realized that she was gnawing it raw, and let go.

The dive computer was about eight inches long, made of stainless steel and featureless black plastic formed into a low wedge shape. Of itself, not unusual. Holden spun it between his hands. The front held a wide LCD screen. Atop it was a compass set at an odd angle, some twenty degrees off the main body.

"Oceanic Pro," he said, reading the maker's logo. "This isn't anything the ship supplies, is it?"

"I haven't seen it on an inventory list. He probably brought it on board himself."

"Not unusual. I brought my own dive computers and mask. A lot of divers prefer familiar kit."

"As long as the divers also wear the electronic gear that relays to the ship," she said, "Larry wouldn't care if they wore six personal computers and lit up like a Christmas tree."

"The navy was more exacting, but yes, some divers wear backup upon backup," Holden said.

He noted the purple ring that was painted around the bottom of the unit, where it would attach by hose to the diving rig. The computer would read and relay to a wrist unit the gas levels, temperature, location, estimated time in tank—all the information a diver would need to stay safe underwater, or at least able to make informed decisions. It also recorded where you went and how to return if you wanted to go back.

Kate stuck her head in the empty locker. "There's something on the floor of the locker. The drawer would have covered it. I can't really see anything but a kind of reflection, about the size of a big watch face."

"Let me," he said, pulling her back.

"I can—"

"Wires," he cut in. "Did you see any wires?"

Hastily she backed up.

Holden knelt and peered inside, then delicately felt about with his fingertips. No wires, just dirt.

And more tape.

He probed, found an edge of tape, and pulled. With a slow, sucking sound, an oversized watch came free. It was nearly half an inch thick, made out of a gray metal, but not chromed or reflective. Its finish was pebbled, not smooth.

"An Atlantis 530," Holden said. "Thing weighs like a pistol and does everything but get you laid. Very fancy."

"Some divers equate the number of gadgets to the size of their, um, more personal equipment."

His smile flashed. "I've noticed that. Not standard Donnelly issue, either, I take it."

"Too pricey for Grandpa. As he has said more than once, he 'doesn't care about the pressure on the back side of the moon or the underside of God.' "

Holden laughed. "Did he still plan his dives with analog decompression tables?"

"Pretty much." She looked at the expensive piece of dive gear. "Mingo will definitely be coming back for that."

Holden didn't say anything.

"Won't he?" she insisted.

"The evidence is mixed."

"What does that mean?"

"You know as well as I do," he said matter-of-factly. "You just don't want to think about it."

There was a tight silence and then words rushed out of Kate like a dam had broken. "I've thought and thought and thought and nothing makes any sense! Mingo and a dive suit are gone and one of our tenders has vanished, but his personal dive electronics are hidden in his locker. No one has seen him in his usual haunts on the island. No one has found the boat he took. About all I can conclude is that he went overboard in the usual manner and drowned on the way back to St. Vincent."

"Precisely what is the 'usual manner'?" Holden asked.

"Peeing over the gunwale while drunk, losing balance, and going into the water. Alcohol isn't a good swimming partner."

"Ah, that way. Yes, it happens. Usually the boat is found adrift, or the body, or both."

"Usually."

"Usually a diver who decides to run off for a binge at least takes his cash with him," Holden said. "And why would he take a dive suit and canister that belong to the ship? The bloody things are unwieldy out of water and old gear isn't worth much at pawn. That doesn't even touch on the theft of a ship's tender."

"Precisely," she said.

Black eyebrows lifted and he said carefully, "On what, precisely, are we in agreement?"

"None of it makes sense!" she said, frustration in every syllable.

"Right. Let's have a go at the mattresses."

"Yuck." But searching old bedding was better than chasing her thoughts—all questions, no answers, and the clammy fear that something was very, very wrong.

*It's just the air coming from the porthole,* she told herself. *Clammy and ripe with the probability of a storm.*

All the upper bunk mattress revealed was a bunch of lumps that had nothing to do with contraband and everything to do with age. The mattress on the lower bunk had seams that were slit in a few places. Nothing huge, just enough to stick two fingers in. Poking around revealed stuffing and two small plastic bags.

Empty.

"He could have stored really small goods in there," Holden said. "Unimaginative, given the clever wedge on the locker drawer, but possible."

"Hide in plain sight?"

With a shrug, Holden continued. "It could have been drugs. It could have been that he scooped up the small stuff—gems and the like—and took them ashore when he left. It would explain the lack of a shaving kit."

"It would?"

"No matter how horny, angry, or drunk, I doubt that Mingo would be foolish enough to cart off stolen goods in plain sight. A shaving bag is convenient and unremarkable."

"Male version of a purse. That makes sense. Finally. I like it." She nodded. "Mingo is the rat gnawing at the Crown's cheese."

Holden smiled and wished it was that simple.

"So Mingo is finding stuff and yet not finding it," she said. "As you pointed out, that part would be simple enough, especially as Volkert is stupefied by sound and spends more time opening snacks than watching the screens."

"Or he's on the take. Even simpler."

"Whatever. So Mingo is maybe seeing things down below and leaving them there and making off-the-record dives to pick up the goodies," she said.

"You can do it for a while," Holden agreed, "but using different dive computers—or turning off and restarting a single dive computer—bollixes up built-in algorithms, which assume eighteen hours between dives."

"So the new or restarted dive computer wouldn't allow for residual gases in the diver's blood."

"I do love a smart woman," he said, touching her abused lip with his forefinger. "No matter how you compute it, you must be very careful about the number of dives you make in any given interval of time. It's not rocket science, but there are some laws of physics you can't get around no matter how many gadgets you wear."

"Like oxygen poisoning."

Holden nodded, hesitated, then said, "So you're pleased with the Mingo-as-rat theory?"

"Pleased is the wrong word. Yet he managed to pull off trysts with Raul and nobody knew."

"There is a difference between ignoring an affair and ignoring someone whose thievery diminishes your share of a dive bonus."

Kate fought against going where Holden and her own thoughts kept pushing her, but there really wasn't any way to ignore the elephant much longer.

"Okay. Probably someone else in the dive crew, or even more than one, benefited from the high-grading," she said. "They wouldn't have been happy when you were called in."

"No. They wouldn't want me aboard, especially at night."

She would have liked to ignore the fact that it had been her family who had refused to let Holden sleep aboard, but the elephant just kept getting bigger.

"There wasn't any room for you," she pointed out.

"Perhaps not a week ago. Since then, there has been steady attrition in the crew quarters. I could have insisted on sleeping aboard, but I didn't. That is on me. At first I told myself that I was investigating whether you were complicit in anything illegal, which was mostly true. Even after I knew you were innocent, I stayed ashore because you were there and I very much wanted you. I still do, more each time."

A gust of humid wind through the porthole did little to cool Kate's blush.

"Then there was the chain Mingo conveniently found," Holden said, as though he hadn't spoken about his soul-deep need for her, "just when AO was looking for an excuse to shut down the dive. They probably thought I'd pass out commendations and fly back to jolly old England, leaving them to strip the wreck before the storm came."

"That would require planning and foresight and . . . planning," she said.

Suddenly she felt hemmed in, chest tight. The elephant was getting bigger and she was going to end up under its crushing feet.

*I can see Mingo high-grading and paying off Volkert to look the other way,* she thought, *but the rest points to someone with real brains and a systematic plan for pillaging a wreck. Mingo is an ad hoc sort of guy.*

*Petty thief, not mastermind.*

*Breathe. Slow. Easy. Running and hiding doesn't work, remember?*

But that's what she wanted to do.

Holden waited, feeling Kate's struggle as though it was his own. He couldn't imagine how difficult it would be to admit that your blood relations were liars and thieves, and uncaring enough to drag you down with them.

She made a low sound, like someone absorbing a body blow. "Mingo alone doesn't add up. *If* there was real treasure in the wreck. That's a big if." *And my last hope.*

Silently, Holden waited, hoping he wouldn't have to be the one to rub her face in her rotten family.

"If the night dives were fairly frequent," she said in a voice thick with unshed tears, "somebody, sometime, would have noticed lights beneath the water, even little ones ninety feet down under a full moon. Grandpa can't be the only one who pees off the deck in the middle of the night."

A silent breath of relief went out of Holden. She was taking off her I-refuse-to-know blinders. It gave him hope that what was growing between himself and Kate would survive what was to come.

"Yes," he said.

"When did you stop suspecting me?" she asked. "Or have you?"

"After a few days you went to the bottom of my list. You have many qualities, Kate, but sustained duplicity isn't one of them. Willful blindness and loyalty when it comes to family, yes. Complicity, no."

She closed her eyes for a moment, then opened them. "I really don't like thinking about Larry as a crook. Or Grandpa."

"As you said, life is rarely about what we like."

The probability of Larry's innocence kept shrinking to the vanishing point and beyond, into the realm of anything is possible, but not at all probable. Holden was watching her with compassionate eyes whose color had changed to sea green shot with gold shards.

Turning away, she whispered, "What a foul mess this is. I hate it. But it's better than hiding my head in the sand." She hesitated. "Isn't it?"

He pulled her against him and buried his face in her hair. She let herself sag into his strength for long moments. He felt the shudders that went through her, the warmth of her tears sliding from her face to his arms, and then she straightened, wiping her eyes impatiently. She flicked the watch he was holding with a determined fingertip.

"Let's plug this into the dive center," she said, "and see what we get."

# Chapter 18

Volkert must have been watching the door, because the instant it swung open he turned down the Techno.

"Captain Donnelly," he said respectfully, "I sincerely hope that you're down here to tell me in person that we're pulling anchor and heading back to shore."

"We have plenty of time," Kate said, "and a reserved space in a lee marina. The island might lose a few trees and tourists, but the rest is secure."

"Any word about the other Captain Donnelly?"

"Just a text from him that he's really all right and they're running a battery of tests."

With a nod, Volkert looked at her as though she was the only one in the room. Holden didn't take it personally; it was clear that Volkert knew who was buying his crisps and cookies now.

"I want the dive track of the entire operation," she said. Whatever doubts she had showed to Holden, she wasn't showing anyone else.

"All of it?" Volker asked.

"Every single one," she said.

Holden smiled when the other man went immediately to work. No doubt he was already wishing he hadn't been so pissy with the pretty lady earlier.

"Getting it." Volkert chewed on some jerky that looked and smelled like it had come from long-dead fish. "I'll just go off the pings from dive comps, since I don't have the plan entered in yet."

"Oh, and we need to know the coordinates in this dive computer and see where, if anywhere, they match up on our grid." Holden placed Mingo's watch on the workspace. It hit with a cold, hard sound.

"Whatever you find doesn't go beyond the three of us," Kate said bluntly. "Got it?"

"Yes, Captain," Volkert said.

Holden knew it was too late for secrecy, but he didn't say anything. Whatever had been happening on this ship had to be an open secret whose occasional leaks were sealed with money or threats. But Volkert wasn't entirely stupid. He wouldn't get on the radio as soon as Kate was out of sight.

"Fortunately, the new units all have USB connectivity." Volkert fumbled around in a nest of collected cables in a drawer. He then unscrewed the access panel on the watch and pulled it open. "This is the hardest part. But you have to engineer for real pressure down there, yah?"

"One would hope," Holden said.

"Here. Connect this." Volkert handed her the cable. "And while we're waiting for it to mount I'll try to get the dive logs overlaid." He leaned over and punched some keys. Then he looked at her sidelong as he turned up his music.

"Fink you freeeeky and I like you a lot," cooed an alien female voice.

"No louder," Kate said.

The beat was insistent but not overwhelming, pulsing away as Volkert matched it with the tapping of keys.

*Maybe he uses the noise as a sort of caffeine,* Kate thought. *Whatever, he works faster with a backbeat.*

Volkert put up a view of the wreck and surrounding seascape that had been patched together from a series of photographs taken by the original survey crew. There were gaps and seams and the whole thing was vaguely murky, though whether that was through lens distortion or compression was unclear.

"The might of the Empire and that's the best we could get," he said scornfully.

"The Empire has many things to do, aesthetics not being high on that list," Holden said. "If this happened to be enemy troop movement, you would be able to count the legs on a flea."

Volkert grunted. "Yah. Okay, I've got dive records that were lifted off the computers and the plans that were filed. I'll post the filed plans first."

A series of lime-green paths snaked across the grid with small white text lines indicating the date and time.

Silently Kate wondered why the hell she hadn't gotten something like this the last time she asked.

*Because I wasn't the captain,* she realized, furious.

And this was no time to lose her temper. Volkert was the quickest way to get the information she needed. She could fire his insubordinate ass later.

"What's the oldest track you have?" she asked.

He moved the mouse so that the arrow touched a path and lit up, showing a date.

She took the mouse and began passing the arrow over paths at random. As she touched them, they lit up and the date flashed. The more lines she touched, the more her temper slipped.

"Despite the impressive snarl of lines, I don't see much more than forty dives here," she said in a clipped voice. "Two shifts a day, that's only twenty dives. The *Golden Bough* was anchored on the wreck while it was cleared. Salvage diving began at least eleven weeks ago.

Even if we were only able to do one dive on some days, it doesn't add up."

"Actually it's forty-three dives," Volkert said, returning to his natural surly state. "The early survey plus two other passes made after most of the wreck was cleared. That's all I have. Remember, there was at least one computer dive specialist before I came on board. From what I've heard, there were several. Heavy drinkers, if you believe ship gossip. The only records I have are from my tenure."

*Which began about a week before I arrived,* Holden realized. *Interesting coincidence. Like the gold chain.*

*Pity that I find coincidences so unsatisfying.*

"So we're missing all of the dive tracks before you came aboard?" Kate asked.

Volkert lifted one shoulder. "Probably they're filed under a different protocol or protocols. I wasn't given any instructions how to proceed when I came on. I was left to create my own protocol and follow it. If there were others used before me, I haven't had time to dig them out and nobody asked me to until now."

*Bottom of the employable barrel,* Kate reminded herself. *You get what you pay for, and we're paying this lazy ape with bananas.*

*Breathe in.*

*Out.*

*In.*

With a wary eye on Kate, Holden studied the pattern on the screen. At first glance, the grid was being well covered by dive plans, with concentrations on the center, but a lot of activity even at the grid edges.

"What's this down here?" He pointed at an area of the map that looked like a jittery mix of pixels. Only one of the early dive paths led across it. "Is that part of the seafloor or is the file bad?"

"Looks like it's being left alone," Kate said. "The early survey done after the overburden was cleared is the only one that went there. Must be a big lump of lava with a coral overgrowth."

"Dodgy diving," Holden said. "A large drop-off is very close by. To cover the area thoroughly, you would have to go more than one hundred feet deep. Unless the slope levels off very quickly, you would find yourself a hundred meters down, or more, before you realized it. The difficulty and expense of recovery goes up with every centimeter you go down."

She frowned, remembering long dinners around the galley table with three generations of Donnellys sharing hopes and old maps.

"Difficult, technical diving, and probably not useful," she said. "If the ship sank right over that lava outcrop, the wreck would either slide off into the deep blue or bump off the other side and stay on the shallow plain as it rotted and broke apart."

"Since the wreck came to rest slightly east and north of that area, apparently intact and in the shallows," Holden said, "there would be no economically compelling reason to investigate the technical diving territory. A few passes for thoroughness would satisfy most captains."

Apparently through with the protein portion of his daily grazing, Volkert opened another bag of cookies. "I can zoom in, but that's as good as we have. The more the zoom, the more blurred the detail. E1 is mainly coral, rock, and a drop into the black. Nothing pinged, even for iron, at least on the survey I found for you."

"Can we see the plans as they were filed off of dive computers, not as they were planned ahead of time?" Kate asked.

Volkert hammered on the keyboard, cursed, and started over again several times. Finally he found the magic combination of commands. "This is what I have."

Cobalt-blue lines now filled the screen, but these were more jagged, uneven, organic. Instead of straight lines or simple arcs, these were less distinct, marked out in a series of line segments, looking almost like lazy lightning. For the most part, there were no surprises here, though they did deviate from the dive plans in places.

"The green lines are the plans and the blue lines are where the divers actually went," Volkert said into the silence as he ground another cookie enthusiastically between his teeth. "The white grid hasn't changed."

She and Holden nodded. Both of them understood the difference between what happened on plans and what happened underwater. Plans were direct. Reality meandered.

"Divers are human," she said. "If something catches your eye and you investigate, the amount of allotted time underwater doesn't change. Some other portion of the dive plan gets shorted or ignored."

She leaned in for a closer look at the tangle of blue and green lines, then backed off for a different perspective.

"What is it?" Holden asked.

"There are a few weird deviations, like this one, the day before you and I arrived." She took the mouse and lit up the date, then shifted the mouse. "And this one." She looked at Volkert. "Change these two to another color or blank out the other lines."

More hard clacking from Volkert as he chewed loudly. "Highlighting."

The lines she was pursuing became neon pink, making it easier to see the deviation between the dive plan and the actual dive. The diver had abandoned the plan, crossed several grid squares to the rocky outcrop, and crossed back to his assigned grid. It hadn't particularly jumped out of the original tangle of dive/planned versus dive/reality tracks, but with the other lines dimmed, the deviation was quite clear.

"Someone went wandering," Holden said. *Like a bee to a honeypot.*

"Volkert, do we have an ID on that dive track?" she asked, even though she was virtually certain who it was.

*Mingo.*

"Yah, okay. The swaggering one."

"Mingo," Holden said, unsurprised.

"Did someone call down a change in dive plan?" Kate asked.

"Don't remember it," Volkert said. "But there's a lot of chatter."

*Or you were chewing too loud to hear anything,* she thought. *Or paid to forget. Same result no matter the reason.*

"What made him move that far over?" Holden asked. "Did he want a look at the drop-off? Did he go to tease Benchley? Was gold just jumping out of the ground for him to see?"

A sinking, twisting feeling wrapped around Kate's throat. "He went there only once on the record, then probably brought something back to another grid and 'discovered' it."

"So he knew there was something to find. A happy welcome aboard, as it were. Mingo carefully removed his loot so that it could be 'discovered' in a mostly unproductive area of the wreck, where Larry, as per my orders, has been concentrating ever since."

"Maybe Larry didn't . . ." Kate's voice died. *He had to know. And Grandpa. He as much as told me when he said secrets are impossible to keep on a ship.*

*I just didn't want to listen then. I don't want to listen now, but I will.*

*No more hiding from savage truths.*

"I would give a great deal to question Mingo," she said with aching calm.

"We can, after a fashion," Holden said. He looked at Volkert. "Has that watch mounted yet?

Techno beat filled the unnatural silence of the ship. There were no divers reporting to the dive center. No sounds of men working on the stern. No footsteps overhead as someone hurried from one part of the ship to another on a task.

Kate shivered, feeling like she was on a ghost ship as she stared at the computer screen. Even Holden's nearby warmth wasn't enough to penetrate a sudden chill.

*Because I am aboard a ghost ship, waiting to hear from one of the spirits.*

"What color do you want Mingo's dive track?" Volkert asked.

She thought of the brightly enameled door to the diver's quarters. "Yellow."

Volkert clacked some keys. "Yah, okay. Here it is."

Yellow tracks jumped up onto the screen, laid on top of all the others. Many of the yellow traces were simple spot markings. Some were fuzzy, indistinct clouds left by concentrated activity in a single area. Some yellow lines were long slashes, but most of them were simple single-location markings.

Holden calculated where he had been on his own dive, plus the overview of the wreck he had paused to memorize on his way down. "A lot of those aren't a dive track," he said.

"Are you sure this information isn't already on computer records somewhere?" Kate asked.

Volkert shook his head hard enough to make his jowls quiver. "This isn't your notation structure. Doesn't match up to any of the coding that Donnelly uses."

She digested that in silence.

"Mingo's been busy," Holden said.

"Mingo's been making a treasure map," she said bitterly. "And here, look. He's been over in that rocky corner a lot." She pointed at the screen where the markings were clustered around the odd formation. "Holden, you've been down there. What's visible in that grid?"

"Mainly that it's less a grid than it looks on the dive plan."

"Could you see it on descent or ascent?"

He thought back past the memory of pain like a white-hot crochet hook digging inside his thigh. "I would have noticed Benchley, but what I saw otherwise was a grid that only looks like neat squares on the plans. The truth is more like a net, pulled here and there to accommodate the reality of the seabed itself."

"Nothing about the rocks at the edge of the grid jumped out?"

"Not on the descent. On the ascent, I had my mind on . . . other things." Like breathing through the pain. "Volkert, you have my dive record, do you not?"

"Yah, if you filed it." More keystrokes and an orange dive track came up.

Kate studied it, then let out a pent breath. "You were in a grid that never even touched where Mingo went off his dive plan. In fact, you were as far away from the outcropping and drop-off as you can be and still be diving the same wreck. All you found was junk."

*And pain,* he thought, *but that's of no value to anyone, especially myself.*

"And that's all you were going to find," Kate continued. "Because you were given a dive plan in a dry grid."

"The gold chain was found near there," Volkert said.

The keys clacked and violet dots appeared, one for each valuable find. All the recorded dive tracks also appeared with the dots. The screen now looked like an electric rainbow had thrown up.

"The gold chain was almost certainly a red herring," Holden said neutrally.

"Yes." She frowned, studying the violent colors.

He saw that her face was a pale mask of revulsion and loss, her few remaining childhood illusions cracking and falling about her feet. He touched her arm, silently telling her that she wouldn't be alone in this storm.

"Larry made and assigned dive plans," she said bleakly. "With Grandpa's input, of course, and whatever information my parents had left that might have been pertinent to this wreck. They researched it for years before they died. Years of dreaming of emeralds and sapphires, rubies and pearls, a woman's weight in gold and gems . . ."

She shook off the past and its mistakes, the hopes and greed centered on the treasures of the Spanish

Main, the past gleaming and flashing as wealth was pulled from a saltwater grave.

"Anything else we should know?" Holden asked Volkert, tapping him on the shoulder.

He cleared his throat. "I'm not looking for trouble."

"Then don't make us come back on you when we find something you bloody well should have told us," Holden said, his voice as hard as his eyes.

The Afrikaner shifted uneasily, making his chair groan. "Yah, okay. I can try to see if there are any old files from before I came."

*Which we have already requested,* Holden thought. He didn't bother to say it aloud. Volkert knew his ass was in a vise.

"The survey you Brits made is shite," Volkert said.

"Already noted."

"Someone must have made a better one," the man continued, stuffing a cookie into his mouth. "I'll look for it again."

"Please do," Holden said, his request as sardonic as his voice. "And do notify us immediately when you find something or give up."

When Kate started to say something more, he guided her from the dive center and shut the door behind her.

"All right," he said. "Tell me."

"Larry might forget to delete all records of a second survey, but Grandpa wouldn't," she said. "And he would keep a hard copy somewhere. That's just his old-fashioned way."

"The dive has found a good weight of silver ingots, plus the odd bit of gold here and there," Holden pointed out. *I'll bet they went ashore in his valise.*

"The ingots were chemically cemented together by seawater," she said, her voice empty. "Lifting them would require heavy tackle and the work of several divers. Hard to handle, hard to conceal, hard to sell. As for the rest that we've found . . ." She shrugged.

"Pretty little cake crumbs to keep the overlords happy and the dive funded," he finished for her. "If we check the dates, I'm rather certain we will find that whenever it was time for a dive disbursement, up came the crumbs to placate the overlords."

"But the rest of the cake is hidden away."

"Or already eaten by the black market, or both," he said. "Until we—"

The squawk box in the hallway went off, burying Holden's words in static.

"Is the captain down there?" Raul asked in a metallic voice.

She went over to the nearest intercom, which was on the wall near the crew's head. "Kate here."

"Weather is getting bad. Wind's steady and strong, and we're getting some real chop. The period between waves has changed. Cook wants ashore. So do we. Malcolm packed up his speedboat and left."

*Good thing I have the keys to the tenders,* she thought. But all she said was, "I'll be up to check the weather."

She disconnected and headed up toward the wheelhouse and Grandpa's special—and specially hated—weather computer.

# Chapter 19

Grandpa's computer didn't tell Kate anything new. The storm had indeed settled in to throw a tantrum. It was picking up speed faster than had been predicted. The sea had gone from clear to cloudy. Small, chaotic ripples of energy passed through the boat, warning of the storm surge that was coming. The air tasted different, heavier. A smoky mist concealed the horizon.

"This is just the start of it," Kate said unhappily to Holden as she stepped out of the wheelhouse. "If it keeps up like this, the next twenty-four hours will be quite a ride."

"You feeling okay?" Holden asked as she looked out over the ocean.

"Aside from being ripped up and lied to, I'm just fine, why?"

"Because you're looking at the leading edge of a tropical storm while standing as the captain on a ship, and a handful of days ago you were fighting yourself on placid seas belowdecks."

"The sea is nothing compared to how angry I am right now."

"Give it some hours," he said softly. "I may be from the opposite coast and considerably farther north, but when I see weather like this, I begin checking that everything nearby is nailed down."

"Give me a few more hours like the last ones, and I could stand toe-to-toe with this storm and scream it down." She blew out a long breath, took in another, blew it out slowly. "It's over. We're going in."

"There's time for a short dive," Holden said. "I'd like to take a look at that pile of rocks."

"Raul is the only diver left aboard. Even if I ordered him to go with you, I doubt that he would. They're frightened by more than just the storm. And they don't know me well enough to trust me."

Holden wanted to argue, but he knew she was right.

*The storm will blow out, just as storms have always done,* he told himself. *We can come back when it is calmer and see what is left. Surely that coral-covered lava formation isn't going to wash away.*

*I'd very much like to see what Mingo found that was valuable enough to lure him into night diving off the books.*

Aware of being watched by the crew, Kate gripped the rail and forced herself to live in only this one moment, not in the lost past or the near future when the last lie would be revealed and she would stand alone and bleeding in the wreckage of her childhood beliefs.

Holden's arm brushed her, hot and strong and alive, reminding her that she was alone only if she chose to be. She leaned into him for a moment before she faced the crew that had gathered below. They needed leadership and that meant her.

The wind flexed casually and lashed her hair across her face like a thousand stinging whips.

"They're calling this Tropical Storm Davida," Kate said. "She'll make life miserable for anyone on the beach in Venezuela."

The crew stirred and glanced uneasily at the stormy horizon. Raul crossed himself as the cook cursed loud enough to be heard above the storm. Even Volkert had come out of his cave for a look.

"What about us?" called the cook.

"We're taking the *Golden Bough* to a lee marina."

Holden's phone rang and vibrated against his leg. He ignored it. Whoever wanted him could wait. The unhappy crew could not.

"But we won't leave until everything on the ship is stowed and secure, including the two tenders," Kate said. "Get to it!"

As the crew dispersed, Holden's phone rang again. He took it out of his pocket and saw that it was Antiquities.

*Probably going to tell me what I already know. Davida is a right bitch.*

He stepped back from Kate and the crew, turning into the bulkhead to minimize the noise.

"Cameron here."

"Finally," Chatham said with a grim kind of cheer. "We have a spot of trouble here. We need you to return soonest."

"I must have heard incorrectly. Say again."

"You are to return to London before Davida grounds all aircraft on St. Vincent. Then you will report directly to the office."

"This is rather sudden."

"The expedition is over," Chatham said, his voice edged with malice. "It has been rubbish from the start. We will throw no more good money after bad."

"There are some developments that—"

"Developments," Chatham cut in. "Is that the new term for shagging the Donnelly bint?"

"She is not a—"

"While that peccadillo could be overlooked in a spectacularly successful operation," Chatham said, ignoring the interruption, "the *Golden Bough* has proven to be anything but."

"My personal life has no bearing on the work that I'm doing out here."

"Bollocks."

Holden was aware of Kate waiting a step away from him, but he didn't bother to lower his voice. "We have recently discovered a thief operating from within the dive team, a thief who could very well be responsible for any perceived shortfall in small, valuable salvage."

"Utter rot. *Moon Rose* is a historical fantasy. As the Yanks say, it is time for a reality check. After the lack of return on investment, your misjudgment is as notable as it is disappointing."

Holden gripped his phone and wished it was Chatham's neck.

"Our sources have also brought up certain irregularities in your recovery reports," the man continued in his clipped voice. "At this point it is more circumstance than fact. If you would like to keep it that way, be on the next plane out of St. Vincent and we will put this unhappiness

behind us. I would not want to see an honored and hon-
orable member of our navy disgraced. Am I clear?"

"Quite, sir. Just as it is clear that you have only part
of the available information, and not the important part
at that."

"Rubbish. Take your bruising like a man along with
the rest of the department and I'll see what I can do to
smooth this over. There is a flight from Kingston in
less than three hours. Do be on it."

Chatham disconnected.

*Bugger,* Holden thought savagely.

He turned and saw Kate watching him, worry drawing her face into tight lines.

"What's wrong?" she asked.

Mist breathed over them, forerunner of the long,
twisting curtains of rain that would follow.

"I have been ordered back to London," he said.
"Immediately."

"Why?"

"It doesn't matter. I'm not going."

"I don't understand."

"As my commander used to say, the whys and where-
fores are not terribly important when you have a device
at hand to defuse." Holden smiled faintly. "We didn't
call them bombs or mines; device is a less threatening term. The commander drilled into us that our job

wasn't to worry about how the device got to where it is, only to prevent it from working and to keep ourselves alive, in that order. In all, it is rather excellent advice for many things."

She came closer, her hair and eyes radiant against the coming storm. "What do you need to keep yourself alive?"

"You," he said, wrapping her close. "Nothing else amounts to a tinker's damn."

She put her hands on his face and looked into his incredible eyes. "I'm yours."

He hoped it was true, that the fragile roots of their relationship weren't ripped out in the storm—or its aftermath.

*You can't see the future, boyo. Take what you have and thank God for it.*

"AO ordered me to shut down the dive," he said.

"For the duration of the storm?"

"There was no mention of resumption."

"What if the site survives the storm with only a little damage?"

"They have washed their hands of this dive. Chatham refused to hear of any thief or other new information. I rather believe that as far as AO is concerned, the sooner the storm buries everything, the better, and me along with it."

"Bastards," she said.

She stood on tiptoe and kissed Holden until they were warmer than the light rain slicking the deck.

"Kate, if I want to keep asking questions despite the storm, questions that include your family, will it change things with us?"

"I have some questions of my own." She wiped damp hair back from her face. "We can compare notes once we're ashore. I hope to see Larry, or at least Grandpa, before the storm shakes the island like a terrier with a rat. I don't like being lied to." The words were more forceful because of her calm.

"I would like permission to search Larry's quarters," Holden said.

"Now?"

"Yes."

"Then do it. I have a ship to secure." She turned away.

"Thank you, Kate. Captain."

"No thanks required. I've had a gut full of playing with shadows on a wall."

Her words echoed in Holden's head as he went to Larry's quarters on the main deck. Like the crew quarters, the door only unlocked from the inside. Other than having more room and an adjoining head—and the fact that the area didn't look like it had been searched—there was little difference between the captain's cabin and Mingo's.

Larry's bed was adequately made, though hardly up to navy standards. His clothes were folded or hung, shoes stashed, nothing to trip over even if the going got rough. Nothing was taped along the back or sides of the locker drawers.

As he headed for the small, two-drawer desk in the corner between the outer wall and the head, a color photo secured to the wall caught Holden's eye. A much younger Kate was hanging upside down on the railing of the *Golden Bough* while Larry made a great show of trying to pry her loose. Her hair hung in a wild red tangle and she was laughing with the carefree contagiousness of a child. Larry was laughing, too. In the background their grandfather was watching them with an indulgent grin.

Holden felt more like an intruder than before, losing all appetite for the process. But he kept going because it had to be done.

The first drawer of the desk held the usual mix of stuff that had been useful once or might be useful again—pens, ruler, paper clips, rubber bands, a magnifying glass, an old cell phone that had died, various pads of sticky notes. It also held a small black plastic box. Inside the box was a dive watch like Mingo's.

Feeling like a thief, Holden pocketed the watch and replaced the box.

The second drawer held old magazine and newspaper articles about Spanish treasure finds, plus an assortment of dubious treasure maps of the sort sold by con men to gullible divers. None of the maps were for areas in St. Vincent and the Grenadines.

By the time Holden headed for the wheelhouse, the workboats had been hoisted aboard into cradles and tied down, as had the siphon and its coils of hose. The decks were cleared, ready for sailing.

"What about the dive buoy?" Luis yelled to Kate as she climbed up to the wheelhouse.

"Leave it," she called. "It should ride out this storm without a problem."

Holden stood on the deck with Larry's watch feeling like a lead weight belt in his pocket. As he went down to the dive center, the *Golden Bough* growled to life. Heavy metal links clanked into the chain locker as the winch worked, the sound even louder than the Techno beat. Vibration shook the deck plates and the whole ship shuddered as the anchor finally came off the bottom. Instantly the motion of the ship changed, becoming more alive, a force set free.

"Where is the plug you used to connect Mingo's watch to the computer USB port?" Holden asked Volkert.

The Afrikaner shut a drawer, tested that it was secure, and opened a deeper drawer, where various cables and cords lay coiled. Without a word he pulled one out, handed it to Holden, and went back to checking that all the computers and screens were secured.

"Did you send the content from Mingo's watch to my e-mail?" asked Holden.

"Yah."

"Excellent," Holden said, stuffing the cord into a pocket with the watch. "Need any help here?"

Volkert shook his head and said, "I've been preparing for the past day."

Chain stopped rattling into the locker, and the anchor clanked into place in its holder at the bow.

Holden turned away and began climbing to the wheelhouse. With every step up from the ship's center of gravity, the motion became stronger. By the time he reached the wheelhouse, the horizon was tilting and straightening with rhythmic regularity. When a bigger wave came along, the motion increased.

He realized he was grinning. Despite the burning ache in his leg and the damning weight of Larry's watch, Holden felt the elation of being at sea in a good blow. And that was all the storm was now, well under thirty knots, just an exhilarating ride on nature's own roller coaster.

When he opened the door to the wheelhouse, Kate nodded to him and returned her attention to the ship's dials, checking that both engines were working evenly and all dials were in the green. She looked natural at the wheel, her hands steady as she brought the ship around and guided it on course for St. Vincent's aptly named Lee Harbor. The *Golden Bough* might not be elegant in looks, but she took the waves and wind like the sturdy workhorse she had been designed to be.

Holden settled himself on the long bench seat at the back of the wheelhouse. From the looks of it, lately the bench had served as Grandpa Donnelly's bed. Holden thought of ways to bring up Larry's watch and decided that until he had a chance to download the information and compare it to Mingo's, there was no point in upsetting Kate. She had enough to do handling ship and storm.

The radio crackled with one-sided conversations and warnings from the local marine stations for small craft to stay ashore.

"You do that very well," he said after a few minutes.

"Like riding a bike," she said, smiling faintly as she repeated her grandfather's words. "The fear is still there, but it's more an echo than a scream. I always loved to be at the wheel."

"Heady stuff for the youngest by far in the family."

"Yes. They used to tease me about it. Mom loved when the wind and waves would come up and she could take one of the workboats out and surf the breaking storm waves. I used to ride with her, then I learned how to do it myself. Incredible fun, better than any carnival ride."

Holden watched as her smile widened, then turned upside down.

"Life aboard the *Golden Bough* was good right up until it wasn't." She turned on one of the windshield wipers, then turned it off. "I'd forgotten the good."

"It is how we humans are wired," Holden said. "Bad experiences go all the way to the bone, nature's way of making sure that lessons stay learned."

In his voice she heard echoes of his own nightmare, his own pain.

A captain called over the radio to another ship, planning an evening in town.

"Sometimes we learn too well," she said, automatically adjusting the wheel to keep the ship on course as the wind and waves played their natural, heedless games. "We lose the good."

"Like the feeling of holding a sound ship in uncertain seas?"

Her smile flashed in the dim light. "Just like that. Only Grandpa understood. Dad was like Larry. A ship was just a way to get dive gear from one place to another."

Again, Holden felt the weight of Larry's watch—and its implications—heavy in the pocket of his cargo pants.

*There's nothing I can do until I see what's stored on the bloody thing. Worrying Kate about it is unnecessary and cruel.*

The radio crackled but the words were indistinct, a background noise like the wind and wash of water against the hull.

"Did your mother like handling the wheel of the dive ship?"

"She preferred charts and books and dreams. I was the one who spent hours up here with Grandpa." Kate paused. "We rarely talked. I just remembered that. We didn't have to chatter. I learned quickly, and after I learned, we just watched the endless dance of ocean and weather and light on water. In some ways, Grandpa and I were alike."

"You love him."

Shadows flickered over her face as she adjusted the wheel to meet a gust of wind. "Yes, very much, and sometimes I don't like him at all. And Larry . . ." She shook her head. "I don't know what to think about it and can't do anything about it anyway."

"Blood relationships are never as simple as they look on paper," Holden said, memories coloring his voice. "My parents have made choices I don't like, and I've made plenty they don't like. It has little to do with loving them or their loving me. Liking and loving are different emotions. One doesn't require the other."

"But when you have both with one person . . ."

He leaned forward and touched her cheek with his fingertips. "Yes. It is very good."

The radio muttered words and static that added up to a small craft announcing it was entering the breakwater of a small marina ashore.

Kate saw the first squall line descending and flipped on the radar overlay and the running lights. Though night was hours away, the storm's twilight was deep.

The steady beat of rain and windshield wipers became part of the background as she turned the *Golden Bough* on a line that made even the big boat shudder with beam seas. Nothing dangerous, but not particularly comfortable either.

Holden took the portside watch so that Kate could concentrate on starboard. Radar would pick up big objects, but rain and spray from the wave tops could conceal debris and small boats that didn't carry radar reflectors.

They finished the run to Lee Harbor in a companionable silence, tied off the boat, paid the crew, and eyed the weather. It was markedly calmer on the lee side.

"Two miles walking in the rain or a mile in the uncertain shelter of the workboat to the fuel dock where the truck is parked," Kate said.

"Workboat has my vote. If I had wanted to slog through rain on foot, I would have joined the infantry."

# Chapter 20

When Holden and Kate finally reached the dirt ruts leading to the cottage, the perpetual twilight of the storm seemed almost normal, as did the rain. The temperature was hot enough to make them sweat, and too humid to absorb the sweat.

Or maybe it was simply that Kate was still steaming from her grandfather's call.

"Did he say anything else about Larry?" Holden asked.

"No. Grandpa was too busy telling me how I had plenty of fuel and should have just ridden the storm out."

"I overheard that part," Holden said. It would have been hard not to, as she had put the phone on speaker in order to drive. "I also heard you telling him that no one gives out blue ribbons for slamming around in a tropical storm when a safe port is nearby. At least Larry is recovering quickly."

"So Grandpa says. I'd feel better if I could talk to Larry myself," she said, bumping slowly down the ruts, "but he was sleeping."

"Did the doctors say what happened to him?"

"Still examining test results."

Holden's duffel pinged from where he had crammed it between his feet. He pulled out his computer. Between bumps he checked the latest weather bulletin.

"Now what?" Kate asked.

"All flights in or out are canceled until further notice. It's still safe enough for bigger planes, but no commercial airline executives want to explain to an insurance carrier that they decided to spin the wheel with a tropical storm that is sliding toward hurricane territory."

"Storms feed on warm water," she said, turning off the truck. "The longer they stall out at sea, the bigger they get."

"It's like plugging into a vast energy grid," he agreed. "Only landfall deflates the storms. In any case, it takes the urgency out of talking with"—*questioning*—"your family about what was happening during the off-books dives."

"It does?"

"Nobody is going anywhere until the storm passes. We can sort it out tomorrow and decide which, if any, authorities require notification," Holden said. "Or, if the storm stalls out off the coast, we'll go to the hospital and sort out everything tonight."

"First I have to sort it out in my head," Kate said. *And my heart.* "I feel like I've been grabbing at air since Mingo took off."

"You're good at spreadsheets," he said. "Perhaps we should try to fit all our facts and probabilities and such into one of them?"

"Or a flowchart."

"If I knew what you were talking about, I'd quite likely agree."

"I'll show you," she said.

When she opened the truck's door, it seemed like grass and shrubs, ocean and leaves, even the ground trembled in the soft roar of the coming storm. Although the first squall line had passed, water still fell from uncountable thousands of leaves, gathering and swelling and dropping to puddles below. The air tasted of salt, and electricity gathered heavy on it, though there was neither thunder nor lightning nearby.

Farnsworth's speedboat wasn't at the cottage's dock, which was just as well. The floating dock was rippling like a snake on the restless water. While the cottage wasn't on the storm side of the island, it wasn't really in the lee, either.

"Guess Malcolm is going to ride it out in town," Kate said.

"With all the tourists fleeing before the airport shut down, there should be plenty of rooms. Or perhaps his female has a sturdy house."

"I'm just glad he isn't here. I don't feel like being genial to someone I barely know when my brother is ill and the family business is headed into bankruptcy." *And it looks like there is a thief or two just to keep things interesting.*

Holden ran his hand soothingly down her spine, but his mind was on the moment when he would plug in his computer and mount Larry's dive watch. "I don't fancy a long night with Farnsworth, either."

After they changed into dry clothes, Kate threw together the usual meal of cold chicken, fruit, and rice. Holden settled at the tiny bar, plugged in his computer, attached the dive watch, and waited.

"Why did you bring Mingo's watch?" she asked, seeing the setup.

"It's Larry's watch. Or, to be precise, I found it in his quarters."

Her stomach clenched. "Hidden?"

"No. In a box in his unlocked desk."

She let out her breath and went back to work.

Holden scanned his e-mail, pulled up the file Volkert had made of the contents of Mingo's watch, and opened the dive log on Larry's watch.

In silence, she poured cold tea into glasses and set out the plates of food. She couldn't read Holden's expression, which told her how accustomed she had become to picking up the small cues of his mood that other people missed. She went around the counter, stood behind him, and watched the screen until tears blurred her vision.

Without a word he reached back and pulled her across his lap, ignoring the pressure on his aching thigh. She looked sad and angry and tired to her soul. He needed to hold her, to silently tell her that she wasn't alone.

"Larry was working with Mingo," she said.

"It's possible that your brother was set up," Holden said carefully.

"Possible." The word broke on a choked sob. "But not very damn probable, is it?"

He didn't answer because the truth wouldn't comfort her, and he wanted very much to do just that.

"Mingo's and Larry's dives covered the same territory," Holden said, "but the times are different. Each was either diving solo or had a different partner."

"Mingo was arrogant enough to dive at night alone," she said after a moment. "But Larry was a careful diver. Once or twice he might have done it, but nearly every night since we arrived? No wonder he looked half dead. I can't believe it took this long to bring him down."

Holden started to point out that Larry hadn't necessarily been wearing the watch every time it recorded a night dive, but kept silent, simply rubbing the tight muscles of her back and shoulders. She leaned against him, but she didn't take her eyes off the damning trails on the computer screen.

After a long silence she asked, "Do you think Mingo is alive?"

"Until there is a body, there is always the possibility of life."

"I'm beginning to hate that word."

"Possibility?" Holden asked.

She nodded. "It offers too many ways to duck the overwhelmingly probable truth."

"If Mingo drowned during a solo dive, who took the *Golden Bough*'s missing tender?" Holden asked. "And why wasn't a body found? The currents in the wreck area flow toward St. Vincent."

"The weight belt would keep him down."

"Until the natural processes of decomposition created gas, which creates buoyancy."

Kate grimaced.

"Sorry, love," he said. "I forgot the American fastidiousness about natural processes."

"So Mingo is hiding out somewhere?"

"Or foul play is involved."

She stared at him with shocked turquoise eyes. "I might be forced to accept that my brother is a thief, but a murderer? No way."

Holden's arms tightened around her. "Remember, Mingo had to deal with some very dodgy people in order to sell the stolen goods."

"Has more appeared on the black market that you haven't mentioned?"

"AO hasn't given me any updates on that front."

"So anywhere from a little to a zillion dollars of stuff could have been skimmed, or not," she said. "Mingo could be alive or dead. Larry may not have been but likely was part of the stealing." She rubbed her forehead. "I'm getting a really big headache, and it's not just the pressure drop from the coming storm. I doubt if the winds are even thirty miles an hour on a sustained basis on the lee side. Gusts are a different story. We've had some pretty good ones."

Holden hesitated, then said, "There is one more thing to be considered."

"I'm sitting down," she said, joking and bracing herself at the same time. She had a feeling she wouldn't like what he had to say.

"Yes, I can feel that," he said, stroking her and nuzzling her neck. Then he pulled back from temptation. "We also have to make an assessment of the possible danger to your family."

"This is becoming a tropical storm, not a big hurricane. Even if it gets to Cat One, we'll be fine. But if you're worried, we can go to higher ground or one of the new hotels."

A gust of wind rattled the louvered windows and sent currents of air stirring.

"Excellent idea," he said. "A few more gusts like that and the tin sheets on the roof will take flight."

She looked at his ever-changing, fascinating eyes and wondered if she would have time to get used to them. "In Charlotte," she said absently, "this would be a welcome break from stultifying heat and humidity."

He lifted his black eyebrows. "Lovely place you live. In any case I was thinking more of dangers of the human variety."

"Such as?"

"If Mingo is alive and he's been stealing treasure that's worth thousands or even millions of pounds, he would want to cover his tracks."

"You don't think that he'd actually murder anyone, do you? I mean, he's an ass, but I don't see him as a stone killer."

"For some people, greed excuses all manner of crimes."

A shudder went through her. "I feel like the night I was alone on the ship and knew that my parents needed help and was terrified I wouldn't be able to get to them. Only now it's Larry who's lost and in danger and desperately in need of a helping hand."

Holden stroked her damp hair that still burned like embers. He wanted to tell her that none of this was her fault but knew it wouldn't help. In her place he would have felt the same.

"I'm calling the hospital," she said. "I have to talk to Grandpa and Larry. I can't spend the night wondering."

After a brief hug, Holden released her. She dug her cell phone out of a pants pocket and got the information for the hospital.

"I am the sister of Larry Donnelly, who was admitted this morning after something went wrong on a salvage dive. I need to speak to him. It is urgent. Yes, I'll wait."

Another gust hit, bringing with it rain that sounded like nails dropped onto the tin roof. The lights went out.

In the silence that followed, his computer pinged with a weather update. The storm had a thirty-five percent chance of coming ashore as a Category One, but landfall wouldn't be until morning. By the time the center passed and they got the wash, it would be almost noon. The storm was sucking energy from the warm water and taking its own time getting anywhere but bigger.

"What?" Kate asked, her voice climbing.

He looked up and saw that she was unnaturally still.

"Are you certain?" Her voice was tight. "Please double-check. Of course I'll wait."

"What is it?" Holden asked.

"Larry checked out of the hospital against the doctor's—yes, I'm here. I understand. What time was that again? And was anyone with him?" She paused. "Thank you. Sorry to have bothered you."

A flush burned along Kate's cheekbones, and her eyes flashed with anger. "He checked himself out a few hours ago and never so much as called me. Grandpa might have been with him, but the nurse couldn't say for sure."

"Then there's no reason to stay here," Holden said. "The worst of the storm won't come until after the eye passes, but it won't be particularly nice until then, especially with the electricity out. Let's find a hotel with a backup generator and—"

Kate's phone rang. She didn't recognize the caller. "Kate Donnelly," she said.

She listened, swayed, and straightened even as Holden came to his feet to steady her.

"Yes? *What?* Are you sure? No, I knew nothing about this. No, don't call the police. Apparently my brother felt like taking a ride in a storm." She disconnected. "Well, I guess that answers some of our questions," she said in a flat, disconnected tone.

Holden waited. If she had been angry before, she was somewhere between rage and shock now.

"That was the harbormaster," she said. "He was doing a storm check on the large boats when he saw the *Golden Bough* pull away from the dock and head out." Her hand shook just a bit, then steadied as she thumbed through the phone's contact list and punched Larry's number. "The harbormaster was calling to chew me out for not telling him I planned to leave."

"Was it Larry?" Holden asked.

She listened to the phone ringing and ringing. "All the harbormaster said was that he saw a man in the wheelhouse, but it was too far away to see a face."

"Kate, I'm sorry that—"

"So am I," she said savagely as she counted ten rings and hung up. "But I have time to find them and tell them to go to hell."

"There's a small craft warning out."

"The workboat is bigger than the minimum recommended," she said impatiently. "I'll have time to go out and back well before the really dirty weather comes."

"You're mental."

"No. I'm fed up with being left adrift by my family."

"Kate," he said gently, "you don't even know where the ship is."

"Larry and Grandpa are going to the wreck of the *Moon Rose*," she said with bitter certainty. "They'll pull up the real treasure they've stashed and take off before the worst of the storm hits. As Grandpa told me, he's ridden out storms before. Sometimes it's safer at sea than tied up at the wrong port."

Holden thought about it a moment. "Quite shrewd, actually. He heads out into a storm and vanishes. The trail goes cold and he gets away with the treasure. Always assuming the captain doesn't misjudge the storm and sink."

"I'd bet on Grandpa and the *Golden Bough* in anything less than a Cat 2."

"You won't be on the *Golden Bough*, though. You will be on a much smaller craft."

"The workboat can take a lot of weather. I should know. I spent hours in the dark during a storm like this one. Alone."

"Kate, I can't let you—"

"I wasn't asking permission," she said, turning away. "You can stay here or drop me at Lee Harbor and go on to a hotel."

"The sun is setting," he said with more patience than he felt, "and the storm could make landfall sooner than predicted."

"Or later. If it gets bad too quickly, I'll stay aboard the ship until it's safe to return."

"That's—"

"No," she cut in. "I'm not staying here and wondering if they're alive and being left behind again with too many questions, no answers, and a lifetime thinking I could have made a difference."

"The longer we argue, the stronger the storm will get."

"Then why are we doing it? It's not like I'm asking you to go with me," she pointed out.

"Excellent, because I'm not going with you. You're staying here. I'll drive the workboat to the wreck."

"If you leave me behind, I'll get a boat and follow you."

Holden looked at her and knew she would do exactly as she said.

"*Bugger,*" he said savagely. "Let's go."

# Chapter 21

The sun was below the horizon, yet an orange glow persisted beneath the wild sky. Clouds lit up like slow-motion napalm, gold at the lowest layers, purple and bruised above. For a moment the evening was held in thrall by an unearthly calm. Then the wind churned, blurring all boundaries, blending whitecaps with mist into a salty sideways rain.

Both Holden and Kate were wearing flotation devices that sent a GPS signal when inflated. Underneath they wore lightweight jackets that repelled most of the rain. Not that it mattered. Between body heat and the extreme humidity, their skin was far from dry.

The water was peppered by squall lines, and whitecaps turned over without any rhythm, carried by swells that increased in size with the strengthening wind. Holden held the wheel, his hands steady and his expression bleak in the dying light. The bow hammered into the rising swell, sending sheets of water into the air.

Kate braced herself as best she could. "How is your leg?"

"Chatty, but being the pilot helps."

She winced at his clipped words and reminded herself that he was the one who had insisted on coming along on this "mental" ride. All she could do was hang on and try to see anything small that the radar missed in all the chop.

"Have you considered that instead of a chirpy family reunion, we may be headed into an armed and unhappy duo of thieves?" he asked.

"Grandpa and Larry won't hurt me."

"In my experience, humans are considerably less predictable than bombs. Survival is a hope, not a certainty."

"They won't physically harm me," she insisted. Psychic harm was another matter entirely, but she wasn't going to talk about it.

The running lights on a distant boat flickered in and out of view with each swell.

"Delighted to know we aren't the only idiots blundering about in the storm," he said.

She checked the radar and the lights. "Looks like they're heading in to St. Vincent, but not from the direction of the wreck of the *Moon Rose.*"

Holden didn't say anything, concentrating on evening out the ride. It was rough, but not dangerous. That would come later, on the ride back, when the storm was stronger and the direction of wind and water would force the workboat to literally surf one breaking wave to another.

The boat slammed down into a trough between unusually large swells.

"I see the work lights where the *Golden Bough* was anchored," she said, staring through the salt spray on the windscreen. "It must be lit up like Christmas."

Holden checked the radar screen and saw a faint blip right where the *Golden Bough* should be. His hand flicked out to the console and all the lights went off, including the required red and green running lights.

"They can still pick us up on radar," Kate said neutrally.

"If they're diving in this weather, they will be busier than a one-legged man in an ass-kicking contest," Holden said, his accent mirroring that of his American mother. "I doubt that anyone will be hanging about the radar display looking for visitors."

"That's probably why the ship is lit up so well," she agreed. "Wet decks and a lumpy ocean make for a slippery work surface."

Kate and Holden watched the glowing area that was the *Golden Bough* slowly grow in size until they could see enough detail to make out the deck as well as what looked like a speedboat tied off the stern. The work lights were concentrated on the port side, leaving the starboard in darkness.

"That fancy runabout always did irritate Grandpa," she said. "Looks like he decided to get his money's worth by bringing it with him."

Holden hoped that was the case. "Why didn't he put it in the second cradle instead of snubbing it off on the stern?"

"The hull of a speedboat and a cradle made for a workboat would be a bad match."

The *Golden Bough* rose and fell as swells swept from bow to stern.

"Will the anchor hold?" he asked.

"No problem in these winds. Twenty, thirty miles an hour more and the anchor would likely begin dragging until it hit coral. But winds like that aren't expected for twelve hours."

*Unless the storm doesn't follow the computer model's carefully calculated, four-color charts.*

"Let me know if you see anybody," Holden said as he made a circle around the *Golden Bough*. "The lower deck door on the starboard side is shut."

"And the diver down flag is up," she said grimly. "Damn it all to hell. Go to the stern. I'll go aboard from there, open the starboard gate, and help you tie off."

"You take the wheel. I'll go aboard."

"But your leg—"

"Has survived much worse," he finished impatiently. "In some things, strength does matter. Take the wheel."

Kate shifted places with him and eased close enough to the stern dive step that Holden could scramble onto it with his duffel. He waited until his bad leg quit twitching before he climbed up to the lower deck.

He saw no one and heard nothing but the rumble of the generator, a bass companion to the contralto wail of the wind. As quickly as possible on the shifting, wet deck, he went to the starboard side and latched a section of the gunwale into open position. Then he braced himself and watched while Kate brought the workboat alongside with a skill he silently applauded.

"Watch it," she called. "I tied a weight on the line."

A few moments later the weighted line flew over the gunwale in spite of the contrary wind and landed on the deck with a clang. If anyone else noticed, there was no sign as Holden swiftly tied off the workboat and helped Kate make the step up. An inexperienced person would have ended up in the water or under the boat, but she had the reflexes of someone who had known the sea better than the land for half her life.

"Well, whoever's here, no one seems to be on deck now," he said.

"Maybe that diver down flag isn't just for show."

"Being stark mental isn't required to night dive in a storm," he said, "but it would be a great aid in explaining the amount of bloody idiocy that has occurred up to this point."

A gust of wind came out of the darkness, ripping spray off whitecaps and whistling around the bulkheads. It appeared as if nothing but the wind was aboard to greet them.

"I guess they're too busy to notice us," she said.

"Or have chosen not to shoot us at this moment."

"Not a glass-half-full sort of guy, are you?"

He made a sound that could have been a laugh or a curse.

"The only gun on *Golden Bough* is in the wheelhouse, locked away," she said. "Grandpa is probably in the dive center with nothing more dangerous than a microphone in his hand."

Holden had his doubts, but he kept them to himself. The fact that Grandpa Donnelly was over seventy didn't mean that he was harmless. Quite the opposite, in fact. The sea had little patience with the stupid or slow.

"Dive center or wheelhouse?" Holden asked.

"Dive center. If Grandpa or Larry isn't there, we'll try the crew quarters."

After ten minutes and a fast run through the ship, they found nothing alive but the wind and water.

"They must be diving," Kate said tightly. "They both know better! Grandpa was told by his doctor that diving could kill him and Larry is half dead from diving too much. I can't believe that whatever is aboard the *Moon Rose* is worth dying for."

But what really frightened her was that her family was down below, she was above, they could be in terrible danger and she wouldn't be able to save them . . . *again, past and future swallowing each other in an endless circle of terror and futility and death and she could only stand in the storm and scream . . .*

From a distance she heard Holden saying her name, calling her back from nightmare and horror. She shuddered and stepped back from him.

"I'm all right," she said. "Just a—"

"Flashback," he said.

"Yes. Stupid."

"No, simply human, love. Go to the dive center while I suit up."

She stared at him with eyes that were haunted in a pale face. "You can't go down there alone."

"Apparently, I won't be alone," he said with faint humor. "I'll be tripping over Donnellys."

The thought of Holden diving alone at night in a stormy sea went through her like a bolt of lightning, showing her things about herself that she hadn't known until this moment.

She could survive the loss of her brother and grandfather, but she would not survive Holden's death.

"I'll be with you every inch of the way," Kate said.

"That's asking too much of yourself."

"Standing up here while you dive alone is asking too much of me. No matter what, I'd rather be with you, Holden. I love you."

He kissed her gently. "I am completely in love with you. Hell of a time to discover it."

She hugged him, held on hard, and said, "Better now than never."

The ship lurched in a sudden blast of wind.

As one, they turned and headed for the dive locker. Kate found that Holden had been correct; Larry had kept her suit well cared for. She was bigger in the bust and hips than she had been ten years ago, but the suit was still a better fit than any of the other available ones would be.

Neither of them discussed the dive suits that were missing from the lockers. Holden was just grateful that the suit he'd used before was still aboard.

"Do you have any glow sticks?" Holden asked. "They're quite handy for being seen down below, especially since these suits lack reflective tape."

She went to a bin that held odds and ends of spare diving equipment and emerged with a bundle of glow sticks. She gave him half and put half in her own mesh diving bag.

"Have you dived at night with only your own personal headlamp and glow sticks?" Holden asked as he suited up.

"Yes, but I never went beyond sixty feet or so."

"How did you feel about it?"

"Excited. Some nerves, but that went away after a few minutes. In the end, I really enjoyed night diving and did it whenever I could. Everything is different at night. Magic."

He smiled. "Excellent. Some people simply aren't suited for night dives. They see only their own fears."

He didn't mention anything about the years since she had last dived, or the way her parents had died. He couldn't know how she would take night diving until she was underwater. Neither could she.

Even as he wished she would stay aboard, he silently saluted her courage in attempting the dive.

Kate checked the gas levels in the tanks. They weren't planning on a long dive, but divers used more gas at night than they did in daylight. Some of that was anxiety. Most of it was simply a daylight creature's need to see more than a single small cone of light. She didn't want to be one of the divers who fell prey to his own imagination, or in her case, memories . . . *the cough and shudder of her father as he came aboard, the slipperiness of the deck in the storm, the aching question of where her mother's body actually lay.*

But none of that was as bad as the present, the feeling that she'd been set up and betrayed by her own family, brought in as a redheaded puppet show to divert attention from Donnelly crimes.

"Our mystery square is SSE of our current position," Holden said as he zipped up and flexed his leg, trying to ease the ache. "What do you think we should be looking for?"

"I don't know. It could be loose, but I doubt it. If I was going to run an operation like this, I'd bundle up the salvage with lift bags," she said, referring to a sturdy balloon that was attached to a large metal hook, waiting to be secured to a net full of salvage, "and stash them beneath a shelf of coral or lava. Even a cave. That rock pile looked like it would be good for hiding things."

"Handy bit of kit, those lift bags," Holden said, checking his tank and then hers. "But not for the inexperienced. Should we take extra canisters for anything we might find?"

"Might as well. We have gas to spare."

They went out on the stern to finish suiting up. Rain was coming down in sheets. They ignored it. They would be underwater soon enough.

"I've rarely used the lift balloons," he said. "In my line of work, we'd bring up devices in nets and cables. Very slowly, mind you. We didn't want the pressure change to cause the whole works to go off."

"Gold doesn't have a problem," she said. "It can go to the surface like a rocket."

"Check me, if you would," he said, turning around so she would look over the connections and the tank setup.

"Your backside is fine," she said, a smile in her voice.

And nerves. She was going to dive, but she wasn't looking forward to it.

Holden checked her out. "Don't fight the water, love. It always wins."

She let out a sigh. "I know."

"If you can't see me, light up a stick."

"Same goes for you."

Before Holden put on his dive mask, he asked, "Are you ready to do this?"

"Ready as I ever will be. Not eager, though."

"You would be mental if you were."

They hugged awkwardly, feeling neoprene and plastic instead of heat and skin. Around them was darkness with only a hint of purple behind the layers and layers of clouds.

"Eyes down, gentle descent, let your vision adjust." His voice was slightly high and chopped on the communication system and air mix. He turned on his headlamp. "And don't look—"

"Into the work lights," she said, turning her head aside as she activated her own light.

They shuffled off an edge of the stern that wasn't occupied by the speedboat. As they finned out toward the dive buoy, the *Golden Bough* loomed above them like the silhouette of some great leviathan, haloed in storm and light.

Kate concentrated on counting, only allowing herself to breathe on even numbers, not thinking about anything except maintaining a regular rhythm. It was a dive trick she had used many times on land, where it had helped her through some very bad moments.

When Holden bent and went fins up to go below, she waited one breath before she followed. It took her a moment to find him within the cone of her headlamp. Energized by the storm, the water moved both of them

about with the ease of infinite strength. They didn't
fight the push and pull of the swell. They just finned
steadily down, pausing for compression stops. The grip
of the storm on the water lessened with every downward kick.

Later, the force of the wind might reach all the way
to the bottom, churning it up and making visibility nil,
ripping out coral chunks and rocks and scattering the
fragile remains of the *Moon Rose*.

But not yet. Though the water wasn't as clear as
it had been yesterday, it was transparent enough
that Kate didn't feel claustrophobic. She could catch
glimpses of motion from Holden's fins perhaps ten feet
below her. His light was a nimbus of pale gold that
dissipated a few yards ahead of him, scattered by particles suspended in the water. When she looked back
up toward the surface, there was no silvery disk of
light, only a gloaming kind of darkness where sky met
water.

She went back to counting and keeping her breath
steady, tasting the dryness of the gas as it went from
pressurized containment to breathable inside her mask.
The weight of the water grew with each downward
stroke of her fins. When she felt her anxiety increase
because her beam was almost immediately scattered
by suspended particles stirred up by the storm, she put
her fingertips at the edge of the beam to give herself

something to focus on besides the particles streaming by. Immediately her sense of vertigo faded.

"Are you all right?" Holden asked.

"Yes. Just trying to stay centered despite the haze of stuff suspended in the water."

Their voices were disembodied, even her own lungs sounding otherworldly to her. She kept counting and realized that her body already knew what to do—legs slightly apart, fins out and flat to slow her descent to a manageable rate.

Light gleamed off Holden's faceplate as he turned his head to look back at her. She put her thumb up to reassure him. The gesture glowing brightly in the dive light's beam. He did the same in return.

The next time Kate looked down, she saw another light below. Its location was fixed, but the amount of light ebbed and flowed in a slow, reliable rhythm.

*Marker beacon,* she thought. *Divers swim to it, then up to the mother ship. Very useful if someone doesn't want to be given away by a dive buoy.*

Her family didn't generally use such beacons, but nothing about this dive was ordinary.

"Is that one of yours?" Holden asked, indicating the light.

"I guess so. Normally we use tethers or follow the dredge or siphon line."

"We departed from normal when we met," he said.

She smiled behind her mask. "Look away from the beacon. Don't burn out your night vision."

Holden already had glanced elsewhere, but he didn't say anything. He would rather have redundant advice than forget something critical.

At the second compression stop, the seafloor appeared to be rising to meet them. Though it was mostly dark above, some bit of light was still making it through, as well as illumination from the beacon. Traces of motion flickered around them, schools of tiny fish attracted by the light, which then reflected back from silver or colored scales.

*It's like being in a swirl of gems,* Kate thought in wonder.

To her, the beauty was both unearthly and relaxing, slowing the racing of her mind until it was more in sync with the easy, deliberate motions that were required underwater.

After the compression stop, the seafloor grew up toward them, appearing as a flat, limited horizon that stretched off in uneven shapes as far as their lights would reach. The bones of *Moon Rose* were black and misshapen.

Her breath rushed in as she looked at the wreck, stabbed by a feeling she hadn't experienced in years. It was the moment when she had gone from looking at pictures of things that her parents and grandfather had been exploring to actually being there. That feeling never went away, even if she'd made herself try to forget it in her years on dry land.

But it came back now, and she was shocked by the strength of it.

Here was history in three dimensions. There had been men and women on the *Moon Rose*. Each of them had a life and memories of other pasts, and then it had all ended in storm and wreckage. All that was left of it now was scattered timbers that could only be reassembled with imagination and wonder.

The spars and ribs jutted out of the sandy and rocky bottom like a fantastic garden of coral. Fish swam around the wreck lazily, some glowing in the near darkness. It was like being in a dream, with a disconnect between thought and action, constant pressure, and the weight of past and present.

*I can choose what to emphasize, what to accept, what to forget,* Kate told herself. *I can choose what I want to be mine.*

*Holden.*

*The future.*

*I can have both after the dive. All I have to do is to get from this moment to the moment we are both aboard the* Golden Bough *again.*

At the corner of her vision she saw Holden. She checked her dive watch, which now glowed with a green-yellow light. He was heading off to the southeast.

"It shouldn't be too far to the edge of the grid where everything drops down," he said.

"As the crow flies," she said. "Too bad we're swimming in slow motion."

"Impatience is the enemy."

She smiled behind her mask.

They were close enough to get an idea of the scale of the ship now. It felt like swimming through a whale's skeleton. The whole wreck swarmed with life. Coral growth covered what had once been exposed wood, blooming like flowers on a battlefield commemorating the dead.

"No one is working the wreck," she said.

"There's light in the distance at ten o'clock," he said.

"I see. Look's like the hip light Larry prefers."

"He's right about where we thought. Almost off the grid at the rock pile, very close to the drop-off to the deep."

Even considering the distortion of the communications system, something in his voice made her pause.

"How is your leg?"

"Still taking orders, which is all that matters."

He didn't mention the pain radiating through his thigh with each heartbeat. He had known that diving would hurt, and it did. Talking about it made it harder to focus on what had to be done.

Following his dive compass and the blurry cone of his headlamp, he headed for a rock rise that was almost buried by fan corals and random hunks of lava sporting smaller coral decorations. The light that had once been distant grew more distinct. When Kate started for it, he caught her arm.

"Wait," he said. "Do you see any other light?"

Both of them checked above, below, and at all sides.

"No," she said. "You?"

"Nothing. Go back up to the top and mind your decompression times. I'll be up shortly."

"You go. I'll deal with Larry."

Holden barely held back what he thought of that idea. "We'll stay together."

He finned toward a figure that held position in the mouth of a small grotto. The opening was barely tall enough for someone to work upright in. From what Holden could see with the other man's work light, the grotto would be a right bastard to move around in without banging tanks, limbs, and dive bag against coral and stone.

"Be extremely careful," Holden said to Kate. "Things that look solid underwater often aren't, and if they are, mashing a valve or a hose or a hand against them could be very bad."

*Is that what happened to my mother?*

Kate put the thought out of her mind. It was the present that mattered, the living, this moment when Holden was approaching the grotto at a shallow side angle with deliberate stokes of his fins.

He stopped well short of the dangerous grotto and touched his right calf to make certain his dive knife was secure. If it came down to a physical argument, he wanted to have a sharp blade at hand.

Inside the grotto, Larry's hip light flapped in slow motion as he worked a netted bag onto a hook that he was holding with one hand. When the hook grabbed solidly, he swam away from the cave, dragging net and hook well into the clear. He checked the hook again, hanging in the water several meters from the outcropping, surrounded by large flat fans of coral.

Then Larry moved, looking rather like a man signaling for a flying saucer to come take him home. His arms extended upward, net and lift bag in one hand. His other hand came across his body to touch a switch on the lift bag. A bright blue light came on, burning like a flare.

Holden had been expecting it and had closed his eyes. When he opened them seconds later, the bag was rising upward. Self-inflating and illuminated, the bundle gathered speed and shot toward the surface.

Kate's distorted words had more rage than meaning as they buzzed over the com. The shadow to his right told him that she had joined him by the grotto. A hard light flashed above as the bag's LEDs became a beacon to guide someone on top to pick up the package, or to help Larry find it alone.

She finned hard past Holden and swept her headlamp at the side of Larry's vision in a demand for attention. He turned to look and stiffened in shock, almost falling over in slow motion. At any other time, it might have been funny.

Then he pointed at her angrily and waved her off.

She held up three fingers, indicating the com channel she and Holden had been using. He hovered in place, waving his arms slowly, his face mask locked in her direction. His body posture was as angry as a man could be in slow motion.

Kate held the beam of her searchlight down, though she was tempted to drill him in the eyes with it.

*Switch channels, you lying—* Her thought was cut off as a voice shouted through the com system, voice driven high because of the trimix he was breathing.

"You shouldn'a come here!"

"Grandpa? What are you doing down? No, scratch that. You're stealing. I get it. But is whatever you put in that lift net worth dying for?"

"You should have stayed out of it!"

"Really? Then why did you and Larry call me in the first place?"

"We didn't want—"

"Shut it," Holden said, his voice harsh despite the trimix distortion. "We can have this discussion up top. The longer we're down here, the more chance that Grandpa will throw an embolism on the way up."

"I have to send up one more thing," Grandpa said.

"But—" she began.

"No buts. If I don't get everything up top, Larry will die. Hell, we all will."

"Explain," Holden said curtly, afraid that he already knew the truth.

"The god-rotting, gut-eating vulture has a gun on Larry."

# Chapter 22

Kate was too shocked to say anything.

"Farnsworth?" Holden asked.

Grandpa signaled yes. Obviously his outburst had taken what extra energy he had. He turned away slowly, the pressure of the water giving everything a sort of regal leisure as he finned back to the cave.

"You start up," Kate said. "I'll help Grandpa with whatever is left."

"I'll help."

"There's no room. For once, being smaller is an advantage." With that, she finned toward the grotto.

Holden wanted to argue, but she was correct. The less time he spent on the bottom, the less his leg would be weakened. He wanted to be as strong as possible before he faced a bureaucrat holding a gun.

Grandpa's heavy breathing came over the com. Whatever he was trying to get was taxing his strength.

"Coming in on your left," she said.

Grandpa moved over as far as was safe. Together they worked a small trunk free of the grotto. Most of the surface was covered in corrosion, turning what had once been silver or bronze to a blackish green, pitted and ugly. The trunk was perhaps three feet at its longest side, eighteen inches deep, and eighteen inches high.

The weight of it was surprising.

A chill went over her. "Is that what I think it is?"

"Won't know until we open it. Hope it survives the trip up. No time to pressurize. I'm running low on air. Not as fast as I used to be."

Grandpa and Kate wound a length of orange line around the chest, wrapping it like a package. As she tied it off, he secured the last of his lift bags to it and motioned her away.

"From what I've heard, it will be a right bastard to drag aboard," Holden said as he hung at the first decompression station.

"Move back," was all Grandpa said.

Kate pushed away.

He deployed the lift bag's canister of propellant and swam away from it. The buoy opened up like an undersea mushroom and then slowly drifted up toward the surface.

The sound in their headsets shifted.

"Ah, there you are," Farnsworth said cheerfully. "Took a bit to get the correct channel, but we're all back together now."

After hearing voices made high by trimix, Farnsworth's sounded unnaturally deep.

Since Holden had nothing useful to say to Farnsworth, he didn't speak, saving his energy for dealing with the pain his thigh was delivering.

"Where is Larry?" Kate demanded as she followed Grandpa on his slow ascent.

"With me. Say hello, Larry."

The sound Larry made was close to a snarl.

"Are you all right?" she asked.

"Tied up like a pig, headache, and wishing I'd never set eyes on that Brit son of a bitch," Larry said.

Farnsworth laughed. "Such a nancy. You walked out of the hospital without problem."

"Because you were holding a gun under your wind jacket," Grandpa said.

"How very American of you," Holden finally said.

"Unfortunate, but we are all together now," Farnsworth said. "Do make a sprightly ascent. I am low on patience."

"Grandpa can't push the decompression times," Kate said. "He shouldn't even be down here!"

"Don't even think of stalling," Farnsworth said. "I've heard that unpleasant things happen to divers who hang around the grotto too long. Ask Mingo. Oh, right. He's gone. I would imagine that Benchley is still shitting neoprene."

"The shark got Mingo?" Kate asked. "Are you sure?"

"Which would you rather believe, dearie? That I gutted Mingo and sank him with a cannonball or that Benchley had the midnight munchies?"

"You murderous bastard," she said.

"Mingo earned worse. He was stealing from me and selling on the black market. Stupid bugger nearly ruined the whole operation."

"Rot in hell," Grandpa said.

"Paraguay, actually," Farnsworth. "I have a pilot and plane standing by. But don't fret. I find I have no taste for killing. If you solve the puzzle I have created, you will all survive nicely."

The sound of Grandpa's breathing became too loud.

"Turn off your com unit, old man," Farnsworth said. "I can't hear myself think."

"Leave him alone," Kate said. "You're lucky you haven't killed him."

"Do stop whining," Farnsworth said. "It is unattractive and irritating. I will give Holden credit for a stiff upper lip. From what I saw of his medical records, his thigh must be unbearably painful."

Holden thought of the ways he knew to share his pain with Farnsworth. Every one of them required getting close, which wasn't going to happen right away.

"It was quite a surprise that you would dive at all," Farnsworth continued with his relentless cheer. "AO certainly wasn't expecting it. You were chosen quite carefully, you know."

For all the response Holden made, Farnsworth could have been talking to himself.

"Hurts that much, old chap?" He chuckled.

"Sod off," Holden said. He had other things to think about than the cheery sadist—like how Kate was going to survive this mess.

"Chatham was rather unhappy that you suited up," Farnsworth said. "In addition to slowing our productive sideline, work injuries are a blot on his records. Shagging the bint was a mistake, too. You have made quite of few of them, you know."

Silence.

Farnsworth laughed. "Never mind, mate. I have enjoyed watching you bungle the job. Quite entertaining, actually. I will be waiting at the stern when your decompression time is up. Don't disappoint me by being late or trying to come aboard before then."

Farnsworth cut out of the circuit.

Or seemed to. There was no way to be certain.

Holden counted time and breathed through the pain until everyone reached the final decompression stop. The water was more active at this level, surging and falling and surging again with the energy of the storm swell, telling them that it would be a lot worse on top.

Before they were ready to ascend to the surface, Holden held up seven fingers and pointed to Kate. When Grandpa lifted his hand to switch along with them, Holden signaled a firm negative. After a few moments, Grandpa signaled agreement. Kate and Holden switched to channel seven.

"When we reach the surface, I'm going to act like I can barely walk," he said quickly. He didn't say that it wouldn't be entirely a charade, because she didn't need anything more to worry about. His thigh felt like it held a tiny, white-hot sun trying to burn through skin and bone. "Stay away from me so Farnsworth has to divide his attention. I'll watch for a chance to take him out."

"Larry," she said.

Holden understood. "We'll untie him as soon as we can, but our first job is to neutralize Farnsworth. Tell him that Grandpa and I both need help getting into the boat." *Not likely that Farnsworth will fall for that, but better than nothing.*

She signaled agreement and they both switched back to the channel Farnsworth expected them to be on.

Kate hung on to the line at the decompression station and tried to get herself under control. It wasn't fear she fought against, but a kind of primal savagery she had never felt. She didn't consider herself a violent person, yet the need to hurt Farnsworth was a fire in her blood.

She passed the decompression thinking about ways to separate Farnsworth from his life or his gun—she didn't really care which. As she finned slowly toward the surface, yellow work lights and slices of silvery moonlight created a quicksilver-and-gold ceiling that warned of the wind chop and deep swells. When her head broke surface and she swam toward the stern, it was a roller-coaster ride over black swells scratched white at the top by the wind. Yellow light spilled off the port side of the ship, giving a clear beacon to swim to.

As the other two ahead of him broke surface, Holden considered switching off his headlamp and trying to get aboard without Farnsworth being aware of it, but he discarded the notion as soon as it came. All the bastard had to do was threaten Kate, and Holden would be helpless. Better to let Farnsworth think they were docile.

"First the old man, then the bint, then Cameron," Farnsworth said through the com unit.

"Grandpa can't get out of the water alone," Kate said. "Neither can Holden."

"Pity. I'll have to shoot them where they are."

"Wait!" she said. "Let me help them."

Grimly Holden thought that being shot sounded almost good. His thigh felt like all of his tendons and muscles were slowly being burned to ash, yet the agony remained even after the flesh had been consumed.

*In half an hour or so it will be better,* he reminded himself. All he had to do was to get from here to there. *I've done it before and survived. This time will be no different.*

Kate helped Grandpa as much as she could, then threw her fins onto the stern and dragged herself aboard with Grandpa's help. Both of them peeled back their masks and head coverings and took off their tanks.

The air was wet and cold and sweet and tasted of electricity. No surprise since lightning stabbed repeatedly through the storm.

"If I see anyone wearing a weight belt come on deck, he or she will be shot. Dump them in the water."

Two weight belts clattered onto the stern and slid into the water.

*Bugger,* Holden thought, releasing his belt.

He had been looking forward to swinging the lead belt at Farnsworth's head.

*There are other ways,* Holden thought.

His dive knife was one of them. He held on to the stern dive step as rain washed his face. One of the dive tanks washed over and sank in the water. No one made a move to recover it.

"You first, Grandpa," Farnsworth ordered. "Come aboard and sit under the work light by the winch."

Grandpa went aboard and sat where Farnsworth pointed. The older man's face looked pale, almost skull-like in the light.

"You next," he said to Kate. "Sit next to him and hug your knees."

A single look told her that Farnsworth was dressed in a wetsuit, braced against the wind and waves, and his gun hand was steady enough that she wouldn't risk Grandpa's life.

"Holden needs help getting onto the dive step," she said.

"Then he stays in the water. Move."

By the time Kate was aboard, Holden had abandoned his dive tanks and heaved himself onto the stern. He hung on to whatever he could as the world spun from more than the motion of waves and wind. Now that he was free of the mask, he didn't fight the nausea racking him. He threw up, letting the waves take the mess, and immediately felt better.

*I'll be making an appointment with the surgeon just as soon as I get ashore,* he told himself.

Assuming he got ashore. But worrying about that wouldn't help and could damage his chances, so he stopped thinking about anything but survival.

He peeled down his clumsy dive gloves and checked that his dive knife was still in place. After releasing the tab that kept the knife secure in its sheath, he tried to decide on the best way to get aboard. Not trusting his thigh to support him at the moment—and hoping to conceal the dive knife strapped to his calf—he crawled aboard on his hands and knees. Rain peppered across the deck, followed by a spray of salt water from an unusually large swell. The motion of the boat was sluggish, despite the fact that wind, current, and tide were working together instead of smacking the hull around like dice in a cup.

"Stand up and get to the main cabin," Farnsworth said. The direction of his voice told Holden that the other man had climbed the stairs to the main deck. "If you can't, I'll—"

"Shoot me," Holden said wearily.

"Actually, I'll shoot the bint. You aren't worth wasting a bullet on."

*You just keep believing that, you sneering sod,* Holden thought.

Making unnecessary work of it, he pulled himself onto his feet and slowly followed Kate and her grandfather up the stairs.

The wind threw rain like grapeshot across the open deck. Despite that, Kate was sweating. She blamed it on the neoprene covering her, but knew Farnsworth's gun was the real cause. She peeled off her heavy gloves, noting that Grandpa already had dropped his.

Farnsworth waited just inside the main cabin, watching them as they balanced against the sway of the boat and entered the cabin. He kept most of his attention on Holden, despite the obvious pain in his expression.

"Larry!" Kate said.

Without waiting for permission, she rushed to where her brother lay on the long couch that was bolted to one side of the main cabin. He was pale, obviously exhausted, and having trouble focusing. He was also soaked from shoes to dripping hair.

And tied hand and foot to the legs of the sofa.

"Don't worry," her brother said, slurring words. "Breathing okay. Just tired. Bastard made me . . . pull lift nets . . ."

"I'll get a blanket."

"You will back away from your brother now." Farnsworth's voice was almost eerie in its lack of emotion.

"Do it, Kate," Holden said. "He's looking for an excuse to shoot. Holding a pistol does that to some people."

"Temptation is a wicked bitch," Farnsworth said, glaring at Larry. "So shut it and keep it shut. I've heard more than enough of your whining."

Larry slumped against his ties and went back to his semiconscious state.

Rain and spray spit through open portholes each time the wind shifted. People in regular clothing would have been cool, but everyone except Larry was wearing neoprene. The chilly blasts from the portholes were refreshing.

Frowning, worried, Kate backed away from her brother through the sporadic spray coming in from various openings. Without warning the ship pitched and she went backward against the main cabin's long table. When she put her hands behind her to brace herself, she felt the unmistakable weight and smoothness of gold against her fingers. She turned, saw what was heaped carelessly on the wood, and stood frozen in astonishment.

"Pretty, isn't it?" Farnsworth said.

"Pretty?" she said. "It's . . . impossible."

The gold looked alive, sliding and shifting with the motion of the boat, barely held in check by the half-inch rail that rimmed the table. Chains, coins, bracelets, earrings, breastplates, arm cuffs, rings, necklaces, figurines—every shape of gold imaginable, supple, gleaming, mesmerizing, heavy with the weight of time and the nature of the metal itself. Gems shimmered in bolts of pure color from some of the pieces. Other pieces were valuable for the pure workmanship of the gold itself.

As though from a distance, she heard Farnsworth order Grandpa and Holden to stand near Larry. She tried to shake off the spell of the past and beauty and focus on the dangerous present, yet the lure of history was too compelling. She could do nothing about Farnsworth and his modern pistol, but she could absorb the presence of the kind of treasure that had driven men for millennia, the shining reason for so many deaths and dreams revolving around the wealth of the New World.

"Go ahead, touch it," Farnsworth said, amusement and vindication in his voice. "More gold than most people ever see in a lifetime."

"The history," she said. "It's staggering. My mother collected centuries-old drawings of jewelry like this."

She touched a crown that sat atop a pile of gold chain instead of resting on a regal skull. The crown was made with long, almost delicate tendrils of gold that curled up at the coronet points like flame frozen in metal. Standing at each point was a richly colored cabochon emerald . . . dark tears of long-dead ambitions still glowing with rich promises. As metal and gems, the crown had considerable monetary value. As history it was priceless.

Holden breathed more easily with each passing second as pain began to loosen its paralyzing grip on his leg. The occasional spray of water from the portholes felt good against his sweaty face.

*Keep everyone distracted for a bit longer,* he silently urged Kate. *I'm getting stronger by the second.*

"Lovely, isn't it?" Farnsworth said, eyes wide as gold coins while he stared, resting the gun against his thigh. "That filigreed piece will have buyers salivating."

She followed the direction of his eyes. The jewelry he was looking at was large enough to be a breastplate, meant to ride low over a lady's breasts. Emeralds, sapphires, and rubies bloomed like a miniature garden kissed by dewdrops of diamond.

"The goldwork is incredibly fine," Kate said. "It looks very like the drawing my mother used to dream about. It was commissioned by an old Spanish lord for his spoiled young wife. She wanted to outshine even the queen at the Mid-May ball held in Seville in 1685. No goldsmith in all of Spain could make the young bride's design, so it was sent to Venice. The rumor was that making the piece nearly beggared her husband."

The jewelry ran like a liquid dream over Kate's fingers, untouched by the black corruption of human vanity and lust and envy.

"More likely," she said, "the lord was punished by the queen when a pretty young upstart wore jewels that put royalty in the shade. Court courtesy demanded that the bride make a gift of the necklace to the queen. That didn't happen. Legend has it that the lord and his young bride were allowed to keep the necklace, but they were banished to the New World. There is no record that their ship ever arrived. Yet here the necklace is, side by side with a solid gold mask of an Inca god or king."

Rain came in a whispering roar over the deck as the ship rose up and up to meet a swell, then slid slowly down the back of the invisible force. The *Golden Bough* seemed a bit slow in responding. Grandpa frowned and looked at the wood beneath his feet as though he could see through down to the bilge.

"Pity I have to leave," Malcolm said. "My understanding is that there is much more down there, but I don't have the time to dive for it. I should have left days ago, but the nights . . . the nights were so bloody lucrative. They more than repaid my patience. Just as I'll repay your cooperation. Most of this is yours."

"What?" Kate said, shocked.

"I'll take some, but not all," he said, gesturing to the table. "I'm a runner, not a weight lifter."

Wind gusted from an unexpected quarter, shoving the ship like a toy against the pull of the anchor until everyone had to brace themselves as the deck tipped hard to port. Farnsworth lurched into the galley counter and went to his knees in a thin puddle of salt spray and rain. His knuckles turned white around the pistol.

Holden lunged for the gun even though stars flared at the edges of his vision as he demanded strength that his thigh didn't have. Farnsworth brought the weapon up just in time to give Holden a good look at the black mouth of the barrel. The weapon wasn't wet enough to affect anything that mattered.

"Get back," Farnsworth snarled above the whine of wind across the open portholes.

Silently raging at missing his chance, Holden stepped backward until his leg gave way and he went to the deck.

"Sucks to be weak, doesn't it?" Farnsworth said, relishing the American slang. "All those brute muscles useless against a skinny nerd holding a gun."

Pain bit into Holden, but it wasn't as great as his anger at not taking the other man down.

*There will be another chance,* Holden promised himself grimly. *He's too busy swaggering not to screw up. A professional would have shot us in the water and taken off with whatever treasure he could carry.*

Fortunately, Farnsworth was an amateur at the killing game.

"Crawl over and sit in one of the swivel chairs," Farnsworth said, gesturing to the table heaped with gold. "You too, Grandpa. Sit so that you two are back to back. Kate, stand by Larry."

Holden could have walked but saw no reason to waste the effort. He crawled to one of the swivel chairs and pulled himself into it. Grandpa moved carefully, his legs wide to help him balance on the shifting deck.

"Swivel the chairs so that you're facing away from each other," Farnsworth said. "Kate, take the line I hung on the hook by the door and bring it here. Be very careful. I would hate to shoot you or your brother because you tripped and fell in my direction."

She glanced at Holden from the corner of her eye. He was watching Farnsworth with predatory intensity.

Barely audible beneath the sound of the generator and the storm, the automatic bilge pumps started. In the wheelhouse, an alarm kicked in. The bilge pumps choked and died.

"Let me up or this ship will sink under our feet!" Grandpa said fiercely.

# Chapter 23

"Shut it, old man. You'll have plenty of time if Cameron's half as clever as he thinks he is," Malcolm said carelessly. "I am certain the brawny hero is planning madly. Put your arms behind your back, hero. You, too, Grandpa."

Holden turned his wrists and stacked them to make extra room.

"Chop-chop, Kate. Tie them together."

The sound of the bilge pump cutting in and out and the feel of the ship itself was more frightening than Farnsworth and his tiresome weapon. Kate went to work quickly, ignoring the fact that both men leaned slightly away from the back of his chair. In addition, Holden took a deep, silent breath and held it while she coiled orange safety line around chairs and men.

She glanced down at Holden's leg, where a knife waited in its sheath. When she looked up, he shook his head very slightly.

"Tighter," Farnsworth said, then staggered when water broke over the ship's bow and ran in a green-white torrent over the main deck. "Sod it. Just get the job done."

Quickly she tied a very impressive-looking knot on her grandfather's chest.

"I taught you too well, Kitty," he said. "That's as neat a viceroy knot as I've ever seen."

"I always loved the pattern," she said.

Holden thought quickly back to his days of learning knots and almost smiled despite the pain. One sharp pull and the fancy knot would unravel—as soon as they found a way to get enough slack to work someone's hand free to reach the knot. Not as easy as it sounded, but at least a fighting chance.

"Isn't that sweet," Farnsworth said. "Now back off, bint." He gave her a shove.

"Real brave with a girl, aren't you?" Grandpa said. "Gutter slime."

"I can buy this ship a thousand times over. What makes you think I care what a pissant mick like you thinks?"

"All mouth and no trousers," Grandpa said. "Untie me and say that."

With a mean smile Farnsworth slapped the old man hard.

Kate made a shocked sound. She grabbed the first piece of treasure that caught her eye.

Without pausing, Farnsworth backhanded Holden, raking a line of red across his cheekbone with the pistol.

"I've been wanting to do that since you came aboard," Farnsworth said, "you with your family connections and medals and London accent. I came up the hard way, getting my arse kicked by my old man and learning to imitate my 'betters.' Guess who is better now?" Taking his time, relishing the moment, he drew back his gun hand to deliver another brutal blow.

Holden had let himself go with the first hit, lessening its force. But a few more like it and he would have the wits of a scrambled egg.

"Stop it!" she yelled, holding her hand high.

Her fingers were clenched around a priceless, palm-size golden frog that was set with cabochon emeralds. The jewels had an uncanny resemblance to the real animal's skin. Its two round ruby eyes glinted, washed by spray from the nearby porthole.

Farnsworth looked up just before the second blow descended. "Are you mental?"

She measured the heft of the jeweled creature in her hand. It felt like pure wealth, like the heady ability to create a bit of jeweled whimsy from the wealth of kings. It felt like power.

She threw it out the open porthole.

Farnsworth goggled at her, his mouth opening and closing without sound.

Blindly she grabbed another piece, something heavy and solid—the mask. "Leave them alone or more goes overboard. How much is it worth to you to beat helpless people?"

The ship lurched into another swell. All that kept Kate on her feet was her one-handed grip on an open porthole and the piece of treasure hooked through it.

Farnsworth dug his fingers into Holden's hair and brought the gun to his cheek. "How much is it worth to keep him alive?"

Slowly she brought her hand in from the porthole. She wanted to throw the heavy mask at Farnsworth's head but was afraid of hitting Holden instead. At least Farnsworth was distracted from beating Holden. She would have to be satisfied with that.

Farnsworth went to her, casually kicked her legs out from under her and smacked the gun along the side of her head as she fell. He lifted her by her hair, saw the dazed look in her eyes, and dropped her.

"If I see you move, you'll get more."

She went slack on the floor only a few feet from Holden. Bitterly, silently, fighting the lines and the sticky neoprene, he separated and flattened his wrists. Then he slammed his back against his own chair and let out all his breath, giving Grandpa Donnelly every bit of slack he could, for the knot was on the older man's chest. From the tugging and twisting of the lines, the old man was all but turning himself inside out to work a hand free.

Farnsworth ignored them. He seemed in a hurry now, sweating visibly as he pulled a beautifully made aluminum case from beneath the couch. Cases like that were created to protect weapons, delicate electronics, or anything small and portable that required coddling.

The ship lurched again. Hard. Lightning exploded and thunder instantly followed, deafening. Artifacts slid and skittered on the tabletop. A few bounced free to shoot across the floor. Farnsworth's foot came down on some gold chain and he fell on his back. His weapon slammed onto the floor but didn't go off. The metal case bounced and bloodied the knuckles of the hand holding it.

Cursing, he retrieved the gun, glared around the cabin, saw no one threatening, and dismissed everything but the treasure in front of him. He put his gun on the table and opened the case. Loose gems already gleamed inside, as though a rainbow had been captured and cut into jewels. Quickly he grabbed handfuls of jewelry from the table and dumped the glittering piles in the case.

The bilge alarm came on as the pumps shut down again.

Sweating, swearing, Farnsworth heaped wealth into the case until it overflowed. When he tried to latch the top, it wouldn't close. He made a sound that was more animal than human and clawed frantically at the excess gold.

Holden hadn't taken his attention off Kate since she had been kicked to the floor. She was only a few feet away from him when her eyes opened, dazed. Slowly they cleared. He saw her take in the room from her ankle-high view.

*Stay down, Kate. Farnsworth is mental, barely one breath from losing all self-control.*

The ocean itself shuddered and heaved beneath the storm, the ship a toy anchored in hell's own washing machine. The *Golden Bough* rode it, but not gracefully.

"Can't do it," Grandpa groaned. "Joints too stiff."

"Then give the slack to me," Holden said in a low voice.

He wouldn't be able to reach behind him to the knot on Grandpa's chest or free his right hand to get his knife, but he could move his left hand enough to grab Farnsworth if he was foolish enough to step a little closer.

With the metal case securely closed, Farnsworth glanced around. When he saw Holden's fierce golden eyes, Farnsworth closed the few feet between them, unable to resist the opportunity to rake the gun over the other man's handsome face again.

Holden's fingers shot up to lock around the pistol, shoving it toward to the ceiling. "Kate, go outside and hide! Don't come back! Farnsworth is going to kill everyone he can see before he leaves."

The slackened lines rode up on Holden's bicep and bound tight. He thought he heard a metallic snicking from somewhere behind Farnsworth but lost it in the ring of the gunshot. Though the gun wasn't a hand cannon like he'd seen in his time in the navy, the report was loud enough to set his ears to ringing.

Half stunned by the unfamiliar report, Farnsworth cursed and grunted, trying to twist free.

Grimly Holden held on to the gun. He felt a tug at his calf and swore silently. Instead of escaping, Kate had gone for his dive knife.

Farnsworth was smaller but had more freedom, leverage, and a leg that wasn't immobilized by pain. Holden had only moments before he lost control of the pistol, and he hung on to each one.

Suddenly the lines around him went slack. He shoved off on his good leg and yelled at Grandpa to do the same while shots fired wildly around them. The knot was undone, but the loops of line were getting in the way of both men.

Inside and out, lightning flashed repeatedly, blinding Holden until all he saw were purple afterimages of the gun levering slowly down toward him.

"Give my regards to the AO," Farnsworth said through clenched teeth as he managed to bring the gun to bear on Holden.

Kate lunged up off the floor and slashed at Farnsworth's gun hand, trying to deflect his aim away from Holden. A shot came like thunder just as Grandpa shoved Holden to the side. Both men dropped in a tangle of orange line and blood.

There was a clatter of metal on metal followed by Farnsworth's yell of shock and surprise as Kate's knife scored across his knuckles. He knocked her off her feet, staggered as the ship took an unusually large swell over the bow, and aimed at Holden again.

In the silence between lightning and thunder came the dry sound of a trigger being pulled again and again.

Empty.

With a savage word, Farnsworth tried to bring the butt of the pistol down on Holden's head, but tripped in the coils of safety line. When Farnsworth gave up and tried to grab Kate, she dove under the table and scrambled out of reach while the ship rose sullenly into another black swell.

Off balance, Farnsworth staggered. The metal case slammed into the rim of the table and white water rushed by on the deck like a cataract.

"Too soon!" he wailed, fear and anger fighting to control him.

He pushed himself upright and clawed his way to the outer door. It clanged against the wall, letting the storm pour in. With a desperate lunge, he disappeared.

The ship tilted and the door slammed shut.

"Kate," Holden said as he rolled out from underneath Grandpa. "Are you all right?"

"You have blood all over you," she said, horrified.

"Your grandfather took the shot meant for me." As Holden spoke, he began checking the older man for injuries. "Neoprene split over the ribs." He probed lightly. "Bloody, but no entry wound."

Grandpa batted his hand away. "Help me to my feet. I have to get to the engine room and see what's wrong with the bilge pump. I don't like the way the ship is riding."

The sound of the speedboat's engine thrummed above the storm.

"I'll check the pumps," Kate said.

"Wait," Holden said, grabbing her wrist. "Farnsworth said he left a little puzzle for me. From other things he said, it's clear he had access to my files. I want to be certain the puzzle isn't the kind that blows up."

"You're paranoid," she said.

"I'm alive. Cut Larry free and see to your family."

"Tools are in the storeroom right next to the engine room. Faster to go through the stern deck entry." She pointed to another door. "I'm leaving Larry where he is. He's too sick to keep himself on the couch without the ropes."

"Go start the engines," Grandpa said to her.

"No," Holden said from the doorway. "Don't touch any buttons or levers until I've checked things out."

Rain hit him like fists and wind tried to shove him off balance. He used the rail as a crutch while he worked his way to the engine room. The footing was uncertain and the hatch handle slippery, but he managed to wrestle the hatch open. He went partway down the ladder, using the strength of his arms more than anything else because he didn't want to use his bad leg until he had to.

He pulled the hatch shut. Light gleamed weakly behind him.

*Thanks for leaving a light on, Farnsworth. Wanted to make it easy to find, didn't you.*

The corridor was narrow enough for Holden to brace himself with his hands, sparing his leg. Since walls, ceiling, and floor were in constant, unpredictable motion, he was grateful for the support. The engine room door was open, latched to the side wall, yellow-green light spilling out the doorway. A gray canvas satchel of tools lay where Farnsworth had left it. Ear protectors were perched on top.

*He really enjoyed setting this up. I can practically hear him giggling at his own cleverness.*

Holden ignored what could have been bait. The generator rumbled like the workhorse it was. The room was warm with the small engine's heat. If the main engines had been running, it would feel like the deafening anteroom of hell.

Without moving any closer, he braced himself in the doorway and surveyed the area. Even if Farnsworth had brought a device from shore, he hadn't had time to set up anything elaborate before Holden and Kate arrived. While they were underwater, Farnsworth must have spent most of his time rounding up the lift sacks. Whatever he had devised for Holden couldn't be too intricate.

*The device will be placed where an explosion could take out the fuel system or controls.* Holden knew he could drop a match into diesel and the flame would just go out. Given a cold day and a steady hand, he could do the same with gasoline. So to be effective, the device would have to have both an explosive and an accelerant for the diesel.

Ignoring the shift and slide of the ship, he stood and looked for something irregular in the twin giant engines, something tucked among the long cylinders and wires and tubes. His eyes darted between the engines, comparing them, seeking any anomaly.

*There.*

The fuel pump on the port engine was a translucent plastic dome filled with diesel swirling around a large conical filter. The device was a small brick of paper-wrapped explosive, studded with a series of wires, some attached to the detonator cap, some leading to a gutted clock radio.

*Internet special,* Holden thought. *Any twit with a computer can find the directions. Hope that C4 isn't homemade.*

*I hate amateurs. Ninety percent of what they make doesn't work.*

But finding out if this device was part of the murderous ten percent took time and the kind of careful attention and probing that a ship at anchor being tossed around by tropical storm didn't allow.

*It will take time, a lot of time, and I'd be as likely to set off the device as to disarm it.*

He looked for anything that could receive a radio transmission. Garage door openers were a favorite.

*I hope Farnsworth is stupid enough to try to activate it at a distance. The atmospherics of the storm and all the metal of the hull and the engine room will baffle any simple means of reception.*

Easing closer, bracing himself against the boat's constant, eccentric motions, Holden studied the device and remembered Farnsworth's cheerful voice telling everyone that they would be able to get to shore, even if they had to swim the last bit.

Like everything Farnsworth worked on, the bomb was anal-retentive perfect. The device could have come from a textbook for anarchists and jihadists. Every weld was signed with a teardrop of solder. The wrapping for the C4 retained its sharp corners. It certainly looked like one of the ten percent of devices that would actually explode.

*The amount of C4 is smallish. Yes, it could kill any luckless chap standing next to it, and would likely blow out the fuel system, but. . .*

For a few long moments, Holden frowned. The device didn't make sense, and the silvery tube that was part of it kept nagging at him. Then he understood.

*Thermite.*

Holden's Pashto phrases competed with the other sounds in the engine room as he cursed Farnsworth and his ancestors back to the beginning of time. Thermite would transform diesel into a raging demon. No place to go. Nowhere to survive. A fast death by flame or a slower death by drowning.

*The bastardized timer isn't counting down in any obvious way, but that doesn't mean anything. Flashy timers are for the cinema.*

*Farnsworth wasn't in a hurry to get away from anything but us, and there was no way to predict how long recovery of the lift balloons would take, so he must have a wide margin of safety built in for his escape.*

Mentally Holden went through the steps he would take in defusing the device, but he found it hard to concentrate. Something Grandpa Donnelly had said kept picking at him, demanding that he add it to the equations of device and ship and storm and time.

*Bilge pumps.*

*Sinking.*

The ship staggered in a series of big swells. It met each one more sluggishly than the last, as though the *Golden Bough* was slowly, slowly settling deeper into the sea.

*The device is a red herring. The real danger is foundering, but Farnsworth expected me to be so fixated on his pretty device that I wouldn't notice his other sabotage until it was too late.*

Abruptly Holden realized that there was water sloshing around his neoprene-covered feet. He bent down quickly, skimmed a finger through the liquid and tasted it, hoping it was simply coming from the machine that converted seawater to drinking water. He touched his fingertip to his tongue.

*Salt.*

The engine room hadn't been wet when he entered and the neoprene had prevented him from noticing the slow, inexorable rising of water—water that would kill much less dramatically but just as finally as any explosive devised by man.

Ignoring the pain in his thigh, Holden went outside as fast as he could and checked that the workboat was still tied to the ship. It would need some bailing, but it was safe. Ignoring his twitching thigh, he went up the stairs as fast as the wallowing ship would allow. By the time he opened the main cabin door, he felt like he'd been in a particularly nasty rugby scrum.

"We're abandoning ship immediately," he said.

"What?" Kate looked up from tying off a final strip of cloth over her grandfather's ribs.

"That's crazy!" Grandpa said over her.

"No," Holden said flatly. "Crazy is staying aboard a sinking ship. Water is at least a centimeter deep in the engine room and rising as we speak. The bilges are flooded and the pump has packed it in."

"Sabotage?" Grandpa asked, his face flushed, furious.

"It doesn't matter." Holden grabbed his dive knife off the table that was still awash in a pirate's private hoard and headed for Larry. "The workboat is alongside. The silly sod took the flashy speedboat. Hope it swamps in the following sea on the way to St. Vincent."

"Let me up," Grandpa sputtered. "I can save my ship."

"No time. We could founder in the next big set of waves." Holden began cutting through Larry's bindings. "Get your grandfather to the workboat, Kate. I'll be along with your brother."

Methodically he set about slapping Larry into consciousness.

More than anything else, the sharp sounds of flesh on flesh told Kate how much trouble they were in. Holden wasn't the kind to smack around a helpless man.

"Let's go," she said Grandpa. "You can lean on me."

"But—my ship—the treasure."

"Sod the treasure," Holden snarled as he sheathed the knife and hauled Larry upright. "The only thing worth saving is our lives."

The *Golden Bough* staggered as she struggled to meet more black cliffs of seawater rushing toward the bow.

Tears ran down the old man's face as he felt the ship he loved struggling for her life, fighting every wave.

Losing.

"I can make it to the workboat myself," he said gruffly to Kate. "Help with Larry." Grandpa stepped through the open door and into the storm.

She turned and grabbed one of her brother's arms. He was on his feet, responding in the manner of a child wakened from a deep sleep by an adult and guided toward another bed. He could walk when ordered, but he wasn't truly aware.

"Wait with him near the door," Holden said to her. He bent and scooped up the safety line that had recently imprisoned him.

"The stairs," she said.

It was all she said. It was enough.

"I know," Holden said. "My leg's too dodgy to carry him." His hands moved quickly, surely, fashioning a makeshift harness from one end of the safety line.

She saw what he was doing and worked with him to put the harness on Larry. Her brother neither struggled nor helped. She understood the cause of his passivity, but it clawed at her just the same.

"I'll go down first and belay him on the stairs," Holden said. "You keep him aimed right."

She waited until Holden had rigged a rough belay on the stair railing. Larry might get banged around, but he wouldn't fall and break his neck.

"Belay on!" Holden shouted above the storm.

Kate did what she could to guide her brother on the first step while the deck tilted and swayed crazily. Holden threw his weight against the belay line, allowing Larry to descend in a more or less controlled fall.

The ship rose to another wall of water, but not far enough. A wave broke over the bow and washed in a wild black-and-white river over the lower deck.

"Holden!" she screamed.

Holden kept himself and Larry from washing overboard by leaning against the belay line and hooking one arm through the railing. When he felt the weight of the water falling away, he called up to Kate.

"Down!"

She shot down the stairs with the speed of a child who had grown up on a ship. Together she and Holden held, pushed, and bullied Larry over the deck. Even with its special grip coating, the footing was treacherous, especially during the torrent of the larger waves breaking over the lower deck. Holden used the rough belay to get Larry into the workboat, then all but fell into it himself. Kate came in on his heels.

Grandpa had already started the engines. "Cast off!"

Untying the line despite the jerk and shudder of the boat against the larger ship would take too much time. Holden pulled the dive knife from its sheath and slashed the lines. With a bob and a shake, the workboat sprang free of the slowly sinking ship.

"I programmed a course to Lee Harbor," Grandpa said to Kate as he guided the workboat away from the *Golden Bough,* his hands sure despite the steady fall of tears down his leathery cheeks. "Take the wheel, Kate. Nobody surfs a small boat better than you do. And that's what we'll be doing most of the way in, surfing."

While they switched places, Holden stuffed Larry into a life jacket and braced his slack body under the dashboard. It wasn't comfortable, but it was safer than slamming about the boat. Grandpa pulled out more flotation gear and handed it to Holden. He put his on quickly and helped Kate into hers while she kept her attention on timing the swells.

"If you get tired, I'll take it," he said against her ear. "I have had some experience."

"Rest your leg as much as you can. I used to do this for fun."

But when lightning came, there was no pleasure on her starkly illuminated features. It took attention and skill to catch the following waves that surged up beneath the stern of the boat, lifting and thrusting it forward. Too much throttle and she would overrun the wave and end up burying the bow in the water and flipping the boat. Too little throttle and the next wave would break over the workboat, swamping it.

For a moment Holden watched her, admiring her skill and courage even as he wanted to spare her. If the wind and current had been going in contrary directions, the workboat would have been riding the edge of its design capabilities just staying afloat. As it was, they made good progress toward shore, thanks to Kate's steady hands.

He took a plastic bailing container off its clip and went to work bailing despite the white-hot star that was eating its way through his flesh.

*It will pass. It always does.*

So did life, but Holden didn't dwell on it. Right now, survival took every bit of his will and concentration.

# Chapter 24

Kate looked out the rear window of the old pickup and saw Lee Harbor washed by curtains of rain and wind. She stared for a long, frustrated moment.

"I told you to stay with them," Holden said.

"The ambulance is on its way," she said, starting the pickup. "I can't do anything for Grandpa and Larry, but I can drive a manual shift vehicle more easily than you right now."

They had already had this argument on the way into the harbor, so Holden saved his energy for what was coming. The sky outside was black with only loose tendrils of clouds showing when inky purple lightning stabbed in the distance. Wind skated across the water, making moored boats toss and rigging wail. Even away from the sea, the taste of brine was in the air.

*Or maybe it's just the salt crust running down from my hair,* he thought, licking his lips.

It took his mind off his thigh, which was settling down more slowly than a spoiled child.

Lightning flashed nearby, bleaching everything white, leaving incandescent afterimages. Simultaneous thunder hammered down, shaking the world. Debris from the streets and then the forests cracked against the truck at unpredictable intervals.

Kate flinched at the most recent hit and told herself she was better off in the truck than she had been in a metal workboat on a wild sea. In either case the visibility was about the same—forward-facing lights revealing quicksilver rain and looming darkness. There was no real scale, nothing to help judge how far away the watery lights that glimmered occasionally really were. There was just rain and wind, night and lightning.

"Are you sure this is still only a tropical storm?" she asked.

"Last time I checked, yes. But some of the gusts are above the upper limit of one hundred and eighteen kilometers. Sustained winds are still below that."

"Feels like more than seventy miles an hour to me," she said grimly as she fought to keep the lightweight pickup on the road. "Do you really think that Farnsworth is going to try and fly out in this?"

"He doesn't have much choice. Even if we all had gone down with the *Golden Bough*, he couldn't be certain that we didn't air every bit of his dirty linen by radio or even cell phone before we drowned. He's an amateur, and I thank God for it. A pro would have killed us, waited for the storm to blow over, then boarded the first plane out with a new identity and a suitcase full of gems."

"Okay, he's crazy and an amateur." She swerved to avoid a flying piece of something unidentifiable. "Apparently he could dive. Is he a pilot, too?"

"I doubt it. From what your grandfather said, Farnsworth learned to dive from a book and a swimming pool. It will take one hell of a good, lucky pilot and plane to fly in this weather."

"But it could be done?"

"Certainly," Holden said, thinking of some of the reports he had heard from combat zones. "Necessity is a cruel mistress. If there is a plane and a runway on St. Vincent, we have to assume that Farnsworth is headed for it."

"I don't think any of the gypsy strips will be usable," she said.

"Excuse me?"

"The runways carved out of the forest for private—often illegal—use. They aren't paved. The only public strip that I know of that will be usable is the one we flew in on, but the flights have been shut down."

"Commercial carriers have. The assumption is that small airplane pilots have enough sense to stay on the ground." Holden's grin was more of a grimace. "Farnsworth is desperate. If he can get a kite into the air, he will fly it."

"We can't be sure he even made it to shore."

"And we have had that argument, too, shortly before the one about my driving the truck."

Kate shut up and concentrated on driving. She knew that Holden somehow felt responsible for what Farnsworth had done, as though being from the same country and working for the same government department meant that he and Farnsworth were equally guilty for what only one of them had done.

As if Holden knew what she was thinking, he said, "I'm sorry, Kate. I should have figured out the game sooner."

"You've done everything you could," she said.

"Not yet."

Rain poured over the truck, overwhelming the wipers. Flying palm fronds smacked into the windshield and clung to the glass like giant bats. One wiper quit working before more rain and wind peeled the fronds away. Fortunately, the dead wiper was on the passenger side.

The cry of the wind rose and fell like a caged animal. Lightning turned the world white, and thunder battered everything in its wake. Water on the road became so deep that the wheels fought for traction.

"Hang on, this might get rough," she said.

"Thank goodness. I was about to expire from boredom."

Kate would have sworn she had lost the ability to laugh, but she hadn't. As she laughed, she discovered that it released the pressure growing in her, improved her reflexes, and allowed her to concentrate better.

"Thank you," she said.

He touched her cheek with fingers that were damp. "My pleasure. One of the first things combat teaches is that laughter keeps you sane."

The truck plowed through the low spot and kept on going. A faint blur of light in the distance slowly became the airport. As they pulled into the nearly empty lot, curtains of rain gleamed like liquid gold in the parking lot lights. Palm fronds and other unidentifiable debris flew horizontally across pools of light and dove into darkness.

Then the grasp of the wind slowly, slowly eased, as if the storm itself was taking time to draw breath. Through curtains of rain, the headlights picked out a car parked at the far side of the main terminal lot, where there was a smaller building for private planes and passengers. The car appeared black, but the make and model were right.

"Farnsworth rented a screaming red Mustang," she said.

"Are you certain?"

"It was listed in the expense file. Not the red part. That was something Grandpa mentioned when he was complaining about Farnsworth's pricey speedboat."

"In this light, red looks black," Holden said.

The instant she stopped next to the car, he got out and put his hand on the vehicle's hood—almost hot enough to make rain steam. A car rental decal showed in the corner of the windshield.

Kate came out and stood beside him. He was speaking in what she assumed was Pashto. He turned to her.

"I really hoped I was wrong and the psychotic sod had drowned," Holden said.

Her mouth turned down. "Sometimes being right is a bitch."

"Now will you wait in the truck?"

"If you do."

Old argument. Again.

Holden switched to Pashto again and headed toward the rattling aluminum structure that catered to charter outfits. It was the only one that had lights on.

As Kate followed, she didn't ask for a translation of his seething words. She imagined she wouldn't like it. But at least he was barely limping now. Obviously the adrenaline ride to Lee Harbor and the storm-shaken trip in the pickup had given his leg a chance to recover from diving.

*And fighting,* she thought. *Don't forget that.*

The memory of fists and shots shuddered through her. She really hoped there wouldn't be any more of it.

And she knew she wasn't leaving Holden to face a madman alone.

Between the building and the main terminal, outlined by runway lights, loose junk skidded and cartwheeled across the apron like kids out at play. The rain poured down so heavily that simply being in it made Kate feel like she was wading through mud carrying a heavy pack. Water trickled down the neck opening of her dive gear and mixed with the sweat beneath.

*At least our gear is black,* she thought. Both of them were like shadows trudging through the rain.

Holden stopped at the small building whose lights barely made a dent in the darkness of the storm. The weak illumination was enough to read the sign nailed over the door.

"What's in there?" she asked.

"Paradise Air, which boasts having tours for every budget, including a jet available for the impatient. Likely the jet is older than we are."

"Could it take off in this?"

"A trash bin could get off the ground in this," he said. "Staying aloft is a different matter."

She looked at the front door. "Is it locked?"

"I haven't checked. Several of the louvered windows on the downwind side are open."

"Most ventilation, least water," she said. "Do you think Farnsworth is working with someone on the ground?"

"He doesn't seem like a share-the-pie sort of fellow. I'm going to have a listen while you wait here or in the truck. If there's a commotion, for the love of Christ get your beautiful ass out of here."

He didn't give her a chance to answer before he walked off into sheets of rain and vanished.

Kate followed. Even if she couldn't see him, she could see the lights that were his destination. When she found him, he looked like one more lump of tropical greenery being mashed down by rain. A few hundred feet beyond the building, a line of three planes shuddered against their tie-downs. Hangars were for rich people and corporations. Paradise Air didn't qualify.

She eased into the shrubbery close to Holden. Eavesdropping wasn't difficult. The corrugated tin roof guaranteed that anyone inside had to nearly shout to be heard over staccato explosions of rain on metal.

Holden stood to the side of the window, watching louvered slices of what was inside. Farnsworth was arguing with someone. He must have taken the time to change out of his dive gear, because he was in casual dress now, and rather wilted from running from his car to the building.

"We had an agreement," Farnsworth yelled.

"That was before my equipment clocked a one-hundred-and-twenty-kilometer wind." A woman's voice, even more clipped and upper class than Farnsworth at his best.

"It was just a gust, not a steady blow. See? We're only at ninety kilometers now."

"When it holds steady at eighty, I'll fly you to South America. You may have a death wish, but I do not."

As though to emphasize her statement, she came and stood toe-to-toe with Farnsworth. She was nearly his height, mixed race, and determined.

"I'll double the fee we agreed on," Farnsworth said.

"The dead don't need money."

He pulled his pistol from beneath his rain jacket. "Die here now or live and fly me out of here. Your choice."

The woman paled beneath her normal warm coloring. "You are mental."

"Not your problem. Which will it be—die now for certain or trust your skill and live?"

The pilot began trying to reason with Farnsworth.

Holden didn't wait to hear anymore. It was obvious that Farnsworth had switched the magazine in his pistol when he changed his clothes. Pulling Kate after him, Holden moved until they couldn't be overheard. It wasn't very far; the wind howled with renewed force. They staggered and leaned into it to keep their feet. Branches, pebbles, leaves, and sticks whipped at them.

"We have to help her," she said before he could speak. "But if we jump in there, we're likely to get shot."

"Do you have a hammer or wire cutters in that rusty box in the pickup?"

"I haven't checked because the truck hasn't broken down. Why?"

"Let's have a look," he said.

He grabbed her arm both to help her in the renewed wind and to make sure she didn't decide to try to rescue the pilot without him. The wind pushed them at a good clip to the nearby pickup. A few curses and fist slams were all it took to open the rusty box. He ignored the pliers and volt tester and screwdriver and wrenches as he dug to the bottom of the box. There, among random washers and bolts, were small wire cutters and a hammer.

Ignoring the pain in his thigh, which had been awakened by slogging through the storm, Holden grabbed the wire cutters and hammer in one hand and Kate in the other.

"Hurry," he said urgently. "We have to get to the planes before Farnsworth does."

They leaned into the wind and plowed through water and rain-sodden landscaping to the apron. The three planes quivered against their tie-downs, dipping and weaving like fish holding against a powerful current. Each plane carried the Paradise Air logo.

Lightning flashed randomly across the darkness, followed by a cannonade of thunder. In the relative silence that followed, Holden and Kate heard a shot and a woman's scream.

"My God," she said. "He shot her."

"Doubtful."

"But I heard it."

"Farnsworth is mental but not stupid," Holden said. "He needs the pilot. He's just tired of her arguments. Take the hammer and stand back. When I draw him out, you get the pilot to cover."

Kate had an idea of what Holden planned and her blood chilled. "Be careful. One of those wires could take off your head."

"I never run with scissors, love. Knives are much more thrilling. Signal me if you see the door open."

He waited until she staggered upwind and clung to one of the rows of metal posts sunk into the apron to separate passengers from planes. Then he turned to the first in the row of planes.

The tie-downs were guy wires that ran from a metal half loop on each wing to an anchor sunk into the cement. The thin cables hummed with strain, singing rather like the rigging in the harbor. There was too much tension on the tie-downs to release them in the normal manner. He gripped the wire cutters, shoved them around the cable, and turned his face away.

Then he squeezed with the strength of adrenaline and necessity.

# Chapter 25

Thin metal cable parted with a deadly whiplash that sliced toward Holden. It cut through tough neoprene like it was a shadow. Even as blood seeped out, the small propeller plane flipped in the wind and flailed around like a bird with one wingtip pinned to the ground. The tie-down on the tail ripped free.

The racket of two planes repeatedly crashing into each other rose above the storm.

Holden ran to the back door of the building and waited behind it. The burning along his left arm was minor, barely a shadow of the pain pulsing in his thigh from crouching and then running.

*Irrelevant,* he thought. *Everything will hold together for a few more minutes.*

If Farnsworth had been alone, Holden would have tried to cut the throat of the first person through the door with his dive knife, but there was no way to be certain who would be the first in line.

With a wet slide and a crunch, one of the planes turned perpendicular in a gust. Sparks leaped where metal skidded over concrete. Something big whisked past Holden's head, close enough to sting. A piece of corrugated aluminum, bent from a previous collision, made a graceful arc to the ground, where it continued to tumble on its corners, warped and deadly.

And loud.

Kate signaled frantically.

Holden tensed. Between the dark and the motion of the rain and wind, he should be invisible. He watched the slice of light that grew as the door opened.

Farnsworth screamed curses when he saw the jumble of planes. His leather-shod foot poked out.

Holden crashed into the door, slamming it back. His injured leg slowed the momentum of the strike.

Farnsworth howled as his foot was being smashed between metal doorframe and door. From the front of the building came the sound of a slamming door as the pilot ran off in the opposite direction.

*Smart lady,* Holden thought.

Sweating, he leaned harder on the door, trying to cripple the other man. Farnsworth shoved back with surprising strength until Holden's weakened leg give just a little.

Just enough.

With a yank, Farnsworth freed his foot from the loafer and slammed back at Holden, sending him off balance. He barely managed to duck the backswing of the metal door.

He heard Kate call his name and yelled at her as he rolled to the ground, "Run!"

Farnsworth limped through the door, one foot shoeless, his gun in his right hand and the handle of the metal case in his left. He looked for targets but his eyes hadn't adjusted to the darkness outside.

In an uneven rush, Holden came up off the ground and tackled the other man. There was an audible crunch as his shoulder slammed into Farnsworth's ribs. Holden saw the gleam of a pistol in the other man's hand as he flew sideways and off his feet, coming down hard on his tailbone and one elbow. The metal case slammed on concrete.

Holden leaped for the gun but his leg wasn't up to it. He went sprawling on the concrete hard enough to make stars explode in his vision. Suddenly his head was filled with broken glass and his leg was on fire. The only way he could locate his opponent was from his curses and mocking words.

"Long way from the rugby pitch, old boy," Farnsworth grunted. "And I never played by the rules there, either."

Holden pulled his knife and lunged up at the amateur who was wasting his breath gloating. Steel connected with Farnsworth's left wrist, twisted and squeezed until bone ground. He shrieked in pain, dropped the case, and brought the pistol butt down on Holden's right shoulder. It was a glancing blow, but enough to make his arm numb for an instant.

The knife slid soundlessly onto the concrete.

Holden brought his left elbow up, aiming for Farnsworth's throat. Instinctively the other man tucked his chin, but the blow knocked him down. Holden followed him, wrestling for control of the gun. Like deadly pieces of debris, the two rolled over and over, grappling for position.

Unnoticed, Kate circled the writhing men, waiting for a chance to use the small hammer on Farnsworth. He might have been thin, but he was tougher than she would have believed.

When Holden saw the gun descending again, he wrenched at Farnsworth's arm as they rolled and kicked and rain poured over them like a sea turned upside down. Black swirled in Holden's vision as his biceps strained. When they finally stopped rolling, Holden was on top. The other man clawed and kicked but he couldn't match Holden's sheer strength. As Farnsworth's fingers slipped away from Holden's neck, he brought his knee up and slammed it below Holden's ribs.

Pain, raw and purple, exploded when Holden's diaphragm took the hit. Even as the world began to go black, he knew he couldn't let Farnsworth shoot him. At this range, he couldn't miss. Holden's fingers clamped around Farnsworth's gun hand. Holden squeezed with every bit of his strength—until a knee slammed into his bad thigh and the night shattered. He felt his hands slipping and the world sliding away and prayed that Kate had run fast and far.

"Upper. Class. Sod," Farnsworth said, hitting Holden with each word.

Then Farnsworth shoved the other man off him and scrambled to his knees, swaying. He tried to bring the gun up to Holden's face with both hands, but his left was useless, slippery with blood from the knife wounds on his wrist.

Kate swung the hammer at the back of Farnsworth's head.

At the last instant, Farnsworth realized the new danger and rolled himself aside. Her blow connected, but only with his shoulder.

*My God, he's fast,* she thought.

The roll turned into something close to a somersault until he was out of reach and far enough away that he would be able to aim the gun at either one of them. He chose Holden.

"Drop whatever you're holding," Farnsworth said to her.

The hammer fell to the cement, but the sound that drew Farnsworth's attention was that of the aluminum case full of gems skidding and sliding toward him, driven by the wind.

*That son of a bitch is shot through with luck,* Kate thought bitterly, watching the case come to him like a dog to his master.

The case waltzed past Farnsworth, just out of reach.

Automatically he stepped after it, landed on his bad foot, and yelped. But even as she turned to run, he pointed the gun at her.

She froze.

"You're smarter than you look," Farnsworth said.

Kate watched him and waited for another chance. Rain came down on her like water from a hose, but she barely noticed it. All that mattered was separating Farnsworth from his gun.

Just out of Farnsworth's reach, the case picked up speed over the watery apron. The wind was powerful enough that standing upright was a struggle. Kate barely noticed, letting her body shift and rebalance like she was on the deck of a ship. Her whole focus was on the gun Farnsworth held on Holden. Using the wind as an excuse, she allowed herself to inch closer. Lucky or not, Farnsworth was bruised, bloodied, and barely able to stand. All that was keeping him going was adrenaline.

She would wait, watch, and be ready for the moment he lost concentration.

From his position on the pavement, Holden saw Kate glide closer to Farnsworth and wanted to howl in frustration. Even battered, Farnsworth was more than a match for her.

"You two really should have gone down with the ship," Farnsworth said, dividing his attention among the sliding case and the two people. "This will require a bit more explaining than I planned."

Holden rolled onto his side and groaned to divert Farnsworth's attention from Kate.

"No farther, Cameron." The gun leveled at him.

She inched closer.

Farnsworth backed away from both of them, nearly fell, but recovered with the help of the wind. His eyes were glazed and glittering in the random flashes of lightning. His glance jumped between the case, which had snagged on a piece of debris, and his two prisoners. But it was the case that drew him most, the wealth of centuries waiting just out of reach.

The suitcase jumped like it had been kicked, pulling free from the debris and slowly spinning down the concrete.

"No!" Farnsworth yelled.

The case kept going.

"Get it!" Kate urged. "It's not too late. You can grab it before the police come."

"And who are they going to bloody believe?" Farnsworth asked, watching the case from the corner of his eye as the case inched down the runway, farther and farther away. "An upstanding agent of the British government like me or a man in a diving suit who was stopped in the process of absconding with a treasure of incalculable value? And let's not forget the thief's American slut, the one who got him onto a good thing through her grandfather and brother."

"They won't believe you," she said.

"I'll be the only one alive to talk."

Kate watched the gun barrel swing toward her until it seemed so big it swallowed the storm. Nothing existed but the jutting piece of metal and that terrifying black circle at the center of it.

"To the victor and all that," he said, grinning.

With a savage roar Holden hit Farnsworth like an avalanche, knocking his feet out from under him. She lunged for the gun to make sure it was pointed anywhere but at them. Her weight bent Farnsworth's arm back and made him fall on it awkwardly. The sound of snapping bone was thicker than the rattle of debris on concrete.

Holden crawled to his hands and knees. Distantly he realized that he was in pain, but he didn't care. Somebody was screaming.

Farnsworth.

Airborne debris whipped by, sometimes missing them, sometimes connecting. Everything that the wind could lift, it did, then whirled it about with casual power. Holden ignored the pelting and buffeting as he yanked the pistol from Farnsworth's fingers, causing him to scream again. With an automatic motion, Holden popped out the magazine and hurled it down the runway, where the wind took it like a new toy and skipped away with it into darkness.

Holden turned to Kate and touched her face gently. "Where are you hurt?"

"Everywhere, but nothing vital. What about your thigh?"

"Still there."

She sat up and got to her feet. "I'll get the case. You watch the snake."

Even as she headed for it, the case retreated into the darkness. Branches lashed sky and ground alike as the wind strengthened even more. It smashed against the island now, raking claws into the ground and lifting away anything that hadn't been torn free yet. The gun scraped, metal on concrete, before being whipped up and into the swirling sky.

"The case!" she cried.

It moved away from her, gaining momentum. She reached for it but the wind pushed her down. Even years of living on an unstable ocean couldn't prepare her for the strength of the storm now. It was all but sucking the breath from her lungs. She staggered and scrambled after the case as it bounced along. Lightning bleached everything to white until thunder and darkness and wind consumed the world.

Half blind, she went on hands and knees after the faint, mocking shimmer of the case bouncing away from her like a misshapen ball.

*Everything that Larry and Grandpa stole for, that my parents died for, that Farnsworth killed for, that Bloody Green let a sea of blood over . . .*

Part of Kate wanted to laugh and sob and let the storm take the treasure.

A bigger part of her wanted to see Farnsworth hang.

The case stopped just beyond the side of the runway, caught by grass and a shrub too tough for the storm to beat it flat. She fell on the case and lay there, panting.

Sirens whooped off in the night. With a groan, she slowly struggled to her feet with the case. Leaning into the wind she half crawled, half lunged back to Holden.

When she all but fell until his lap, he wrapped his arms around her. Both of them ignored Farnsworth moaning nearby.

"Your grandpa will be proud of you," Holden said when he saw the case.

"I didn't do it for my family. I just wanted to make sure there was enough evidence to hang Farnsworth."

"Bloodthirsty." Holden's teeth gleamed. "I do enjoy that in a woman."

Sirens whooped, closer with every second.

"I used Farnsworth's phone to make a few calls," Holden said.

Several official-looking vehicles rushed onto the apron, lights flashing.

"I hope they're on our side," she said.

"Either way, it will be a long night."

She looked over at the pale shape that was Farnsworth and shook her head. "At first he seemed so nice."

"They always do."

The winds shook the pillars of the world, making the ground itself tremble, and the rain tasted of brine. Clinging to one another, Holden and Kate waited for the officers to arrive and the questions to begin.

# Chapter 26

Kate awoke to the feel of Holden's morning arousal nudging her hip and his hands caressing her breasts. She smiled and rolled over to face him. Her teeth closed lightly against his chin.

"Somebody is an early riser," she said, snuggling close.

"Somebody," he said wryly, "spends most of the time around you aroused."

Laughing softly, she tasted the curve where his neck met his muscular shoulder. The past week locked in one wing of a private home with Holden had been a revelation to her. Despite the polite, squared-away men who shared the residence with them, the accommodations were excellent—good food, daily linen service, and responsive staff.

The fact that Holden and Kate couldn't leave without an escort was irritating but understandable.

Larry and Grandpa were stuck in the hospital with equally polite, out-of-uniform military men to assure that neither Donnelly suddenly decided to leave. Communications with her family had been limited and monitored while British and Vincentian authorities tried to sort out accusations and counteraccusations.

Malcolm Farnsworth was in the same hospital as Grandpa and Larry, with attentive guards at his bedside.

Kate wished Farnsworth was behind bars. A medieval dungeon, for instance, complete with rats and screams.

"You're thinking too hard," Holden said, nuzzling her ear, then nibbling on the random freckles on her shoulder. "Breathe, love. Breathe me."

She arched into his caress and smiled, letting go of everything but him. "Have I told you what a really fine night diver you are? Morning, too. And the afternoons are—"

The room phone rang.

Holden began speaking in Pashto.

"Taylor, no doubt," she said, sighing. "After a week, you would think he would have run out of questions."

"You would be wrong. The British bureaucracy has raised repetition to a fine art, particularly where a man of Chatham's lineage is concerned."

The phone vibrated with impatience.

"Really?" she said, admiring the blue-green-gold gleam of Holden's eyes in the light pouring through the big bedroom window. "I've heard the English are avid dog breeders, but their tender concern for Chatham's bloodlines is tiresome."

Holden gave a crack of laughter. "I'll be sure to tell Taylor. He doesn't like Chatham any more than we do. His superiors, however, are another matter."

The phone kept ringing as Holden gave her a lingering kiss.

"Bugger," he said. "It's not going to go away."

"I guess Taylor hasn't read Rumi."

"The thought of Harrison Taylor and love poetry boggles." Still lying on his side, Holden picked up the phone. "What is it that couldn't wait until a civilized hour?"

She propped her chin on Holden's naked hip and looked out the window while he tried to talk Taylor out of an immediate meeting.

The second-story room gave her a view of the beach, where there was still a tangle of debris marking the highest margin of the storm surge. If not for that, the memory of torrents of rain and occasional hurricane-force winds would have seemed impossible, a wild nightmare. Now the sea was calm, transparent in the shallows before going through every tint and tone of blue out to the depths. Fair-weather clouds sailed lazily across an endlessly blue sky. The sun ruled over everything, making the air brilliant and the sand blinding.

Holden hung up.

"Now what do they want?" she asked.

"I wasn't informed."

"Do they ever?"

He ran his fingertips down her silky cheek. "Only when protocol requires it."

She nuzzled his hand. "What time?"

"They will graciously permit us to dress."

"The difference between this and jail would be what?"

"We're together," he said.

"Good answer." She got up and walked to her suitcase. "I'm not sure I'm going to be civil. I'm tired of giving variations of the same answers to variations of the same questions."

"As am I. Taylor seems heartily sick of it, too. Yet certain formalities are required when investigating murder, massive theft of Crown properties by a very distant cousin to royalty, and the like."

"Ah, yes. Gotta love those doggy bloodlines." She pulled on underwear and lightweight clothes. "At least Larry is well again. The doctor said he has gained five kilos, slept most of the early days and all of the nights, and shows no lingering effects of oxygen poisoning."

"And your grandfather is as salty as ever. I do believe the nurses will be relieved to see him ushered from the hospital."

Kate laughed. Despite the uncertain future, she had been doing a lot more laughing lately. "You're good for me, Holden."

"It is very mutual."

She turned and found him right behind her. Dressed, unfortunately.

"Onward to slay British dragons with American slang," she said.

He laughed and gave her a hug. "You're good to be with, in and out of bed, diving, walking, swimming, breathing, just being." He could see the worry in her eyes and in the subtle tightness of her body. "Whatever happens, I love you."

She clung to him and murmured her love against his mouth.

The knock on the door was a reminder that their time wasn't their own.

She looked at her rather rumpled self in the mirror and shrugged. When she had packed for the trip, she hadn't known she would be spending so much time as a coddled guest of the British authorities.

Taylor waited just outside the large dining room with its extraordinary view of the beach. Medium height, muscular, with the carriage of a former military man and the intensity of a ferret on the hunt, Taylor nodded to her. Surprisingly, he smiled at Holden.

"Thank you for your promptness, sir," Taylor said. "You have been a gentleman in a situation in which many of your peers would have sulked and pouted."

Black eyebrows rose. "Does that mean I may call you by your given name?"

"As long as it isn't Stinky, yes."

Holden laughed and exchanged a warm handshake with Taylor. "Please give my best to your aunt and uncle."

Kate tried not to stare, but she did feel like she had taken a header down a particularly odd rabbit hole. Holden and Taylor had never given any indication that they knew each other.

"Apologies," Taylor said. "Circumstances required that certain procedures and appearances must be maintained."

"Understood and accepted. I take it that circumstances have changed?" Holden asked.

"Quite. As the pearl-fondling MP kept saying, this is a frightful embarrassment, but now it has resolved. We just need one further thing from you."

One of the squared-away men stepped out of the dining room. "Ready, sir."

"Please," Taylor said, nodding to Kate.

Still feeling more than a little unreal, she stepped into the dining room. Instead of the meal she had expected on the damask-covered table, she saw a stunning array of gems and gold. She walked closer, started to touch a shimmering mound of loose jewels, then snatched her hand back.

"Go ahead," Taylor said. "Touch as you please. As I have repeatedly stated to Chatham's solicitors and less formal advocates, if you had stolen this material in the first place, you never would have handed it over to us. It would have been quite easy to stash it somewhere during the storm and retrieve it at your leisure."

"It was my only proof that Farnsworth is a lying, murderous son of a bitch," she said.

Taylor laughed. "I see why Holden is so taken with you. Your American candor is as delightful as your beauty."

Her head turned toward Taylor so swiftly that her hair shimmered and rippled like flame. "I—thank you?"

"Does she always say that as a question?" Taylor asked Holden.

"Only when confronted by a surprising flirt."

"I am married, not blind," Taylor said, winking at Kate. "I know the circumstances under which you first viewed the treasure were less than ideal, but can you positively identify any of the pieces as ones you saw aboard the *Golden Bough*?"

She blinked and realized that the social niceties were over. "There were gems lining the bottom of the case, yet I can't swear that these are the same ones. The gold chains are as anonymous in their way as a stack of dollars. But this"—her voice dropped as she touched a necklace spread against the white damask—"is unforgettable. Not simply the rainbow beauty of the jewels, but the extraordinary workmanship."

"You said that your mother had a drawing of a similar piece?"

"Nearly identical. She was fascinated by the combination of the modern—for the times—use of gems and the nod to a past when workmanship was prized above gems."

"Do you still have the drawing?" Taylor asked.

"You would have to ask my grandfather or my brother."

Taylor nodded and waited expectantly.

"The gold mask is the same as I remember," she said. "I wanted to smash it into Farnsworth's smug face."

Taylor muffled laughter with a cough. "I understand the impulse. He is a piece of work."

"The crown with the emerald tears is a bit more bent than I remember, but otherwise the same. He panicked at the end and just smashed the lid down and ran."

"Farnsworth is a swine," Holden said, remembering the gyrating deck and the thunderous wash of water over the slowly dying ship. "No matter what happens to him, he deserves worse."

"Amen," Kate said below her breath. "That's all I really recognize. The gorgeous cross set with emeralds, the tight geometry of that big ruby brooch, that knife hilt inlaid with sapphires and diamonds . . ." She shook her head. "I don't remember them."

Taylor smiled. "Excellent. Those were borrowed from various collections."

"I told you she had a keen eye," Holden said.

"Can you identify any other pieces?" Taylor asked.

She gave a last, lingering look at the treasure that had lured her parents to their deaths and nearly killed the rest of the Donnelly family. And Holden, who was worth more to her than she had believed possible.

"Not with certainty," she said.

She didn't say anything about the emerald-encrusted frog that now lay at the bottom of the ocean. If it would have saved their lives, she would have thrown every bit of treasure back to the hungry sea.

"Thank you," Taylor said. "Your cooperation is appreciated by the Crown."

"Has Farnsworth admitted to killing Mingo yet?" Holden asked.

"No. Pity, that. His solicitors insist he is innocent of murder. As for the rest, Chatham made him do it."

"Shocking," Holden said dryly. "What does Chatham say?"

"His solicitors still vigorously assert that he was just gathering evidence of Farnsworth's malfeasance." Taylor smiled slowly. "However, you were correct when you said that it was doubtful that this was either man's 'first rodeo.' We have found and interviewed the unhappy recipients of Chatham's past contracts. He was systematically looting the projects under his control."

"I told you he was a god-rotting bureaucrat," Grandpa said, walking into the room. "Vultures feeding on honest men."

Kate left the treasure without another look and ran to hug him, then Larry, who came in just behind him.

"I'm sorry, Kitty Kat," Larry said, hugging her close. "I never should have brought you into this. I didn't know that Farnsworth was crazy. I caught him as he was coming up from a night dive with Mingo. Farnsworth said if I went to the authorities, he would frame Grandpa and me for the theft and make it stick. He said he had a lot of connections and you know Grandpa's reputation." Larry shrugged. "Then Farnsworth learned that Cameron was coming and told me I'd better have a nice set of books to show or it was over."

"It's okay," she said, hugging him again. "But if you sign another contract without me, you're on your own."

"Um . . ." Larry said.

"You weren't the first," Taylor said. "This was not the only time that Chatham has stolen from an ongoing project. As far as such things go, it was a rather elegant sort of theft. Whether on a land dig or an ocean salvage, Farnsworth arranged for costly artifacts to disappear. The project itself ultimately is written off as a failure. In the case of more than a few contractors, assets were seized on the pretext of breach of agreement. Chatham was good at finding companies that were on the ragged edge of survival, getting them to sign hopeless contracts, and then ruining their reputations when the project failed."

"Are the solicitors finished wrangling yet?" Holden asked.

"Yes." Taylor turned to Kate. "As someone explained to your family earlier, the previous contract has been torn up with the assent of all parties. A new one has been signed."

She winced and looked at Larry. "This time I will kill you."

Taylor laughed. "The contract was negotiated by Holden's solicitors, who are fiercely competent. The treasure will be priced at fair market value, which will be determined in excruciating detail. After expenses, which have also been negotiated and agreed upon, Moon Rose Limited will be paid half the market value of the treasure, plus the cost of replacing the *Golden Bough.* The salvage of the wreck of the *Moon Rose* will continue at Crown cost, under your brother's guidance and Holden's occasional oversight."

"Holy crap," Kate said, eyes wide. "Are you pulling my leg?"

Grandpa laughed around the pipe stem clamped between his teeth.

"More nuggets of slang to add to my collection," Taylor said, smiling. "No, I'm not pulling your leg or any other part of you. Holden's solicitors are a fearsome lot."

She stared at the man who had been questioning them for a week without a single break in his correct armor until this morning. "How long has Chatham been screwing over his government and everyone else?"

"At least twelve years," Taylor said. "We are still digging, I assure you."

"Nobody knows how to steal like a god-rotting bureaucrat," Grandpa said.

"Vultures," Larry said.

Grandpa walked over to look at the treasure. Larry followed to stand beside him. The family connection showed in both posture and familiarity.

"How did Chatham get away with it so long?" Kate asked Taylor angrily. "Surely there is some oversight in that bureaucracy."

Taylor hesitated.

"Connections," Holden said. "The failure of some of Chatham's projects was chalked up to incompetence. He was kept on, but he knew he would never rise further than he had, even with his family's influence."

Quietly the Donnellys speculated about the worth of one piece or another.

"What made this time different?" Kate asked. "Why did they listen to us rather than Chatham?"

Holden looked uncomfortable.

"Holden's connections," Taylor said. "His family has a long military tradition and considerable wealth from commerce during the salad days of the British Empire. When Chatham chose Holden to be an incompetent dive supervisor due to his injury, Chatham had no idea that Holden was one of 'the' Camerons."

"Enough," Holden said.

Taylor gave him a sideways look. "One cannot help the family into which one is born."

"One tires of the subject," Holden shot back.

"This one doesn't," Kate said, confronting Holden. "When, if ever, were you going to tell me about your apparently illustrious family?"

"When I had my ring upon your finger and not a moment before. My family is large and can be intimidating. They have been terribly keen on the subject of my marriage for the last few years. I have not. Then I met a woman courageous enough to overcome her nightmares and lovely enough to stop my heart."

"Does this paragon have red hair?" she asked softly.

"Like sunset," he said, then whispered against her ear, "and freckles I've yet to taste."

Grandpa looked up. "You have the real treasure," he said to Holden. "Make damn sure she doesn't slip through your fingers."

"That is entirely up to her." Without looking away from her turquoise eyes, Holden said, "Taylor, please take everyone but Kate and close the door behind you."

"Yes, sir. Come along, gentlemen. There is a salvage dive to plan."

Grandpa and Larry looked at Kate.

"Shoo," she said. "I'm a big girl now."

When the door closed, Holden reached into his pocket and took out two gold rings.

"With the blessing of the British government, I had these made from a bit of money chain from the *Moon Rose*," he said. "Will you take one, and me?"

She let out a long breath. Her eyes sparkled with laughter and tears and her throat was tight with emotion.

He waited for her to take the ring that gleamed so softly against his palm.

"The writing inside," she managed. "It's elegant and beautiful, but I can't read it. What does it say?"

"Let the lover be."

"Yes," she whispered against his lips. "Let the lover be."